研究生"十四五"规划精品系列教材

研究生汉诗英译鉴赏实践教程

主编 田荣昌 冯广宜
编者 李小棉 王芙蓉 孙　燕
　　　王和私 王春霞 李菁林

西安交通大学出版社
XI'AN JIAOTONG UNIVERSITY PRESS

图书在版编目(CIP)数据

研究生汉诗英译鉴赏实践教程 / 田荣昌，冯广宜主编.
— 西安：西安交通大学出版社，2023.8
ISBN 978-7-5693-3155-4

Ⅰ.①研… Ⅱ.①田… ②冯… Ⅲ.①古典诗歌-英语-文学翻译-中国-研究生-教材 Ⅳ.①I207.22②H315.9

中国国家版本馆 CIP 数据核字(2023)第 054139 号

书　　名	研究生汉诗英译鉴赏实践教程
	YANJIUSHENG HANSHI YINGYI JIANSHANG SHIJIAN JIAOCHENG
主　　编	田荣昌　冯广宜
责任编辑	李　蕊
责任校对	张静静
装帧设计	伍　胜
出版发行	西安交通大学出版社
	（西安市兴庆南路1号　邮政编码710048）
网　　址	http://www.xjtupress.com
电　　话	(029)82668357　82667874(市场营销中心)
	(029)82668315(总编办)
传　　真	(029)82668280
印　　刷	西安日报社印务中心
开　　本	787mm×1092mm　1/16　印张 19.375　字数 411千字
版次印次	2023年8月第1版　2023年8月第1次印刷
书　　号	ISBN 978-7-5693-3155-4
定　　价	52.80元

如发现印装质量问题，请与本社市场营销中心联系。

订购热线：(029)82665248　(029)82667874
投稿热线：(029)82668531

版权所有　侵权必究

前 言

中国历来有"诗之国度"之美誉，诗词歌赋，代代传承，生生不息，时至今日，诗歌已有三千余年的悠久历史。诗歌是中华文化圣殿的一颗明珠，是语言中最为凝练最为优美的核心内容，是中国文学艺术精髓之所在，凝聚着无数中国人的睿智思想和民族情怀，再现了中国人的集体价值观、哲学观、道德观、人生观，以及独特的艺术品位和审美情趣。

何谓"诗"？东汉许慎《说文解字》释："诗，志也。《毛诗序》曰：'诗者，志之所之也。在心为志，发言为诗，情动于中而形于言。'"南朝梁刘勰说："诗者，持也，持人情性"（《文心雕龙·明诗》）。古人对"诗"之概念的解释言简意赅。析言之，诗乃人心之所持，志趣之所寄，心智之所表，情感之所依。中华诗词，承载着中国人精神世界中抽象而含蓄的内容，是中华民族家国情怀和群体智慧最为集约、最为精妙、最为艺术的一种文字折射，也是每一个曾经生活在这片乐土上的个体心路历程的文字记录和情志感悟的语言外化。

从古到今，中华民族都是善于作诗的民族，而善于作诗的民族一定也是尊重自然、敬畏生命、倡导和平、热爱生活、追求美好、积极向上、乐观豁达的民族。中华民族正是这样一个热爱诗歌且擅长作诗的伟大民族：地域广袤，江山如画，有诗歌得以生成的地理条件；文化悠久，历史厚重，有适合诗歌孕育成长的人文资源；语言文字，发达成熟，具有诗歌需要的"诗性"元素；民众想象力丰富，精神追求至为高尚，具备诗歌艺术的先天气质——"诗性"的土地和民族。"诗性"的文化和语言，自然成就"诗性"的国家。

汉语诗歌，蕴藉深厚，意味隽永，辞藻华丽，音韵铿锵，可歌可咏，乃成就中华传统文化之瑰宝，蓄储中华人文精神之阆苑，典呈中华文学艺术之精华。汉语诗歌蕴含着丰富而复杂的汉语语言创作和运用技巧，重修辞，多用典，精措词，尚音律，崇哲理，妙玄义，非长期沉浸于中国文化和汉语语言体系之中者往往不得章法，不领要义，不通诗理，不辨表里，不解本事，只好望诗兴叹，仅仅会识读汉字，不过是作囫囵吞枣或一知半解式的浅层阅读而已。因此，只有深入系统地学习和研读汉语诗歌，才意味着真正踏入中华文化的艺术宝库，方能真正了解、理解中华文化之精髓，这也是传承发扬中华文化的必由之路。汉诗英译是借助英语翻译，向世界其他民族和国家呈现映丽隽永的中华诗词的必要方式，也是传播和发扬中华民族集体智慧和精神思想的重要途径之一，是"中华文化走出去"得以实现的端口之一。

《研究生汉诗英译鉴赏实践教程》（以下简称"本教程"），以中华传统诗词英译鉴赏为对象，以传承和弘扬中华优秀传统文化为宗旨，帮助学生熟悉并清楚认识中华诗词的历史发展脉络，领会经典诗词中蕴涵的丰富而深邃的中华思想和智慧，理解中华优秀传统文化的精髓，培养学生的人文情怀，促进其双语创新思维和应用能力的提升，增强其跨文化交际意识与比较文化的敏感度，促进学生英汉思维模式的双重构建，提升学生用英语传播中华文化的综合语言能力。

本教程以中华汉语古典诗词的历史发展脉络为主线，每一章选取五首能够体现不同历史时代的诗词特质和风格的经典篇章，每一首汉诗均附有详细的注释和主题解读，之后平行列出若干首由中西方知名翻译家或学者翻译的英译文本作为实践环节的对照和延伸学习内容。鉴赏实践环节要求学生采用简易平实的语言，从诗歌主题，诗歌作者和译者的生平、创作及翻译风格，汉诗和对应英译文本的音、意系统，汉诗和英译文本的美学效果对比等不同角度做课堂鉴赏演示。通过几种英译文本与汉诗的对比性鉴赏，学生将比较深入且系统地掌握阅读和鉴赏汉英诗歌的基本技巧，大致掌握汉诗的不同英译文本之间在语言表达、词语转换、文化交互及文学色彩等方面的异同，洞悉英汉两种语言在诗歌层面的语法、句法、时态、语态、修辞等的运用技巧，体会英汉之间同质或异质的语言要素、表情达意功能的差异、文化层面的区别和关联，从而加深学生对母语文化的参悟度，提升其用英语表达中国文化的能力，使学生在不同场合具有更强的语言应变力和表达力，增强学生对中华优秀传统文化的自信，为国际化科研人才参与国际学术交流提供一个全新的途径和视角。

研究生的英语教学，在本质上依然属于人文教育。因此，在英语语言教学过程中，既要重视语言技能的培养，更不能忽视对研究生人文素质的培养。"研究生汉诗英译鉴赏实践"课程作为教改试点课程之一，是本教程所依托的重要实践基础，它完全区别于过去传统型英语语法、写作等理论性课程，是以研究生"语言实践"为核心教学目标，将语言学习的重心放在个体参与和体验活动之中，充分调动研究生学习和钻研英语的主动性，赋予研究生自主学习的自由和选择权，开展与其兴趣相关联的自主探索、主动学习、深入探究和现场演示等的语言实践活动。

本教程紧扣"研究生汉诗英译鉴赏实践"课程的总体思路和框架，严格遵循"思政研究与汉诗英译鉴赏"相结合的主导思想，将"思政内容与研究生英语教学有机融合"，以研究生"课堂实践演示"的实战型教学模式为编写理念，充分关注每一位学生的个性和兴趣，结合其各自专业特点，从文化、历史、哲学、文学、社会学、语言学等不同维度入手，既重视学生的英语语言文化的学习，又关注学生各自的学术专长和专业特点，两相结合，互为参鉴，深化学生对中华优秀传统文化的认知，增加中国传统文化因子在英语教学实践中的比重和分量，让学生将专业知识灵活适当地融入英语语言的学习和实践环节之中，在夯实英语语言技能的同时，帮助学生系统化了解中华汉语诗词的架构和脉络。

通过"探索→识别→分析→阐释→评价→应用→创造→表达"这一渐进式英语语言课堂实践推进模式，帮助学生以汉语语言和文化为参照物，以英语为语言输出载体，准确而全面地理解中华传统文化中最值得继承、最需要向世界广泛推广的经典诗词内容。

　　本教程注重培养学生的双语语言运用和再现能力，所选汉语诗篇均具有较高的知名度和传播性，所选英译文本也同样具有较高的权威性和可信度，对于诗歌范例的鉴赏力求简洁易懂，使实践诗篇与学生语言水平基本保持一致。在编写体例上，仅第二章"《诗经》英译鉴赏实践"包含从诗歌原文、注释、释义，到主题鉴赏、英译文本及英译鉴赏的完整鉴赏实践环节，因不同的人对不同诗歌的理解和喜好也不一致，故其后各章节略去一部分环节，以供学生自行鉴赏提升。

　　汉语诗歌是记录中华历史的刻录机，也是反映不同历史时代社会现实的一面镜子。在21世纪的今天，我们应重温经典，追古抚今，重新认识并深度挖掘中华优秀诗词文化的精神价值，让它在新的时代焕发新的活力。同时，还应积极主动地向外输出中华汉语诗词，让更多的人了解这种瑰丽迷人的东方文学体裁与众不同的艺术魅力。

　　本教程在编写过程中参考了大量的国内外文献资料，在此对所有文献的作者和出版机构表示衷心的感谢！同时感谢西安交通大学研究生院对本教程的编写和出版给予的慷慨资助，最后由衷地感谢西安交通大学外国语学院诸位领导对本教程编写工作的大力支持！

　　中华诗词名传千古，优秀诗篇灿若星辰，编者团队在选择每个时代的代表诗篇时，精挑细选，却也诚惶诚恐，所选诗篇及鉴赏评析，未必尽如读者所愿，如有舛误谬见之处，望各位专家和热心读者不吝赐教！

田荣昌

2022年10月1日

于西安交通大学逸夫外文楼

目 录

第一章 绪 论	（ 1 ）
第二章 《诗经》英译鉴赏实践	（ 13 ）
导 读	（ 13 ）
《诗经》英译鉴赏实践之一	（ 20 ）
《诗经》英译鉴赏实践之二	（ 32 ）
《诗经》英译鉴赏实践之三	（ 43 ）
《诗经》英译鉴赏实践之四	（ 51 ）
《诗经》英译鉴赏实践之五	（ 60 ）
单元扩展实践练习	（ 70 ）
第三章 建安诗英译鉴赏实践	（ 71 ）
导 读	（ 71 ）
建安诗英译鉴赏实践之一	（ 78 ）
建安诗英译鉴赏实践之二	（ 85 ）
建安诗英译鉴赏实践之三	（ 92 ）
建安诗英译鉴赏实践之四	（ 103 ）
建安诗英译鉴赏实践之五	（ 109 ）
单元扩展实践练习	（ 116 ）
第四章 唐诗英译鉴赏实践（上）	（ 118 ）
导 读	（ 118 ）
唐诗英译鉴赏实践之一	（ 125 ）
唐诗英译鉴赏实践之二	（ 131 ）
唐诗英译鉴赏实践之三	（ 137 ）
唐诗英译鉴赏实践之四	（ 141 ）
唐诗英译鉴赏实践之五	（ 148 ）

  单元扩展实践练习 …………………………………………………（155）

第五章　唐诗英译鉴赏实践(下) …………………………………（156）
  导　读 ………………………………………………………………（156）
  唐诗英译鉴赏实践之六 ……………………………………………（166）
  唐诗英译鉴赏实践之七 ……………………………………………（171）
  唐诗英译鉴赏实践之八 ……………………………………………（178）
  唐诗英译鉴赏实践之九 ……………………………………………（184）
  唐诗英译鉴赏实践之十 ……………………………………………（191）
  单元扩展实践练习 …………………………………………………（197）

第六章　宋词(豪放派)英译鉴赏实践 ……………………………（199）
  导　读 ………………………………………………………………（199）
  宋词(豪放派)英译鉴赏实践之一 …………………………………（208）
  宋词(豪放派)英译鉴赏实践之二 …………………………………（220）
  宋词(豪放派)英译鉴赏实践之三 …………………………………（227）
  宋词(豪放派)英译鉴赏实践之四 …………………………………（235）
  宋词(豪放派)英译鉴赏实践之五 …………………………………（241）
  单元扩展实践练习 …………………………………………………（249）

第七章　宋词(婉约派)英译鉴赏实践 ……………………………（251）
  导　读 ………………………………………………………………（251）
  宋词(婉约派)英译鉴赏实践之一 …………………………………（261）
  宋词(婉约派)英译鉴赏实践之二 …………………………………（267）
  宋词(婉约派)英译鉴赏实践之三 …………………………………（277）
  宋词(婉约派)英译鉴赏实践之四 …………………………………（284）
  宋词(婉约派)英译鉴赏实践之五 …………………………………（291）
  单元扩展实践练习 …………………………………………………（297）

附录　阅读文献 ………………………………………………………（298）

第一章

绪 论

Literature is a country's most complicated and superb "spiritual invention", distinguished from any other forms of knowledge or civilization. Then poetry is the last thing understood about a country's literature. It is easier to think in a foreign language than to feel in it. Therefore no art is more stubbornly national than poetry. But what is poetry? This is a tough question. Very few people could satisfactorily define or interpret poetry although they try to make some fruitless efforts. Even proficient poets sometimes have trouble defining poetry.

Some ancient Chinese classics such as *The Literary Mind and the Carving of Dragons* (《文心雕龙·明诗》) define poetry in this way: "Poetry is to culture people's temperament" [1]. This of course is not a definition but the educational function of poetry. A better one is "诗,心之止也", which means that poetry is what people feel about the external natural objects or what the natural objects reflect through human minds; poetry is where people's mind dwells or rests upon.

Western poets have also tried to define poetry in many different ways. The famous English Lake Poet William Wordsworth (1770 – 1850) said, "All good poetry is the spontaneous overflow of powerful feelings." For this definition, the inspiration of poetry is heightened, which is quite close to Chinese literary term

---

[1] 诗者,持也,持人性情。

"天机" (motive force of Heaven) presented by Lu Ji (陆机) in his great work *Rhapsody on Literature* (《文赋》): "When the motive force of Heaven becomes swift and smooth, there is no confusion that cannot be put into order."① Inspiration is the ideas suddenly and unaccountably flashing into the light of consciousness. Wordsworth's best friend Samuel Taylor Coleridge (1772 – 1834) made an egotistically shorter one: "The best words in the best order", which stresses the sequence of words. No matter inspiration or order, the poetry should follow all human common sense. Thomas Carlyle (1795 – 1881) explained poetry from its music effect: "Musical thought." Robert Browning (1812 – 1889) seemed to put poetry into philosophic category: "Poetry is the inclusion of the infinite into the finite." American modernist poet T. S. Eliot (1888 – 1965) spoke as an idealist when he explained poetry as "not the assertion that something is true, but the making of that truth more fully real to us." Robert Lee Frost (1874 – 1963) commented: "Poetry is what is lost in translation." Percy Bysshe Shelley (1792 – 1822) defended that "Poetry is the record of the best and happiest moments of the happiest and best minds. A poem is the very image of life expressed in its eternal truth." The average reader sees poetry as, "the literature that is written in some kind of verse form." The poets speak abstractly and romantically when defining their domain, but no one could have adequately defined poetry.

Whatever the definition is given for poetry, the above-mentioned features all meet the ends of poetry: a literary form; written in short or long lines; compressed content; rich image; beautiful harmony; great artistic appeal; sensual pleasure... Briefly speaking, poetry is often considered beautiful, lyrical, rhythmic and mesmerizing.

Chinese is a hieroglyphic language, best-written in the character-based *hanzi* system which is characteristic of pictograms or ideograms. Chinese characters represent rich ideas on the basis of their flexible morphemes and vivid images, so it is innate to be the language of poetry and can be a good source to best fit the needs of producing or composing a good poem: it has a power of suggestion by the use of figurative language, structure, pictorial images, diction, sounds, and rhythm. These indispensable features help Chinese to be an ideal medium of

---

① 方天机之骏利,夫何纷而不理?

poetic expression, as compared with other languages. Therefore, Chinese poetry is "the most literary, the most artistic, the longest-established civilization that exists."

It's said that the earliest recorded Chinese verse was produced at least five thousands years ago in Emperor Yao's period:

Playing the Clay Shoe	**击壤歌**
When the sun gets up, I get up;	日出而作,
When the sun retreats, I retreat.	日入而息,
I dig a well wherefrom I drink;	凿井而饮,
I do farming so that I can eat.	耕田而食,
Whatever force can Mound exert on me?	帝力于我何有哉?

(Tr. by Zhao Yanchun)

There is another version:

Song of Clay Darting

At daytime (dawn), we work;
At nighttime (dusk), we break.
We sink a well for drink;
We till the field for food.
What's the use of crown for us?

(Tr. by Tian Rongchang)

This poem depicts the earliest plain agricultural life of Chinese ancestors.

The first collection of Chinese poetry the *Book of Songs* tells us a romantic love story: "The fishhawks sing gwan gwan//on sandbars of the stream. Gentle maiden, pure and fair//fit pair for a prince" (Tr. by Stephen Owen).① The greatest romanticist Qu Yuan uttered his last call before his drowning, "Long, long had been my road and far, far was the journey; I will go up and down to seek my heart's desire"(Tr. by David Hawkes).② This verse is the unyielding cry of a patriotic poet for his unfinished ambition to unify his mother land. We can hear the same voice from another ambitious politician and military genius Cao Cao: "The aged steed that lies in the stable//Aspires to race a thousand miles.

---

① 《诗经·关雎》:关关雎鸠,在河之洲。窈窕淑女,君子好逑。
② 《离骚》屈原:路漫漫其修远兮,吾将上下而求索。

The hero in his evening years//Never lets droop his noble ideal "(Ty. by Roxane Witke). ①

As the first rhapsody of the Tang dynasty, the "Preface to Prince Teng's Pavilion"(《滕王阁序》) presented a wondrous landscape of our country: "The sunset glow flows together with a solitary goose; the autumn water infuses with the high sky into siren hues."② The second greatest romantic poet Li Bai depicts the grandeur image of the Yellow River:"Do you not see the Yellow River come from the sky//Rushing into the sea and never come back?" (Tr. by Xu Yuanchong) ③ His peer poet, Du Fu, who is widely reputed as "Poet-historian" has made a vivid account of the devastation and social dislocation caused by the Anshi Rebellion(755 – 763):

  The nation shattered, mountains and rivers remains;

  City in spring, grass and trees burgeoning.

  Feeling the times, blossoms draw tears;

  Hating separation, birds alarm the heart.

         (Tr. by Burton Watson)④

After the flourishing age of Tang poetry, the history has witnessed another charismatic moment of Song lyrics in the Southern and Northern Song dynasties. One of the leading figures of the *Ci* or Song lyrics is Su Shi, the well-known sage of Song lyrics in the Northern Song dynasty, has created hundreds of bold and unrestrained *Ci* lyrics. The most fabulous one is "Tune: Charm of a Maiden Singer—Memories of the Past at Red Cliff":

  The Great River eastward flows,

  With its waves are gone all those

  Gallant heroes of bygone years. ⑤

Therefore, for his unconventional, vigorous and masculine genre of lyrical poems, in the history of the Song lyrics, Su Shi is well-known as the founder and leading exponent of the "heroic school"(豪放派, unrestrained school) of lyrical

---

① 《龟虽寿》曹操:老骥伏枥,志在千里。烈士暮年,壮心不已。
② 《滕王阁序》王勃:落霞与孤鹜齐飞,秋水共长天一色。
③ 《将进酒》李白:君不见,黄河之水天上来,奔流到海不复回?
④ 《春望》杜甫:国破山河在,城春草木深。感时花溅泪,恨别鸟惊心。
⑤ 《念奴娇·赤壁怀古》苏轼:大江东去,浪淘尽,千古风流人物。

第一章 绪 论

composition.

Xin Qiji (1140 – 1207), one of his ardent followers in the Southern Song dynasty won a lasting name for similarly unrestrained Song lyrics creation, which may be better read and enjoyed than Su Shi's lyric works. Less lucky than Su Shi, Xin Qiji was born in a more turbulent and chaotic time and has witnessed the humiliating living conditions of people in the Jurchens (女真)-occupied hometown Shandong. Throughout his life, he served only low official positions in the government, and most of his lifetime, he was demoted and located in different places, nearly living a retiring life. While luckily, his reclusive life style helped him write a number of fine Song lyrics full of expansive and heroic spirit and ambition, as in the following lines from a song lyric set to the tune of "Congratulations the Groom"[①]:

At midnight I sang wildly, as a stirring solemn wind rises-
I hear the clanking of the row of metal horses hung from the eaves.
The south and the north
Are still split at this moment.

(Tr. by Ronald Egan)

Another patriotic poet as influential as Xin Qiji is Lu You (1125 – 1210), who is 15 years older than Xin. Lu You has left to later generations more than 9300 poems, and was particularly obsessed with the aspiration to defeat the Jurchens in order to shame off the national humiliation and recover the lost territory. His official career was also a frustration and failure as Xin Qiji did and only occupied mostly low positions in local governments. His patriotic fever has been a lifelong theme in most of his poems, which was even reflected in his deathbed poem entitled "An Instruction for My Son"[②]:

I know in death all will turn to nothing;
Still I grieve that I'll never see all of China united.
On the day the king's armies bring peace to the Central Plain,
Don't forget to tell your old man at the family sacrifice.

---

① 《贺新郎·用前韵送杜叔高》辛弃疾:夜半狂歌悲风起,听铮铮、阵马檐间铁。南共北,正分裂。
② 《示儿》陆游:死去元知万事空,但悲不见九州同。王师北定中原日,家祭无忘告乃翁。

The most representative patriotic verse of Lu You is "Telling of Innermost Feeling"①:

  Years ago I travelled ten thousand miles in search of honour;
  Riding alone, I guarded the Liangzhou frontier.
  Where are my broken dreams of mountain passes and rivers?
  Dust has darkened my old stable coat.
  The Tartars have not been defeated.
  My hair has turned grey first.
  My tears flow in vain.
  Who would have thought that in this life.
  My heart should be with the Tian Mountains
  And my body grow old by the seashore!
      (Tr. by James J. Y. Liu)

Su Shi and Xin Qiji both made great contributions to the genre of Song lyrics, while the latter has broadened it to a far wider scope than the former, further liberating the genre from its chief conventional subject matter of romance and love. Another supreme master of the style of romance and love is a woman lyricist: Li Qingzhao, who closely adhered to the style of delicate and feminine taste. Li Qingzhao (1084 – c. 1151), born in a family of government officials with a heavy cultural atmosphere, was gifted and talented when she was a young girl. After she grew up, she married Zhao Mingcheng, also from an official family, who was fond of the study of inscriptions on ancient bronzes and stone tablets. At the downfall of the Northern Song, Li Qingzhao fled south with her husband who served as the Prefect of Jiankang, but Zhao died shortly afterwards. Li Qingzhao was known by her romantic love song lyric, but she also wrote mannish poem as other male poets and lyricists, the following lines is a superb virile poem of her:

Quatrain on a Summer Day

  While alive, one should be a hero among men.
  To die, still a gallant one among spirits.
  Even today I have in mind the great Xiang Yu

---

① 《诉衷情·当年万里觅封侯》陆游:当年万里觅封侯,匹马戍梁州。关河梦断何处?尘暗旧貂裘。胡未灭,鬓先秋,泪空流。此生谁料,心在天山,身老沧州。

第一章 绪 论

Who refused to move to the east of the Yangtze.

(Tr. by Ye Yang)①

But her most readable romantic lyric is undeniably "Sound by Sound: in Slow Tempo"②:

To search, to seek,

In such cold and solitude,

How wretched, how dreary, how desolate!

(Tr. by Ye Yang)

Another translated version is more beautiful in both sound and rhyme:

Note after Note (shengshengman)

Search, search, seek, seek,

cold, cold, desolate, desolate,

bleak, bleak, wretched, wretched, sad, sad.

The set of seven reduplicated words describe the parallel complex state of the lyric speaker's heart and the outside world in autumn with a strong sense of sorrow, loneliness and helplessness.

Literary critics claimed that Li Qingzhao was the unprecedented master of *Wanyue* or Graceful and Restrained School (婉约派) of Song lyrics in Chinese literature history for her uncanny craftsmanship, prominent artistry and feminine delicacy and refinement.

Romantic love between man and woman is one of the commonest themes in the Song lyrics, but the most remarkable lyricist who is reputed for writing plain and vulgar folk love lyrics is Liu Yong. His birth and life remain unknown, but his works are well-known for individual flavor and artful taste. It is rather rare for a male poet to compose lyrics with a strong sense of womanhood, which seems to be the long exclusive property of female poets like Li Qingzhao. On this account, Liu Yong had been contemptuously scorned by some scholarly literati and poets. Liu Yong often combines a description of events or scenes in real life with his representation of his character's feeling and emotions, making it easily appealing to the reader. For this reason, his song lyrics were quite popular with

---

① 《夏日绝句》李清照:生当作人杰,死亦为鬼雄。至今思项羽,不肯过江东。
② 《声声慢·寻寻觅觅》李清照:寻寻觅觅,冷冷清清,凄凄惨惨戚戚。

the commoners. There was the saying: "At every place where there was a drinking well, there was someone who was able to sing Liu's songs."① The most elegant piece of his romantic lyric is "Bells in Continuous Rain"②:

> Cicadas droned sadly in the cold;
> In front, night fell at the traveler's pavilion,
> While a shower had just stopped.
> No heart to drink beneath the tent at the city gate,
> We found it hard to part
> But was hurried up by the magnolia boat that was about to leave.
> Holding hands, we looked at each other with teary eyes,
> And we choked in utter silence.
>
> (Tr. by Ye Yang)

When the Yuan dynasty was founded, it has witnessed a history of more than a hundred years of booming economy and culture. The literature of the Yuan dynasty showed extraordinary vitality with diverse forms of popular marketplace literature and arts like the variety play, storytelling, the *chantefable* (弹词) and *sanqu* (the colloquial song). *Sanqu*, as a new genre of literature was heavily brewed in the Yuan dynasty, which was different from the previous *Shi* poetry or *Ci* (Song lyrics) in Tang and Song dynasties, although they share some common poetic features. *Sanqu* is sometimes mistakenly called "leftovers of the Song lyric" (ciyu, 词余), but it is more colloquial and vernacular (everyday speech as distinguished from literary language). This new style is considered a combination of the classically elegant (ya) and the common (su). Among the leading figures of *Sanqu*, Ma Zhiyuan (c. 1250 – 1324) and Zhang Yanghao (1269 – 1329) are recommended here with their representative works.

Zhang Yanghao's "Tune: Sheep on a Hillside—Lamenting the Past at Tong Pass"③:

> Peaks and pinnacles seem to rush together,

---

① 《避暑录话》叶梦得:凡有井水处,皆能歌柳词。
② 《雨霖铃》柳永:寒蝉凄切,对长亭晚,骤雨初歇。都门帐饮无绪,留恋处,兰舟催发。执手相看泪眼,竟无语凝噎。
③ 《山坡羊·潼关怀古》张养浩:峰峦如聚,波涛如怒,……兴,百姓苦。亡,百姓苦。

第一章 绪 论

    Waves and breakers seem to be angry.

    ...

    They arose — the common people suffered,

    They fell — the common people suffered.

(Tr. by Stephen H. West)

Ma Zhiyuan's "Tune: Sand and Sky—Autumn Thoughts"①:

    Dry vine, old tree, crows at dusk,

    Low bridge, stream running, cottages,

    Ancient road, west wind, lean nag,

    The sun westering,

    And one with breaking heart at the sky's edge.

(Tr. by Cyril Birch)

    Generally speaking, Chinese classical poetry has a history of no less than three thousand years, until the shifting age of Ming and Qing dynasties, when the vernacular and popular forms of literature gradually take up the place of conventional classical works. Chinese poetry has gone further away from the elegant and graceful literati's restraint but nearer to the spoken and vulgar poetics.

    So another question would naturally expect a brief discussion: Why do people read poetry? The great master Confucius said: "My little ones, why don't you study the *Book of Songs*? By the Songs you can stir, you can consider, you can express fellowship, you can show resentment."② As the following explanation goes, "Poetry is not cut off form real life but basically concerned with life, that is — with the lived fullness of the world. It extends our own limited experience by means of imagination. By imagination, it sharpens our sense of the physical world on the one hand, and on the other hand, it deepens our sense of the emotional, intellectual, and moral implications of human situations and actions.... Poetry enables us to know what it 'feels like' to be alive in the world. What does it 'feel like,' for instance, to be in love, to hate somebody, to be conscience-stricken, to watch a sunset or stand by a death-bed, to be willing to

---

① 《天净沙·秋思》马致远:枯藤老树昏鸦,小桥流水人家,古道西风瘦马,夕阳西下,断肠人在天涯。

② 《论语·阳货》:小子何莫学夫《诗》?《诗》,可以兴,可以观,可以群,可以怨。

die for a cause or to live in a passionate devotion to some chosen ideal?... We, as readers, may grow as we continue to explore the poetry of the past and the new poetry that will be written tomorrow."

While, what poem can be called good one? By John Frederick Nims, a good poem is likely to seem so spontaneous, so easy, so natural, that we can hardly imagine the poet sweating over it — crossing out lines, scrawling in between them, making out lists of rhymes or synonyms. Essentially, most poets work hard over their lines to produce a "good" one which seems to be not worked at all. A poem, however, should not be regarded as a marriage of technical devices and ideas; but an impulse to utter artistic words with sensory beauty and musical effect. The devices should enhance or expose the poem's meaning(s). But, for convenience's sake, the elements of poetry will be focused on separately in the following so that the reader can devote his/her attention to the effects achieved by certain poetic conventions.

In a word, what can poetry do for people? T. S. Eliot once said, "Poetry may make us from time to time a little more aware of the deeper, unnamed feelings which form the substratum of our being, to which we rarely penetrate; for our lives are mostly a constant evasion of ourselves." Plato remarked, "Poetry is nearer to vital truth than history." Francis Bacon commented, "Poetry (makes men) witty." So poetry can touch people's deepest heart, sooth their crying spirit and ease their disturbed mind when they're trapped in sorrowfulness and disappointment. It's a way of saying and uttering of personal feelings by reading poetry.

This textbook is chiefly intended for non-English majored graduates to provide them practice opportunities to learn English through a new vision and approach other than the traditional grammar-based reading or skill-targeted writing class. Those who have interest in poetry translation or appreciation may also find the textbook very helpful. From an academic view, to appraise poetry demands not only a superb taste in the ever-shifting symbolic system of the connotations of language and an instinct for the aesthetic significance of abstract forms and patterns, but also a deep and abiding understanding of the rhythmic psychology and even physiology of readers in general, however, the technical mastery is not so common a gift for most people.

第一章 绪 论

This textbook therefore targets to guide and encourage graduate students to study the themes of the selected poems, the feelings and the craftsmanship of Chinese poets at a non-professional level. It helps to stir students to actively participate in reading, reciting, appreciating poetry and sharing their personal ideas about the translated versions of selected Chinese poetic masterpieces. It is also intended to train students' fundamental thinking and efficient reading competence and to help students to enjoy English as part of their living experience.

The selected Chinese poems and the matched English versions in this textbook are based upon editors' personal preference and longtime teaching experience of the related courses for graduates, referring to the masterpieces of some well-known Chinese poets and Western translators or sinologists. These literary figures have created gorgeous enlightenment and vision on how human nature was defined in a beautiful and interesting manner; how the natural world is viewed through their delicate verses and musical tempos; and how their voices about the inner reflection were spontaneously uttered and expressed.

The appreciation of these poets' works in English versions might not offer any so-called professional analytic criteria to criticize and appreciate English translated poems, but very individual and even subjective insights to read, understand and enjoy the chosen English versions of these fabulous Chinese poetic creations. Students are to be acquainted with the rudimentary skills to enjoy the English versions of the Chinese poetry with a relatively larger readership, so as to enhance their interest in learning English and understanding Chinese and English literature and culture, with the purpose to establish them a habit of learning and using English in their whole life and career, further to enhance their cultural confidence.

Poetry may have no exact interpretation, so students are not expected to understand or analyse the selected poems in an academically accurate and professional way, but to find the greatest expressions and ideas in these English versions of beautiful Chinese poetry.

As for the students' practice activities, the following points are suggested to be included into students' presentation tasks:

1. Background knowledge and warm-up questions/activities.

The background knowledge can be about the poet's family/social background, the translator's nationality, translating style(s) or methods, skills, masterpieces, and appraisals etc. Some simple questions can be asked to the class to warm up for the poem reading and appreciating.

2. Structure of the selected poem.

   How does the poem develop? What is the main idea of the poem? How are these lines and sections related to each other? How is the poem read by different readers?

3. Learning of language in the translated versions of the selected poem.

   The group for this task should explain in details the new words and phrases in the translated versions.

   (1) New words: Find out the new words in the English versions to explain their meanings, give some examples, compare with synonyms and/or antonyms, and explain what do these words mean in the poem.

   (2) Lines: Find out the difficult lines in the poem to explain their meanings.

   (3) Language features and writing style: What features can you find about the language used in each English version? What rhetorical devices are used and what effects do they achieve? What style does the translator use in the poem? Why does the translator use that particular style?

   (4) Translation: Translate the Chinese poem into English version in your own words. You are supposed to compare your translated version with one or two published professional versions.

《诗经》英译鉴赏实践

  Shijing (*Shih-ching*), *Book of Songs* (or *Book of Poetry*, *Book of Odes*), also known as *Maoshi* (Mao's version of the Book of Songs, 毛诗), is one of the Confucian Classics (Five Classics, 五经). It is the first Chinese collection of three different types of songs with the total number of 305 pieces, originating in the Shang and the early and middle phase of the Zhou period. None of the 305 songs is attributed to a particular author. The anthology of poetry encompasses the voices of rulers as well as those of the common people, verses of mythological remembrance and celebration, as well as lyrics of love and hope, solitude and despair. It is this all-embracing view of human existence, expressed in the solemn and straightforward diction of pre-classical Chinese, that has established the Poetry as the foundational text of Chinese literature.

  Much of this pre-classical literature was composed out of a desire by early authors to preserve and transmit, both orally and in writing, the accumulated wisdom of their culture. Of all the early forms of literary expression, poetry perhaps best embodies the didactic purposes of ancient Chinese authors and the capacity of artful language to accomplish them. To read the lyrics preserved in the *Shijing* is both to learn the wisdom that the Chinese ancients held dear and to hear the preaching voice of the poet, instructing one to do this and not that, reminding one of the right course and warning against straying into evil ways. Because Confucius appreciated its didactic essence, he recommended the poetry of the *Shijing* to his disciples and relied on it to illustrate the principles and methods of moral cultivation he was trying to impart. Confucius's use of the ancient collection of poetry effectively made it a text of the Confucian school.

During the period of Warring States, no particular written version of the Poetry was considered primary or authoritative. Only the institutionalization of official learning (*guanxue*, 官学) at the Qin and Han imperial courts led to written versions of the Classics taught at court, especially at the Imperial Academy founded in 124 BC, and called for textual stabilization and standardization. From his time on, it became increasingly difficult to separate *Shijing* poetry from the moral lessons of Confucius's philosophy.

As shown in Table 2.1, the poetic anthology consists of three types of songs—Airs (*feng*, 风), Odes (*ya*, 雅), Hymns (*song*, 颂). The 160 Airs are arranged according to the state they originated from (hence called *guofeng*, 国风, "Airs of the states"). The Odes are divided into Major Odes (*daya*, 大雅) and Minor Odes (*xiaoya*, 小雅) and arranged in decades (*shi*, 什). The Hymns are religious chants sung in the ancestral temples of the royal house of Zhou, as well as Lu (鲁), the regional state of the Duke of Zhou (周公) and the home state of Confucius, as well as the royal house of Shang, whose descendants lived in the state of Song (宋). The Airs of the states are folk songs, often concerned with a love theme. The Odes are said to come from the aristocratic class, the Major Odes being sung at the royal court, the Minor Odes at the courts of the regional rulers. The songs collected in the *Shijing* are not only of a high literary value as the oldest songs in China, but they also reveal much of the activities of different social strata in early China. All poems are accompanied by a short preface (*xiaoxu*, 小序), the first poem also a long preface (*daxu*, 大序). With the ancient songs, "one can inspire, observe, unite, and express resentment"[①] as well as learn "in great numbers the names of fish, birds, beasts, plants, and

---

① 《论语·阳货》:《诗》,可以兴,可以观,可以群,可以怨。

trees"①; those who fail to study them "have nothing to express themselves with"② and are like a man who "stands with his face straight to the wall"③; moreover, the goal was not mere memorization but the ability to properly apply the songs in social intercourse.

Table 2.1　The Types of Songs in *Shijing*

Types	Contents	Number
Airs	South of Zhou（周南）	11
	South of Zhao（召南）	14
	Songs of Bèi（邶风）	19
	Songs of Yong（鄘风）	10
	Songs of Wei（卫风）	10
	Songs of the Kings（王风）	10
	Songs of Zheng（郑风）	21
	Songs of Qi（齐风）	11
	Songs of Wei（魏风）	7
	Songs of Tang（唐风）	10
	Songs of Qin（秦风）	10
	Songs of Chen（陈风）	10
	Songs of Kuai（桧风）	4
	Songs of Cao（曹风）	4
	Songs of Bin（豳风）	7
\multicolumn{3}{l}{Airs has generally been defined as local airs of the states, i.e., songs with musical features of various geographical regions, which are mostly shorter lyrics composed in simple formulaic language that frequently seem to assume the voice of the common folk: songs of love, courtship, pleasure and joy, frustration and anguish, dating and longing; songs of soldiers on campaign and hard-working farmers; songs of political satire and bitter protest. Their simple and often charming diction has conveyed a sense of dignity and sincerity, endowing the poetic voice with a superior capacity for truth, immediacy, and compassion that has inspired the Chinese literary tradition to the present day.}		

---

① 《论语·阳货》:多识于鸟兽草木之名。
② 《论语·季氏》:不学《诗》，无以言。
③ 《论语·阳货》:其犹正墙面而立。

续表

Types	Contents	Number
Odes	Major Odes（大雅）	31
	Minor Odes（小雅）	74
Odes, also known as *ya*, referred to the music from the Kings' Estates of Western Zhou. The word *ya* was also defined as proper（正）. At the time, the music of the Kings' Estates was regarded as the proper sounds, the music that served as model, offering relatively unproblematic narratives of morality and virtuous rulership. The division of Major Odes and Minor Odes has been quite controversial, but there were definitely differences between the two in terms of their musical features and occasions of usage.		
Hymns	Hymns of Zhou（周颂）	31
	Hymns of Shang（商颂）	5
	Hymns of Lu（鲁颂）	4
Hymns were the music used exclusively for sacrificial offerings, extensive court panegyrics of the royal house in ancestral temples, recalling the foundation and rise of the Zhou. Besides singing the praises of the accomplishments of ancestors, some of the Hymns were used as a prayer to divinity for a bumper harvest year between spring and summer, or as a tribute to divinities between autumn and winter. These songs, while being solemn in tone, are stiff and dull in sentiment, and not so appealing.		

  Shijing had always attracted the interest of all groups of persons. Confucius once said that without the *Shijing* there was nothing to talk about. With many examples from the *Shijing* he even taught his disciples.

  During the so-called literary inquisition under the First Emperor of Qin（秦始皇）, the *Shijing* survived virtually without damage, certainly because most of its songs were mainly passed on orally, which is easier for songs than for prose texts. During the early Han period（西汉）there were four different versions available: the Qi（齐）, Lu（鲁）, Han（韩）, and Mao（毛）versions. The former three were written in the modern chancery script style（*lishu*,隶书）and therefore considered as new-script texts, while the *Shijing* of Mao Heng（毛亨）and his son Mao Chang（毛苌）, was written in ancient characters and thus considered to be from the old-text tradition. For the Qi, Lu and Han versions there were "professorships"（erudites or *boshi*,博士）established at the National University

第二章 《诗经》英译鉴赏实践

(*taixue*,太学), which means that they were the imperially acknowledged versions. The Lu version was already lost in the 4th century AD, while the Han version survived until the end of the Northern Song period.

A kind of commentary on the Han version (*Hanshi Waizhuan*,《韩诗外传》) compiled by Han Ying(韩婴) has lived on, which was treated as a sub-classic writing ever since. The Qi version was lost during the 3rd century. The Mao version had been transmitted by descendants of Zixia(子夏), a disciple of Confucius. Mao Heng introduced this version of the *Shijing* to Han period scholars, but it only obtained official status during the Later Han period(东汉) and was revised and commented by Zheng Zhong(郑众), Jia Kui(贾逵), Ma Rong(马融) and Zheng Xuan(郑玄). The latter wrote a commentary called *Maoshi Zhuanjian*(《毛诗传笺》). The most important commentary is Kong Yingda's *Maoshi Zhengyi*(唐·孔颖达《毛诗正义》). Today the Mao version is the only surviving one. The Neo-Confucian master Zhu Xi(朱熹) assembled all Song period commentaries on the Maoshi and published them as *Shijizhuan*(《诗集传》).

Apart from the Airs, Odes, and Hymns, there must have been other types of songs(altogether six types of songs,诗经六义) of which no examples are preserved, namely the types of *fu*(赋) or "straightforward," which during the Han period reappears as the genre of prose rhapsody, and is a very descriptive and often didactic type of poem, and *bi*(比) or "simile, parable", and *xing*(兴), "an atmospherical introduction".

Table 2.2 Other Types of Songs

	Stylistic Devices	Function	Example
赋	straightforward	narrative, description of the lyric （叙事描写或议论抒情）	蒹葭苍苍,白露为霜。 所谓伊人,在水一方。 《秦风·蒹葭》
比	parable	comparison or analogy （以彼物比此物,同类列举,以比其义）	硕鼠硕鼠,无食我黍! 三岁贯女,莫我肯顾。 《魏风·硕鼠》 手如柔荑,肤如凝脂。 领如蝤蛴,齿如瓠犀。 《卫风·硕人》

续表

Stylistic Devices		Function	Example
兴	atmospherical introduction, stimulus	expression or evocation （触景生情，因物起兴）	风雨凄凄，鸡鸣喈喈； 风雨潇潇，鸡鸣胶胶； 风雨如晦，鸡鸣不已。 《郑风·风雨》

The great Tang period commentator Kong Yingda (孔颖达) interprets those terms in the following way: *feng*, *ya* and *song* referred to certain external compositional forms or functions, while *fu*, *bi* and *xing* were designations for certain methods of how the content of the poem was approached, or stylistic devices. During the Han period, when only the four designations of *feng*, *daya*, *xiaoya* and *song* were used, they were interpreted as the "four beginnings" (*sishi*, 四始), describing the flourishing and decline of the royal house of Zhou (周).

A very good example for the *xing* is the beginning of the Air "Guanju" (《关雎》).

Quotation 1 "Guanju" (Tr. by James Legge)

关关雎鸠，	*Kwan-kwan* go the ospreys,
在河之洲。	On the islet in the river.
窈窕淑女，	The modest, retiring, virtuous, young lady:—
君子好逑。	For our prince a good mate she.
参差荇菜，	Here long, there short, is the duckweed,
左右流之。	To the left, to the right, borne about by the current.
窈窕淑女，	The modest, retiring, virtuous, young lady:—
寤寐求之。	Waking and sleeping, he sought her.
求之不得，	He sought her and found her not,
寤寐思服。	And waking and sleeping he thought about her.
悠哉悠哉，	Long he thought; oh! long and anxiously;
辗转反侧。	On his side, on his back, he turned, and back again.
参差荇菜，	Here long, there short, is the duckweed;
左右采之。	On the left, on the right, we gather it.

第二章 《诗经》英译鉴赏实践

窈窕淑女，	The modest, retiring, virtuous, young lady:—
琴瑟友之。	With lutes, small and large, let us give her friendly welcome.
参差荇菜，	Here long, there short, is the duckweed;
左右芼之。	On the left, on the right, we cook and present it.
窈窕淑女，	The modest, retiring, virtuous, young lady:—
钟鼓乐之。	With bells and drums let us show our delight in her.

An example for the *bi* is the Air "Shuoshu"(《硕鼠》), where scheming and exploitative aristocrats are compared to "large rats".

Quotation 2 "Large Rats" (Tr. by James Legge)

硕鼠硕鼠，无食我黍！	Large rats! Large rats! Do not eat our millet.
三岁贯女，莫我肯顾。	Three years have we had to do with you,
	And you have not been willing to show any regard for us.

The Air "Qiyue"(《七月》) proves an example for the *fu* with the beginning.

Quotation 3 "Qiyue" (Tr. by James Legge)

七月流火，	In the seventh month, the Fire Star passes the meridian;
九月授衣。	In the 9th month, clothes are given out.

Especially the Hymns, and also the Odes, can be used as historiographical sources for the late Shang and early Zhou periods. Information about institutional history, leisure time activities of the upper class, as well as the hardships of the life of ordinary people can be found. Many of the Airs are simple love songs, the most famous of which being the first song of the *Shijing*. Very typical for the Airs, and also for some of the Minor Odes, is the repetition of verses in each of the stanzas, a phenomenon which is known in the West in poems of the rondo(回旋,往复) type. Another phenomenon very common in the Airs are double rhymes (*dieyun*, 叠韵), like in the verse *yaotiao shunü* (窈窕淑女) in the Air "Guanju" (《关雎》), multiple or special readings (*shuangsheng*, 双声), like in the verse *cenci xingcai* (参差荇菜) in the same Air, and repeated words (*diezi*, 叠字), like in the Air "Fengyu" (《风雨》).

Quotation 4　"Fung yu"(Tr. by James Legge)

　　风雨凄凄，　　Cold are the wind and the rain,
　　鸡鸣喈喈。　　And shrilly crows the cock.

A large part of the verses has four syllables, especially among the Airs. The songs in the *Shijing* are the oldest example for regular poems that later became so popular. From a linguistic viewpoint the rhymes of the songs are an important help for the reconstruction of archaic Chinese.

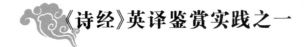

《诗经》英译鉴赏实践之一

国风·周南·关雎

关关雎鸠①，在河之洲②。

窈窕③淑女，君子好逑④。

参差荇菜⑤，左右流⑥之。

窈窕淑女，寤寐⑦求之。

求之不得，寤寐思服⑧。

悠哉悠哉⑨，辗转反侧⑩。

参差荇菜，左右采之。

窈窕淑女，琴瑟友之⑪。

参差荇菜，左右芼⑫之。

窈窕淑女，钟鼓乐⑬之。

【注释】

①〔关关〕雄雌水鸟相互应和的鸣叫声。〔雎鸠〕亦称王鴡，一种水鸟，上体暗褐，下体白色，善捕鱼。

②〔洲〕水中的陆地。

第二章 《诗经》英译鉴赏实践

③〔窈窕〕娴静貌,美好貌。窈,喻女子心灵美。窕,喻女子仪表美。
④〔逑〕"仇"的假借字,配偶,匹配。
⑤〔参差〕长短不齐的样子。〔荇菜〕又名莕菜,多年生水生草本,圆叶细茎,叶浮于水面,可食用。
⑥〔左右流之〕流,义同"求",此指顺水势摘采,时而向左时而向右地择取荇菜,这里是以勉励求取荇菜,隐喻"君子"努力追求"淑女";之,指荇菜。
⑦〔寤寐〕日夜;寤,醒时;寐,睡时,入睡。马瑞辰《毛诗传笺注通释》说:"寤寐,犹梦寐。"
⑧〔思服〕思,语气助词,无实义;服,思念。《毛传》:"服,思之也。"
⑨〔悠哉悠哉〕悠,感思,此指悠长;哉,语气助词。此句意为思念绵绵不断。
⑩〔辗转反侧〕辗,古字作"展";展转,即反侧;反侧,犹翻覆。此句意即翻来覆去无法入眠。
⑪〔琴瑟〕皆弦乐器,琴五或七弦,瑟二十五或五十弦。〔友〕用作动词,此处有亲近、结交之意。〔之〕指诗中的"淑女"。
⑫〔芼〕以手指或指尖采摘。
⑬〔钟鼓乐之〕用钟奏乐来使她快乐。乐,使动用法,使……快乐。

白话释义

关关鸣叫的雎鸠鸟,
双栖在水中的沙洲上。
美丽善良的姑娘哟,
小伙子把你记心上。

荇菜参差水面长,
采荇人左右采摘忙。
美丽善良的姑娘哟,
醒来睡着都难忘。

追求的愿望挂心上,
睡着醒来都把你想。
长夜漫漫真思念,
翻来覆去难入眠。

荇菜参差水面漂,
采荇人左右找啊找。
美丽善良的姑娘哟,
鼓瑟弹琴把你邀。

荇菜有短也有长,
采荇人前后采撷忙。
美丽善良的姑娘哟,
敲锣打鼓心欢畅。

主题鉴赏

《周南·关雎》为《诗经》十五"国风"之首篇,也是"诗三百"中最为读者所熟知的一首诗。孔子《论语·八佾》中评价《关雎》:"乐而不淫,哀而不伤"。《毛诗序》称:"《关雎》,后妃之德也,《风》之始也,所以风天下而正夫妇也。……是以《关雎》乐得淑女,以配君子,忧在进贤,不淫其色,哀窈窕,思贤才,而无伤善之心焉。是《关雎》之义也。"唐代孔颖达《毛诗正义》曰:"此诗之作,主美后妃进贤。思贤才,谓思贤才之善女。"宋代朱熹《诗集传》言:"孔子曰'《关雎》乐而不淫,哀而不伤',愚谓此言为此诗者,得其性情之正,声气之和也。"清代方玉润《诗经原始》说:"此诗佳处,全在首四句,多少和平中正之音,细咏自见,取冠《三百》,真绝唱也。"

古人解诗,多从政教德化入手,或言此诗乃颂后妃贤淑之德,或言王者求贤若渴,或言宣倡人伦之风谨严男女之行,而以情诗着眼者鲜见。正如汉儒在《毛诗序》中所说,"《风》之始也,所以风天下而正夫妇也",古人认为夫妇之德乃人伦之始,一切德行成就的根基即在于夫妇之德,而《关雎》也正是因为在"厚人伦,美教化,移风易俗"方面具有一定的典范作用,才被列为《国风》之首篇。这种解读放在古代的政教背景下,自然无可厚非。

但若以今人视角,此为歌颂纯美无瑕的男女爱情诗又何尝不可:一位翩翩君子,爱慕追求一位窈窕淑女,因此对其魂牵梦绕,念念不忘,幻想有朝一日可以与佳人携手相伴,琴瑟相和,结为连理。这种解读并未逾越"思无邪"的道德框架。

诗歌第一节以一对雌雄雎鸠于河洲和鸣的情景起兴,渲染了一种情意绵绵、痴心相恋、不离不弃的浪漫情调。雎鸠鸟儿的相鸣声——"关关",从听觉上触动了诗人的情怀。"兴"对于渲染诗歌中的和鸣气氛和触发意境乃诗经惯用之手法。此后随声望去——"在河之洲",又从视觉上引起诗人的遐思——窈窕淑女,成为君子眼

第二章 《诗经》英译鉴赏实践

中理想的求偶对象!此节重点刻画了"窈窕淑女"贤淑温婉的美好形象,惟妙惟肖地反映出君子追求淑女的心理活动。爱美之心,人皆有之,君子对于淑女的追求,可谓极尽"煎熬",虽然"寤寐求之""辗转反侧",却仍能"发乎情,止乎礼"。在与淑女相识之后,也是以演奏"琴瑟""钟鼓"这种代表高雅和礼节的乐器与她相知,体现了一位谦谦君子遵循礼法而又不失风雅的动人作风。

从艺术表现和创作手法来看,诗歌运用了双声叠韵的联绵字,即重言"关关"、双声"参差"、叠韵"窈窕",既是双声又是叠韵的"辗转"、重章复唱等手法,以增强诗歌音调的和谐美和描写人物的生动性。用这类词修饰动作,如"辗转反侧"来模拟形象,如"窈窕淑女"来描写人物,如"参差荇菜"描写场景,无不活泼逼真,声情并茂。诗歌反复交替出现采摘荇菜的忙活场景,也为本诗增添了一种别样的灵动和生机,体现出上古诗歌创作的高超水准和精湛的艺术表现力。"一切景语皆情语",从关雎、参差荇菜这些沙洲上的事物即能触景生情,从"求"这个全篇的中心到"友""乐"二字的逐渐加深,表现了一个男子对女子从爱慕,到思念,再到追求的动态心路历程,那种求之不得的焦虑和梦中求得后的喜悦,形象逼真,惹人艳羡,谓其为中国古代情诗之首,的确是实至名归。

整体而言,全诗意境清新优美,健康积极,语言含蓄隽永,情调婉转自然,流露出上古民风的淳朴和乐,读来朗朗上口,余韵不绝。

English Interpretation

"*Guanju* of Zhou Nan"(《周南·关雎》) ranks first in the *Book of Songs*, perhaps because *The Analects of Confucius* commented on it as "happiness but not lust, sorrow but not hurt."① In a word, the 305 pieces of the *Book of Songs* are pure and innocent to be used as vehicles of moral education. Conventionally, this poem is considered a political satire. American professor of Asian Studies in Princeton University Martin Kern explained this poem from the conventional perspective, as for the *Classic of Poetry* (*Book of Songs*), he paid particular attention to newly discovered manuscripts from antiquity that help us rethink the fundamentals of the Chinese poetic tradition. "In this song in four-syllable lines, the Mao commentary glosses the first word, a reduplicative binome(双声词), as

---

① 《论语·八佾》:乐而不淫,哀而不伤。

'harmonious sound'①, and the second word, an assonant binome (叠韵词), as a kind of bird that lives in separation. This nature image, filling the entire first line, is then interpreted as evocative of the virtue of the queen: she is in harmonious company with her lord but keeps the appropriate distance in order not to debauch him②. With line three, this reading is further solidified in the description of the lady. The first word, the near-rhyming binome *yaotiao* (窈窕), is glossed as 'secluded and noble'③, while the epithet for the lady is read as 'good.' Together, these word glosses generate the meaning that the 'Minor Preface'（诗小序）then elaborates upon, establishing a specific hermeneutic procedure in which evocative nature images are decoded as illustrations of human relations and behavior. The interpretation of 'Fishhawks'（Guanju）also sets the tone for the first section of the anthology, the eleven 'South of Zhou'（周南）poems that have been hailed as the paradigm of the 'orthodox airs（正风）' since Zheng Xuan（郑玄）. Furthermore, the Mao Tradition, transmitted through Zheng Xuan's commentary, came to serve as a model of reading not only for the ancient songs but also for poetry in general, including new compositions from late Eastern Han times onward." Yet up to then, the Mao reading had been the exception, not the rule. The Lu tradition — the dominant reading of the "Airs" in Han times — took the song as specific criticism of King Kang's sexual indulgence and neglect of duties; similarly, the Qi and Han interpretations read the song as a satire on excessive behavior. Some Eastern Han and later texts such as Zhang Chao's（张超）"Fu Ridiculing 'Fu on a Maidservant'"（《诮青衣赋》）maintained that "Fishhawks"（《关雎》）functioned as a satire because it confronted King Kang with an illustration of true virtue — a reading that could thus accommodate Mao glosses such as "goodness" "harmonious separation" or "secluded and pure." The later tradition reacted in mixed ways to the Mao Tradition, which had become orthodox by Tang times. Song scholars such as Ouyang Xiu（欧阳修）, Su Zhe（苏辙）, Zheng Qiao（郑樵）, Lü Zuqian（吕祖谦）, and Zhu Xi（朱熹）were critical of many of the Mao historical readings of the

---

① 《玉篇》：关关，和声也。
② 《毛诗·关雎序》：《关雎》，后妃之德也，风之始也，所以风天下而正夫妇也。
③ 《毛传》：窈窕，幽娴也。

第二章 《诗经》英译鉴赏实践

Airs. They proposed to free the Poetry from the Mao readings that they judged as obscuring straightforward expressions of folk sentiment. In the minds of these scholars, the meaning of the Airs was still open to direct access.

At present, especially the modern reading of the Airs (风) as original folk songs that express their meaning on the plain surface of their words. So this poem is popularly regarded as a love song describing the love between men and women, which inspires people to love virtue and beauty in accordance with the rites to the accompaniment of music. For according to Confucius, music imitates the harmony of the universe and the rites, its order, the ritual property and proper social conduct. The rites may serve to secure the mean in one's desires and music, in one's sentiments. The former may regulate one's mind and the latter may harmonize one's feelings. With both, man could live a happy life in a peaceful world.

In the first stanza of this poem, the technique of association is used. Human emotion is associated with the crying of love birds *jujiu* (雎鸠) or turtledoves: Turtledoves sing to each other, depend on each other and love each other, raising the association of love between a maiden and a gentlemen. The second stanza depicts the picture of the young maiden gathering cress left and right in the river. This might be the imagination of the young man missing the maiden, so his thoughts are wandering about her. The third stanza is the evocation of the happy union or grandeur wedding ceremony of the young man and the maiden at last. Music of lutes, drums and bells are taken as the solemn rite to welcome the maiden's coming. The whole poem shows a romantic love story and the open folk sentiment of the ancient Chinese in the Zhou dynasty.

学生英译实践园地

第二章 《诗经》英译鉴赏实践

英译实践版本选读

译文 1　詹姆斯·理雅各

Kwan ts'eu

Kwan-Kwan go the ospreys,
On the islet in the river.
The modest, retiring, virtuous, young lady:—
For our prince a good mate she.

Here long, there short, is the duckweed,
To the left, to the right, borne about by the current.
The modest, retiring, virtuous, young lady:—
Waking and sleeping, he sought her.

He sought her and found her not,
And waking and sleeping he thought about her.
Long he thought; oh! long and anxiously;
On his side, on his back, he turned, and back again.

Here long, there short, is the duckweed;
On the left, on the right, we gather it.
The modest, retiring, virtuous, young lady:—
With lutes, small and large, let us give her friendly welcome.

Here long, there short, is the duckweed;
On the left, on the right, we cook and present it.
The modest, retiring, virtuous, young lady:—
With bells and drums let us show our delight in her.

译文 2　威廉姆·詹宁斯

Song of Welcome to the Bride of King Wen

Waterfowl their mates are calling,
On the islets in the stream.
Chaste and modest maid! fit partner
For our lord (thyself we deem).

Waterlilies, long or short ones,—
Seek them left and seek them right.
'Twas this chaste and modest maiden
He hath sought for, morn and night.
Seeking for her, yet not finding,
Night and morning he would yearn
Ah, so long, so long! —and restless
On his couch would toss and turn.

Waterlilies, long or short ones,—
Gather, right and left, their flowers.
Now the chaste and modest maiden
Lute and harp shall hail as ours.
Long or short the waterlilies,
Pluck them left and pluck them right.
To the chaste and modest maiden
Bell and drum shall give delight.

译文 3　汪榕培　任秀桦

The Cooing

The waterfowl would coo
Upon an islet in the brook.
A lad would like to woo
A lass with pretty look.

第二章 《诗经》英译鉴赏实践

  There grows the water grass
  The folk are fond to pick;
  There lives the pretty lass
  For whom the lad is sick.

  Ignored by the pretty lass,
  The lad would truly yearn.
  The day is hard to pass;
  All night he'll toss and turn.

  There grows the water grass
  The folk are fond to choose;
  There lives the pretty lass
  Whom the lad pursues.

  There grows the water grass
  The folk are fond to gain;
  There lives the pretty lass
  The lad would entertain.

译文 4　许渊冲

Cooing and Wooing

  By riverside a pair
  Of turtledoves are cooing;
  There is a maiden fair
  Whom a young man is wooing.

  Water flows left and right
  Of cresses here and there;
  The youth yearns day and night
  For the good maiden so fair.

His yearning grows so strong,
He cannot fall asleep,
But tosses all night long,
So deep in love, so deep!

Now gather left and right
Cress long or short and tender!
O lute, play music light
For the fiancée so slender!

Feast friends at left and right
On cresses cooked tender!
O bells and drums, delight
The bride so sweet and slender!

英译鉴赏简析

四种英译文本,前两则为西方汉学家翻译,后两则为中国著名翻译家翻译,各有优劣,伯仲叔季,实难定夺。在此,仅对许渊冲先生的译文做鉴赏品评。

许先生有"诗译英法唯一人"之美誉,他终身致力于中英、中法文学翻译,向全世界译介中国传统诗词文化,一生曾翻译过《诗经》《楚辞》《李白诗选》《西厢记》等中华名著。他于2010年获中国翻译文化终身成就奖,2014年获国际翻译家联盟"北极光"杰出文学翻译奖,是首位获此殊荣的亚洲翻译家。许先生深谙汉诗之精髓,译文用词朴实无华,却语义精准,不伤原诗之意;音律和谐清朗,贴近原诗之妙;句式简短和拍,一词一字恰到好处。

诗题"关雎"译为"Cooing and Wooing",实在妙不可言。"关关"为拟声词,指雎鸠水鸟的和鸣声;"雎鸠",又名"王雎""鱼鹰",雌雄相伴,一生定偶,生活于河湖水泽边,因此,它们常用来象征不离不弃,忠贞不贰的爱情。从字面上,"关雎"指的是"关关鸣叫的水鸟",但要再现中国文化的含义,就要突出这一对"求偶鸟"的文化象征义。"cooing"既指鸽子或水鸟的叫声(cry softly, as of pigeons),又引申为男女之间说情话(speak softly or lovingly);"wooing"本意为"求助"(ask for someone's favor),引申义为"求爱"(make amorous advances towards; court):if a man woos a woman, he tries to start a romantic relationship with her and to persuade her to marry him。如此看来,"Cooing and Wooing"表达出了"关雎"的两层语义:表层意象语义和深层文化语义。在音韵上,coo 读音为[ku:],woo 读音为[wu:],属于同韵词(words with the same phonetic ending),发同一单音节长元音(the same long monosyllabic vowels),又称为元音叠韵词(vowel-rhymed words),长元音[u:]声音舒缓悠长,声情并茂地呈现出雎鸠雌雄相鸣、生机盎然的求偶景象,为君子对心慕淑女的求爱场景做好了铺垫。这也是诗经常用的"赋比兴"手法的经典范例。

第一节"关关雎鸠,在河之洲。窈窕淑女,君子好逑"中,水鸟的一唱一和与君子对淑女的爱慕相一致。许先生的译文成功保留了这一比兴手法:

By riverside a pair
Of turtledoves are cooing;
There is a maiden fair
Whom a young man is wooing.

原诗的第二节、第四节、第五节都延续了比兴的手法,都运用了"荇菜"这一核心意象,采取换词法,以"流之""采之""芼之"加以区别,在语义上,层层递进。许渊冲先生忠实原诗,在翻译这三节时,他保留了核心意象"荇菜",统一译为"cresses","左右"则译为"left and right"。同时,他对于"荇菜"在这三节中的比喻义分别采用不同的翻译方法:在第二节中,"左右流之"译为"flow left and right...here and there",比喻现实中淑女之难求;在第四节中,他以荇菜的甜美"tender"映衬淑女之"sweet",温柔贤淑,成熟待"摘",即"gather",象征君子迎娶淑女后,宴请宾朋,欢聚一堂的大喜场景。

在第一节和第二节中将"窈窕淑女"译作"a fair maiden"。"窈窕"指的是女子美丽娴静的样子,强调的是外貌;"fair"一词形容女子外貌姣好,切合"窈窕"之意。定下"fair"之后,许渊冲先生没有选用"a fair lady",而是选用"maiden"一词,"lady"使人联想起西方文化中的贵族女子,用"maiden"简单却不简陋,符合中国传统中的"淑女"形象。在第四节和第五节中,"窈窕淑女"从"fair maiden"改译为"fiancée"和"bride",此"窈窕淑女"非彼"窈窕淑女",自然要从未婚的"maiden"变成将要结婚的"bride",译文的变换也是对原诗时间过渡的精准再现。因为,大多数诗经篇章的一唱三叹,往往带有情节的变换性或递增性,所以,译者对原诗的理解程度直接决定译文的优劣。

译文整体句式每句不超过四个词,词数长短非常契合诗经"四字句"(four-character line)的句法特点。尾韵的处理更为精当,将原诗的韵表现得更加出彩:pair/fair/there;cooing/wooing;right/night/light/delight;strong/long;asleep/deep;tender/slender。

《诗经》英译鉴赏实践之二

国风·秦风·蒹葭

蒹葭①苍苍②,白露③为霜④。
所谓伊人⑤,在水一方⑥。
溯洄⑦从之,道阻⑧且长。
溯游⑨从之,宛在水中央。
蒹葭萋萋⑩,白露未晞⑪。
所谓伊人,在水之湄⑫。
溯洄从之,道阻且跻⑬。
溯游从之,宛在水中坻⑭。
蒹葭采采⑮,白露未已。
所谓伊人,在水之涘⑯。
溯洄从之,道阻且右⑰。
溯游从之,宛在水中沚⑱。

【注释】

①〔蒹葭〕蒹,又名"荻(dí)""菼(tǎn)",初生的芦苇。《说文》:葭,苇之未秀者。蒹葭,笼统言之意为初生的芦苇;细言之,幼小时叫"蒹",蒹长成后称"萑(huán)",葭长成后称"苇"。

②〔苍苍〕草色深的样子。《说文》:苍,草色也。此处引申为青黑色。

③〔白露〕中国二十四节气之一,农历八九月间。古语云:"八月白露节,秋分八月中;九月寒露节,霜降九月中。"《礼记·月令》:"孟秋之月(中略)凉风至,白露降,寒蝉鸣。(中略)是月也,以立秋。(中略)霜始降,则百工休。"《月令七十二候集解》:"白露,水土湿气凝而为露,秋属金,金色白,白者露之色,而气始寒也。"《孝

第二章 《诗经》英译鉴赏实践

纬经》："处暑后十五日为白露,阴气渐重,露凝而白也。"
④〔霜〕露水凝戾为霜。
⑤〔伊人〕伊,语助词。谓"是"之意,表强调。
⑥〔在水一方〕方,古与"旁"通用,即言在河对岸,隔河而望,不可触及。下节"在水中央""在水之湄""在水中坻""在水之涘""在水中沚"均言在河之旁,可望而不可即,全诗上下同义复用。
⑦〔溯洄〕逆流而上,故道路阻隔,心生愁忧。
⑧〔道阻〕韩诗释"阻"为"忧""险"。《疏》:皮嘉佑云:"《释文》《说文》俱云:'阻,险也。'《释诂》及《诗传》皆云:'阻,难也。'道难则心有忧危之意,故韩以忧险并释之。"
⑨〔溯游〕顺流而下。
⑩〔萋萋〕草木生长茂盛的样子。《说文》:萋,草盛,从艹从妻声。诗曰:菶菶萋萋。大雅文谓梧桐也,草木同类。毛曰:菶菶(běng)萋萋,梧桐盛也。
⑪〔晞〕晞,干。白露未晞,意指尚未成霜。《笺》云:未晞,未为霜也。
⑫〔湄〕古通"澺"。《说文》:水草交为湄。《释水》:水草交为湄。水草交际之处,即水岸;又释为"厓",水边高地。与下文"道阻且跻"义通。
⑬〔跻〕登,上升。《疏》:言其难至如升高地。
⑭〔坻〕水中小洲或高地(读 dǐ 时指山坡或地名)。《释水》云:小洲曰渚,小渚曰沚,小沚曰坻。
⑮〔采采〕茂盛,众多。
⑯〔涘〕水边高地。《说文》:涘,水厓也。
⑰〔右〕《笺》云:右者,言其迂回也。《释名》:水出其右,曰沚丘,同于沚。
⑱〔沚〕水中的小块陆地。《说文》:沚,小渚曰沚。

白话释义

初生芦苇颜色青,白露凝霜挂叶上。
心上人儿在哪方,就在河水那一旁。
逆流而上去见她,河水蜿蜒路好长。
逆流而上去看她,就在河水那一旁。
芦苇新生色青葱,霜露挂在叶梢上。
逆流而上去见她,河水蜿蜒路好长。
逆流而上去看她,就在河水那一旁。

芦苇丛簇好茂盛，露珠还在叶脉上。
心上人儿在哪方，就在河水那一旁。
逆流而上去见她，河水蜿蜒路好长。

主题鉴赏

  古希腊称诗人为"词语的运动员"(athlete of the word)，即言诗人是用词语的高手。因此，当我们在欣赏一首诗歌时，如果能意识到这位"运动员"高超的竞技技术，那么对于诗歌主题的把握应该不至于偏离太远。但实则针对《诗经》所生发的多元解读已成为千余年来中国语言、艺术、诗学、文字学、动植物学、政治学等领域极为常见的现象，《诗经》之所以能够被传颂千载，魅力永驻，与其丰富多彩的文化内涵不无关系，也与对其多元化解读紧密相关；不同时代，不同读者，不同目的，自然会产生不同的认识和理解。尤其自清代起，诸多学者摒弃了前代学者矫枉过正的学术见解，更多利用比较科学的文字音韵学、语言学、文化学等正流学术成果来重新解读《诗经》本事和主题思想，产生了许多解而有凭、释而有据的新认识、新观点，无疑为今人理解和欣赏《诗经》创造了极为有利的条件，成为当代研究《诗经》的重要学术资源和理论依托。

  也许正如约翰·弗雷德里克·尼姆斯(John Frederick Nims)所说，"任何一首诗都有可能被用来表达多重意图"，因此，对于《蒹葭》一诗的解读，同样有多种不同的见解和声音。如姚际恒《诗经通论》评《蒹葭》曰："此自是贤人隐居水滨，而人慕而思见之诗。"即所谓"思见贤人"之诗。方玉润《诗经原始》曰："《蒹葭》，惜招隐难致也。"

  又说《蒹葭》一诗三章，一唱三叹，首唱"蒹葭苍苍，白露为霜。所谓伊人，在水一方"已成千古绝唱，其余两章同意附和，不必深究。

  "伊人"在中国传统诗歌中，多指受人爱慕的美丽女子。但"所谓伊人"句，似乎与"贤人"相距甚远。因此，此说似乎不足为凭，情诗说更符合现代人的阅读视角。诗歌以清秋为背景，着力于描写主人公对心慕女子的企盼。一开始，他若有所思地站在水边，向对岸望去，看到他所爱慕的那个姑娘正向水边走来，心里很高兴；可不久，芦苇挡住了他的视线，他看不到她了。他以为那姑娘正向上游走去，也就沿着河岸向上走；走了长长的一段艰难而又曲折的路，却依旧是什么也没有看见。他不灰心，又折回来去追寻女子，最后终于看到她正站在河中的一个小洲上，这时他内心便充满了喜悦。全诗抒发了诗中男主人公对心中佳人的倾慕之情，表现出佳人难期怅然若失的情感变化，揭示了人类永恒的主题之一——爱情的独特意义。

第二章 《诗经》英译鉴赏实践

English Interpretation

The theme of "Jian Jia" remains a controversial one for over two thousand years. The well-known British sinologist James Legge said, "this piece reads very much like a riddle." "Someone tells how he sought another whom it seemed easy to find, and yet could not find him." If we believe what he said, this poem may become a narrative dealing with friendship. But most Chinese critics agree that this poem is a love song, of which opinions differ only as to whether the lover is a man or a woman.

The famous Chinese translator Xu Yuanchong held the idea that this poem is simply a love song of a man in search of his lover, as in his brief comment: "The first two lines of the three stanzas describe the season when the reeds turned from green to frost-white. The dreariness of autumn may be easily associated with the weariness of the man in search of his love. The next two lines tell us vaguely where his love is without describing her physical beauty. The last four lines depict his fruitless, hard, long journey in search of his love. The harder and the longer his journey, the more fruitless his search would appear. The more inaccessible his love, the more beautiful she would appear, not only in the eyes of the searcher but also of the reader."

学生英译实践园地

第二章 《诗经》英译鉴赏实践

英译实践版本选读

译文1 詹姆斯·理雅各

Këen Këa

The reeds and rushes are deeply green,
And the white dew is turned into hoarfrost.
The man of whom I think
Is somewhere about the water.
I go up the stream in quest of him,
But the way is difficult and long.
I go down the stream in quest of him,
And lo! he is right in the midst of the water.

The reeds and rushes are luxuriant,
And the white dew is not yet dry.
The man of whom I think
Is on the margin of the water.
I go up the stream in quest of him,
But the way is difficult and steep.
I go down the stream in quest of him,
And lo! he is on the islet in the midst of the water.

The reeds and rushes are abundant,
And the white dew is not yet ceased.
The man of whom I think
Is on the bank of the river.
I go up the stream in quest of him,
But the way is difficult and turns to the right.
I go down the stream in quest of him,
And lo! he is on the island in the midst of the water.

译文 2　威廉姆·詹宁斯

Chasing the Phantom

When reed and rush grew green, grew green,
And dews to hoar-frost changed,
One whom they speak of as "that man"
Somewhere the river ranged.
Upstream they went in quest of him,
A long and toilsome way;
Downstream they went in quest of him;—
In *mid*-stream there he lay!
When reed and rush grew tall, grew tall,
And dews lay yet undried,
He whom they speak of as "that man"
Was by the riverside.
Upstream they searched for him, along
The toilsome, deep defile;
Downstream again — and there he lay,
Midway, upon the isle!
When reed and rush were cut and gone,
And dews still lingered dank,
He whom they speak of as "that man"
Was on the river's bank.
Upstream they searched for him, along
The toilsome right-hand road;
Downstream, — and on the island there,
In *mid*-stream, he abode!

译文 3　杨宪益　戴乃迭

The Reeds

The reeds are luxuriant and green,
The white dew has turned to frost.

第二章 《诗经》英译鉴赏实践

My beloved so dear to me
Is somewhere beyond the waters.
Upriver I search for him,
The way is arduous and long.
Downriver I search for him,
He seems to be in the middle of the waters.

The reeds are exuberant and strong,
The white dew has not yet dried.
My beloved so dear to me
Is somewhere near the river-bank.
Upriver I search for him,
The way is arduous and hard.
Downriver I search for him,
He seems to be on a shoal in the waters.

The reeds are flourishing and lush,
The white dew is still falling.
My beloved so dear to me
Is somewhere near the riverside.
Upriver I search for him,
The way is arduous and tortuous.
Downriver I search for him,
He seems to be on an islet in the waters.

译文 4　许渊冲

Where is She?

Green, green the reed,
Frost and dew gleam
Where's she I need?
Beyond the stream.
Upstream I go;

> The way's so long.
> And downstream, lo!
> She's thereamong.
>
> White, white the reed,
> Dew not yet dried.
> Where's she I need?
> On the other side.
> Upstream I go;
> Hard is the way.
> And downstream, lo!
> She's far away.
>
> Bright, bright the reed,
> With frost dews blend.
> Where's she I need?
> At river's end.
> Upstream I go;
> The way does wind.
> And downstream, lo!
> She's far behind.

英译鉴赏简析

  这首诗以秋水、蒹葭、霜、白露等一系列秋天的自然意象营造了一种朦胧、清新而又神秘的意境。主人公和伊人的身份、关系、空间位置等均为未知数，给人以雾里看花、若隐若现、朦胧缥缈之感，使诗歌的主题显得难以捉摸。不同时代的学者所作的解读众说纷纭，因此，《蒹葭》可能是"诗三百"中争议比较多的诗篇之一。

  《毛诗序》《郑笺》均认为此诗为"刺世"之作："《蒹葭》刺襄公也。未能用周礼将无以固其国焉。"朱熹《诗集传》："言秋水方盛之时，所谓彼人者，乃在水之一方，上下求之皆不可得。然不知其所指也。"钟惺《评点诗经》："异人异境，使人欲仙。"姚际恒《诗经通论》云："此自是贤人隐居水滨，而人慕而思见之诗。"方玉润《诗经原始》曰："蒹葭，惜招隐难致也。……此诗在《秦风》中，气味绝不相类。以好战乐斗

第二章 《诗经》英译鉴赏实践

之邦,忽遇高超远举之作,可谓鹤立鸡群,翛然自异者矣。然意必有所指,非泛然者。《序》谓'刺襄公,未能用周礼。'吕氏祖谦遂谓'伊人犹此理'。"陈继揆《读风臆补》:"意境空旷,寄托元淡。秦川咫尺,宛然有三山云气,竹影仙风。故此诗在《国风》为第一篇缥缈文字,宜以恍惚迷离读之。"王国维《人间词话》评:"《诗·蒹葭》一篇,最得风人深致。晏同叔之'昨夜西风凋碧树。独上高楼,望尽天涯路',意颇近之。但一洒落,一悲壮耳。"陈子展《诗三百解题》说:"《蒹葭》一诗,无疑的是诗人想见一个人而竟不得见之作。这个人是谁呢?他是知周礼的故都遗老呢,还是思宗周、念故主的西周旧臣呢?是秦国的贤人隐士呢,还是诗人的一个朋友呢?或者诗人自己是贤人隐士一流、作诗明志呢?抑或是我们把它简单化、庸俗化,硬指是爱情诗,说成诗人思念自己的爱人呢?众说纷纭,难以判定。"

以上各种解读若归纳起来,大概有如下三种说法。

一为"刺襄公"说。苏东天在《诗经辨义》中阐述:"'在水一方'的'所谓伊人'是隐喻周王朝礼制。如果逆周礼而治国那就'道阻且长''且跻''且右',意思是走不通、治不好的;如果顺从周礼那就'宛在水中央''水中坻''水中沚',意思是治国有希望。"

二是"招贤"说。姚际恒和方玉润持此观点。"伊人"即"贤才","贤人隐居水滨而人慕而思见之"。所谓"征求逸隐不以其道,隐者避而不见。"

三是"情诗"说。蓝菊有、杨任之、樊树云、高亨、吕恢文等均持"恋歌"说。如吕恢文说"这是一首恋歌,由于所追求的心上人可望而不可即,诗人陷入烦恼。河水阻隔是含蓄的隐喻。"

"诗无达诂",无论哪一种解说,在其时代背景下,自有其存在的理由。或许情诗说更加接近今天的阅读视角,以此来看,这首诗的主题在于表现主人公对美好爱情的执着追求和追求不得的惆怅心情。

诗的每章开头都采用了赋中见兴的笔法,通过对眼前所见自然秋景的描写,以及对伊人的无限遐想,营造出一个空灵缥缈、怀人难见、心生惆怅的情歌意境。

四种译文,各有千秋,此举几例,以作说明。

《蒹葭》一诗意象妍丽,诗境详雅,韵律整饬,堪称《诗经》"秦风"之至篇。诗歌第一小节押同一后鼻音韵[ang]:"苍""霜""方""长"和"央"。气流经口腔入喉部,至胸腔共鸣,厚重沉吟而余音未绝。第二小节和第三小节均押元音韵[i]:"凄""晞""跻""坻""已""涘"和"沚"。第一小节是一韵到底,第二小节是一、三、四句押韵,第三小节是一、二、四句押韵。从中可以看出,第一、二节的声调变化几乎是一致的,除了一个地方有所不同,韵脚处完全一致。同一韵的优点在于整首诗的音律和谐动听,产生乐音效果,更易于歌唱或吟咏,"诗三百"甚至汉魏乐府诗大多数诗篇都是同韵一通到底。偶有变韵或跳韵现象，应属于诗歌的节拍变化或音变现象。这首诗从第三小节开始发生变韵，韵脚由原先的平声全变成了仄声，给人一种谐和转变的过渡感和跳跃感。

　　许渊冲先生一贯主张译诗"三美论"，主张之一为"音（韵律）美"。在音韵和节奏方面，他的这篇译文可谓上乘之作。首先，诗题译为"Where is She?"，而非音译为"Jian Jia"或意译为 rushes（灯芯草）或 reeds（芦苇，茅草，秸秆）等，可谓直达诗意，便于读者理解此诗的主题。其次，原诗韵律为 aaba baba，对应的英译文三节均押英诗常用谐韵 abab cdcd，如 white//bright, green//sheen, gleam//stream, hard//apart，完全再现了全诗尾韵，彰显许先生翻译之功非同一般。三节诗，双行和隔行统一韵[iː]/[əʊ]/[ʌn]，元音清朗饱满，鼻音顿挫厚重，情感从内向外，意味悠长。原诗所有的诗行都是由四或五个音节构成，许先生保留了原文四言诗的风格，译文富有歌咏性，节奏感强，符合诗经句式特点。

　　许先生的译文也特别关照叠词的音效和语义，选词简洁，语义传神，音效清朗，非常符合《诗经》诗篇的用词和音韵特点。如"苍苍""萋萋""采采"等双声叠韵词，均有"芦苇茂盛"之意，但在语体情感色彩上带有递进的目的，因此又略有差异。如何在英译中表现出这种语义层进关系，并非易事。许先生将其分别译为"green/green""white/white"及"bright/bright"，既保留了叠词的诗歌音效，又准确再现了语义推进关系。

　　相比之下，西方汉学家的译文，从整体上看，无论句式、用词、音韵等，多带有维多利亚时期英诗的浓郁风格。在音律上，采用英诗头韵法（alliteration），如"reeds and rushes"，保留了"蒹葭"二字的双声特点，较好地展现了汉诗的音韵特点。在句式上，基本遵守原诗的句子结构和顺序，更注重于对原诗意思的表达，因此，句式显得冗长，不够简洁。但理雅各基本采用逐字逐句直译法，他坚持语义忠实，这对于西方读者理解汉语原诗当然有积极的作用。但因中西文化的隔阂，其译文有不少误译之处，比如"道阻且长""道阻且跻""道阻且右"句，"阻"与"长""跻""右"，实际为合并语义，都带有"难行"之意，中间的"且"属于诗经常用的语气助词，用于衬字或补足音节，但理雅各均采取分译法，即逐字对应，分别译为"the way is difficult and long""the way is difficult and steep""the way is difficult and turns to the right"。同时，"道阻且右"之"右"，并非"右边"之意，而是"绕行，路远"之意，理雅各译为"turns to the right"实为误译。另外，理雅各译文将"伊人"译为"he"或"him"，主要原因可能在于他认为这首诗并非爱情诗，而是友谊诗，因此，诗中的主人公和伊人身份界定为男性也不足为奇。

　　总体而言，许渊冲的译文以其凝练的语言将原文犹如一幅优美的画卷呈现于

第二章 《诗经》英译鉴赏实践

读者面前，在较高程度上保持了原文的美感。同时，他将蒹葭的颜色变化从春季的绿色描绘到秋季的白色，使读者联想到主人公寻觅"伊人"的时间之漫长和过程之艰辛。在意象上，许渊冲先生在译文的意象传递上非常贴近原诗，更能以简洁平实同时又富有韵律的译文传达中国古典诗歌的意境和神韵，使西方人更易于接受和感知中国诗词的艺术魅力。理雅各的译文采用散体形式，更像是一则娓娓道来的故事，牵引着读者走入诗人的内心世界。当然，不同的社会历史背景、民族、文化和译语读者的接受现状，都将影响译者对诗歌的理解和翻译，任何一种译文都很难全面再现原诗从神韵到形式诸方面的美感。

《诗经》英译鉴赏实践之三

国风·周南·桃夭

桃之夭夭①，灼灼②其华③。
之子于归④，宜其室家⑤。

桃之夭夭，有蕡⑥其实。
之子于归，宜其家室。

桃之夭夭，其叶蓁蓁⑦。
之子于归，宜其家人。

【注释】
①〔夭夭〕夭，少也。夭夭，盛貌，桃之少壮也，即桃树含苞待放貌。鲁诗、韩诗"夭夭"作"枖枖"，草木盛茂。又曰女子笑貌。
②〔灼灼〕灼，明亮，此指花之盛放貌。经传谓：灼为焯之假借字也。
③〔华〕通"花"。
④〔之子于归〕之子，指出嫁的姑娘。归，女子出嫁。

⑤〔宜其室家〕宜,和顺,和善。室家,指夫妇。
⑥〔蕡〕果实丰硕貌。
⑦〔蓁蓁〕树叶茂盛的样子。

白话释义

桃树繁茂,桃花烂漫。
有女出嫁,夫妇美满。
桃树繁茂,果实累累。
有女嫁人,家庭和睦。
桃树繁茂,桃叶密实。
姑娘嫁人,兴家旺族。

主题鉴赏

　　这是一首祝贺年轻姑娘出嫁之诗。据《周礼》云:"仲春,令会男女。"朱熹《诗集传》云:"然则桃之有华(花),正婚姻之时也。"古语云:"父母之命,媒妁之言。"可见婚姻之事实非儿戏。据说,那时人们一般在春光明媚、桃花盛开的季节为闺阁待嫁的姑娘举办婚礼,故此诗以桃花起兴,一唱三叹,歌咏女子婚姻之喜,嫁人之庆。《毛诗序》等旧说以为本诗与后妃君王之德有关,或不可取。

　　全诗分为三章。首章以鲜艳的桃花比喻新娘的娇媚之貌。娇艳欲滴的桃花,花蕊绽放,香气馥郁,一如巧着脂粉、两腮红润、心情欢愉的待嫁新娘,既羞赧又兴奋的内心与面若桃花的外貌两相辉映,美丽动人。诗中景与人,情景交融,烘托出欢乐祥和的大喜氛围。第二章则是对婚后美好生活的期盼和祝愿。桃花盛放之后就是累累硕果。诗人说它的果子结得又肥又大,象征着新娘早生贵子。第三章以桃叶的茂盛祝愿新婚家庭的兴旺发达。桃树枝头的累累硕果和桃树枝叶的茂密成荫象征着新娘婚后生活的美满幸福,真是最美的比喻,最好的颂辞。

　　从桃花到桃实,再到桃叶,三次变换比兴,勾勒出男婚女嫁一派兴旺的景象。古人将桃花似的外"美",巧妙地和"宜"的内"善"结合起来,表达了人们对家庭和睦安居乐业生活的美好向往。

　　朱熹《诗集传》认为该诗每一章都是用的"兴"。此说固然有理,然细玩诗意,确是兴中有比,比兴兼用。全诗三章,每章都先以桃起兴,继以花、果、叶兼作比喻,极

第二章 《诗经》英译鉴赏实践

有层次:由花开到结果,再由果落到叶盛。全诗所喻诗意也渐次变化,与桃花的生长规律相适应,自然浑成,融为一体。

诗人在歌咏桃花之后,更以当时的口语,道出贺词。第一章云:"之子于归,宜其室家。"也就是说这位姑娘要出嫁,和和美美成个家。第二、三章因为押韵关系,改为"家室"和"家人",巧妙地将"室家"变为各种倒文和同义词,语义从小到大,从两个人的小家,到包括公婆在内的大家,再到丈夫的整个家族。古礼男以女为室,女以男为家,男女结合才组成家庭。女子出嫁,是组成小家庭的开始。而且,诗中反复用一"宜"字,这个"宜"字,揭示了新娘能够与家人和睦相处的美好品德,也写出了她的美好品德给新家庭注入了新鲜的血液,带来了和谐欢乐的气氛。朱熹《诗集传》释云:"宜者,和顺之意。室谓夫妇所居,家谓一门之内。"这实际上是说新婚夫妇的小家为室,而与父母等共处为家。今以现代语释为家庭,更易为一般读者所了解。各章的前两句,是全诗的兴句,分别以桃树的花、实、叶,比兴男女盛年,及时嫁娶。诗中运用重章叠句,反复赞咏,更与新婚时的气氛相融合,与新婚夫妇美满的生活相映衬,既体现了歌谣的风格,又体现了农村的物候特征。

姚际恒《诗经通论》:"桃花色最艳,故以取喻女子,开千古词赋咏美人之祖。"这种意象被后世的诗人反复使用,如《文心雕龙》:"故'灼灼'状桃花之鲜……"总之,这首短诗,言简意赅,意象练达,体现了周代社会特有的婚俗。同时,《桃夭》篇也是中国文学史上第一个用桃花比喻女子美貌的诗作。自此,"桃花"一词,成为汉语古诗中反复出现的文学意象,后世以此入诗者不在少数。三国魏阮籍《咏怀·昔日繁华子》有:"天天桃李花,灼灼有辉光。"唐代崔护《题都城南庄》云:"去年今日此门中,人面桃花相映红。"宋代陈师道《菩萨蛮》词曰:"玉腕枕香腮,桃花脸上开。"这些诗作,无一不受到《诗经·桃夭》的影响。

"诗三百"写尽了古人爱情与婚姻生活的方方面面,说明家庭和婚姻的重要性,表达了人们对美好生活的期盼,所谓"宜其家人,而后可以教国人。""宜家""宜室""宜人",层层推进,乃至最后要"宜国"。儒家传统所谓"修身、齐家、治国、平天下"的主张,从此诗可见一斑。即使今天也依旧如此:家和万事兴,有家才有国。社会的安定和祥和,离不开每一个构成社会大集体的"小细胞"——家庭的幸福和安康。桃花般的女子,贤达聪慧,嫁与如意郎君,成家立业,夫妻恩爱,子女成才,生活美满,家庭幸福,"之子于归""宜其室家",这也是和谐社会之根本。

English Interpretation

American translator Martin Kern had the following comments on "Tao

Yao": A specific feature of many "Airs" is an opening nature image followed by a juxtaposed human situation. Here, nature imagery serves as an implicit analogy to human affairs, a rhetorical technique identified as "evocation" or "stimulus" (*xing*) in the poetic tradition. Due to its indirect nature, "evocation" has proven a rather difficult concept to define, but according to the Mao reading, it governs a song like "The Peach Tree Lush":

The peach tree lush, lush,

Blazing, blazing its flowers.

This girl goes out to marry,

Suiting well her [new] house and family.

The following two stanzas are close repetitions of the first but develop the "blazing flowers" first into "ripening fruits" and then into "luxurious leaves." In Mao's interpretation, these images evoke the vitality of youth together with the appropriate timeliness of growth and development: As the fruits ripen to their fullness, so does the girl reach the proper time of marriage. This analogy is then further developed into a praise of morality and social order, as it radiates from the royal court downward to the common folk: In the ideal world of the early Zhou, the young women will not miss the right time of marriage.①

---

① 《诗集传》：文王之化，自家而国，男女以正，婚姻以时，故诗人因所见以起兴，而叹其女子之贤，知其必有以宜其室家也。……然则桃之有华（花），正婚姻之时也。

第二章 《诗经》英译鉴赏实践

学生英译实践园地

英译实践版本选读

译文 1 詹姆斯·理雅各

T'aou yaou

The peach tree is young and elegant;
Brilliant are its flowers.
This young lady is going to her future home,
And will order well her chamber and house.

The peach tree is young and elegant;
Abundant will be its fruits.
This young lady is going to her future home,
And will order well her chamber and house.

The peach tree is young and elegant;
Luxuriant are its leaves.
This young lady is going to her future home,
And will order well her family.

译文 2 威廉姆·詹宁斯

BRIDAL-SONG

Ho, graceful little peach-tree,
Brightly thy blossoms bloom!
Go, maiden, to thy husband;
Adorn his hall, his room.

Ho, graceful little peach-tree,
Thy fruit abundant fall!
Go, maiden, to thy husband;
Adorn his room, his hall.

第二章 《诗经》英译鉴赏实践

Ho, graceful little peach-tree,
With foliage far and wide!
Go, maiden, to thy husband;
His household well to guide.

译文 3 杨宪益 戴乃迭

The Peach Tree is Slender and Sturdy

The peach tree is slender and sturdy,
Flaming red are its blossoms.
The girl is getting married,
Most suitable for the house.

The peach tree is slender and sturdy,
Luscious and abundant is its fruit.
The girl is getting married,
Most suitable for the home.

The peach tree is slender and sturdy,
Exuberant and green are its leaves.
The girl is getting married,
Most suitable for the family.

译文 4 许渊冲

The Newly-Wed

The peach tree beams so red;
How brilliant are its flowers!
The maiden's getting wed,
Good for the nuptial bowers.

The peach tree beams so red;

How plentiful its fruit!
The maiden's getting wed;
She's the family's root.

The peach tree beams so red;
Its leaves are lush and green.
The maiden's getting wed;
On household she'll be keen.

英译鉴赏简析

中国古典诗词英译一直是翻译界的热门话题。以上《桃夭》一诗的英译版本共有四篇，前两篇为英国汉学家理雅各和詹宁斯所译，后两篇为中国当代翻译名家杨宪益、戴乃迭夫妇和许渊冲所译。总体而言，西方汉学家的译文读起来有一种"隔阂"的感觉。

全诗共三节，每节前两行"桃之夭夭，灼灼其华""桃之夭夭，有蕡其实""桃之夭夭，其叶蓁蓁"，有一种内在的层进关系。四篇译文，首行"桃之夭夭"均无句式、用词和音韵的变化："夭夭"意为"桃花盛放，娇艳无比"，从诗意的准确性和音韵的谐律上看，许渊冲先生的译文当最为贴近原诗。从选词的音节效果上，理雅各的译文均采用多音节形容词，统一用倒装句式，有古典英诗的特点；詹宁斯的译文句式和选词均不够整齐划一，形音皆显凌乱；杨宪益、戴乃迭和许渊冲的译文多音节、单音节词混用，音律失衡。许渊冲的译文中若能将"其叶蓁蓁"改为"How luxuriant are its leaves"似乎更佳，更能表现出诗经一唱三叹的诗节特点。

该诗的翻译难点在于每一节的后两句："之子于归，宜其室家""之子于归，宜其家室""之子于归，宜其家人"。其中，"于归"意为"姑娘出嫁"。"于"属于虚词，用在动词前，协调或补足音节；"归"的含义源于古代女子把丈夫家看作自己的归宿。前两篇译文均未直接译出"出嫁"这一层意思，后两篇译文分别使用两个关键用词"marry"与"wed"，区别如何？两个词作为动词，词义无大的差别，都有"娶妻；嫁人；男女双方结婚"的意思，而"wed"比较古雅，也偏于口语体，经常用于文学作品，"marry"一词则稍显正式。每节诗的最后一句"宜其室家""宜其家室""宜其家人"，有些学者认为没有区别，但编者以为，词序差异和变词现象并非浅层的诗歌形式的变化，应包含有时间的推进性和过渡性：女主人公从闺阁待嫁的美丽少女，到嫁与夫家的贤淑新娘，再到生儿育女、操持家庭的主妇，这一过程应该在译文中有所体

第二章 《诗经》英译鉴赏实践

现。但是,前两篇译文的前两节均无变化,仅第三节有所体现。而后两篇译文均能非常准确地再现这种时间的递进关系或过程的变化性,尤其是许渊冲的译文最能反映出三个诗节的逻辑关系。音律上,也是许渊冲的译文最为谐律:red/wed;flowers/bowers;fruit/root;green/keen。

《诗经》英译鉴赏实践之四

国风·郑风·子衿

青青子衿①,悠悠②我心。
纵③我不往④,子宁⑤不嗣音⑥?

青青子佩⑦,悠悠我思。
纵我不往,子宁不来?

挑兮达兮⑧,在城阙⑨兮。
一日不见,如三月⑩兮。

【注释】

①〔青青〕朱熹《诗集传》释"青青"为"纯绿之色"。〔子〕古时男子的美称,此诗指"你"。〔衿〕衣服的交领,周代未获取功名的读书人所穿的衣服一般称为"布衣";读书人的着装称为"青衿",一般指青色(青黑色)的衣服。
②〔悠悠〕形容忧伤,忧思难忘的样子。
③〔纵〕即使。
④〔不往〕不前往去看望你。
⑤〔宁〕岂,难道。
⑥〔嗣音〕嗣,韩诗、鲁诗"嗣"作"诒",通"贻","给""寄"的意思。此为保持音信之意。

⑦〔佩〕古代男子系在衣带上的玉饰。此指用以系佩玉的绶带。
⑧〔挑达〕挑（一说读 tāo），亦作"佻"（tiāo）。达，来回踱步的样子。亦作"挑闼""挑挞"。
⑨〔城阙〕城门两侧的用来瞭望放哨的阁楼。或特指京城。
⑩〔三月〕隔了三个月，多为虚指，即言时间很久。

白话释义

　　青青的是你的衣领，悠悠的是我的心境。
　　纵然我不曾去看你，你难道就不给我传递音讯？
　　青青的是你的佩带，悠悠的是我的情怀。
　　纵然我不曾去看你，难道你不能到我这儿来吗？
　　走来走去张眼望啊，在这高高的观楼上。
　　一天不见你的面啊，好像有几个月那么长！

主题鉴赏

　　《诗序》言："子衿，刺学校废也。乱世则学校不修焉。"要说本诗是"刺学校废"，无论如何也看不出学校废的迹象来。姚际恒在《诗经通论》说："小序谓'刺学校废'，无据。"他认为此诗大概为"思友之诗"。朱熹认为本篇"亦淫奔之诗"，他解释"挑兮达兮"是"轻儇（xuān）跳跃之貌"，"放恣也"（《诗集传》）。立场不同，所持观点也不同。朱熹把"情歌"一律视为"淫诗"，当然，《子衿》也难逃此"难"。王先谦在《诗三家义集疏》中引用曹操的《短歌行》和《北史》里的有关记载，连同朱熹的《白鹿洞赋》等史料，证实"皆用《序》说。三家无异义"。从汉魏到唐宋明清各代，一些解说《诗经》者，大多数继承了《毛诗》中"青衿，学子之所服"的说法。只有方玉润略加修改此说：他认为不是"刺"，而是"伤学校废也"。他在《诗经原始》中说："愚谓《序》言原未尝错，特谓'刺学校'则失诗人语气。此盖学校久废不修，学者散处四方，或去或留，不能复聚如平日之盛，故其师伤之而作是诗。"这种说法也没离开《诗序》主旨，仍然认为是"学校废"。

　　今人多不从此说。余冠英认为："这诗写一个女子在城阙等候她的情人，久等不见他来，急得她来回走个不停。一天不见面就像隔了三个月似的。末章写出她的烦乱情绪。"

　　由此，以男女间的爱恋之情来解读《郑风·子衿》的主题亦未尝不可。从诗歌

第二章 《诗经》英译鉴赏实践

的语气口吻来判断,此诗是写一位女子对心上人的思念似乎更加贴近当代人的阅读趣味:心上人青青的衣领和青青的佩玉令女子思念悠悠,于是独自登上城楼,遥望心上人所在的地方,一天见不到,便觉得如隔三月之久。

从创作手法来看,全诗采用倒叙,细致入微地描述了女子对心上人无限相思的微妙感人的心理活动,可谓惟妙惟肖,意境悠远,耐人寻味,的确是一首简单却淳朴至美的思念情歌,因此被称为中国文学史上描写相思之情的经典作品之一也是实至名归。

全诗共三章,前两章以"我"的口气自述怀人。"青青子衿""青青子佩",是以恋人的衣饰借代恋人。对方的衣饰给她留下如此深刻的印象,使她念念不忘,可想见其相思萦怀之情。如今因受阻不能前去赴约,只好等恋人过来相会,可望穿秋水,却不见踪影,浓浓的爱意不由地转化为惆怅与幽怨:"纵然我没有去找你,你为何就不能捎个音信?纵然我没有去找你,你为何就不能主动前来?"第三章点明地点,写她在城楼上因久候恋人不至而心烦意乱,来来回回地走个不停,觉得虽然只有一天不见面,却好像分别了三个月那么漫长。

全诗五十字不到,但女主人公等待恋人时的焦灼万分的情状如在眼前。产生这种艺术效果,有赖于诗人在创作中运用了大量的心理描写。诗中表现这个女子的动作行为仅用"挑""达"二字,主要笔墨都用在刻画她的心理活动上,如前两章对恋人既全无音问又不见踪影的埋怨,末章"一日不见,如三月兮"的独白。两段埋怨之辞,以"纵我"与"子宁"对举,急盼之情中不无矜持之态,令人生出无限想象,可谓言简而意丰。末尾的内心独白,则通过夸张的修辞技巧,造成主观时间与客观时间的反差,从而将其强烈的情绪心理形象地表现了出来,可谓因夸以成状,沿饰而得奇。

有研究者称,《子衿》是《诗经》众多情爱诗篇中较有代表性的一篇,女主人公在诗中大胆表达了自己对心上人直白、强烈、无遮无拦的浓浓思念,表现出两千多年前的女性大胆独立、自主平等、纯洁无邪、情真意切的爱情观,体现出端正美好的道德观念和精神实质。这在《诗经》以后的历代文学作品中是少见的。诗歌突出的结构特点也是《诗经》诸多诗篇一贯采用的重章迭唱法,一唱三叹,余音不绝。叠字的使用令主人公抽象难述的思念之情具象化、实体化、可触化:"青青子衿",以男子衣服的颜色触及人物内心的情感色彩,突出其与众不同的心境变化;"悠悠我心",寥寥数语即镂刻出女主人公丰富的内心活动。叠字的使用,不仅使人物形象和其心理活动更加入微可见,而且生动逼真,活灵活现,极大地增加了诗歌语言的音乐性、艺术性和共情性。

English Interpretation

The greatest Master Confucius once said that "Three hundred poems, in a word, are thoughts of innocence."[①] (*Analects*) and "With the ancient songs, 'one can inspire, observe, unite, and express resentment[②]' as well as learn 'in great numbers the names of fish, birds, beasts, plants, and trees[③]'" (*Analects*). So the traditional Confucian scholars tend to interpret every poem in the *Book of Songs* from the perspective of didactic functions, therefore it has become a moral textbook of Confucianism. As for "Zi Jin" (《子衿》), "Mao's Preface"(《毛诗序》) claimed that "Zi Jin is to satirize the wasted school, that is, in chaotic times the school is abandoned." Kong Yingda in the Tang dynasty further explained that "The state of Zheng declined, so the schools were deserted, and some scholars left, some remained. Those who have left were blamed by those who stayed on. It's to criticize the abolition of the schools." But it is hard to see any sign of abandoned schools in the poem. Zhu Xi corrected the distortion of predecessors' viewpoints as "This is also a poem of erotic lust" (《诗集传》). This explanation approximates the theme of romantic love between men and women, but goes too far.

Simply speaking, this poem is a romantic love story between a maiden and a young Confucian scholar. It portrays a maiden who has been waiting for her lover, the young scholar on the city tower because she hasn't seen him for a long time and missed him so much.

The poem consists of three chapters with the poetic technique of flashback. In the first two chapters, "Qingqing Zi Jin" and "Qingqing Zi Pei" describe the young scholar's blue clothes to recall the beautiful past memory of them and vividly reflect her love-sickness to him. The clothes of her lover has left such a deep impression on her that she wishes to meet him as they have appointed. But because of some unknown reasons, he could not go to the appointment, so the

---

① 诗三百,一言以蔽之,思无邪。
② 诗,可以兴,可以观,可以群,可以怨。
③ 多识于鸟兽草木之名。

第二章 《诗经》英译鉴赏实践

young lady became impatient and complained why he couldn't come to see her. Her strong love seems transformed into womanish melancholy and lovers' resentment: Even if I did not go to you, why can't you send a message? Even if I don't go to see you, why couldn't you come to me? The third chapter pointed out the location, where she was awaiting alone on the city tower for a long time, pacing up and down, walking back and forth with an upset and annoying mind. The last image pushed the poem into a climax: although only one day without meeting him seemed to be separated for three months.

The whole poem has less than fifty words, but the image of the heroine waiting for her lover is successfully portrayed as anxious and perplexed as at present. The acquisition of the artistic contrast lies in the poet's skillful use of a lot of psychological descriptions and lifelike verbal expressions.

学生英译实践园地

英译实践版本选读

译文 1　詹姆斯·理雅各

Tsze K'in

O you, with the blue collar,
Prolonged is the anxiety of my heart.
Although I do not go [to you],
Why do you not continue your messages [to me]?

O you with the blue [strings to your] girdle-gems,
Long, long do I think of you.
O you, with the blue collar,
Although I do not go [to you],
Why do you not come [to me]?

How volatile are you and dissipated,
By the look-out tower on the wall!
One day without the sight of you
Is like three months.

译文 2　伯顿·华兹生

Blue Blue Your Collar

Blue blue your collar,
sad sad my heart:
though I do not go to you,
why don't you send word?

Blue blue your belt-stone,
sad sad my heart:
though I do not go to you,

第二章 《诗经》英译鉴赏实践

why don't you come?

Restless, heedless,
I walk the gate tower.
One day not seeing you
is three months long.

译文 3　亚瑟·韦利

You with the Collar

Oh, you with the blue collar,
On and on I think of you.
Even though I do not go to you,
You might surely send me news?

Oh, you with the blue collar,
Always and ever I long for you.
Even though I do not go to you,
You might surely sometimes come?

Here by the wall-gate
I pace to and fro.
One day when I do not see you
Is like three months.

译文 4　许渊冲

To a Scholar

Student with collar blue,
How much I long for you!
Though to see you I am not free,
why don't you send word to me?

Scholar with belt-stone blue,
How long I think of you!
Though to see you I am not free,
why don't you come to see me?

I'm pacing up and down
On the wall of the town.
When to see you I am not free,
One day seems like three months to me.

译文 3　汪榕培　潘智丹

The Blue Collar

You wear a collar blue;
At ease I cannot be.
Though I come not to you,
Why don't you ask for me?

You wear a collar blue;
At peace I cannot be.
Though I come not to you,
Why don't you come to me?

I'm looking far away;
On the City Wall I plea.
If you come not one day,
Three months it seems to be.

英译鉴赏简析

　　《子衿》一诗的英译文本共选五首，前三个译本为外国译者翻译，后两个为中国译者翻译。总体而言，外国译者基本采取散体诗译法，忽略了原诗的音韵效果，更注重原诗的字面语义，而国内译者在选词上更加注意再现原诗的音韵效果，用词多

第二章 《诗经》英译鉴赏实践

数为单音节词,音调、音律更贴近原诗。以下就理雅各的译文和华兹生的译文做一简析:

理雅各的译文基本采用直译法,在词语的选用上,侧重于对诗行语义的剖解,而忽略了原诗的诗韵,多选用多音节词,语意凝重端庄,音节叠沓古雅。比如将"悠悠我心"译为"prolonged anxiety":"prolonged"意为"延长的,持久的",隐含着漫长等待的感觉;"anxiety"不但有"渴望"之意,还有"忧虑,担心",更能显示出女主人公久未见到心上人,既有思念又有担心不安的那种复杂心理。"嗣音"指传音信,理雅各选用了"message"(书面或口头的消息;音讯)一词,比较符合原诗的文化背景。"挑达"选用了"volatile"(易变的,尤指人的情感)和"dissipated"(沉迷于酒色的;闲游浪荡的),这两个词均源于古法语较为典雅的文体,从语义上似乎在暗示女主人公所思慕的男子对情感不够执着,因此才会令女主人公"挑达不安"。虽能够译出主人公独自等待却不见爱人的抱怨之情,但似乎语义有些夸张和失真,与诗歌主题有所偏离。

另外,理雅各的译文中还增译了感叹词"O",带有低吟舒缓的语音效果的感叹词,表达了女子思慕恋人情浓意切却久未见面的哀怨情感,使诗歌的整体气氛更加饱满。

华兹生的译文同样采用直译法,但更加注意译文与原诗结构、诗意和节奏的逐词逐句的对应关系。形容词的重复使用和消减英语 be 动词的译法,与汉诗诗行长度、音节保持高度一致,如 blue blue your collar; sad sad my heart; restless, heedless。这种译法明显有悖于英文的常规语法规则,但却成功复制了汉诗隐性语法的句法特点,诗意上再现了女主人公急切焦灼的心理状态,故而华兹生的译文不失为一种翻译汉语古诗的大胆尝试。尤其突出的亮点是他巧妙捕捉到"挑兮达兮"的丰富情感内涵,因此其翻译准确而精当,无须使用无助于表达的任何修饰词,仅仅通过"restless"(不安的,坐卧不宁的)和"heedless"(心不在焉的)这两个带有同样后缀-less且长度相等、语义近似的形容词,即能活灵活现地表现出女子期盼与心上人见上一面的急迫不安,魂不守舍的焦灼心态。而且在音节上,与"挑""达"的双声效果和"……兮……兮"的同韵效果巧妙吻合,可谓形、音、义的精妙之译。

《诗经》英译鉴赏实践之五

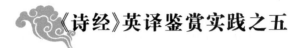

国风·鄘风·载驰

载驰载驱①,归唁卫侯②。
驱马悠悠③,言至于漕④。
大夫跋涉⑤,我心则忧。

既不我嘉⑥,不能旋反⑦。
视尔不臧⑧,我思不远⑨。

既不我嘉,不能旋济⑩?
视尔不臧,我思不閟⑪。

陟彼阿丘⑫,言采其蝱⑬。
女子善怀⑭,亦各有行⑮。
许人尤之⑯,众稺且狂⑰。

我行其野,芃芃⑱其麦。
控⑲于大邦,谁因谁极⑳?
大夫君子,无我有尤㉑。
百尔所思㉒,不如我所之㉓。

【注释】

①〔载驰载驱〕语助词。孔疏:走马谓之驰,策马谓之驱。高亨注:载,犹乃也,发语

第二章 《诗经》英译鉴赏实践

词；驰，驱，车马疾行。
② 〔唁〕吊唁。一说许穆公夫人归宗国吊唁其去世的父亲卫懿公（卫侯）；一说为许穆夫人悼宗国危亡之意。韩诗：吊生曰唁，吊失国亦曰唁。
③ 〔悠悠〕路途遥远。
④ 〔漕〕地名。毛传：漕，卫东邑。《诗三家义疏》："毛序：……卫懿公为狄人所灭，国人分散，露于漕邑。……（露于漕邑者，谓戴公也。）"
⑤ 〔大夫〕指许国赶来阻止许穆夫人去卫国吊唁的大臣们。〔跋涉〕草行曰跋，水行曰涉，合而用之，意为事急不问水之浅深，直前济度，视水行如陆行。
⑥ 〔嘉〕同意，赞许。《释诂》：嘉，美也。
⑦ 〔旋反〕旋反，同"还返"。还归，返回。
⑧ 〔视〕表示比较（双方的观点）。〔臧〕好，善。一说许穆夫人追念旧事，之所以请嫁于齐国，为日后宗国有事，可得齐国之援救，因此自己的想法乃是"嘉美也"。果然，宗国今日"不臧"（被狄人入侵），也无法"旋济"（不能旋反）。
⑨ 〔思〕忧思。〔远〕摆脱。
⑩ 〔济〕渡河；有益。另释为"止"。
⑪ 〔閟〕同"闭"，闭塞不通。一说"閟与祕同，密也。"
⑫ 〔陟〕登山。〔阿丘〕一侧高一侧矮的山丘。
⑬ 〔言〕语助词。〔虻〕贝母草，产于高山苔原地带。《毛诗传》："偏高曰阿丘。……升至偏高之丘，采其虻者，将以疗疾。"古人采虻以治病，此喻指许穆夫人设法挽救宗国。
⑭ 〔善怀〕善，多。怀，思考。女子多思念其父母之国。
⑮ 〔行〕指做事的准则；另释为"道路"。
⑯ 〔许人〕许国大夫。〔尤〕古同"訧"，意为过失，指责，怪罪。
⑰ 〔众〕一说同"终"，一说"众人"。〔稚〕引申为愚妄，不能见事理之大。
⑱ 〔芃芃〕芃，草盛貌。《郑笺》："麦芃芃者，言未收刈，民将困也。"此指卫国丧乱已久，救援无人。
⑲ 〔控〕往告，赴告。
⑳ 〔因〕亲也，依靠。〔极〕至，指来援者的到达。
㉑ 〔无我有尤〕无过我者，对我不要怪罪。
㉒ 〔百尔所思〕（虽然）你们有百种想法。尔，女（汝），此指许国的大夫们。
㉓ 〔之〕前往，指许穆夫人祈求于大国以救邦危。

白话释义

驾车急急去赶路,回家吊唁我卫侯。
路途遥远马快跑,终于到达漕城下。
许国大臣挡前路,令我心急如火焚。

即使反对我想法,怎能就此驱马还。
各人想法均不同,我的想法行得通。

登上高高的山丘,采些母贝把病治。
女人善于细思量,想法有理又有据。
许国大夫不明白,想法幼稚欠思虑。

穿过卫国的田野,麦苗葳蕤还未割。
祈求大国能出手,解救卫国于危亡。
各位大夫听清楚,不要对我硬阻挠。
思前想后多犹豫,不如让我去行动。

主题鉴赏

该诗是"诗三百"中彰显爱国情怀主题的代表性诗歌。《诗三家义集疏》载:

"鲁说曰:许穆夫人者,卫懿公之女、许穆公之夫人也。初,许求之,齐亦求之,懿公将与许,女因其傅母而言曰:'古者诸侯之有女子也,所以苞苴玩弄,系援于大国也。今者许小而远,齐大而近,若今之世,强者为雄,如使边境有寇戎之事,惟是四方之故,赴告大国,妾在不犹愈乎?今舍近而就远,离大而附小,一旦有车驰之难,孰可与虑社稷?'卫侯不听,而嫁之于许。其后翟人攻卫,大破之,而许不能救,卫侯遂奔走涉河,而南至楚丘。齐桓往而存之,遂城楚丘以居,卫侯于是悔不用其言。当败之时,许夫人驰驱而吊唁卫侯,因疾之而作诗。"

许穆夫人被称为中国文学史上的第一位爱国女诗人。《载驰》在强烈的矛盾冲突中表现了深厚的爱国主义思想。许子东先生说,"诗人的个人情感,一旦进入文学,便会具有社会意义。"《载驰》即是一篇以个人情感为微观视角却洋溢着爱国情怀的伟大诗篇,也是《诗经》诸多篇章在独特的社会背景下所承载的教化民众、针砭

第二章 《诗经》英译鉴赏实践

时事的社会功能的体现,即所谓"微言大义",实现"寓褒贬,别善恶"这样的社会功能。

身为卫国之女,但嫁与许国的许穆夫人,在获悉父母之邦卫国被狄(翟)人所灭之时,能够力排众议,冲破重阻,跋山涉水,毅然决然地返回宗国,亲自吊唁兄长戴公,并向齐国求救,竭尽全力拯救祖国于危亡之际。

此诗为许穆夫人到达漕邑城楼之下,被后面赶来的许国大夫所阻时创作的感人诗篇。个人的情绪,一旦投放到宏大的历史背景下,便产生了非常深远的社会意义,因此,这首诗便不再是一篇表达个人怨怒的个人作品,而是一种承载着可歌可泣的爱国精神的诗篇。虽为弱小女子,她却大胆地冲破传统礼教和道德对女性的束缚,号召卫国民众上下一心,团结一致,积极迎战,共御国辱,保全社稷。但许国那些固守封建礼教的大夫们,却在家国存亡之际,仍禁守着限制女子抛头露面的传统礼教,对她百般阻挠,不让其亲自去祈请大国之助。一边是心系宗国,敢于冲破礼教束缚的女子,一边是冥顽不化,胆小羸弱的许国大夫,两股力量的矛盾冲突随章节逐次升级,为读者烘托出一位有胆有识的豪情女子的高大形象,让人不禁肃然起敬。

诗歌以第一人称叙事口吻切入,截取重大历史事件的瞬间记忆,读者无须深究诗歌背后具体的历史事件的内容,只需将关注点投射于许穆夫人这一焦点之上,便能被其独特的胆识和勇气所折服,所感动。

文学的作用不仅仅在于怡情,更应在于其对人的精神和意志的唤起和激活功能。有学者评论道:"《载驰》是许穆夫人悯其宗国颠覆,归唁卫侯的纪事之作。……耿耿爱国之心,可质天日。因此,我们不仅称许穆夫人是公元前七世纪我国的爱国女诗人,也是世界上最早的一位爱国女诗人。"

English Interpretation

The British sinologist Arthur Waley had such comments on Zai Chi: "The general situation in this poem is quite clear. The speaker is a lady of Wei, unhappily married in Xu, a small State to the southeast of Wei. She attempts to go back to her own people and home, but is detained by the men of Xu. She speaks of Xu as a 'great land' out of conventional courtesy. Tradition says that she was Mu Fu-jên, a Wei princess married to the Lord of Xu about 671 B. C." So is this poem simply about the unhappy marriage of Lady Xu who wanted to go back to her homeland?

Traditionally, Lady Xu is considered the first patriotic poetess in the history of Chinese literature. As the princess of the State of Wei, she was married with the Duke Mu of the State Xu and became Lady Xu. When she heard that her motherland was invaded and occupied by the foes of Di, she was eager to call upon the court nobles to rescue her motherland from the hand of the invaders, but the coward nobles were unwilling to risk their life to support her. Instead, they made every effort to stop her. However, Lady Xu not only resisted the opposition and broke through the obstacles, but resolutely returned to her country and tried to save the motherland from peril. Zai Chi reveals the profound patriotism of an ancient female to her motherland.

第二章 《诗经》英译鉴赏实践

英译实践版本选读

译文 1　威廉姆·詹宁斯

THWARTED

O forth would I gallop and homeward fly
To cheer in his trouble my lord of Wei;
And urging my steeds the livelong day
Ts'o's city would reach without delay.
But an officer hies o'er stream and plain,
And I, to my sorrow, must needs remain.
My pleasure, it seems, is not your own;
My hopes of return ye have overthrown.
Yet, though it is plain ye disapprove,
The thoughts of my heart no power can move
My pleasure is not your own, it seems,
And now can I not recross the streams.
Yet, though ye approve not, as'tis plain,
The thoughts of my heart can none restrain.
I'd climb to the top of yonder hill,
And gather the lily that care can kill.
We women are full of wants (ye say),
And every want must have its way.
But wrong are ye there, ye men of Hiu;
And childish and headstrong all are you!
I'd travel across the wide, wide plain,
Now clad in its rich long waving grain,
And make my appeal to the sovereign State;
For whose is the cause—the need so great?
Ye officers, ye of high degree,
Say not that the error lay with me:
For the counsels of all of you combined

Fall short of the course I had in mind.

译文 2　詹姆斯·理雅各

Tsae ch'e

I would have galloped my horses and whipt them,
Returning to condole with the marquis of Wei.
I would have urged them all the long way,
Till I arrived at Ts'aou.
A great officer has gone, over the hills and through the rivers;
But my heart is full of sorrow.

You disapproved of my [proposal],
And I cannot return [to Wei];
But I regard you as in the wrong,
And cannot forget my purpose.
You disapproved of my purpose,
And I cannot return across the streams;
But I regard you as in the wrong,
And cannot shut out my thoughts.

I will ascend that mound with the steep side,
And gather the mother-of-pearl lilies.
I might, as a woman, have many thoughts,
But every one of them was practicable.
The people of Heu blame me,
But they are all childish and hasty [in their conclusions].

I would have gone through the country,
Amidst the wheat so luxuriant.
I would have carried the case before the great State.
On whom should I have relied? Who would come [to the help of Wei]?
Ye great officers and gentlemen,

第二章 《诗经》英译鉴赏实践

Do not condemn me.
The hundred plans you think of
Are not equal to the course I was going to take.

译文 3　亚瑟·韦利

(Untitled)

I ride home, I gallop
To lay my plaint before the lord of Wei,
I gallop my horses on and on
Till I come to Ts'ao.
A great Minister, post-haste![①]
How sad my heart.

He[②] no longer delights in me;
I cannot go back.
And now, seeing how ill you use me,
Surely my plan is not far-fetched!

He no longer delights in me;
1 cannot go back across the river.
And now, seeing how ill you use me,
Surely my plan is not rash!

I climb that sloping mound,
I pick the toad-lilies.
A Woman of good intent
Has always the right to go.
That the people of Hsü should prevent it
Is childish, nay, mad.

---

① Sent to bring her back.
② Her husband in Hsü.

I walk in the wilderness;
Thick grows the caltrop.
Empty-handed in a great land,
To whom could I go, on whom rely?
Oh, you great officers and gentlemen,
It is not I who am at fault;
All your many plans
Are not equal to what I propose.

译文 4　许渊冲

Patriotic Baroness Mu of Xu

I gallop while I go
To share my brother's woe.
I ride down a long road
To my bother's abode.
The deputies will thwart
My plan and fret my heart.

"Although you say me nay,
I won't go backward the other way.
Conservative are you
While farsight'd is my view?

"Although you say me nay,
I won't stop on my way.
Conservative are you
I can't accept your view."

I climb the sloping mound
To pick toad-lilies round.
Of woman don't make light!

第二章 《诗经》英译鉴赏实践

My heart knows what is right.
My countrymen put blame
On me and feel no shame.

I go across the plains;
Thick and green grow the grains.
I'll plead to mighty land.
Who'd hold out helping hand.
"Deputies, don't you see
The fault lies not with me?
Whatever may think you,
It's not so good as my view."

英译鉴赏简析

首先,从诗歌题目来看,四种译文对"载驰"的处理方法迥然有别。

译文 1 中,詹宁斯译为"THWARTED"(thwart 的过去式和过去分词),意为"阻挠;使受挫折;挫败",与许穆夫人试图挽救母国于危亡之际却遭遇母国朝廷苟且贪生的大臣们百般阻挠这一诗歌主题思想比较贴近,但仍显得隔靴搔痒,未达要义。

译文 2 中,理雅各按照"忠实"原则,采用威妥玛拼音(Wade — Giles romanization)译法译为"Tsae ch'e",但此译法在语义上无助于读者理解许穆夫人快马加鞭马不停蹄(载驰)地奔回母国的主题。

译文 3 中,韦利以"Untitled"(无题)为题,主要原因可能在于韦利英译《诗经》时(1960 年版),根据诗歌的不同内容主题,打乱重排,分成爱情、婚姻、战争、宴饮、农桑等十几个主题,因此,每一首该主题下的诗篇基本都是"Untitled"。

译文 4 中,许渊冲先生作为中华典籍资深译者,深得翻译之道,把"载驰"译为"Patriotic Baroness Mu of Xu",意为"爱国的许穆夫人",许穆夫人的身份、爵位,以及诗歌的主题一目了然。同时,从译文用韵来看,詹宁斯严格遵循韵体诗译法,采用双行体(couplet rhymes)尾韵,以及头韵、腹韵等独特的音效词:

fly/Wei[eɪ]
day/delay [leɪ]
plain/remain [eɪn]

own/overthrown [əʊn]

disapprove/move [uːv]

seems/streams [iːmz]

……

从音效上，整体音乐感非常接近原诗，节奏明快而紧凑，紧张而飞驰。

理雅各和韦利的译文，均未遵守原诗的诗歌韵律，而是采用散体诗译法。理雅各的译文译法细密，用词考究，但同时也显得句式冗赘，用词复杂。在语义再现方面，这种译法有其优点，但对于汉语原诗的"形"而言，的确较为偏离。

相较而言，许渊冲先生一贯遵循其"三美主义"翻译原则，即"音、形、义"三个维度，完美再现了汉诗之"诗歌性""文学性"。具体而言，用词上，许渊冲先生的译文尽力保持四字行（four-character line），比如首句"载驰载驱，归唁卫侯"（I gallop while I go//To share my brother's woe），"gallop//go"动词妙用，形意俱佳，言简意赅地再现了主人公"I"驾马驱驰的动态感和急迫感，"while"一词不仅符合"载……载"的并列功能，而且在音效上堪称完美，行内"while//I [aɪ]"，双行体尾韵"go/woe [əʊ]"均非常谐韵。词义准确度、贴近度上，许渊冲先生的译文最佳。

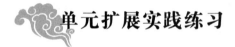

单元扩展实践练习

一、请试译以下诗经名句。

1. 执子之手，与子偕老。（《邶风·击鼓》）
2. 一日不见，如三秋兮！（《王风·采葛》）
3. 爱而不见，搔首踟蹰。（《邶风·静女》）
4. 桃之夭夭，灼灼其华。（《周南·桃夭》）
5. 未见君子，忧心忡忡。（《召南·草虫》）
6. 巧笑倩兮，美目盼兮。（《卫风·硕人》）
7. 谁谓河广，一苇杭之。（《卫风·河广》）
8. 榖则异室，死则同穴。（《王风·大车》）

第三章

建安诗英译鉴赏实践

 导 读

  The Han dynasty can be divided into two periods, the Western Han and the Eastern Han. The Western Han dynasty, also known as the former Han, began in 202 BC, which was established by Liu Bang（刘邦）. The Eastern Han, also known as the later Han, was established in 25 AD with the accession of Emperor Guangwu of Han. During this period, the political system was established, the society was stable, and the economy developed at a faster pace than the previous times. The feudal autocracy and ideological control in some sense severely restricted the academic learning and cultural development during the period of the Western and Eastern Han dynasties.

  The culture has been largely influenced by the Study of Classics, especially the thought of Confucianism. Although it witnessed setbacks in its development, the culture has made some remarkable achievements. During the age of the Han, the court was the center of literary creation. There existed various forms of poetry, including the four-character line poems, Chuci (Chu Lyrics，楚辞), the five-character line poems, and the seven-character line poems. Many of the poetry in the Han dynasty focused on beautiful language, orderly syntax, and layered structure to depict various objects, spectacular scenes of nature, court occasions, and imperial activities, stimulating the reader's sensibility and imagination to achieve aesthetic pleasure. There were many well-known poets in the Han dynasty, for instance, Sima Xiangru, Jia Yi, and Yang Xiong, etc. They promoted the development of ancient Chinese poetry and had a great influence on the literature of the subsequent dynasties.

The "Three Kingdoms" were three states that succeeded the Eastern Han dynasty (东汉) and came into being as the only surviving dominions of three warlords that contended for imperial power. The Kingdom of Wei (魏), founded by Cao Pi (曹丕, known as Emperor Wen of Wei, 魏文帝), is normally seen as the rightful successor of the Han dynasty. It ruled over northern China, while the south was controlled by the Kingdom of Wu (吴), founded by Sun Quan (孙权). The region of Sichuan and Yunnan was dominated by the Kingdom of Shuhan (蜀汉), established by Liu Bei (刘备). The name "Three Kingdoms" has become a common term because it is the popular translation of the historical novel *The Romance of the Three Kingdoms* (《三国演义》).

The division between north and south in the early 3rd century intensified the cultural, political and economic differences between these two parts of China. The Kingdom of Wei saw the introduction of a pseudo-moral ranking of eminent families in nine grades (九品). The highest of them had the exclusive access to eminent state offices. The 3rd century also experienced a general militarization of society. The Kingdom of Wu in the southeast was characterized by an antagonism between the imperial court and the local gentry. The Kingdom of Shuhan, whose rulers claimed the inheritance of the Han dynasty, instead perpetuated the solitary standing of the society in the Sichuan Basin. The latter was conquered by the Kingdom of Wei. The Kingdom of Wei succumbed to internal quarrels and was replaced by the Jin dynasty (晋), founded by a powerful general of the Sima clan (司马家族).

Generally, the literature of the Wei and Jin Dynasties has been considered flourished from the Jian'an period, which is the last period of Eastern Han. At that time, five-character-line poems have reached maturity, and *fu* has gained great development. Moreover, the prose like the letter, petitions, inscriptions, etc. was flourished during the Jian'an period. It is often assumed that the

第三章 建安诗英译鉴赏实践

flourishing culture of the Jian'an period had much to do with the interests of Cao clans including Cao Cao and his two sons Cao Pi and Cao Zhi. The content of the Cao clans' literature is mainly related to their personal experience and is closely connected with the contemporary political and historical events. Cao Cao was not only an aggressive and strategic politician and militarist in northern China, but one of the most influential figures in the literary world during the Jian'an period. He was uninhibited by nature, unrestrained, and practical. His literary works reflect his thoughts and personality to a certain extent. And his poems often show a macroscopic vision, broad-mindedness, and majestic grandeur. Cao Pi, the son to Cao Cao, was also an accomplished figure in old-styled poetry. Most of his poems are verbal texts for Music Bureau songs. The language of his poems is concise and easy to understand, with detailed descriptions and vivid images. Cao Zhi was Cao Pi's younger brother. He was a talented poet and left a great number of superb poems for later generation. His poems focus on diction, imagery, structure, and rhetoric.

Cao Cao

Cao Cao (155-220), courtesy name Cao Mengde (曹孟德), posthumously entitled "Emperor Wei Wudi" (谥号魏武帝), was one of the powerful warlords at the end of the Eastern Han dynasty. Although Cao Cao's intention was to protect the under-age emperor of the Han dynasty, his son Cao Pi (曹丕) ended the Han dynasty by his proclamation of the Kingdom of Wei in 220 AD that was to be one of the so-called Three Kingdoms (三国时期). Cao Cao was not the founder, but the ancestor of the Wei (魏) or Cao-Wei dynasty (曹魏). Cao Cao is known as a formidable politician and military leader.

Cao Cao came from Pei (沛县) in present Anhui Province. His father Cao Song (曹嵩) had been raised by a court eunuch called Cao Teng (曹腾) and was able to climb the ladder of official career to the position of Defender-in-chief (太尉). Cao Cao himself became a court gentleman and took part in the suppression of the Yellow Turban Uprising (黄巾起义). For his successful campaign he was appointed commandant of the control army (典军校尉). When Dong Zhuo (董卓) destroyed the eunuch faction at the imperial court and assumed dictatorial power of the central government, Cao Cao fled to Luoyang where he assembled an army to attack Dong Zhuo, jointly with the powerful warlord Yuan Shao (袁绍). Cao Cao was the only commander of the rebel armies who dared to attack Dong Zhuo. When he successfully drove Dong Zhuo out of the capital, he was rewarded with the post of governor (taishou, 太守) of the commandery of Dongjun (东郡). In 192, Cao Cao was again dispatched to the field to suppress the Yellow Turban Uprising in the eastern part of the empire. In the subsequent years, Cao Cao demonstrated his superior military skills in the campaigns against a series of local potentates that challenged the Han dynasty. He defeated Yuan Shu (袁术), Tao Qian (陶谦), Zhang Miao (张邈) and Lü Bu (吕布) and finally became the sole military leader that could challenge the powerful general Yuan Shao. In 200, he defeated the vastly superior army of Yuan Shao in the battle of Guandu (官渡之战) and was able to secure the whole of northern China for the dynasty. He also forced the tribal federation of the Wuhuan (乌桓) into submission that controlled China's northeastern land.

In 208 Cao Cao was appointed Counsellor-in-chief (丞相). In the following years he tried to conquer southern China that was controlled by Liu Biao (刘表), Sun Quan (孙权) and Liu Bei (刘备). Liu Biao's son Liu Cong (刘琮) submitted to Cao Cao, but the two others were able to resist the ruler of the north. In the battle of the Red Cliff (赤壁之战) in 208, Cao Cao's army was heavily defeated, and a conquest of the south was from then on impossible. Instead, Cao Cao solidified his rule over the north, suppressed rebellions like Ma Chao (马超) and Han Sui's (韩遂) uprising in the west and the secular state of the Daoist leader Zhang Lu (张鲁) in the region of Hanzhong (汉中).

Although he was still theoretically a subject of the Han dynasty, Cao Cao factually ruled as an emperor. He was given the title of Duke of Wei, later as Prince of Wei (魏王). He used the banner of an emperor, wore the robes and caps of an emperor and was revered with all honors only a ruler was allowed to be addressed with. Yet it was only his son who formally made an end to the Han and proclaimed the Kingdom of Wei.

Cao Cao was the first person to comment the military classic *Sunzi Bingfa* (《孙子兵法》) and also compiled a lot of military treatises by himself. He was also a renowned poet and composed a lot of elegies like "Xielu Xing" (《薤露行》),

"Haoli Xing"(《蒿里行》) or "Buchu Xiamen Xing"(《步出夏门行》). He supported a lot of poets at his court and thus induced the flourishing age of poetry during the Jian'an reign (建安时期).

Cao Pi

Emperor Wen (魏文帝), personal name Cao Pi (曹丕), courtesy name Cao Zihuan (曹子桓), was the son of the warlord Cao Cao and founder of the Kingdom of Wei (魏) that ruled over one of the Three Kingdoms. He came from the district of Qiaoxian (谯县) and was made Commander in Charge of Imperial Official (五官中郎将) and Vice Counsellor-in-chief (副丞相) during the time when his father already dominated the court of the Eastern Han dynasty. In 217 he was nominated heir (crown prince, 太子) of Cao Cao. On the death of his father, he succeeded his father as Prince of Wei (魏王) and Counsellor-in-chief. Shortly later he deposed Emperor Xian (汉献帝) and proclaimed the Wei dynasty. As an emperor, he also proclaimed a new reign motto and shifted the capital back from the provisional seat in Xuxian (许县), where his father had his stronghold, back to Luoyang (洛阳). Cao Pi tried strengthening the power of the emperor by cutting the importance of the offices of the Three Dukes (三公) and giving more responsibility to the imperial secretariat (尚书台). He could thus reign through a bureaucratic institution of clerks rather than with the support of powerful persons, and, in a very legalist manner, gained more power by making himself free of the influence of generals and relatives of empresses which had been a problem through the whole Han period. Cao Pi was also very careful with granting titles of nobility and only gave territories to princes and meritorious officials that would not provide them with sufficient economical and military resources to challenge the central government. At the same time, state officials supervised all activities of the princes and marquesses. Disobedience among the nobility was ruthlessly punished. For the recruitment of able persons staffing the bureaucracy, Cao Pi introduced the system of the nine ranks (九品中正制), by which all eminent families were classified into one of nine categories and officials could be recruited for all nine ranks of the bureaucracy.

Cao Pi personally led three campaigns against the Kingdom of Wu in China's southwest, but he failed three times to defeat emperor Sun Quan (孙权), not to speak of conquering his empire.

Cao Pi's posthumous title is "Cultivated Emperor" (Emperor Wen, 魏文帝). This is because Cao Pi is known for his love of literature, especially poetry. Like his brother Cao Zhi (曹植), he wrote a lot of poems, and his "Yan Ge Xing" (《燕歌行》) is one of the first poems written in seven-character verses. His book *Dianlun (On the Standards of Literature*, 《典论》), of which only the chapter "Lunwen" ("Discussing Literature", 《论文》) has survived, is China's oldest literary critique.

Cao Zhi

Cao Zhi (曹植), courtesy name Zijian (子建), was the son of the warlord Cao Cao (曹操) and Empress Bian (卞后), and the younger brother of Emperor Wen (魏文帝). As a young boy he was very intelligent and able to recite poems, essays, and rhapsodies (赋) from memory. Cao Zhi was called the "embroidered tiger" (绣虎) because his writings were so beautiful.

Cao Pi and Cao Zhi are conventionally portrayed as rivals who competed to be named their father's successor. The competition between Cao Pi and Cao Zhi for designation as heir was fierce and involved intrigue and scheming on both sides. Cao Zhi's reckless behavior eventually resulted in the loss of his father's favor. His father loved him so much that he planned to name Cao Zhi his successor, and was in this plan supported by Ding Yi (丁仪). Yet Cao Zhi was not reverent and assertive enough and fond of wine.

His elder brother Cao Pi often envied him, thought about killing him, and once—planning to humiliate Cao Zhi—ordered him to compose a poem within seven paces. Cao Zhi just pondered a few seconds to reflect, and then answered by presenting the "Seven-Pace Poem" (《七步诗》), in which he compared the two brothers as the bean straw that should not be used to cook beans. When Cao Pi mounted the throne, he made his brother Prince of Dong'e (东阿王), later of Chen (陈王). Cao Zhi asked several times to be appointed to a real government post, but was never granted this favour. His posthumous title is Prince Si (陈思王). Some of the poems of this period do have a clear connection with contemporary events.

Most of Cao Zhi's regular poems are five-character verses (五言诗) and use comparisons (比) and descriptive associations (兴) as stylistic devices. His language is very refined and rich in terms. They can be seen as an advancement of the Han period music-bureau poems (乐府) to a higher literary level. Representing the apogee of Han period poetry, Cao Zhi's poems are also the precursor of the very rich and complex poetry and prose-poetry of the Southern and Northern dynasties (南北朝), and also influenced the famous Tang poetry. The critic Zhong Rong (钟嵘) wrote in the book *Shipin* (《诗品》) that the structure of Cao's poems was "extraordinarily high", and his words "brilliant and multifaceted" (骨气奇高,词采华茂).

Part of Cao Zhi's early poems were written in an optimistic mood that the newly-founded Wei Kingdom might guarantee peace and prosperity, like in the poem "Bai Ma Pian" ("Ballad of the White Horse", 《白马篇》). At the same time they also reflect the hardship the common people were enduring during the turbulent decades of the early 3rd century, like in "Song Ying Shi" ("Sending off Master Ying", 《送应氏》), "Taishan Liang Fu Yin" (《泰山梁甫吟》), "Xiashan Pian" (《虾鳝篇》), and "Meinü Pian" (《美女篇》). In the second phase of his life, Cao's personal situation is seen as a prince without concrete duties, and thus a lot of frustration about the court intrigues and his own uselessness was reflected. Such a situation is described in "Zashi" (《杂诗》), "Zeng Baimawang Biao" ("Presented to Cao Biao, Prince of Baima", 《赠白马王彪》), "Xujie Pian" (《吁嗟篇》), "Yetian Huangque Xing" (《野田黄雀行》) or "Yuange Xing" (《怨歌行》).

Cao Zhi's most famous rhapsody (赋) is "On the Goddess of River Luo" ("Luoshen Fu", 《洛神赋》). Some of his rhapsodies describe events, like "Dongzheng Fu" (《东征赋》), "Dengtai Fu" ("Fu on Ascending the Terrace", 《登台赋》) or "Shuxing fu" (《述行赋》), others are expressions of his sentiments, like "Lisi Fu" (《离思赋》), "Ganjie Fu" (《感节赋》) or "Xiji Fu" ("Rejoicing at the Clearing Rain", 《喜霁赋》), and a further group describing objects, like "Baodao Fu" (《宝刀赋》), "Midiexiang Fu" (《迷迭香赋》) or "Shengui Fu" (《神龟赋》). In contrast to many earlier Han period rhapsodies, Cao Zhi's are much shorter, and are closer to the daily life than the descriptions of imperial activities in earlier times. They also take in the "romantic" spirit of the saoti rhapsodies（骚体赋）based on the "Elegies of Chu"（楚辞）.

The most important prose writings of Cao Zhi are the letters "Yu Wu Jizhong Shu"（《与吴季重书》）and "Yu Yang Dezu Shu"（《与杨德组书》）.

Cao Zhi also saw himself as a critic, arguing that only a writer would be able to understand what good and bad literature was. Unfortunately he did not write any individual book on literary critique, but his arguments are scattered in letters and other writings, mainly his letter to Yang Dezu. "No one was perfect," was his main proposition, and "writers therefore would have to rely on the advice of supporters and friends. Yet inspiration to poetry came also from the common people," he said.

建安诗英译鉴赏实践之一

七步诗①
曹 植

煮豆燃豆萁②，
豆在釜③中泣④。
本自同根生⑤，
相煎⑥何太急⑦？

【注释】

①南朝刘义庆《世说新语·文学篇》载："文帝（曹丕）尝令东阿王（曹植）七步中作诗，不成者行大法（杀），应声便为诗曰：'煮豆持作羹，漉菽以为汁。萁在釜下燃，豆在釜中泣。本自同根生，相煎何太急？'帝深有惭色。"故此有"七步成诗"之说，后以此为题。

②〔萁〕豆类植物脱粒后剩下的豆茎。

③〔釜〕盛行于汉代的古炊器。敛口圆底，或有二耳。其用于鬲（lì），置于灶上置

第三章 建安诗英译鉴赏实践

甑(zèng)以蒸煮,有铁制的,也有铜或陶制的。
④〔泣〕小声哭泣。
⑤〔本〕原本,本来。〔同根生〕当初曹丕让曹植七步成诗只是一个借口,想借机杀曹植,他认为曹植肯定不能成功。但他没料到,曹植才华如此出众,当时就连曹丕本人也被感动了些许,并且为了保住名声,以安天下,他才放过了曹植。
⑥〔煎〕煎熬,这里指迫害手足兄弟。
⑦〔何〕多么。〔急〕紧迫。

白话释义

锅里煮豆子,豆秸锅底烧,豆子在锅里面哭泣;
豆子和豆秸本来是同一条根上生长出来的,
豆秸怎能这样急迫地煎熬豆子呢!

主题鉴赏

黄初元年(220年)正月,六十六岁的曹操病死,曹丕由世子荣升魏王;同年十月,汉献帝被迫禅让帝位,曹丕上位,称魏文帝。由于争封太子这段经历让曹丕无法释怀,在他称帝后,他仍对曹植耿耿于怀,担心这个有学识又有政治志向的弟弟会威胁自己的皇位,想着法子要除掉他。曹植知道哥哥存心陷害自己,可自己无法开脱,只好在极度悲愤中七步之内应声成诗。

这首诗最早就被记录在《世说新语》之中,后来流传的仅有四句。大概是因为在传播过程中对它是否真出于曹植之手尚难肯定。然《世说新语》的作者去曹魏之世未远,所述自然有一定的依据,而且据《世说新语》中引《魏志》也说曹植"出言为论,下笔成章",曹操曾试之以《登台赋》(《铜雀台赋》),植援笔立成,而且斐然可观,所以曹植在七步之内作出这样一首好诗也是可能的。

《七步诗》纯以比兴的手法出之,语言浅显,寓意明畅,无须多加阐释,只需于个别词句略加疏通,其意自明。全诗语气委婉而深沉,讥讽之中既有提醒规劝,又有质问愤怒。一方面反映了曹植的聪明才智,另一方面也反衬了曹丕迫害手足的残忍。前两句描述了燃萁煮豆这一日常生活场景,后两句话锋一转,集中抒发了曹植内心的悲愤,他显然是在质问曹丕:我与你本是同胞兄弟,为什么要如此苦苦相逼?诗人取譬之妙,用语之巧,而且在刹那间脱口而出,实在令人叹为观止。诗歌以其豆相煎设喻,形象逼真地再现了曹丕对自己和其他众兄弟残酷迫害的历史原貌。

曹植极富技巧地以"豆"自喻其水深火热的悲惨处境,而用"萁"比喻自己的同胞兄弟曹丕对亲兄弟的戕害。"萁"本为"豆"的一部分,豆和豆萁是同一个根上长出来的,但却被晒干后用作柴火来燃烧煮熟与自己同根而生的豆子,就好比同胞兄弟,豆萁燃烧起来却把锅内的豆煮得翻转"哭泣",以此来比喻兄弟相残。这一譬喻可谓入木三分,力透纸背,让人对曹丕残害同胞、违逆天伦、悖反常情的做法感到唾弃和不齿。通过燃萁煮豆这一日常现象,抒发了曹植内心的悲愤。由此,"本是同根生,相煎何太急"语,已成为千百年来人们劝诫避免兄弟阋墙、自相残杀的普遍用语,说明此诗的流传时间之久远。

南北朝时期著名诗人谢灵运曾对曹植有如此评价:"天下才有一石,曹子建独占八斗,我得一斗,天下共分一斗"(《释常谈》)。南朝梁文学批评家刘勰在《文心雕龙·才略》中对曹植评价颇高:"子建思捷而才俊,诗丽而表逸。"南朝文学批评家钟嵘亦赞曹植"骨气奇高,词彩华茂;情兼雅怨,体被文质,粲溢今古,卓尔不群"(《诗品·魏陈思王植》)。明代著名文学家王世贞说:"子建天才流丽,虽誉冠千古,而实逊父兄,何以故?才太高,辞太华"(《艺苑卮言》卷三)。可见前人都指出了曹植才华出众,禀赋异常的特点,而最能表现其才华的诗作应该包括这首传颂千载的《七步诗》。

English Interpretation

Cao Zhi was a prince of the state of Cao Wei in the period of Three Kingdoms, and an accomplished poet in the period of Jian'an. His style of poetry, greatly revered during the Jin dynasty and Southern and Northern Dynasties, came to be known as the Jian'an style. It is said that the first major poet of the new style that emerged at this time was Cao Zhi.

Despite his failure in politics, Cao Zhi was considered one of the representatives of the poetic style of his time, together with his father Cao Cao, his elder brother Cao Pi and several other poets. During the life of the great warlord Cao Cao who dominated northern China towards the end of the Han dynasty, he had shown favor to his son Cao Zhi due to his intelligence and literary talents.

Cao Cao considered making him heir and Cao Zhi had support from a significant fraction of his father's court, even though he was Cao Cao's third son. However, Cao Zhi eventually disappointed his father and the position of heir went

第三章 建安诗英译鉴赏实践

to his elder brother Cao Pi. After Cao Cao's death in 220, Cao Pi would remove all his brothers, including Cao Zhi, from the capital to send them to their fiefs (封地) to ensure they would not be a threat to his power. The poem is set against this historical background, although the poem itself and the story attached to it are not found in the official history *Records of the Three Kingdoms* (《三国志》).

There are two versions of the story attached to the poem of the "Seven-Pace Poem". The first[①] is recorded in *A New Account of the Tales of the World* (《世说新语》). In chapter four of this text, it claims that Cao Pi was jealous of Cao Zhi's artistic talents and sought to execute him:

Cao Pi summoned Cao Zhi and issued an ultimatum (最后通牒) to his little brother, asking him to produce a poem within the timeframe of walking seven steps or otherwise be executed. Cao Zhi complied such a poem, and Cao Pi "showed deep shame on his face".

Another abridged version is recorded in the *Romance of the Three Kingdoms* (《三国演义》) as is shown in this appreciation section.

After Cao Cao's death, Cao Zhi did not bother to show up to his funeral. Cao Pi took this incidence as an excuse to penalize Cao Zhi. Their mother begged him not to take his little brother's life, but Cao Pi's advisors insisted him to make the hard decision. So Cao Pi was reluctant, and was then advised to find an excuse to give his brother a difficult test in public, and either execute or demote him based on whether he succeeded. Cao Pi accordingly summoned his little brother in front of his entire court, accused him of having used ghostwriters to gain fame and secure their father's favor, and challenged him in front of the court to produce a poem on the spot or otherwise be executed for having been a liar about his famed literary talents. The test was based on a painting shown in court, which was one bull killing another after a head-butting fight, and Cao Zhi was asked to produce a poem to describe the painting, without using any of the relevant words, within the timeframe of walking seven steps. Cao Zhi responded with a fairly long poem within the time frame. Cao Pi did not wish to give up, and gave his little brother a harder test by asking him to produce a poem about brothers but without

---

① 《世说新语》：文帝尝令东阿王七步中作诗，不成者行大法。应声便成诗曰："煮豆持作羹，漉菽以为汁。萁在釜下燃，豆在釜中泣。本自同根生，相煎何太急？"帝深有惭色。

referring to the word "brother", but this time Cao Zhi immediately composed this famous poem. Upon hearing the poem, Cao Pi burst into tears in front of the court, and eventually demoted Cao Zhi to a place far from the center of power rather than executing him. Therefore, these two different versions of the "Seven-Pace Poem" were from different origins. It is widely acknowledged that the six-line poem is the original one based on its specific rhyming and the stylistic form closely related to the poetic genre of Jian'an Literature.

"Seven-Pace Poem" was a good example of allegory as a literary device or artistic form. An allegory is a narrative or visual representation in which a character, place, or event can be interpreted to represent a hidden meaning with moral or political significance. Ancient poets typically use allegories to convey (semi-) hidden or complex meanings through symbolic figures, actions, imagery, or events, which together create the moral, spiritual, or political meaning the author wishes to convey. As for the "Seven-Pace Poem", beanstalk and bean are allegorically juxtaposed to convey the meaning that as generic brothers, Cao Pi and Cao Zhi should not be in rivals. So this is just the literary point until today readers still show much interest in reading such a didactic short verse. "同室操戈, 相煎何急" has become a well-known Chinese idiom to express the idea that people of the same origin (brothers, relatives or compatriots) should show mercy to each other.

Wang Shizhen (王世贞), the literary critic in the Ming dynasty claimed Cao Zhi to be the first "poet immortal" succeeded by Li Bai in the Tang dynasty and Su Shi in the Song dynasty.

第三章 建安诗英译鉴赏实践

学生英译实践园地

英译实践版本选读

译文 1　翟理斯

The Brothers

They were boiling beans on a beanstalk fire;
Came a plaintive voice from the pot,
"O why, since we sprang from the selfsame root,
Should you kill me with anger hot?"

译文 2　莫斯·罗伯特

Seven Steps

Beans a simmer on a beanstalk flame,
From inside the pot expressed their ire:
"Alive we sprouted on a single root—
What's your rush to cook us on the fire?"

译文 3　柳无忌

Verses Composed In Seven Paces

A kettle had beans inside,
And stalks of the beans made a fire;
When the beans to the brother-stalks cried,
"We sprang from one root, why such ire?"

译文 4　许渊冲

Written While Taking Seven Steps

Pods burned to cook peas,
Peas weep in the pot:
"Grown from the same trees,
Why boil us so hot?"

第三章　建安诗英译鉴赏实践

译文 5　卓振英

A Seven-Pace Poem

The flames of burning pods malignly leap,
The beans in th' cooking pan do weep:
"Are we not growths of the same stems and roots?
Whereat should you bear us a hate so deep?"

建安诗英译鉴赏实践之二

观沧海
曹　操

东临碣石①，
以观沧海②。
水何澹澹③，
山岛竦峙④。
树木丛生⑤，
　百草丰茂。
秋风萧瑟⑥，
洪波⑦涌起。
日月之行⑧，
若出其中⑨；
星汉⑩灿烂，
若出其里⑪。
幸甚至哉⑫，
歌以咏志⑬。

【注释】

① 〔临〕登上，有游览的意思。〔碣(jié)石〕：山名。碣石山，原渤海边的一座山，位于今河北省昌黎县北。公元207年秋天，曹操征乌桓得胜回师时经过此地。
② 〔沧〕通"苍"，青绿色。〔海〕此指中国的内海渤海，位于辽、冀、鲁、津三省一市之间，东至辽东半岛南端，南至山东半岛北岸。
③ 〔何〕多么。〔澹澹(dàn dàn)〕水波摇动的样子。
④ 〔竦峙(sǒng zhì)〕耸立。竦，通"耸"，高。
⑤ 〔丛生〕草木聚集丰茂貌。
⑥ 〔萧瑟〕树木被秋风吹动的声音。
⑦ 〔洪波〕汹涌澎湃的波浪。
⑧ 〔日月〕太阳和月亮。〔之行〕之，语助词，无实义；行，运行。
⑨ 〔若〕如同，好像是。日月似乎是从大海中升起和落下。
⑩ 〔星汉〕银河，天河。
⑪ 〔若出其里〕好像从大海里出现一般。
⑫ 〔幸〕庆幸。〔甚〕很，程度副词。〔至〕极点。〔哉〕语尾感叹词。
⑬ 〔歌以咏志〕就用诗歌来表达心志吧！（最后两句常见于曹操的诸多诗篇中，与本诗正文的内容没有直接关系。）

白话释义

东行登临碣石山，
遥望大海阔无边。
海水浩渺起波澜，
山岛林立耸云天。
树木葱茏花草盛。
秋风萧瑟草木摇，
海浪翻腾巨浪兴。
日月升起又夕归，
好似源于瀚海中。
银河群星耀天宇，
大海洪波拥其中。

第三章　建安诗英译鉴赏实践

生逢此世有抱负！
高歌一曲志难平。

主题鉴赏

《观沧海》是东汉末年军事家、诗人曹操采用乐府旧题所创作的四言组诗《步出夏门行》的第一章。这组诗作于建安十二年曹操北征乌桓凯旋时。全诗由序曲和四章正文构成。序曲即前奏曲，是歌唱的引子，之后的四章正文包括：《观沧海》《冬十月》《土不同》《龟虽寿》。

序曲《艳》介绍了组诗的创作背景："云行雨步，超越九江之皋。临观异同，心意怀犹豫，不知当复何从？经过至我碣石，心惆怅我东海。"意思是："最初我打算南征荆州，施泽惠给江南人民。面对北伐和南征两种不同意见，便犹豫起来，不知如何为好。到达碣石后，看到百姓所受的压迫，心情更加伤感。"

正文的第一章《观沧海》是曹操北征乌桓凯旋时途径碣石山登山望海有感而发之作。诗歌描绘了大海吞吐日月、包蕴万千的壮丽景象，表达诗人以景托志、胸怀天下、统一江山的积极进取精神。

正文的第二章《冬十月》描写征讨乌桓胜利归来途中所见的风物，充满了生活气息。

正文的第三章《土不同》叙写黄河以北地区冬天的严寒景况与民风特点，表达了诗人哀叹生民，心怀苍生的心情。

正文的第四章《龟虽寿》以慷慨激昂的豪情壮志，抒发了诗人老当益壮、积极进取的豪迈情怀。全诗意境开阔，气势雄浑，堪称汉末乐府题材中的经典作品。

乌桓是当时东北方的大患，建安十一年，乌桓攻破幽州，俘虏了汉民十余万户。同年，袁绍的儿子袁尚和袁熙又勾结辽西乌桓首领蹋顿，屡次骚扰边境，以致曹操不得不在建安十二年五月毅然决定亲率大军北上征伐袁乌贼匪。他先是率军追歼袁尚和袁熙残部，接着誓师讨伐乌桓，七月出卢龙寨，八月直捣乌桓敌营，最终取得决定性的胜利。这次胜利巩固了曹操军队的后方实力，为次年曹军挥戈南下的军事行动奠定了基础。在讨伐敌军凯旋途中，曹操登临当年秦皇汉武亦曾登临的碣石山，面对洪波涌起的大海和秋风萧瑟的景致，不觉触景生情。这位已到中年却仍野心勃勃的政治家、军事家壮志未酬的心境就像沧海一样难以平静，因此他将自己戎马一生的宏伟抱负和远大胸襟倾注于笔端，融入诗歌里，借大海的形象来抒发胸中块垒,为后人留下了这首壮丽恢宏热血沸腾的诗篇。

《观沧海》头二句点明诗人"观沧海"所在的位置:诗人登上碣石山顶,居高临海,视野寥廓,大海的壮阔景象尽收眼底。以下十句描写,概由此拓展而来。"水何澹澹,山岛竦峙"是望海初得的大致印象,有点像绘画的粗线条。在这水波"澹澹"的海上,最先映入眼帘的是那突兀耸立的山岛,它们点缀在平阔的海面上,使大海显得神奇壮观。这两句写出了大海远景的一般轮廓,下面再层层深入描写。

"树木丛生,百草丰茂"二句具体写竦峙的山岛:虽然已到秋风萧瑟,草木摇落的季节,但岛上树木繁茂,百草丰美,给人诗意盎然之感。"秋风萧瑟,洪波涌起"二句则是对"水何澹澹"一句的进一层描写:定神细看,在秋风萧瑟中的海面竟是洪波巨澜,汹涌起伏。虽是秋天的典型环境,却无半点萧瑟凄凉的悲秋意绪。诗人面对萧瑟秋风,极写大海的辽阔壮美:在秋风萧瑟中,大海汹涌澎湃,浩渺接天;山岛高耸挺拔,草木繁茂,没有丝毫凋衰感伤的情调。这种新的境界,新的格调,正反映了他"老骥伏枥,志在千里"的胸襟。

前面的描写,是从海的平面去观察的。"日月之行,若出其中;星汉灿烂,若出其里"四句则联系廓落无垠的宇宙,纵意荡开大笔,将大海的气势和威力展现在读者面前:茫茫大海与天相接,空蒙浑融;在这雄奇壮丽的大海面前,日、月、星、汉(银河)都显得渺小了,它们的运行,似乎都由大海自由吐纳。诗人在这里描写的大海,既是眼前实景,又融进了自己的想象和夸张,展现出一派吞吐宇宙的宏伟气象,大有"五岳起方寸"的势态。这种"笼盖吞吐气象"是诗人"眼中"景和"胸中"情交融而成的艺术境界。言为心声,如果诗人没有宏伟的政治抱负,没有建功立业的雄心壮志,没有对前途充满信心的乐观气度,那是无论如何也写不出这样壮丽的诗境的。沈德潜曾说曹操诗歌"时露霸气",指的就是《观沧海》这类作品。

总体而言,《观沧海》基本沿袭了先秦《诗经》四言诗的创作风格。诗歌主题硬朗,语调昂扬,诗人采用浪漫主义手法,勾勒出沧海辽远、山岛竦峙、吞吐日月、包蕴万千的壮丽景象,描绘了中华河山的雄奇瑰丽,表达了诗人以景托志,借物言志,胸怀天下,乐观进取的精神风貌。全诗语言质朴,想象丰富,气势磅礴,苍凉悲壮。

第三章 建安诗英译鉴赏实践

学生英译实践园地

英译实践版本选读

译文 1　叶　扬

Watching the Deep Blue Sea

Eastward we went up Mt. Tablet
to watch the deep blue sea.
How the waters ripple
among the standing hilly islets!
Trees grow in clusters;
all plants are so lush.
The autumn wind is soughing
while big waves arise.
The sun and the moon move
as if right in its middle.
The bright river of stars
seems to flow from its depth.
How extremely fortunate I am
to sing this song of praise!

译文 2　许渊冲

Viewing the Boundless Sea

I come to view the boundless ocean
From Stony Hill on eastern shore.
Its water rolls in rhythmic motion
And islands stand amid its roar.
Tree on tree grows from peak to peak;
Grass on grass looks lush far and nigh.
The autumn wind blows drear and bleak;
The monstrous billows surge up high.
The sun by day, the moon by night

第三章　建安诗英译鉴赏实践

Appear to rise from the sea deep.
The Milky Way with stars so bright
Sinks down into the sea in sleep.
How happy I feel at this sight!
I croon this poem in delight.

译文 3　赵彦春

The Blue Sea

On the East Hill I stand,
O'erlooking the blue sea.
The waters far expand;
The isle juts up like T.
The trees grow upon trees;
The grass sprawls on so lush.
Now soughs an autumn breeze
That spurs the waves to rush.
O Sun, o Moon, so light,
Have you risen from there?
O Milky Way, so bright,
Have you taken their glare?
How happy, O hurray!
I sing, sing up this lay.

译文 4　汪榕培

Viewing the Sea

When I climb atop the Rocky Hill,
I view the vast East Sea at will.
The waters quietly ebb and flow;
The island mountains skyward go.
The trees are growing dense and green;
The grass is sprouting lush and clean.

When autumn winds sweep o'er the shore,
Huge waves and billows surge and roar.
The sun and the moon on their way,
Seem to rise there from day to day.
The stars that shine bright in the sky,
Seem to grow there far and nigh.
In such a happy mood I am
That I sing it as an epigram.

建安诗英译鉴赏实践之三

短歌行
曹 操

对酒当歌①，人生几何②！
譬如朝露，去日③苦多。
慨当以慷④，忧思难忘。
何以解忧？唯有杜康⑤。
青青子衿，悠悠我心⑥。
但为君故，沉吟⑦至今。
呦呦鹿鸣，食野之苹。
我有嘉宾，鼓瑟吹笙⑧。
明明如月，何时可掇⑨？
忧从中来，不可断绝。
越陌度阡⑩，枉用相存⑪。
契阔谈䜩⑫，心念旧恩。
月明星稀，乌鹊南飞。
绕树三匝⑬，何枝可依？

第三章 建安诗英译鉴赏实践

山不厌高,海不厌深⑭。

周公吐哺⑮,天下归心。

【注释】

①〔对酒当歌〕一边喝着酒,一边唱着歌。当,是对着的意思。

②〔几何〕多少时日。

③〔去日〕用于感叹光阴易逝之语。过去的日子。〔苦〕患,苦于。

④〔慨当以慷〕指宴会上的歌声激昂慷慨。当以,这里无实际意义。全句意思是,应当用激昂慷慨(的方式来唱歌)。

⑤〔杜康〕相传是最早造酒的人,这里代指美酒。

⑥〔青青子衿(jīn),悠悠我心〕出自《诗经·郑风·子衿》。这里用来比喻渴望得到有才学的人。子,对士人贤才的尊称。衿,衣服的交领。青衿,是周代读书人的服装,这里指代有学识的人。悠悠,长久的样子,形容思虑连绵不断。

⑦〔沉吟〕沉思,深思。这里指对贤才的思念和倾慕。

⑧〔呦(yōu)呦鹿鸣,食野之苹。我有嘉宾,鼓瑟吹笙(shēng)〕出自《诗经·小雅·鹿鸣》。呦呦,鹿叫的声音。苹,艾蒿或地衣。鼓瑟吹笙,指奏起音乐欢迎有识之士的到来。

⑨〔何时可掇(duō)〕什么时候可以摘取呢?掇,拾取,摘取。另解:掇读 chuò,为通假字,通"辍",即停止的意思。

⑩〔越陌度阡〕穿过纵横交错的小路。陌,东西向田间小路。阡,南北向的小路。

⑪〔枉用相存〕屈驾来访。枉,这里是"枉驾"的意思。用,以。存,问候,思念。

⑫〔契阔谈䜩〕契(qì),投合无间的情分。阔,离别,分别。契阔,语出《诗经·邶风·击鼓》:"死生契阔,与子成说。"意为久别重逢。谈䜩,意为一边宴饮,一边交谈。此句意为曹操求贤若渴,希望贤才到来,彼此久别重逢谈心宴饮,畅谈治国的道理。

⑬〔三匝(zā)〕匝,圈。指三周,形容反复盘旋。

⑭〔海不厌深〕一本作"水不厌深"。意思是表示希望尽可能多地接纳人才。

⑮〔周公吐哺(bǔ)〕此为引用典故《史记·鲁周公世家》:"周公戒伯禽曰:'我文王之子,武王之弟,成王之叔父,我于天亦不贱矣。然我一沐三捉发,一饭三吐哺,起以待士,犹恐失天下之贤人。'"极言曹操像周公一样礼贤下士,殷勤待士。

白话释义

　　一边喝酒一边高歌，人生的岁月有多少。
　　好比晨露转瞬即逝，逝去的时光实在太多！
　　宴会上歌声慷慨激昂，心中的忧愁却难以遗忘。
　　靠什么来排解忧闷？唯有豪饮美酒。
　　有学识的才子们啊，你们令我朝夕思慕。
　　只是因为你们的缘故，让我沉痛吟诵至今。
　　阳光下鹿群呦呦欢鸣，在原野吃着艾蒿。
　　一旦四方贤才光临舍下，我将奏瑟吹笙宴请嘉宾。
　　当空悬挂的皓月哟，什么时候可以摘取呢？
　　心中深深的忧思，喷涌而出不能停止。
　　远方宾客穿越纵横交错的田路，屈驾前来探望我。
　　彼此久别重逢谈心宴饮，重温那往日的恩情。
　　月光明亮星光稀疏，一群寻巢喜鹊向南飞去。
　　绕树飞了几周却没敛翅，哪里才有它们栖身之所？
　　高山不辞土石才见巍峨，大海不弃涓流才见壮阔。
　　我愿如周公一般礼贤下士，愿天下的英杰真心归顺于我。

主题鉴赏

　　这首诗的创作时间学术界大致有五种说法。一是在苏轼《赤壁赋》中"横槊赋诗"言语的基础上，《三国演义》称曹操在赤壁大战前吟诵这首《对酒当歌》，时间约为建安十三年末。二是求贤说，出自张可礼《三曹年谱》："抒发延揽人才之激切愿望，盖与《求贤令》作于同时。"时间在建安十五年。三是宾主唱和说，此主张发自万绳楠，他认为此诗作于汉建安元年，曹操迁汉献帝于许都之际，曹操与手下心腹如荀彧等人的唱和之作。四是及时行乐说，但没有考证具体时间。此说由沈德潜发之，《古诗源》卷五："《短歌行》，言当及时为乐也。"五是源自王青，他认为该诗作于招待乌丸行单于普富卢的宴会上，时间在建安二十一年五月。

　　《短歌行》是汉乐府的旧题，属于《相和歌辞·平调曲》。这就是说它本来是一个乐曲的名称，最初的古辞已经失传。乐府里收集的同名诗作有 24 首，最早的是曹操的这首。这种乐曲怎么唱，现在当然是不知道了。但乐府《相和歌辞·平调

第三章 建安诗英译鉴赏实践

曲》中除了《短歌行》还有《长歌行》,唐代吴兢《乐府古题要解》引证古诗"长歌正激烈",魏文帝曹丕《燕歌行》"短歌微吟不能长"和晋代傅玄《艳歌行》"咄来长歌续短歌"等句,认为"长歌""短歌"是指"歌声有长短"。现在也就只能根据这一点点材料来理解《短歌行》的音乐特点。《短歌行》这个乐曲,原来当然也有相应的词,就是"乐府古辞",但这古辞已经失传了。现在所能见到的最早的《短歌行》就是曹操所作的拟乐府《短歌行》。所谓"拟乐府"就是运用乐府旧曲来补作新词,曹操传世的《短歌行》共有两首,这里要介绍的是其中的第一首。

这首《短歌行》的主题非常明确,就是作者求贤若渴,希望人才都来投靠自己。曹操在其政治活动中,为了扩大他在庶族地主中的统治基础,打击反动的世袭豪强势力,曾大力强调"唯才是举",为此而先后发布了"求贤令""举士令""求逸才令"等。而《短歌行》实际上就是一曲"求贤歌",又正因为运用了诗歌的形式,含有丰富的抒情成分,所以就能起到独特的感染作用,有力地宣传了他所坚持的主张,配合了他所颁发的政令。

全诗分为四节。

第一节主要抒写了诗人对人生苦短的忧叹。第一节中有两处都提到了"酒"。在魏晋时期,酒多受到诗人的喜欢,心情愉悦或是悲伤感慨时都不难找到酒的影子。本诗中,第一句就用酒来作开头引出诗人对人生苦短的忧叹。第一节最后一句"何以解忧?唯有杜康。"相传发明酿酒的人名叫杜康,这里的"杜康"也是指代酒的意思。我们如何去理解诗人这种人生苦短的忧叹呢?诗人生逢乱世,目睹百姓颠沛流离,肝肠寸断,渴望建功立业,改变乱世局面,因而发出人生苦短的忧叹。

第二节情味更加缠绵深长了。"青青"二句原来是《诗经·郑风·子衿》中的话,原诗是写一个姑娘在思念她的爱人。曹操在这里引用这首诗,而且还说自己一直低低地吟诵它,这实在是太巧妙了。他说"青青子衿,悠悠我心",固然是直接比喻了对"贤才"的思念,但更重要的是他所省掉的两句话:"纵我不往,子宁不嗣音?"由于曹操事实上不可能一个一个地去找那些"贤才",所以他便用这种含蓄的方法来提醒他们:"就算我没有去找你们,你们为什么不主动来投奔我呢?"由这一层含而不露的意思可以看出,他那"求才"的用心实在是太周到了,的确具有感人的力量。而这感人力量正体现了文艺创作的政治性与艺术性的结合。他这种深细婉转的用心,在《求贤令》之类的文件中当然无法尽情表达;而《短歌行》作为一首诗,就能抒发政治文件所不能抒发的感情,起到政治文件所不能起的作用。紧接着他又引用《诗经·小雅·鹿鸣》中的四句,描写宾主欢宴的情景,意思是说只要你们到我这里来,我是一定会待以"嘉宾"之礼的,我们是能够欢快融洽地相处并合作的。这八句仍然没有明确地说出"求才"二字,因为曹操所写的是诗,所以用了典故来作比喻,这就是"婉而多讽"的表现方法。同时,"但为君故"这个"君"字,在曹操的诗中也具有典型意义。本来在《诗经》中,这"君"只是指一个具体的人;而在这里则具有了广泛的意义;在当时凡是读到曹操此诗的"贤士",都可以自认为他就是曹操为之沉吟《子衿》一诗的思念对象。正因为这样,此诗流传开去,才会起到巨大的社会反响。

  第三节是对以上十六句的强调和照应。以上十六句主要讲了两个意思,即为求贤而愁,又表示要待贤以礼。倘若借用音乐来作比,这可以说是全诗中的两个"主题旋律",而"明明如月"八句就是这两个"主题旋律"的复现和变奏。前四句又在讲忧愁,是照应第一个八句;后四句讲"贤才"到来,是照应第二个八句。表面看来,意思上是与前十六句重复的,但实际上由于"主题旋律"的复现和变奏,因此使全诗更有抑扬低昂、反复咏叹之致,加强了抒情的浓度。再从表达诗的文学主题来看,这八句也不是简单重复,而是含有深意的。那就是说"贤才"已经来了不少,我们也合作得很融洽;然而我并不满足,我仍在为求贤而发愁,希望有更多的"贤才"到来。天上的明月常在运行,不会停止,同样,我的求贤之思也是不会断绝的。说这种话又是用心周到的表现,因为曹操不断在延揽人才,那么后来者会不会顾虑"人满为患"呢?所以曹操在这里进一步表示,他的求贤之心就像明月常行那样不会终止,人们也就不必要有什么顾虑,早来晚来都一样会受到优待。关于这一点,下文还有更加明确的表示,这里不过是承上启下,起到过渡与衬垫的作用。

  第四节求贤如渴的思想感情进一步加深。"月明"四句既是准确而形象的写景笔墨,也有比喻的深意。沈德潜《古诗源》中说:"月明星稀四句,喻客子无所依托。"实际上是说那些犹豫不决的人才,在动荡的时局下一时无所适从。诗人以乌鸦绕树、"何枝可依"的情景来启发他们,不要三心二意,要善于择枝而栖,赶紧到我这边来。最后"周公"四句画龙点睛,明明白白披肝沥胆,希望人才都来归顺我曹操,点明了全诗的主旨。关于"周公吐哺"的典故,据说周公自言:"我文王之子,武王之弟,成王之叔父也;又相天子,我于天下亦不轻矣。然一沐三捉发,一饭三吐哺,犹恐失天下之士。"这话似也表达了诗人的心情。

  总体来说,《短歌行》正像曹操的其他诗作如《蒿里行》《对酒》《苦寒行》等一样,是政治性很强的诗作,主要是为曹操当时所实行的政治路线和政治策略服务的;然而它那政治内容和意义却完全熔铸在浓郁的抒情意境之中,全诗充分发挥了诗歌创作的特长,准确而巧妙地运用了比兴手法,来达到寓理于情,以情感人的目的。在曹操的时代,他就已经能够按照抒情诗的特殊规律来取得预期的社会效果,这一创作经验显然是值得借鉴的。同时因为曹操在当时强调"唯才是举"有一定的进步意义,所以他对"求贤"这一主题所作的高度艺术化的表现,也应得到历史的肯定。

第三章 建安诗英译鉴赏实践

学生英译实践园地

英译实践版本选读

译文 1　莫斯·罗伯特

A Short Song

Here before us, wine and song!
For man does not live long.
Like daybreak dew,
His days are swiftly gone.

Sanguine-souled we have to be!
Though painful memory haunts us yet.
Thoughts and sorrows naught allays,
Save the cup Du Kang first set.

"Deep the hue of the scholar's robe,
Deeper, the longing of my heart."
For all of you, my dearest lords,
I voice again this ancient part.

Nibbling on the duckweed,
"Loo! Loo!" the lowing deer.
At our feast sit honored guests
For string and reed to cheer.

The moon on high beckons bright,
But no man's ever stayed it.
Heart's care rises from within,
And nothing can deny it.

Take our thanks for all your pains;
Your presence does us honour.

第三章 建安诗英译鉴赏实践

Reunited on this feasting day,
We well old loves remember.

The moon is bright, the stars are few,
The magpie black as raven.
It southbound circles thrice a tree,
That offers him no haven.

The mountaintop no height eschews;
The sea eschews no deep.
And the Duke of Zhou spat out his meal,
An empire's trust to keep.

译文 2　许渊冲

A Short Song

We should sing before wine,
For how long can life last?
Like dew on morning fine,
So many days have passed.
How can we unbound
By grief which weighs us down?
Grief can only be drowned
In wine of good renown.

Talents with collars blue,
For you I pine away.
So much I long for you,
My heart aches night and day.
How gaily call the deer
While grazing in the shade!
When I have talents here,
Let lute and lyre be played!

Bright as the moon on high,
How can I bring it down?
Grief from within comes nigh;
Ceaselessly it flows on.
Across the fields and lanes,
You are kind to come here.
Talking of far-off plains,
You cherish friendship dear.

The moon's bright and stars nice,
The crows in southward flight.
They circle the trees thrice,
There's no branch to alight.
With crags high mountain rise;
With water the sea's deep.
With the help of the wise,
An ordered world we'll keep.

译文 3　赵彦春

A Short Song Ballad

Before wine, sing a song,
How long is life, how long?
It seems like morning dew
With bygones gone with woe.
O sing loud and sing free,
And yet my cause frets me.
What can kill sorrow mine?
Nothing but Dukang Wine.

Blue, blue the scholar gown,
Seek, seek I up and down.

第三章 建安诗英译鉴赏实践

In your esteem I bow
And have chanted till now.
The deer each to each bleat,
A field they wormwood eat;
I have good guests today;
The lute and flute we play.

Fair, fair the moon does shine;
Could I have it? I pine!
My heart's laden with care,
Which seems to stay for e'er.
Through the field lies the lane;
It's for you, not in vain.
We talk throughout repast;
Rememb'ring your grace past.

The moon's bright and stars few;
Fly south magpie and crow.
Thrice they go round the birch,
But on which bough to perch?
Let mounts be high and steep
And the seas broad and deep.
O our sage Prince of Chough,
To your side all would go.

译文 4　杨宪益　戴乃迭

A Song

Wine before us, sing a song.
How long does life last?
It is like the morning dew;
Sad so many days have past.

Sing hey, sing ho!
Deep within my heart I pine.
Nothing can dispel my woe,
Save Du Kang, the god of wine.

Blue, blue the scholar's robe;
Long, long for him I ache.
Preoccupied with you, my lord,
Heavy thoughts for your sake.

To each other cry the deer,
Nibbling grass upon the plain.
When a good friend visits me,
We'll play the lyre once again.

In the sky, the moon is bright;
Yet I can reach it never.
In my heart such sorrow dwells;
Remaining with me ever.

In the fields, our paths crossed;
Your visit was so kind.
Together after our long parting,
Your favours come to mind.

Clear the moon, few the stars;
The crows in southward flight.
Circling three times round the tree,
No branch where to alight.

What if the mountain is high,
Or how deep the sea?
When the Duke of Zhou greeted a guest,
In his service all wished to be.

第三章　建安诗英译鉴赏实践

建安诗英译鉴赏实践之四

野田黄雀行①

曹　植

高树多悲风②，
海水扬其波③。
利剑不在掌④，
结友何须多⑤？
不见篱间雀，
见鹞⑥自投罗⑦？
罗家⑧得雀喜，
少年见雀悲。
拔剑捎⑨罗网，
黄雀得飞飞⑩。
飞飞摩苍天⑪，
来下谢少年。

【注释】

①收于《相和歌辞十四·瑟调曲》，是曹植后期的作品。
②〔悲风〕凄厉的寒风。
③〔扬其波〕掀起波浪。此二句比喻环境凶险。
④〔利剑〕锋利的剑。这里比喻权势。此句意为手中未掌握权力。
⑤〔结友〕交朋友。〔何须〕何必，何用。
⑥〔鹞（yào）〕一种非常凶狠的鸟类，鹰的一种，似鹰而小。
⑦〔罗〕捕鸟用的网。此处暗喻落入权势者之手。
⑧〔罗家〕设罗网捕雀的人。

⑨〔捎(shāo)〕挥击;削破;除去。据《说文·第十二上》:自关已西,凡取物之上者为挢捎(jiǎo shāo)。此处当指"用剑挑开":少年拔剑挑开罗网,黄雀得以重获自由。

⑩〔飞飞〕自由飞行貌。

⑪〔摩〕接近;迫近。"摩苍天"形容黄雀飞得很高。黄雀破网而出,直上青天;突然又飞下来,绕在少年周身,以示感谢。

白话释义

高高的树木不幸时常受到狂风的吹袭,平静的海面被吹得不住地波浪迭起。
宝剑虽利却不在我的手掌之中,结交再多的朋友(不能保护他们)又有何用?
你没有看见篱笆上面那可怜的黄雀,为躲避凶狠的鹞却又撞进了网里。
张设罗网的人见到黄雀是多么欢喜,少年见到挣扎的黄雀不由心生怜惜。
拔出利剑对着罗网用力挑去,黄雀才得以飞离那受难之地。
振翅飞上苍茫的天宇,获救的黄雀又飞来向少年表示谢意。

主题鉴赏

本诗《野田黄雀行》被历代学者认为是表达曹植"想救丁仪兄弟却无能为力的愤慨。"

史载,曹操曾经几次想立曹植为太子,不过,最终曹植争立太子失败。而丁仪、丁廙两兄弟是拥护曹植的,二人作为曹植一派,在古代被杀是很正常的事。一般情况下,参与争夺皇位的失败皇子,也会被成功者直接或间接找机会杀掉。曹植之所以没被杀害,最重要的原因当是太后向文帝求情,希望他不要手足相残,体谅她这个做母亲的,放曹植一马,于是曹植免去一死。《魏书》载诏曰:"植,朕之同母弟。朕于天下无所不容,而况植乎?骨肉之亲,舍而不诛,其改封植。"不过此后曹植频繁被贬,不能在一个封地待太久,也不能培养自己的势力,始终被曹丕父子防备着,不受重用。建安二十四年,曹操借故杀了曹植的亲信杨修,次年曹丕继位,曹丕又杀了曹植的好友丁氏兄弟。曹植身处动辄得咎的逆境,无力救助友人,深感愤愤,内心十分痛苦,只能写诗寄意。他苦于手中无权柄,故而在诗中塑造了一位"拔剑捎罗网",拯救无辜者的少年侠士,借以表达自己的心曲。

全诗可分两段。前四句为一段。诗一开端,"高树多悲风,海水扬其波"两句以比兴发端,出语惊人。雄壮悲戚的意象渲染出浓郁孤寂的悲剧气氛,隐喻当时政治

第三章　建安诗英译鉴赏实践

形势的险恶；而少年拔剑捎网的形象则寄寓着诗人冲决罗网、一试身手的热切愿望。可谓意象奇崛，语言警策，急于有为的壮烈情怀跃然纸上。南朝梁刘勰谓诗"格刚才劲，且长于讽喻"（《文心雕龙·隐秀》），确是中肯之论。《易》曰："挠万物者莫疾乎风"（《说卦》）。谚曰："树大招风。"则高树之风，其摧折破坏之力可想而知。"风"前又着一"悲"字，更加强了这自然景观所具的主观感情色彩。

　　大海无边，波涛山立，风吹浪涌，楫摧樯倾。这两句所描绘的恶劣的自然环境，实际是现实政治气候的象征，曲折地反映了宦海的险恶风涛和政治上的挫折所引起的作者内心的悲愤与忧惧。正是在这样一种政治环境里，在这样一种心情支配下，诗人痛定思痛，在百转千回之后，满怀悲愤喊出了"利剑不在掌，结友何须多"这一自身痛苦经历所得出的结论。没有权势便不必交友，这真是石破天惊之论！无论从传统的观念，无论从一般人的生活际遇，都不能得出这样的结论来。儒家一向强调"有朋自远方来，不亦乐乎！"强调"四海之内皆兄弟"。从《诗经·伐木》的"嘤其鸣矣，求其友声"到今天民间流传的"在家靠父母，出门靠朋友"，都是强调朋友越多越好。然而，正是由于它的不合常情常理，反而有了更加强烈的震撼力量，更加深刻地反映了作者内心的悲愤。从曹植作品《赠徐干诗》的"亲交义在敦"、《赠丁仪诗》的"亲交义不薄"、《送应氏》的"念我平生亲"、《箜篌引》的"亲友从我游"等诗句中看，曹植是一个喜交游、重友情的人。这样一个风流倜傥的翩翩佳公子，如今却大声呼喊出与自己本性完全格格不入的话来，不但用以自警，而且用以告诫世人，则其内心的悲苦激烈、创巨痛深，正是不言可知。

　　"不见篱间雀"及其下文为全诗第二段。无权无势就不必结交朋友，这当然不是诗人内心的真实思想，而是在特殊情况下所发出的悲愤至极的牢骚和无奈。这个观点既无法被读者接受，诗人也无法引经据典加以论证。因此他采用寓言手法，用"不见"二字引出了持剑少年救雀的故事。这个故事从表面看，是从反面来论证"利剑不在掌，结友何须多"这一不易为人接受的观点，而实际上却是紧承上段，进一步抒写自己内心的悲愤情绪。"黄雀因是以俯噣（啄）白粒，仰栖茂树，鼓翅奋翼，自以为无患，与人无争也。不知夫公子王孙，左挟弹，右摄丸，将加己乎十仞之上"（刘向《庄辛谓楚襄王》）。黄雀自以为停留在茂树上，与人无争，就不会有生命危险。奈何，富贵人家的公子王孙，早就商量一起拿着弹弓，捕雀以相娱乐。朱乾《乐府正义》："取义于此，大约相戒免祸。"黄雀是温驯的小鸟，加上"篱间"二字，更可见其并无冲天之志，不过在篱间嬉戏度日而已。然而就是这样一只于人于物都无所害的小鸟，竟也不能见容于世人，设下罗网，放出鹞鹰，必欲驱捕逐得而后快。为罗驱雀的鹞鹰何其凶恶，见鹞投罗的黄雀何其可怜，见雀而喜的罗家何其卑劣，诗人虽无一字褒贬，而感情却已深融于叙事之中。诗人对掌权者的痛恨，对无辜被害的弱小者的同情，均不难于词句外得之。因此，诗人又进而想象有一手仗利剑的少年，抉开罗网，放走黄雀。黄雀死里逃生，直飞云霄，却又从天空俯冲而下，绕少年盘旋飞鸣，感谢其救命之恩。显然，"拔剑捎罗网"的英俊少年实际是诗人想象之中自我形象的化身；黄雀"飞飞摩苍天"所表现的轻快、愉悦，实际是诗人在想象中解救了朋友急难之后所感到的轻快和愉悦。诚然，这只是诗人一己的幻想而已，在现实中无权无势无能为力，只好在幻境中求得心灵的解脱和慰藉，其情亦可悲矣。然而，在这虚幻的想象中，也潜藏着诗人对布罗网者的愤怒和反抗。

曹植诗歌的特点，以钟嵘《诗品》"骨气奇高，辞采华茂"八个字概括最为贴切，也最常为人引用。宋人张戒说："……子建诗，微婉之情、洒落之韵、抑扬顿挫之气，固不可以优劣论也"（《岁寒堂诗话》）。但就这首《野田黄雀行》而言，"骨气"（思想内容）确实是高的，而辞采却说不上"华茂"。从总体上看，这首诗更具有汉乐府民歌的质朴风味。首先，拔剑捎网、黄雀谢恩这一情节，就明显受汉乐府民歌中许多带寓言色彩的作品的影响。西汉《铙歌》十八曲中《艾如张》一曲有"山出黄雀亦有罗，雀已高飞奈雀何"之句，对此篇构思的启发，更是显然。其次，此诗的词句也多质朴无华。"罗家得雀喜，少年见雀悲"这种句式完全是纯粹的口语，"黄雀得飞飞，飞飞摩苍天"二句中的叠字及顶真修辞手法也都是乐府民歌中常见的。这些朴实的词句和诗歌所要表现的内容正相适应，如果有意雕琢，其感人的力量也许倒反而会减弱了。于此可见曹植这个才高八斗的诗人向民歌学习所取得的成就。

第三章 建安诗英译鉴赏实践

学生英译实践园地

英译实践版本选读

译文 1　吴伏生　格雷厄姆·哈蒂尔

A Yellow Sparrow in the Wild Fields

The winds mourns in the treetops, the sea is lifting its waves.
No swords in my hand, why I need so many friends?
See there, the sparrow, catching sight of the circling eagle
flaps from the hedgerow into the waiting net.
The trapper dances in delight,
but seeing the bird, the young boy is sad.
With a sudden thrust he cuts the cords,
and the sparrow takes to the sky;
He lifts, then soars, to the edge of the heaven,
down he swoops again, to thank the boy.

译文 2　汪榕培

Sparrows in the Wild Field

Powerful winds will blow at lofty trees;
Violent waves will roar in mighty seas.
As the sword of power is not in my hand,
It is no good to make friends in the land.

Don't you see the sparrow on the hedge
Snared while fleeing a falcon pulling fledge?
While the snarer is glad to catch the sparrow,
The young man feels sorry for the sparrow.

When he draws the sword and cuts the snare,
The sparrow is set free to cut the air.
The sparrow soars as high as eyes can span
And then returns to thank the kind young man.

第三章　建安诗英译鉴赏实践

建安诗英译鉴赏实践之五

短歌行①

曹　丕

仰瞻②帷幕，俯察几筵③。

其物如故④，其人不存。

神灵倏忽⑤，弃我遐迁⑥。

靡瞻靡恃⑦，泣涕涟涟⑧。

呦呦游鹿⑨，衔草鸣麑⑩。

翩翩飞鸟，挟子巢栖⑪。

我独孤茕⑫，怀此百离⑬。

忧心孔疚⑭，莫我能知⑮。

人亦有言："忧令人老"⑯。

嗟我白发⑰，生一何早⑱。

长吟永叹，怀我圣考⑲。

曰："仁者寿"⑳，胡不是保㉑？

【注释】

①《短歌行》为乐府诗旧题，属《相和歌辞·平调曲》。乐府诗里尚有《长歌行》，短歌、长歌的区别在于声调的长短，不是指诗的篇幅长短或词句的多少。

②〔仰瞻（zhān）〕抬起头来谦恭的观看。意同"瞻仰"。

③〔俯察〕低下头来仔细地看。〔几〕矮小的桌子，古代人用以倚靠身体。〔筵（yán）〕竹席。

④〔如故〕同原来一样。

⑤〔神灵倏（shū）忽〕（父亲的）魂魄疾速离去。

⑥〔遐(xiá)迁〕远离。此指诗人的父亲离开人世。
⑦〔靡(mǐ)瞻靡恃〕靡,没有。瞻,恃,依靠。此句意为没有企望了,没有依靠了。
⑧〔泣涕涟涟〕泣涕,眼泪。涟涟,泪流不止的样子。
⑨〔呦呦〕鹿的叫声。语出《诗经·小雅·鹿鸣》:"呦呦鹿鸣,食野之苹。"
⑩〔衔草〕心不能安定。〔麑(ní)〕指小鹿。
⑪〔挟子巢枝〕鸟携带着幼雏栖息在巢里。枝,筑巢之物。一作"栖"。
⑫〔孤茕〕孤独。〔茕〕孑身一人。
⑬〔百离〕种种痛苦。离,同"罹难",忧苦,苦痛。
⑭〔忧心孔疚〕内心忧愁的极其痛苦。孔,甚,很。疚,病痛。
⑮〔莫我能知〕倒装句,莫能知我,即没有人能够懂得我的悲伤。
⑯〔忧令人老〕《古诗》有"思君令人老"句,此为化用。令,使。
⑰〔嗟〕叹息。感叹我的满头白发。
⑱〔一何〕多么,竟然。意即我这么早就满头白发。
⑲〔圣考〕指曹操。父死称"考"。圣,对先父的敬称。
⑳〔仁者寿〕语出《论语·雍也》篇,意为仁者安静,故多长寿。
㉑〔胡不是保〕意即为何(我父亲)不能(像仁者那样)长寿呢!胡,何,为何。

白话释义

　　抬头望着帷幕,低头看着几筵。
　　还是原来的物品,亲人却已离开人间。
　　他的魂魄匆忙离去,把我丢下,渐行渐远。
　　我无依无靠难见一面,不禁泪水涟涟。
　　呦呦鸣叫的母鹿,衔来地衣把小鹿召唤。
　　翩飞的母鸟,护翼着小鸟飞回鸟巢。
　　只有我孤孤单单,心里苦痛难言。
　　内心悲戚苦难言,无人能懂我伤悲。
　　老话说得有道理:"忧愁让人老"。
　　可叹我的白发啊,为何生得这么早!
　　长吁长叹真痛苦,伏念深怀我先父。
　　古语说:"仁德之人可长命",
　　　为何先父难长寿?

第三章 建安诗英译鉴赏实践

主题鉴赏

公元 220 年(建安二十五年)正月,曹操病死。二月,葬高陵。此诗当作于曹操葬后不久。曹操《遗令》:于铜雀台堂上"安六尺床,施穗帐,""月旦十五日,自朝至午,辄向帐中作伎乐"。王僧虔《技录》云:"《短歌行》'仰瞻'一曲,魏氏遗令,使节朔奏乐。魏文制此辞,自抚筝和歌。歌者云:'贵官弹筝。'贵官,即魏文也。此曲声制最美,辞不可入宴乐"(《乐府诗集》卷三十载《古今乐录》)。所以,曹丕写这首乐府诗,并且自己"抚筝和歌"是由于父亲的急速死去使他悲痛不已,同时也是为了践行父亲的遗令。

此诗写思亲之情,每四句为一节,共六节。第一节写睹物思人,而人不在;第二节写失去依怙,泪流不已;第三节以写鹿麂飞鸟之乐,反衬己悲;第四节写孤独无依之哀;第五节写怀忧早衰;末节写痛亲早亡,心痛难抑。全诗写得质朴、本色,且其中有作者诗文"工于言情"的特点,十分细致、生动。

诗人从人亡物在写起,"仰瞻帷幕,俯察几筵。其物如故,其人不存。"俯仰之际,看到死者生前用过的帷幕、桌筵,不禁触物伤情,勾起物在人亡之痛。起笔十分自然。

接着,"神灵倏忽,弃我遐迁。靡瞻靡恃,泣涕涟涟。"点明了丧亲思痛的主题。诗人在极度悲伤中,似乎觉得父亲是在十分短疾的时间里忽然远离自己而去的。"倏忽"一词非常生动地写出了曹丕丧亲之后,惘然若失的心态。失去曹操不仅失去他生活上的引导者,也失去他政治上的扶持者,因此,使他"靡瞻靡恃,泣涕涟涟"。这里,诗人运用《诗经·小雅·小弁》的成语"靡瞻匪父,靡依匪母",来抒写失去父亲的哀伤,显得很贴切。失去了自己所瞻仰倚仗的人,自然使他止不住要"泣涕涟涟"了。于是,这一节紧承开头,进一步展现诗人失去父亲的悲痛心情。

然而,诗人的笔触没有继续顺着第二节直倾自己的哀痛心情,却是突然插入鸣鹿衔草呼唤小鹿,飞鸟挟子归巢的具体形象:"呦呦游鹿,衔草鸣麂。翩翩飞鸟,挟子巢栖。"写出有所"瞻恃"的欢乐,以动物亲子之间的和谐、亲爱来对比,反衬自己的丧亲之哀。笔势跌宕,拓深了诗歌的意境。

接着,"我独孤茕,怀此百离。忧心孔疚,莫我能知。"四句又转入实写,叙述自己孤寂无依,内心的痛苦是人莫能知的。此写出忧苦之多,《诗经·小雅·采薇》中有"忧心孔疚,我行不来"句,是表现征人思念家乡、亲人的心情的,诗人借用此句来表达自己丧亲后的孤茕悲苦是很恰当的。

第五节"人亦有言:'忧令人老。'嗟我白发,生一何早。"紧接上一节中的"忧"字展开,由忧字写到自己白发早生,从忧伤到早衰,还是从自己亡亲之痛着笔的。

最末节,"长吟永叹,怀我圣考。曰:'仁者寿,'胡不是保?"转笔写怀亲,对父亲的离世深感悲切,喟然难抑:既然,古语云仁者可以长寿,而自己的父亲却无法颐养天年。诗歌在浓重的悼亲、思亲的情绪中憾然结尾,令读者无不动容落泪。可以说,曹丕的这首《短歌行》,在感情基调上和艺术手法上,绝不次于被称为中华第一孝诗的《诗经·小雅·谷风之什·蓼莪》。中华孝道,传颂千载,即使被认为善用政治伎俩,迫害手足兄弟的魏文帝曹丕也有忠情孝义、温软敦厚的一面。

第三章 建安诗英译鉴赏实践

英译实践版本选读

译文 1　翟理斯

On the Death of His Father

I look up, the curtains are there as of yore;
I look down, and there is the mat on the floor;
These things I behold, but the man is no more.

To the infinite azure his spirit has flown,
And I am left friendless, uncared-for, alone,
Of solace bereft, save to weep and to moan.

The deer on the hillside caressingly bleat,
And offer the grass for their young ones to eat,
While birds of the air to their nestlings bring meat.

But I a poor orphan must ever remain,
My heart, still so young, overburdened with pain.
For him I shall never set eyes on again.

'Tis a well-worn old saying, which all men allow,
That grief stamps the deepest of lines on the brow.
Alas for my hair, it is silvery now!

Alas for my father, cut off in his pride!
Alas that no more I may stand by his side!
Oh where were the gods when that great hero died?

译文 2　亚瑟·韦利

On the Death of His Father

I look up and see his curtains and bed:
I look down and examine his table and mat.
The things are there just as before.
But the man they belonged to is not there.
His spirit suddenly has taken flight
And left me behind far away.
To whom shall I look on whom rely?
My tears flow in an endless stream.
"Yu, yu" cry the wandering deer
As they carry fodder to their young in the wood.
Flap, flap fly the birds
As they carry their little ones back to the nest.
I alone am desolate
Dreading the days of our long parting:
My grieving heart's settled pain
No one else can understand.
There is a saying among people
"Sorrow makes us grow old."
Alas, alas for my white hairs!
All too early they have come!
Long wailing, long sighing
My thoughts are fixed on my sage parent.
They say the good live long:
Then why was he not spared?

译文 3　赵彦春

A Short Song Ballad

Up, the dome I behold,
And down, I see the stand.

第三章 建安诗英译鉴赏实践

Everything stays as old,
But she's not on this land.
Gods go off or come by;
Why do they desert me?
On whom can I rely?
In tears none I can see,
But hear some stray deer bleat,
A-calling their dear ones,
And a flock of birds fleet,
To feed their nestled sons.
Only I stay alone,
A-suffering this woe,
To deep sorrow I'm thrown,
Who does my status know?
O sadness, as they say,
Makes one age fast, no doubt.
O goodness, my hair gray
Has so early come out
In depth I sing this song;
My old father I miss.
It's said kind men live long;
Why didn't he live as this?

译文 4　佚名

On the Death Of His Father

Raising my eyes, I see his screen;
Bending my head, his table clean.
These things are there just as before,
The man who owned them is no more.

Suddenly his spirit has flown,
And left me fatherless, alone.

Who'd look to me? On whom rely?
Tear upon tear streams from my eyes.

The deer are bleating here and there,
They feed the young ones in their care.
The birds are flying east and west,
Feeding the nestlings in the nest.

Alone I'm desolate the drear,
Severed from the father I revere.
Deep in my heart grief overflows,
But no one knows, no one knows.

'Tis said that sorrow makes us old.
And early grow white hair. Behold!

For the deceased I wail and sigh;
If the good live long, why should he die!

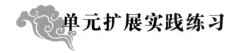

一、请用英语简要评述以下汉诗的两篇英语译文。

杂诗七首（其四）

曹 植

南国有佳人，容华若桃李。
朝游江北岸，夕宿潇湘沚。
时俗薄朱颜，谁为发皓齿？
俯仰岁将暮，荣耀难久恃。

第三章 建安诗英译鉴赏实践

译文 1　许渊冲

Seven Poems (IV)

A beauty lives in southern lands,
As fair as peach in bloom she stands.
At dawn she wanders left and right
Of Rivers Xiao and Xiang till night.
For rosy face the world won't care.
Who would praise her teeth bright and fair?
She sinks or swims, time flies so fast.
Alas! how could her prime long last!

译文 2　高德耀

Unclassified Poem (No. 4)

In a southern kingdom there is a lady fair,
The beauty of her countenance like peach and plum.
At daybreak she wanders the Yangzi's north bank,
In the evening she stays on an islet of the clear Xiang.
The taste of the time disdains a rosy face,
To whom will she reveal her gleaming teeth?
In no time the year draws to an end,
Radiant beauty is hard to rely on for long.

第四章

唐诗英译鉴赏实践(上)

导 读

The Tang dynasty, founded in 618 AD, developed in the subsequent years into a powerful empire in Chinese history. The political structure of the Tang society was somewhat different from either that of the previous age of the Wei, Jin, and the Northern and Southern dynasties, or that of the Song dynasty afterwards.

The unification of the entire country and the prosperity of the nation somehow strengthened the imperial power, and the aristocratic families were in one way or another restricted in their forces. The civil service examinations (科举考试) did not play as strict and significant a role as in times after the Song dynasty, but to some degree they still helped to open up political opportunities for the middle and lower social strata, and thus made it possible for talented people from among them to show more enthusiasm for participating in the political and cultural activities in the society. On the other hand, the imperial power did not become an absolute autocratic force either. Shortly after he was in power, Emperor Taizong (唐太宗) issued a decree to write and compile the *Records of Clans* (《氏族志》), the actual import of which was to make adjustments to the relationship of various interest groups. Aristocratic families,

第四章 唐诗英译鉴赏实践（上）

both new and old, and local forces still wielded their influence in politics. Nor was a singular and powerful ideological control ever established throughout the Tang dynasty. In the Early and High Tang dynasty, in particular, Confucianism was not attached more importance than Taoism and Buddhism by either men of letters or with the rulers at the top.

In general, the Tang society was quite free in thought. Due to the relative liberalness of the social condition, as well as the merging of the cultures of the many different ethnic groups in the country and the frequent exchanges of Chinese and foreign civilizations, the culture of this age gradually displayed its iridescent and lively aspects.

Classical poetry had been the core genre of the literature of the literati since the Wei and Jin. It had developed and changed over a long time, learned valuable lessons through rich experience, and opened up a great variety of possibilities. Therefore classical poetry reached its zenith during the Tang dynasty. From the Early Tang to the High Tang, under favorable conditions in many different aspects, poetry displayed its highest artistic features.

In his anthology, *A Critical Collection of Tang Poetry*(《唐诗品汇》), Gao Bing (高棅) of the Ming dynasty divided the history of the development and evolution of Tang poetry into four stages: the Early Tang, the High Tang, the Mid-Tang and the Late Tang (初唐、盛唐、中唐、晚唐). Later it has become the conventional format of periodization of Tang poetry, and expanded to the other genres of Tang literature.

However, it has often been controversial as regards how these four stages should be divided by specific dates. Considering the age-old convention, we shall continue to use this method of periodization, but we should put more emphasis on the differentiation between the Early/High Tang and the Mid-/Late Tang, with the "An-Shi Rebellion" (安史之乱) that broke out in the last years of the Tianbao reign (天宝年间) as the line of demarcation.

Generally speaking, the literature of the Early/High Tang developed in the same direction as the literature of the Wei, Jin, the Northern and Southern dynasties, with its core spirit in the pursuit after beauty. The early Tang period was also best known for its *lüshi* (regulated verse, 律诗), an eight-line poem with five or seven words in each line; *ci* (verse following strict rules of prosody);

and *jueju* (truncated verse/quatrain, 绝句), a four-line poem with five or seven words in each line.

By the *Mid-Tang*, there appeared a series of complicated changes in literature. On the one hand, there was an obviously increase of the consciousness of regarding literature as an attachment to, or a tool of, politics and morality. On the other hand, the representation of emotions in human life in literature continued its process of expansion and deepening. Such changes continued all the way throughout the Song dynasty. The two best-known poets of this period were Li Bai (李白) and Du Fu (杜甫). Li Bai was well-known for the romanticism of his poetry; Du Fu was seen as a Confucian moralist with a strict sense of duty toward society.

Later Tang poets developed greater realism and social criticism and refined the art of narration. One of the best known of the later Tang poets was Bai Jüyi (白居易), whose poems were an inspired and critical comment on the society of his time.

Subsequent writers of classical poetry lived under the shadow of their great Tang predecessors, and although there were many fine poets in subsequent dynasties, none reached the level of this period. As the classical style of poetry became more stultified, a more flexible poetic medium, the *ci* (lyric poetry, 词), arrived on the scene. The *ci*, a poetic form based on the tunes of popular songs, some of Central Asian origin, was developed to its fullest by the poets of the Song dynasty. The Song era poet Su Shi (苏轼) mastered *ci*, *shi*, and *fu* forms of poetry, as well as prose, calligraphy, and painting.

As the *ci* gradually became more literary and artificial after Song times, Chinese *Sanqu* poetry (散曲), a more free form, based on dramatic arias, developed. The use of *Sanqu* songs in drama marked an important step in the development of vernacular literature.

Poetry of the Early Tang

In the Early Tang, the rulers assumed a liberal attitude toward literature and arts. Li Shimin (Emperor Taizong) personally wrote the "Commentary" on the "Biography of Lu Ji" (《陆机传》) in *History of the Jin* (《晋史》) in which he praised the "beautiful and varied diction" of Lu Ji's works, showing his appreciation of the belles-lettres literature. Afterwards, rulers such as Emperor Gaozong, Empress Wu (武则天) and Emperor Zhongzong were also fond of arts and literature. In order to make a show of the atmosphere of the time of peace and prosperity of the great Tang Empire, they recruited numerous men of letters in the country, commissioned the compilation of encyclopedias and concordances, and composed poems in exchanges with their subjects. Accordingly the imperial court of the Early Tang, just like that during the Southern dynasties and the Sui, became the center of literary activities of the time. The most representative members from the palace literati of the Early Tang were Yu Shi'nan (虞世南) of the Taizong reign, Shangguan Yi (上官仪) of the Gaozong reign, Du Shenyan (杜审言), Song Zhiwen (宋之问), and Shen Quanqi (沈佺期) of the reign of Empress Wu and Zhongzong, etc. Most of their works deal with eulogizing of the court and feasts at imperial palaces and gardens in contents, wherein it was difficult to express feelings in a profound way. However, in terms of the construction of the poetic forms, they still made significant contributions. Also, some of their compositions, which had nothing to do with imperial feasts and gatherings, could be quite moving.

Four Talents of Early Tang

As early as in the circles of Early Tang poetry, there already appeared some whose poems were different from the Palace Style. Poets who truly displayed some new aspects in Early Tang poetry and brought about obvious changes in Tang poetry were the so-called "Four Talents" (初唐四杰) who were active during the reigns of Gaozong and Empress Wu, Lu Zhaolin (卢照邻), Luo Binwang (骆宾王), Wang Bo (王勃), and Yang Jiong (杨炯). They were not a "group" in the later sense, but the four names which, from a later perspective, emerged from this age.

As early as in Song Zhiwen's "Funeral Oration for Academician Du Shenyan", there was a reference to "up-coming youngsters Wang, Yang, Lu and

Luo."① placing the four in one group for the first time. It also touched upon their common features: "Due to destiny, they could not help themselves in terms of blessings and longevity. Probably because of the jealousy of divinity, they could not enjoy both talent and substances in life."② It means that although they were talented, they suffered many setbacks in life. Three of them had the attraction of failure, suffering, and untimely but pitiful deaths. Compared to previous ages, there were certainly more opportunities for an individual to win success by talent during the Tang dynasty. In his *Preface to the Collected Works of the Lord of Nanyang* (《南阳公集序》), Lu Zhaolin mentions how in the early Tang, many renowned officials either "presented themselves with literary compositions" (虞、李、岑、许之俦，以文章进) or "made their reputation by their talent" (王、魏、来、褚之辈，以材术显), all "starting as cotton-clad commoners and rising to senior ministers" (咸能起自布衣，蔚为卿相), which made people like him very excited. However, for those who lacked distinguished family background and yet were too strong in character, there were still hardships and dangers in their life.

Among the Four Talents, Lu Zhaolin, who once served as a District Defender, committed suicide because he could not stand the pain from a killer crippling disease; Luo Binwang participated in Xu Jingye's rebellion and disappeared without a trace; Wang Bo became a convict and later died from drowning when he crossed the sea to visit his father in Jiaozhi; Yang Jiong, who served as a District Magistrate, was the only one who had a peaceful life. Their life's experience, as those with high talents but low in social status or those with great expectations for themselves but faced bad fortunes, had a deep influence on their personality and their literary compositions.

Du Fu paid a tribute to the poetry of the Four Talents, "Wang, Yang, Lu, and Luo were the style of those days; /'not serious in their writing'— the sneering never stops."③

As regards their poetry, they were all best known for their long song forms, such as Lu Zhaolin's heptasyllabic (七言诗) "An Ancient Topic from Chang'an"

---

① 《祭杜学士审言文》宋之问：后复有王、杨、卢、骆。
② 《祭杜学士审言文》宋之问：由运然也，莫以福寿自卫；将神忌也，不得华实斯俱！
③ 《戏为六绝句（其二）》杜甫：王杨卢骆当时体，轻薄为文哂未休。

第四章 唐诗英译鉴赏实践(上)

(《长安古意》), or Luo Binwang's "A Piece on the Imperial Capital"(《帝京篇》) and "A Piece on the Past"(《咏怀》), both in mixed pentasyllabic(五言诗) and heptasyllabic(七言诗) lines. Poems like these have incorporated the special features of song forms since the Qi(齐) and Liang(梁) as well as the scale and grandeur of the rhapsodies on capitals. They are grand in scale, splendid in scenery, with vivid description of things and views of the capital, as well as the prosperous and luxurious life there. These poems hold many levels of implications. For instance, "An Ancient Topic from Chang'an," in its lucid and ornate style, not only praises the pursuit of a happy life, but also laments the brevity of rank and wealth; towards the end, it sets the loneliness of humble and poor commoners in strong contrast against the arrogance and indulgence of the nobilities that have been highlighted previously, revealing the injustice in human society. In short, these poems represent a rich and complex experience of life, and refuse to view life with prejudice, so they are extremely lively and lifelike.

In addition to their long song forms, Lu and Luo also have quite a few outstanding short pentasyllabic poems. For example, Luo Binwang's "Singing about Cicadas While in Prison"(《在狱咏蝉》) is a well known one among them. It assimilates profound feelings about life in the form of poetry on things which used to be focused on entertainment, representing an important change in the poetry on things of the Tang dynasty. In particular, "A Quatrain on Seeing Someone Off at the Yi River"(《于易水送人》) manages to bring out the author's heroic spirit:

  Here at this place, saying farewell to the Yan Prince,
 Bristling with emotions, the warrior's hair stood up against his cap.
  The people of the bygone days have since disappeared,
  But the water of today is still as chilly as usual.

Among the "Four Talents," Wang Bo(649—676) had the shortest life but the highest reputation. He was at his best in his pentasyllabic regulated poems and quatrains, which are neat and trim in prosody, plain but refined in style, and full of vigor in implication. Take, for example, "Seeing District Defender Du off to Shuzhou"(《送杜少府之任蜀州》):

  The city walls, the palaces: encircled by the three Qin regions;
  The wind, the mist: drifting over the five rivers.

My heart is heavy about parting from you, my friend,
Though I know we are both away from home for a career.
With friends who understand each other in this world,
Even if wide apart, they are like next-door neighbors.
There is no need to go to the crossroads
And shed our tears like young children.

Wang Bo was a man of letters with great talent. Besides his pentasyllabic regulated poems and quatrains, his heptasyllabic poem "Pavilion of the Prince of Teng" (《滕王阁序》) is undoubtedly ranked as first-class compositions (天下第一骈文). Later ages, however, remembered him for a few moving, straightforward parallel prose lines such as "Where is he now, the prince in the tower? / Beyond the balcony the long river just keeps flowing on."① and the most eminent couplet is a reference to two lines: "Falling sunset rays fly together with one lone duck, / Distant heavens are the same color as autumn's water."② These lines were part of every schoolboy's lore now, and it is difficult to tell here whether they were used as a direct allusion or simply sprang to mind as a cliche of ordinary classical discourse. Many of Wang Bo's poems are relatively unornamented, and his works in general have a forcefulness that is indeed distinct from the sometimes mechanical exposition we find in court writers of the era. Wang Bo was, however, sometimes a master of the most florid, ornamental style; and in this, "reform" is hard to see.

Less gifted among the "Four Talents," Yang Jiong is almost exclusively better known in his pentasyllabic regulated verse (including the extended regulated poems), like "A Song of Joining the Army" (《从军行》). A heroic spirit is imbued in the poem by the representation of the ideal and passion of life, i. e. , to establish oneself by winning honors:

Watchtower fires shone on the western capital;
In his heart, beyond control, he felt a rising anger.
Following the ivory tally, they departed the Phoenix Palace.
Riding on armor-clad horses, they besieged the Dragon City.

---

① 《滕王阁序》王勃:阁中帝子今何在?槛外长江空自流。
② 《滕王阁序》王勃:落霞与孤鹜齐飞,秋水共长天一色。

第四章 唐诗英译鉴赏实践（上）

  Snow was heavy: painted banners looked so dim;
In gusty winds, the sound of drums was heard.
One'd rather be the commander of a hundred men
Than to be a man of letters, reading books only!

  Generally speaking, the composition of the "Four Talents" of the Early Tang was closely related to the literature of the Six Dynasties. It inherited much from the latter, from form and subject matter to diction and vocabulary. At the same time, it also transformed the latter in a strong manner. The world in their poetry became grander and vaster, their poetic language turned more lucid and refined, and in particular, their poems were filled with more vigor. All this demonstrated that the Tang poetry was taking a course of its own. As regards its relation with contemporary literature, it also rectified, in a powerful fashion, the weakness in the style of the palace poetry, the lack of passion and vigor due to an excessive emphasis on rhetoric and ornamentation.

唐诗英译鉴赏实践之一

从军行[①]

杨　炯

烽火照西京[②]，

心中自不平。

牙璋辞凤阙[③]，

铁骑绕龙城[④]。

雪暗凋旗画[⑤]，

风多杂鼓声[⑥]。

宁为百夫长[⑦]，

胜作一书生。

【注释】

① 〔从军行〕为乐府《相和歌辞·平调曲》旧题,主题为军旅生活。
② 〔烽火〕古代边防告急的烟火。〔西京〕西汉都长安,东汉改都洛阳,因此称洛阳为东京,长安为西京。
③ 〔牙璋〕古代发兵所用之兵符,分为两块,相合处呈牙状咬合,朝廷和主帅各执其半。此处指代奉命出征的将帅。〔凤阙〕宫阙名。汉建章宫的圆阙上有金凤,故以凤阙代指皇宫。
④ 〔龙城〕又称龙庭,在今鄂尔浑河的东岸,汉时匈奴的要地。汉武帝派卫青出击匈奴,曾在此获胜。这里指塞外的敌方据点。
⑤ 〔凋〕原意指草木枯败凋零,此指大雪纷飞,军旗黯然失色。
⑥ 〔杂鼓声〕寒风怒吼,夹杂着咚咚战鼓,形容战事之急。
⑦ 〔百夫长〕一百个士兵的头目,泛指下级军官。

白话释义

边塞战火传京城,
壮士心中难平静。
将军受命辞皇宫,
精兵勇将围敌营。
雪纷军旗失颜色,
狂风夹杂战鼓声。
哪怕做个百夫长,
胜过无用一书生。

主题鉴赏

这首诗借用乐府旧题"从军行",描写一个读书士子从军边塞、参加战斗,保家卫国的心路历程。诗歌的历史背景大致为唐调露、永隆年间,吐蕃、突厥曾多次侵扰甘肃一带,裴行俭奉命出师征讨贼军之事。明代唐汝询在《唐诗解》中认为是杨炯看到朝廷重武轻文,只有武官得宠,心中有所不平,故作诗以发泄牢骚。此为误

第四章 唐诗英译鉴赏实践（上）

读。全诗仅用四十个字就成功渲染了塞外边疆战事荼靡、京城人心凝聚、同仇敌忾的浓郁氛围，揭示出诗人激昂向上、精忠报国的心理变化过程，笔力雄劲，主题硬朗。诗歌以通俗易懂的语言，富于激情的笔调，抒发了诗人胸臆难平，情志高亢的报国情怀。诗歌褪尽六朝绮靡轻颓的诗风，重现了汉魏建安风骨的俊逸雄劲之气，体现出浓郁的时代气息，流露出唐人尚武轻文的观念，表达了初唐读书人内心深处所潜藏的弃笔从戎、征战沙场、策勋扬名、为国效力的强烈意志。

首联写边境战事消息传至京城长安，激起了志士的爱国热情，因此，开首两句是整个事件展开的大背景。诗歌的技巧高人一筹，它并不直言军情紧急，而是以"烽火照西京"这一句独创性的诗句开启了丰富的想象空间。通过"烽火"这一形象化的景物，再加上动词"照"，渲染了一种迫在眉睫的紧张气氛，富有技巧地呈现了军情刻不容缓的急迫感和逼仄感。"心中自不平"是由烽火而引起的：国家兴亡，匹夫有责，他不愿再把青春年华消磨在"两耳不闻窗外事"的读书度日之中。一个"自"字，表现了书生那种由衷的爱国激情，即使被视为"百无一用是书生"的儒生同样有保家卫国抵御外敌的精神境界。由此看来，初唐的书生们并非闭门读死书、心中无块垒的庸常之辈，纵使书生意气，亦能挥斥方遒。许多书生依然怀揣着报国保家、建功立业、守护家园的浓浓热血，看来华夏儿女的爱国情怀千古不变。

颔联写主帅率军辞别京城，奔赴前线作战，以排山倒海之势包围敌军城堡的过程。一个"辞"字，显出奉旨率师远征者的严肃和庄重；一个"绕"字，显见大唐铁骑威力无穷，把敌军的营地团团包围。此处以匈奴名城龙城代指敌军的要塞。

颈联接续颔联，诗人抓住了隆冬自然界的主要表象"雪""风"两者，刻画两军对峙时的紧张场面。上句视觉：大雪纷飞中战旗到处翻舞；下句听觉：风声狂吼中夹杂着进军的战鼓声。两句诗视觉听觉交互生辉，声色并茂，各臻其妙。诗人以象征军队的"旗"和"鼓"，表现出征将士冒雪同敌人搏斗的坚强无畏精神和在战鼓声激励下奋勇杀敌的悲壮激烈场面。

尾联"宁为百夫长，胜作一书生"表达了初唐时期的读书人为国建功的共同心愿。李泽厚说，"当时从高门到寒士，从上层到市井，在初唐东征西讨、大破突厥、战败吐蕃、招安回纥的天可汗（太宗）时代里，一种为国立功的荣誉感和英雄主义弥漫在社会氛围中。"同样的气概在杨炯其他诗篇里也有所表现，例如以旧乐府题所创作的《战城南》：

　　塞北途辽远，城南战苦辛。
　　幡旗如鸟翼，甲胄似鱼鳞。
　　冻水寒伤马，悲风愁煞人。
　　寸心明白日，千里暗黄尘。

这首诗的基调并不亚于《从军行》，诗歌格调雄浑激越，气势轩昂，洋溢着浓郁的爱国之情，表达了诗人豪情满怀、御敌必胜的坚定信心。

总之，《从军行》以生动的笔触，有力的措辞，抒发了书生投笔从戎，出塞参战的强烈意愿。能把如此丰富的内容，浓缩在有限的篇幅里，可见诗人的艺术功力非同一般。然而这种跳跃是十分自然的，每一个跨度之间又给人留下了丰富的想象余地。同时，这种跳跃式的结构，使诗歌具有明快的节奏，如山崖上飞流惊湍，给人一种一气直下、一往无前的气势，有力地突显出诗人满腔的爱国激情和唐军将士保家卫国、御敌千里、气吞山河的精神风貌。全诗立意高远，在内容和艺术风格上均突破了初唐"宫体诗"华丽空泛、绮靡颓废的风格，在中国古典汉诗的发展史上有着承前启后的重要意义。

第四章 唐诗英译鉴赏实践（上）

英译实践版本选读

译文 1　陈伟强

Ballad of Joining the Army

Beacon fires light up the western capital,
And my heart turns uneasy.
With the ivory tally our commander exits Phoenix Watch-tower;
Our ironclad horses encircle Dragon Fort.
As snow darkens the sky, our banners' designs are over-shadowed,
As winds intensify, they mix with the rumblings of drums.
I would rather be appointed a Leader of a Hundred Men,
Than to be a lone bookworm.

译文 2　许渊冲

I Would Rather Fight

The beacon fire spreads to the capital;
My agitated mind can't be calmed down.
By royal order we leave palace wall;
Our armored steeds besiege the Dragon Town.
Darkening snow damages our banners red;
In howling winds are mingled our drumbeats.
I'd rather fight at a hundred men's head;
Than pore o'er books without performing feats.

译文 3　刘　群

To the Military Tune

Upon the capital beacon fires glowed;
My heart but drubbed with the battle lour drawn.
From court the assault orders were bestowed;

Our cavalries besieged the foe's fort town.
Snow dims the sky and flag hue hard to see;
The howling wind blended with drumbeat sounds.
Yet rather a centurion I would be;
Than reading books away from battle grounds.

译文 4　杨宪益　戴乃迭

Following the Army to the Frontier

Flaring beacons relayed the alarm to the West Capital,
The scholar was filled with an ardent fighting spirit.
Holding the tally of command the general bade adieu to the palace,
And soon the iron cavalry besieged the Dragon City of Huns.
Army flags faded and dulled in the whirling snow,
While howling winds were punctured by battle drums.
Better to join the army and be a captain
Than remain a scholar wallowing in books.

译文 5　佚　名

To Be a Commander

Watchtower fires shone on the western capital;
In his heart, beyond control, he felt a rising anger.
Following the ivory tally, they departed the Phoenix Palace.
Riding on armor-clad horses, they besieged the Dragon City.
Snow was heavy, painted banners looked so dim;
In gusty winds, the sound of drums was heard.
One'd rather be the commander of a hundred men,
Than to be a man of letters, reading books only!

第四章 唐诗英译鉴赏实践（上）

唐诗英译鉴赏实践之二

在狱咏蝉
骆宾王

西陆①蝉声唱，
南冠②客思深。
不堪玄鬓影③，
来对白头吟④。
露重飞难进⑤，
风多响易沉⑥。
无人信高洁⑦，
谁为表予心⑧？

【注释】

①〔西陆〕指秋天。《隋书·天文志》载："日循黄道东行一日一夜行一度，三百六十五日有奇而周天。行东陆谓之春，行南陆谓之夏，行西陆谓之秋，行北陆谓之冬。"
②〔南冠〕即楚冠。《左传·成公九年（晋归钟仪）》载："晋侯观于军府，见钟仪，问之曰：'南冠而絷者谁也？'有司对曰：'郑人所献楚囚也。'"此为用典，以楚钟仪戴着南冠被囚于晋国军府事来代指囚徒。
③〔玄鬓影〕指蝉的黑色翅膀，这里比喻自己正当盛年。
④〔白头吟〕乐府曲名，诗中描述了主人公清清白白却遭诬谤的遭遇。此处指诗人感叹自己正当玄鬓之年，却来默诵《白头吟》那样哀怨的诗句。
⑤〔露重〕秋露浓重。〔飞难进〕蝉羽翼因露水凝重而难以高飞。
⑥〔响〕指蝉声。〔沉〕沉没，掩盖。

⑦〔高洁〕清高洁白。古人认为蝉栖高饮露,是高洁之物,作者因以自喻。
⑧〔予心〕我的忠贞之心。

白话释义

　　监外秋蝉鸣不停,身陷囹圄心悲恸。
　　蝉儿羽翼亮铿铿,怎懂我已少白头。
　　秋露浓浓蝉难飞,蝉声岂能压秋风。
　　饮露高飞心高洁,谁能替我洗冤情。

主题鉴赏

　　司马迁在《史记·屈原贾生列传》中说:"蝉蜕于浊秽,以浮游尘埃之外。"蝉能入土生活,又能出土羽化。汉代以来,多以蝉的品性来自喻或喻人,或者以蝉的羽化来比喻人的精神的重生,表达对不同流合污、不趋炎附势、洁身自好者高洁品质的赞颂。唐代诗人虞世南有诗云:"垂緌饮清露,流响出疏桐。居高声自远,非是藉秋风"(《蝉》)。

　　《在狱咏蝉》是"初唐四杰"之一骆宾王的代表诗作之一,也是他身陷囹圄之作。此诗以蝉为喻,以蝉比兴,以蝉寓己,寓情于物,寄托遥深,蝉人浑然一体,抒发了诗人品行高洁却"遭时徽纆"①的哀怨悲伤之情,表达了辨明无辜、昭雪沉冤的愿望。全诗情感充沛,取譬明切,用典自然,语意双关,于咏物中寄情寓兴,由物到人,由人及物,达到了物我一体的境界,是咏物诗中的名作。此诗当是受前代的影响而成,创作此诗的背景如下:

　　唐高宗永徽二年(651),33岁的骆宾王在豫州刺史李元庆(唐高祖李渊第十六子)的府中做了六年的幕僚。学而优则仕,辅佐明君兼济天下,是古代读书人的抱负。若怀才不遇,放下名利弃官而去,则为士之风骨。唐高宗仪凤三年(678),屈居下僚十多年而刚升为侍御史的骆宾王,却因上疏论事触怒武则天,遭诬,以贪赃罪名下狱。闻一多说,骆宾王"天生一副侠骨,专喜欢管闲事,打抱不平……"(《唐诗杂论·宫体诗的自赎》)。这些话道出了骆宾王下狱的根本原因:他敢抗上司,敢动刀笔,敢替弱势群体鸣不平。因此,他被当权者以"贪赃"与"触忤武后"的罪名投入牢狱似乎理由充分。

---

① 〔徽纆〕绳索样的一种狱具。

第四章 唐诗英译鉴赏实践(上)

诗歌首联以蝉声起兴,引起客思。颔联以"不堪"和"来对"构成流水对,"玄鬓影"与"白头吟"鲜明对照。尤其"白头吟"用典之妙,令人拍案叫绝。相传西汉诗赋大家司马相如对卓文君始乱终弃,卓文君作《白头吟》以自况:"凄凄重凄凄,嫁娶不须啼。愿得一心人,白头不相离。""白头吟"三字于此起了双关讽喻的作用,骆宾王极富技巧性地引用这一典故,批评执政者辜负了诗人对国家的一片忠心。内心失望至极,却不着一字,毫不言悲,意在言外,情在字里,充分显示了汉诗的含蓄蕴藉之美。他自伤老大无成,而又受人陷害,身陷囹圄,委婉曲折地表达了自己的凄伤哀怨无人赏识的落寞孤寂无助之痛。

颈联纯用"比"体,以"露重""风多"喻环境恶劣,"飞难进"喻宦海浮沉难进,"响易沉"喻言论受压。两句中无一字不在说蝉,也无一字不在说自己,寄托遥深。尾联以蝉的高洁,喻己的品性,结句以设问点出冤狱未雪之恨。这首诗借咏蝉来寓意,抒发了自己在狱中悲痛、苦闷的心情,语意沉痛之至,读之令人涕下。

骆宾王的一生,浮浮沉沉,没有做过大官,但却充满传奇色彩。他四五岁出口作文,七岁赋诗,写下了流传后世的成名作《咏鹅》。这首诗使七岁的骆宾王一鸣惊人,遂以神童称誉乡里,这在中国历史上都是极为罕见的。白居易写下成名作《赋得古原草送别》时,已经十六岁了;李白写《蜀道难》时已经二十岁;杜甫写下成名作《望岳》时已经二十四岁。可见,骆宾王"神童"的美誉名不虚传。尽管骆宾王在七岁的时候就声名远扬,收获了满满赞誉,但他并没有止步不前,这和他父亲的严格管教密不可分。在骆宾王十岁的时候,他博学多才的父亲骆履元考中进士,担任山东博昌县令一职,他们全家就从义乌迁居到了博昌。他的父亲给他请了当地最好的老师。骆宾王也很争气,读书万卷,经史子集无所不通,并且都能领会其中的要旨和奥妙。不过,书读多了,反而让他有点书呆子气质。虽才华横溢,但骨子里却清高、偏执、认死理,这样的性格注定了他一生的坎坷。

骆宾王十七岁的时候,父亲病死。父亲做官七年,家中竟然没有积蓄,连回老家安葬的钱都没有,他只好将父亲就地葬在了博昌县。三年服孝期满之后,骆宾王带着父亲生前对他的期望进京赶考。他认为自己一定能凭借真才实学考中进士。然而,考试的结果却是他名落孙山。这对他来说无疑是一次沉重的打击。这次考试失败之后,骆宾王再也没有主动参加过科举考试。有的人失败了,会选择继续奋斗,直到证明自己的实力为止。而骆宾王不同,他深知自己的实力,他不需要向任何人证明。后来,有好几次出仕做官的机会,都因为他这种不合作和不屑于自我证明的态度而失之交臂。他在李元庆的府中担任幕僚时,李元庆要他自叙才能,以便提拔他,但骆宾王却认为,一个人才能的高低、品格的优劣,应该由领导明察,并秉公考核,不能听由本人的吹嘘。话外之音分明就是,我什么都能干,你要是足够诚心的话,应该拿着某个职位来求我。

纵览骆宾王的一生,如果没有名主来请自己出山,他是很想当一个高洁的隐士的。他后来多次离家谋官时,都是因为家庭生活压力大,快过不下去了,他才低下他那高傲的头颅去谋求出路。即便是四十九岁满头白发被召入京时,他在三篇对策文中仍然没有以臣子自称。其外表隐忍内在叛逆的性格由此可见,他把个人的尊严看得比命还要重要。到了六十一岁,骆宾王似乎时来运转了,他被提拔为从六品的侍御史。这是朝廷的监察官,负责纠察监督文武百官。但是,上任不到半年,他这个负责纠察百官的侍御史因多次上书纠察,得罪了武氏集团,被对手举报,说他以前在长安担任主簿时有贪污行为,因此锒铛入狱,成为阶下囚,遭受严刑拷打,强迫他亲口认罪。

骆宾王幼承家教,以清正廉洁、清白做人为人生信荷,自然无法接受被人诬陷。但他丝毫不惧怕当权者的淫威,并没有在刑讯逼供中低头,始终坚贞不屈。春去秋来,骆宾王入狱已有一年,始终不能平反昭雪。在诬陷者的淫威之下,也无人敢挺身而出,为他申冤。在阴森恐怖的监狱中,铁窗外面大树上凄哀的蝉鸣引发了诗人与秋蝉之间的共鸣。骆宾王想到自己的处境,于是,他便写下了这首传诵千古的名作《在狱咏蝉》。

骆宾王一生正直不阿,清白高洁,一身正气,却投报无门,从《在狱咏蝉》的主题和基调即可见一斑。最终给他带来厄运的还是他的文字。光宅元年(684),武则天废黜刚登基的中宗李显,另立李旦为帝,自己临朝称制。武则天打算进一步登位称帝,建立大周王朝,引起了一些忠于唐室的大臣勋贵的愤怒。身为开国元勋英国公李绩(后被太宗赐名李勣)嗣孙的李敬业(原名徐敬业),以已故太子李贤为号召,在扬州起兵,建立匡复府,自任匡复府上将、扬州大都督。骆宾王被罗致入幕府,为艺文令,他以笔为刀,写下了《代李敬业传檄天下文》(《讨武曌檄》)这篇直接声讨统治阶级的千古檄文,也是他传世的十卷诗文中最受文人和史学家推崇的名作,檄文事昭而理辩,义正词严,且朗朗上口,一经发出即被广为传诵。《新唐书》中说,连事主武则天本人读到,都忍不住为之惊叹。这篇檄文也成为展示骆宾王不畏武氏威权、匡扶李唐功业的远大志向与社会担当的宣言书。文章千古事,身后千古迷:李敬业兵败身亡后,骆宾王不知所终。

第四章 唐诗英译鉴赏实践(上)

学生英译实践园地

英译实践版本选读

译文 1　威特·宾纳

A Political Prisoner Listening to a Cicada

While the year sinks westward, I hear a cicada
Bid me to be resolute here in my cell,
Yet it needed the song of those black wings
To break a white-haired prisoner's heart....
His flight is heavy through the fog,
His pure voice drowns in the windy world.
Who knows if he be singing still? —
Who listens any more to me?

译文 2　许渊冲

The Cicada Heard in Prison

Of autumn the cicada sings;
In prison I'm worn out with care.
How can I bear its blue-black wings
Which remind me of my grey hair?
Heavy with dew, it cannot fly;
Drowned in the wind, its song's not heard.
Who would believes its spirit high?
Could I express my grief in word?

译文 3　杨宪益　戴乃迭

A Poem about a Cicada Written in Prison

Outside a cicada is stridulating in the depths of autumn,
While in jail I am tortured by a surge of homesickness.
Hoary-haired with grief, how can I endure

第四章 唐诗英译鉴赏实践（上）

Such plaintive singing of the black-headed creature?
Heavy dew has encumbered it from taking wing,
Its sounds easily muffled by strong winds.
Nobody in the world trusts my noble and unsullied nature,
Who is there to vindicate my innocence?

译文 4 刘义庆

On Hearing Cicadas in Prison

The year is sinking west, cicadas sing,
Their songs stir up the prisoner's grief.
I cannot bear the sight of their dark wing,
Their hymn to innocence gives me no relief.

Wings heavy with dew, hard becomes the flight,
Drowned in strong wind, their voice cannot be heard.
None would believe their songs are pure and bright,
Who could express my feeling deep in word?

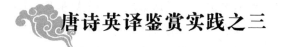
唐诗英译鉴赏实践之三

曲池荷

卢照邻

浮香①绕曲岸②，
圆影③覆华池④。
常恐秋风早，
飘零⑤君⑥不知。

137

【注释】

① 〔浮香〕荷花氤氲的香气。
② 〔曲岸〕曲折的湖岸。
③ 〔圆影〕指圆圆的荷叶映照于水面上的影子。
④ 〔华池〕美丽的池子。
⑤ 〔飘零〕坠落,飘落。
⑥ 〔君〕此处暗示当权者,意即自己空有满腹才华却不被赏识,无人重用。

白话释义

　　　　　　轻幽的芳香围绕在弯曲的池岸,
　　　　　　圆实的花叶覆盖着美丽的水池。
　　　　　　常常担心萧瑟的秋风来得太早,
　　　　　　使你来不及饱赏荷花就凋落了。

主题鉴赏

　　《曲池荷》是初唐四杰之一卢照邻所创作的一首五言绝句。此诗作于唐高宗永徽三年,借荷花来托物言志,表达诗人怀才不遇的失落和怅然,情感真切自然。卢照邻,志大位卑,一生坎坷多舛。他任新都尉时染上风痹病,辞职北返,"羸卧不起,行已十年",痛苦不堪。咸亨四年,他在《病梨树赋·序》中说:"癸酉之岁,余卧病于长安光德坊之官舍。父老云:'是鄱阳公主之邑司,昔公主未嫁而卒,故其邑废。'时有处士孙君思邈居之……余年垂强仕,则有幽忧之疾,椿菌之性,何其辽哉!"此时他虽求助于神医孙思邈,但对自己身体已经不抱什么希望,常常"伏枕十旬,闭门三月。"在《病梨树赋》中他写道:"怯衡飙之摇落,忌炎景之临迫。"这里的"怯摇落"与《曲池荷》诗中的"叹飘零"是一样的含意,其中深深寄寓着诗人一生的忧愤与感慨。

　　诗人采取先扬后抑的艺术手法,前两句写荷花香气馥郁,形容美丽,后两句却突然降格,借花之自悼,写人之自艾。"浮香绕曲岸",未见其形,先闻其香。适逢夏日,曲折的池岸飘溢着阵阵荷花清香,说明花事正盛,景色正美。"圆影覆华池",写月光笼罩着荷池,在水面上投下圆圆的荷影,花与影,影影绰绰,莫能分解。写荷的诗作不在少数,而这首诗采取侧面写法,以香夺人,不着意描绘其优美的形态和动人的纯洁,却传出了荷花独特的香气和姿态,颇具神韵。咏物诗,因物以见我,乃见

第四章 唐诗英译鉴赏实践（上）

其佳处。除余山《竹林问答》中说："咏物诗寓兴为上,传神次之。寓兴者,取照在流连感慨之中,《三百篇》之比兴也。传神者,相赏在牝牡骊黄之外,《三百篇》之赋也。若模形范质,藻绘丹青,直死物耳,斯为下矣。"如此看来,可见卢照邻咏物诗之造诣。

"常恐秋风早,飘零君不知"是沿用屈原《离骚》"惟草木之零落兮,恐美人之迟暮"的句意,但又有所变化,含蓄地抒发了自己怀才不遇、早年零落的感慨。

卢照邻在去世前不久写的《释疾文》中说道："余羸卧不起,行已十年,宛转匡床,婆娑小室。未攀偃蹇桂,一臂连蜷;不学邯郸步,两足铺匐。寸步千里,咫尺山河。每至冬谢春归,暑阑秋至,云壑改色,烟郊变容,辄舆出户庭,悠然一望,覆焘虽广,嗟不容乎此生,亭育虽繁,恩已绝乎斯代。赋命如此,几何可凭?""春秋冬夏兮四序,寒暑荣悴兮万端。春也万物熙熙焉感其生而悼死;夏也百草榛榛焉见其盛而知其阑;秋也严霜降兮殷忧者为之不乐;冬也阴气积兮愁颜者为之解欢。"这不免也有诗人自己的性格原因。由于他被身体的病痛所折磨,同时又饱受仕途无望之折磨,故而对事物变化的反应特别敏感。

《释疾文》深刻地表达了他对生命无常的感慨："神翳翳兮似灰,命绵绵兮若缕。一伸一曲兮,比艰难乎尺蠖。九生九死兮,同变化乎盘古。万物繁茂兮此时,余独何为兮肠遭回而屡腐?""草木扶疏兮如此,余独兰騑兮不自胜。"万物越是繁茂越是生机勃勃,他就越发感觉到自己的形象枯槁。同时他对繁荣的万物是"感其生而悼死","见其盛而知其阑",也有对自己和他人盛时的回忆与感慨。《曲池荷》同样是他对人生遭际的不解和叩问,这种思想在他的不少作品中都有表现。这位位列初唐四杰的大诗人因病痛的折磨痛苦不堪,最终选择了自杀来结束自己的生命,痛呼哀哉!

将这首托物言志诗归为中国咏物诗之正宗手法,自不待言。其略可称道者大致有两点:一是咏花诗最易落入精雕细刻、镂金错彩的细微描写套路,这首诗写曲池荷,虽略带六朝余韵,然能于大处落墨,气象较为阔大;二是这首诗切物抒情,较为真切自然,婉转写来,并无造作,笔未离题而深沉之意尽蕴其中。

唐代诗论家皎然评价这首诗说："以荷之芳洁自比,荷受秋风飘零,不为人知,以喻人负异才,流落无人知也"(《诗式》)。清人沈德潜云："言外有抱才不遇、早年零落之感"(《唐诗别裁》)。近代刘永济说："此诗亦《离骚》'恐美人之迟暮'之意,言为心声,发于不觉也"(《唐人绝句精华》)。

学生英译实践园地

第四章　唐诗英译鉴赏实践（上）

英译实践版本选读

译文1　索姆·杰宁斯

The Lotus in the Winding Pond

The winding bank is permeated with the quiet fragrance of lotus flowers,
Round lotus leaves lie in layers on the pond.
I often worry about the bleak autumn wind coming too early,
Let people have no time to enjoy the lotus withered.

译文2　冯志杰

Ode to Lotus in Pond of Qu

O'er th' bank of the Pond of Qu floats balm of flower,
And the leaves of lotus shadow the clear water.
The chilly autumn wind comes so early, I'm afraid,
That you'll be unable to scent out the flowers fade.

唐诗英译鉴赏实践之四

滕王阁①诗
王　勃

滕王高阁临江渚②，
佩玉鸣鸾③罢歌舞。
画栋朝飞南浦云④，
珠帘暮卷西山⑤雨。
闲云⑥潭影日悠悠⑦，

物换星移⑧几度秋。
阁中帝子⑨今何在⑩？
槛⑪外长江⑫空自流。

【注释】

① 〔滕王阁〕四大名楼之一，位于江西省南昌市，始建于唐永徽四年，由滕王李元婴（唐高祖李渊第二十二子，唐太宗李世民之弟）任洪州（今南昌）都督时修建。因初唐四杰之首王勃的千古第一骈文《滕王阁序》中"落霞与孤鹜齐飞，秋水共长天一色"的经典名句而名扬天下，传世千年。文学家韩愈也撰文述"江南多临观之美，而滕王阁独为第一，有瑰丽绝特之称"，故有"西江第一楼"之美誉。滕王阁又与湖北武汉的黄鹤楼、湖南岳阳的岳阳楼并称"江南三大名楼"。
② 〔渚〕江中小洲。
③ 〔佩玉鸣銮〕身上佩戴的玉饰、响铃。
④ 〔画栋〕有彩绘的栋梁楼阁。〔南浦(pǔ)〕地名，在南昌市西南。浦，水边或河流入海的地方，多用于地名。
⑤ 〔西山〕又名逍遥山、南昌山、厌原山、洪崖山，位于江西省新建区西部，被称为江南最大的"飞来峰"。
⑥ 〔闲云〕悠然飘浮的云。
⑦ 〔日悠悠〕每日无拘无束地游荡。
⑧ 〔物换星移〕形容万物的更替、时代的变迁。物，四季的景物。星，时空，时间。
⑨ 〔帝子〕指滕王李元婴。
⑩ 滕王阁始建于唐高宗永徽四年。李元婴在洪州担任都督约九年，于公元662年，被调往四川隆州（今阆中）。据说，王勃大约在唐高宗咸亨二年创作《滕王阁序》，此时距李元婴任洪州（今南昌）都督已过去八年有余，故有"阁中帝子今何在"之问。
⑪ 〔槛〕高楼供人扶倚的栏杆。
⑫ 〔长江〕此指赣江，是江西省最大河流，经鄱阳湖流入长江。

第四章　唐诗英译鉴赏实践（上）

白话释义

巍峨高耸的滕王阁俯临着江心的沙洲，
佩玉、鸾铃鸣响的华丽歌舞早已停止。
早晨南浦飞来的轻云在画栋边上掠过，
傍晚时分西山的雨吹打着珠帘。
潭中白云的倒影每日悠然浮荡，
时光易逝，人事变迁，不知已经度过几个春秋。
高阁中的滕王如今在哪里呢？
只有那栏杆外的江水空自流淌，日夜不息。

主题鉴赏

《滕王阁诗》是唐代诗人王勃创作的一首七言古诗。滕王阁为江南三大名楼之一，建于唐高宗永徽四年，为滕王李元婴任洪州都督时所建，由此得名。故址在今江西南昌赣江边新建西章江门上，俯视远望，视野均极开阔。唐高宗上元三年，诗人王勃远道去交趾探父，途经洪州，参与都督阎伯舆宴会，即席创作《滕王阁序》，《滕王阁诗》为序末所附诗歌，可以视为文章的"跋尾"，内容多为评介、鉴定、感言之类。

诗歌首联开门见山，用质朴苍老的笔法，点出了滕王阁的形势，并遥想当年兴建此阁时的豪华繁盛的宴会场景。其后的"南浦""西山""闲云""潭影"和"槛外长江"都从第一句"高阁临江渚"生发出来。清晨，滕王阁上雕刻着精美图案的梁木被南浦飞来的云环绕；傍晚，西山的雨打湿用珠玉串成的门帘。这两句诗可谓动静结合，画面感直逼眼前，既表现了滕王阁的高峻和周围自然环境的迷人，又衬托铺垫了滕王阁今日的冷清寂寞。这两句依然暗含着对比，过去，雕梁画栋的楼阁有滕王登临更显其气势非凡，珠帘微雨更显其温婉高贵，可如今人去楼空，一派苍凉。滕王阁如此迷人瑰丽，气势磅礴，但如今阁中又有谁来游赏呢？想当年建阁的滕王和他的官场好友们，坐着鸾铃马车，挂着琳琅玉佩，在阁上举杯庆贺，宾主欢畅。那种豪华场面已成记忆，一去不返，读罢令人慨叹时光再美，终会流逝，筵席欢腾，总会散去。第一句写空间，第二句写时间，第一句兴致勃勃，第二句意兴阑珊，两两对照。

颈联由空间转入时间，"闲云潭影日悠悠，物换星移几度秋"，点出了时日的漫长,岁月的流转,很自然地生出了风物更换季节、星辰转移方位的感慨。同时也引出尾联,"阁中帝子今何在,槛外长江空自流",把人的目光牵引到更加广阔的空间,把人的思绪带领到更加纵深的历史之中。江水一刻不停地流动,时间一秒不息地流逝,历史上无论多么辉煌显赫的生命,都注定悄然逝去。一个"空"字,把悲伤之情抒发到了极致,把消沉之思绪凝结到了顶点,荣华富贵转头空,功名利禄如浮云。景与情、人与物的完美融合,将尾联的情感推至高潮。不由得使人感慨,人去阁在,江水永流,繁华不能永恒,生命总有告别。寥寥两句便把全诗的主题鲜明深刻地予以呈现,使人自然生出生命短暂、繁华易逝、人生无常、曲终人散的喟叹和无奈。读过苏轼《赤壁赋》的读者不禁会想起其中的句子"(曹操)固一世之雄也,而今安在哉?"这是诗人消极心绪的流露。

  诗的结尾用对偶句法作结,很有特色。一般说来,对偶句多用来放在中段,起铺排的作用。这里用来作结束,而且不像两扇门一样地并列(术语称为扇对),而是一开一合,采取"侧势",读者只觉其流动,而不觉其为对偶,显出了王勃过人的文采。后来杜甫的七言律诗和七言绝句,也时常采用这种手法,如"即从巴峡穿巫峡,便下襄阳向洛阳""口脂面药随恩泽,翠管银罂下九霄""流连戏蝶时时舞,自在娇莺恰恰啼"等。可见王勃对唐诗发展的影响至深至远。

  总体而言,这首诗一共只有五十六个字,其中属于空间的有阁、江、栋、帘、云、雨、山、浦、潭影,属于时间的有日悠悠、物换、星移、几度秋、今何在。唐诗多用实字(即名词),这与喜欢多用虚字(尤其是转折词)的宋诗有着明显的区别。例如,三四两句中,除了"飞"字和"卷"字是动词以外,其余十二个字是实字,唐人的善用实字,实而不实,于此可见。这些语词以极高的艺术手法巧妙自然地融合在一起,构思奇巧,境界脱俗,且毫无叠床架屋堆砌词语的感觉。主要的原因,是它们都环绕着一个中心——滕王阁,各自发挥着众星拱月的作用。

  全诗在空间、时间双重维度展开对滕王阁的吟咏,笔意纵横,穷形尽像,语言凝练,感慨遥深。诗意气度高远,境界宏大,与《滕王阁序》真可谓双璧同辉,相得益彰。

第四章 唐诗英译鉴赏实践（上）

学生英译实践园地

研究生汉诗英译鉴赏实践教程

英译实践版本选读

译文 1　翟理斯

Prince Teng's Pavilion

Near these islands a palace was built by a prince,
But its music and song have departed long since.
The hill-mists of morning sweep down on the halls,
At night the red curtains lie furled on the walls.
The clouds o'er the water their shadows still cast,
Things change like the stars: how few autumns have passed
And *yet where is that prince? Where is he? —No reply*,
Save the plash of the stream rolling ceaselessly by.

译文 2　哈　特

The Pavilion of the King of Teng

The high pavilion
Of the King of Teng
Stands on the riverbank.

The tinkle
Of jade ornaments,
The songs of birds,
The strains of music,
And the rhythm of the dance
Are hushed forevermore.
On their southern course
The mists of morning
Drift past its painted beams,
And the rains
From the western hills

第四章 唐诗英译鉴赏实践（上）

At sunset sweep by its lacquered screens.

The lazy clouds
Still cast their shadows
On the pool,
And the same sun
Looks sadly down from heaven.

How all has changed!
For how many autumns
Have the brilliant stars shone out!

Where is the emperor's son
Who dwelt within these walls?

Out the balcony
The long river flows ceaselessly, in silence.

译文 3　许渊冲

Prince Teng's Pavilion

By riverside towers Prince Teng's Pavilion proud,
But gone are cabs with ringing bells and stirring strains.
At dawn its painted beams bar the south-flying cloud;
At dusk its curtains furled face western mountains' rains.
Free clouds cast shadows in the pool from day to day;
The world and seasons change beneath the changing sky.
Where is the prince who in this Pavilion did stay?
Beyond the rails the silent River still rolls by.

译文 4　罗经国

Pavilion of Prince Teng

The lofty King Teng's Tower overlooks the River.
The jade pendants tinkle, and the carriage bells jingle.
The banquet's over, the guests are leaving,
and the singing and the dancing have stopped.
In the morn the rosy clouds from the southern shore flit across the painted pillars.
In the eve the rain in the western mountains are drawn in by the red curtains.
The lazy clouds are reflected in the water and the days pass in leisure.
Things change and stars move;
how many years have passed since the building of the Tower?
Where is its builder, King Teng?
Only the River outside the railing flows to the east all by itself.

唐诗英译鉴赏实践之五

送杜少府之任蜀州①

王　勃

城阙②辅③三秦④,

风烟⑤望五津⑥。

与君⑦离别意,

同⑧是宦游⑨人。

海内⑩存知己,

天涯⑪若比邻⑫。

无为⑬在歧路⑭,

儿女⑮共沾巾⑯。

第四章 唐诗英译鉴赏实践（上）

【注释】

①〔少府〕中国历代政府为皇室管理私财和生活事务的职能机构，秦汉始设。隋唐时"少府"相当于"县尉"。诗中杜少府具体何人，史无具载，应为王勃知己好友。〔之〕到，往。〔蜀州〕今四川崇州。

②〔城阙（què）〕即城楼，此指唐代京师长安城。

③〔辅〕护卫，护佑。

④〔三秦〕指长安城所在的关中腹地，大致为今陕西省秦岭以北、渭河以南、潼关以西、大散关以东区域。秦朝末年，项羽破秦，继而三分关中，立秦三将章邯为雍王、董翳为翟王、司马欣为塞王，此为"三秦"之始。这句是倒装句，意思是京师长安有三秦护佑。

⑤〔风烟〕在风烟迷蒙中。名词用作状语，表示行为状态。

⑥〔五津〕指岷江的五个渡口，即白华津、万里津、江首津、涉头津、江南津。这里泛指蜀川。

⑦〔君〕古时对他人的尊称，相当于"您"，此指杜少府。

⑧〔同〕一作"俱"，都是。

⑨〔宦（huàn）游人〕出外就任做官。

⑩〔海内〕四海之内，即全国各地。古代人认为中国疆土四周环海，所以称天下为四海之内。

⑪〔天涯〕天边，这里比喻极远的地方。"海内存知己，天涯若比邻"句系化用曹植的《赠白马王彪》："丈夫志四海，万里犹比邻。忧思成疾疢，无乃儿女仁。"

⑫〔比邻〕并邻，近邻。比，靠近，挨着。

⑬〔无为〕无须，不必。

⑭〔岐（qí）路〕岔路。古人送行常在大路分岔处告别。

⑮〔儿女〕古代指青年男女，后指子女。北齐颜之推《颜氏家训·音辞》："吾家儿女，虽在孩稚，便渐督正之。"

⑯〔沾巾〕泪沾手巾，形容落泪之多。

白话释义

> 三秦腹地拥长安，
> 风烟千里有蜀川。
> 此去与君相别离，
> 遥隔天涯赴新任。
> 知己情同亲兄弟，
> 山海虽远心不离。
> 就此作别各自去，
> 勿让泪水沾湿衣。

主题鉴赏

《送杜少府之任蜀州》作于唐高宗乾封年间，是王勃为送别一位到蜀地任县令的杜姓朋友而作，是其游蜀之前供职于长安时期的作品。此诗是中国诗歌史上送别诗的上乘之作，为慰勉好友勿在离别之际落泪哀戚所作。

首联描绘出送别地与友人出发地的形势和风貌，隐含送别的情意，对仗整饬，风格潇洒大气。诗从送别的地点落笔，"城阙辅三秦，风烟望五津"。诗人站在京城郊外，看到雄伟的长安城为辽阔的三秦之地所拱卫护佑，向远处眺望，在风烟迷蒙的地方便是蜀地的"五津"，点出杜少府即将赴任的处所。因为朋友要从长安远赴四川，这两个地方在诗人的感情上自然发生了联系。诗的开头不说离别，只描写出这两个地方的形势和风貌，送别的情意便自在其中了。诗人身在长安，连三秦之地也难以一眼望尽，远在千里之外的五津是根本无法看到，超越常人的视力所及，用想象的眼睛看世界，运用夸张手法，开头就展开壮阔的境界，与一般送别诗只着眼于燕羽、杨枝、泪痕、酒盏不相同。

颔联三、四句，"与君离别意，同是宦游人"为宽慰之辞，是说彼此离别的意味同样都有游宦人的情意。以散调承续首联，点明离别的无奈与必然性。此句句法起了变化，表现方法也由写景改为抒情，以实转虚，文情跌宕，令人动容。离乡背井，已有一重别绪，彼此在客居中话别，又多了一重别绪，其中真有无限凄恻。这里，诗人安排了两个联结纽带：感情的一致（与君离别意）和处境的一致（同是宦游人），将自己的心与杜少府的心拉近，也将远隔千里的距离缩短了。这两句对偶不求工整，固然由于当时律诗还没有一套严格的规定，却因此有了其独到的妙处，使人感到矫

第四章 唐诗英译鉴赏实践（上）

夭变化，不可端倪。

颈联"海内存知己，天涯若比邻"，奇峰突起，格调新颖，高度概括了"友情深厚，山河难阻"的温馨情景，境界从狭小转为宏大，情调从凄恻转为豪迈，也使知心好友之间的友情升华到一种更高的美学、哲学境界。即使远离也无法分开知心好友之间的情谊，只要同在四海之内，就是天涯海角也如同近在邻居一样，表现友谊不受时间的限制和空间的阻隔，是永恒且无所不在的，所抒发的情感也是乐观豁达的。这两句因此成为远隔千山万水的朋友之间表达深厚情谊的不朽名句。尽管是化用曹植的《赠白马王彪》的诗句，但是更加精简明快，富有节奏感，这一句远远超过曹植的原创诗句，更多地为后世所传诵。

尾联点出"送"的主题，情感真挚，余味无穷。诗的前六句意境阔大，情调开朗，感情深厚，因此结尾处写出"无为在歧路，儿女共沾巾"这样的诗句，实在是水到渠成，完全扫除了送别诗"流泪""伤感"的余习，一反离愁别恨的常调。"在歧路"三字点出题面上的"送"字，这是诗人临别时对朋友的叮咛，也是自己情怀的吐露。在结构上紧接前两句，于极高峻处忽然又落入舒缓，然后终止。

全诗开合顿挫，气脉流通，意境旷达，将送别诗的悲凉凄怆之气，凝铸于天涯遥隔却情谊永驻的温暖瞬间。诗歌音调明快爽朗，语言清新高远，内容独树一帜，一洗往昔送别诗中悲苦缠绵消极落寞之态，体现出诗人高远的志向、豁达的情趣和旷达的胸怀。仅仅四十个字，却纵横捭阖，变化无穷，仿佛在一张小小的画幅上，包容着无数的丘壑，有看不尽的风光，因此被称为"离别诗"中的经典之作的确实至名归。

有评论者认为，这首送别诗，无论从押韵、平仄、对仗，还是从意境、情感、思想等几个方面衡量，均为一首相当成熟的五言律诗，体现出王勃与众不同的诗歌才华，在初唐新体诗形成的阶段起到了非常重要的转型作用。全诗抒发对友人的真情实感，从胸臆中流出，完全褪去了宫廷诗空洞无实的赞美和绮靡矫揉的做作之风，开创了一种更加贴近生活、更加亲近读者的不凡格调，为初唐诗坛的改革和倡导刚健的诗风迈出了可喜的步伐。明代陆时雍评论说："此是高调，读之不觉其高，以气厚故"（《唐诗镜》）。清末俞陛云称赞道："一气贯注，如娓娓清谈，极行云流水之妙"（《诗境浅说》）。

学生英译实践园地

第四章 唐诗英译鉴赏实践（上）

英译实践版本选读

译文 1　威特・宾纳

Farewell to Vice-prefect Tu

By this wall that surrounds the three ch'-in districts,
Through mist that makes five rivers one.
We bid each other a sad farewell,
We two officials going opposite ways...
And yet, while China holds our friendship
And heaven remains our neighbourhood.
Why should you linger at the fork of the road,
Wipping your eyes like a heart-broken child?

译文 2　许渊冲

Farewell to Prefect Du

You'll leave the town walled far and wide
For mist-veiled land by riverside.
I feel on parting sad and drear,
For both of us are strangers here.
If you have friends who know your heart,
Distance cannot keep you apart.
At crossroads where we bid adieu,
Do not shed tears as women do!

译文 3　杨宪益　戴乃迭

Bidding Deputy Magistrate Du Farewell

The capital and palace are guarded by the land of three Qin kingdoms,
In the distance the Five Ferries are screened by wind and mist.
Now comes the time for us to bid farewell to each other,

And we will both be officials away from home on duty.
So long as we remain bosom friends in our heart of hearts,
We'll still feel like neighbours despite the distance apart.
So don't let us shed silly tears like youngsters
At that last moment when we both wave goodbye.

译文 4　王玉书

Bidding Deputy Magistrate Du Farewell

Here, the walled city is protected by Three Qin;
There, amid wind and mist, five ferries can be seen.
Feeling of parting, it's easy to understand;
For us who are both officials in a strange land.
Throughout the country really exist bosom friends;
Who are like neighbors though at the world's different ends.
On the road where we part, we just can do nothing;
Like those worldly men and women their tears shedding.

译文 5　尹绍东

To See Police Commissioner Du off for Shuzhou

The Three Qins area has protected Chang'an for many a generation.
In the mist, I gaze from afar at the five ferries at your destination.
Seeing you off, I find it hard to part,
Since we both serve in government.
Within the Four Seas, I am lucky to have you as my bosom friend;
We seem to live nearby, though we are at the earth's opposite end.
When we part at a fork in the road,
There is no need to wet the handkerchiefs, like young lovers, with tears shed.

第四章　唐诗英译鉴赏实践（上）

单元扩展实践练习

一、请试译王勃《滕王阁序》中的名句。

1. 落霞与孤鹜齐飞，秋水共长天一色。
2. 关山难越，谁悲失路之人？萍水相逢，尽是他乡之客。
3. 时运不齐，命途多舛。冯唐易老，李广难封。
4. 老当益壮，宁移白首之心？穷且益坚，不坠青云之志。

唐诗英译鉴赏实践(下)

By the Mid-Tang, there appeared a series of complicated changes in literature. On the one hand, there was an obviously increase of the consciousness of regarding literature as an attachment to, or a tool of, politics and morality. On the other hand, the representation of emotions in human life in literature continued its process of expansion and deepening. Such changes continued all the way throughout the Song dynasty.

The two best-known poets of this period are Li Bai and Du Fu. Li Bai is known for the romanticism of his poetry; Du Fu is seen as a Confucian moralist with a strict sense of duty toward society. Later Tang poets developed greater realism and social criticism and refined the art of narration.

Li Bai

Li Bai, the Poet Immortal is often regarded, along with Du Fu, as one of the two greatest poets in China's literary history. Approximately 1,100 of his poems remain today. Li Bai's poetry was introduced to the Western world by the well-

第五章 唐诗英译鉴赏实践（下）

known American Imagist poet Ezra Pound through the very liberal translations of Japanese versions collected by American scholar Ernest Fenollosa.

Li Bai is best known for the extravagant imagination and striking Taoist imagery in his poetry, as well as for his great love for liquor. Like Du Fu, he spent much of his life travelling, although in his case it was because his wealth allowed him to, rather than because his poverty forced him. He is said to have drowned in the Yangtze River, having fallen from his boat while drunkenly trying to embrace the reflection of the moon.

[**Biography**]

However, his family had originally dwelled in what's now southeastern Gansu, and later moved to Jiangyou（江油）, near modern Chengdu in Sichuan province, when he was five years old. He was influenced by Confucian and Taoist thought, but ultimately his family heritage did not provide him with much opportunity in the aristocratic Tang dynasty. Though he expressed the wish to become an official, he did not sit for the Chinese civil service examination. Instead, beginning at age twenty-five, he travelled around China, enjoying wine and leading a carefree life — very much contrary to the prevailing ideas of a proper Confucian gentleman. His personality fascinated the aristocrats and common people alike and he was introduced to the Emperor Xuanzong around 742.

He was given a post at the Hanlin Academy（翰林院）, which served to provide a source of scholarly expertise and poetry for the Emperor. Li Bai remained less than two years as a poet in the Emperor's service before he was dismissed for an unknown indiscretion. Thereafter he wandered throughout China for the rest of his life. He met Du Fu in the autumn of 744, and again the following year. These were the only occasions on which they met, but the friendship remained particularly important for the starstruck Du Fu (a dozen of his poems to or about Li Bai survive, compared to only one by Li Bai to Du Fu). At the time of the An Lushan Rebellion（安史之乱）he became involved in a subsidiary revolt against the Emperor, although the extent to which this was voluntary is unclear. The failure of the rebellion resulted in his being exiled a second time, to Yelang（夜郎）. He was pardoned before the exile journey was complete.

Li Bai died in Dangtu（当涂）. Traditionally he was said to have drowned attempting to embrace the moon's reflection in a river; some scholars believe his death was the result of mercury poisoning due to a long history of imbibing Taoist longevity elixirs.

[**Li Bai's Poetry**]

Over a thousand poems are attributed to him, but the authenticity of many of these is uncertain.

He is best known for his *yuefu* poems, which are intense and often fantastic. He is often associated with Taoism: there is a strong element of this in his works, both in the sentiments they express and in their spontaneous tone. Nevertheless, his *gufeng* ("ancient airs", 古风) often adopt the perspective of the Confucian moralist, and many of his occasional verses are fairly conventional.

Much like the genius of Mozart there exist many legends on how effortlessly Li Bai composed his poetry; he was said to be able to compose at an astounding speed, without correction. His favorite form is the *jueju* (five- or seven-character quatrain, 绝句), of which he composed some 160 pieces. Li Bai's use of language is not as erudite as Du Fu's but impresses equally through an extravagance of imagination and a direct correlation of his free-spirited persona with the reader. Li Bai's interactions with nature, friendship, his love of wine and his acute observations of life inform his best poems. Some, like *Changgan Xing* (translated by Ezra Pound as "A River Merchant's Wife: A Letter", 《长干行》), record the hardships or emotions of common people. He also wrote a number of very oblique poems on women.

One of Li Bai's most famous poems is "Drinking Alone under the Moon" (《月下独酌》), which is a good example of some of the most famous aspects of his poetry — a very spontaneous poem, full of natural imagery and anthropomorphism:

There are four poems Li Bai wrote under this title, this is the most famous.

花间一壶酒，Amongst the flowers is a pot of wine;

独酌无相亲。I pour alone but with no friend at hand;

举杯邀明月，So I lift the cup to invite the shining moon;

对影成三人。Along with my shadow, a fellowship of three.

第五章 唐诗英译鉴赏实践（下）

月既不解饮，The moon understands not the art of drinking;
影徒随我身。The shadow gingerly follows my movements;
暂伴月将影，Still I make the moon and the shadow my company;
行乐须及春。To enjoy the springtime before too late.

我歌月徘徊，The moon lingers while I am singing;
我舞影零乱。The shadow scatters while I am dancing;
醒时同交欢，We share the cheers of delight when sober;
醉后各分散。We separate our ways after getting drunk;
永结无情游，Forever will we keep this unfettered friendship;
相期邈云汉。Till we meet again far in the Milky Way.

(Tr. by Ezra Pound)

[**Comments**]

Li Bai grew up in rural Sichuan and was obviously a voracious reader—though at one point he claimed that he had been a young tough. He was learned but untrained; his writing shows none of the formal discipline that came as second nature to Wang Wei.

For Li Bai this was a liberty that enabled him to write in ways that were unprecedented. Li Bai had a theatrical flair; he invented himself, and through his poetry advertised himself, as an eccentric, a drinker, and a Daoist initiate. In 725, he left Sichuan and traveled down the Yangzi seeking patrons, enjoying himself, and studying Daoism. His reputation steadily grew, and in 742 he was summoned to court and given a place in the Hanlin Academy （翰林院）. He never took the examination; it is unlikely that he would have been recommended to do so or that he would have been successful. By the 740s, however, poetic talent no longer needed the confirmation of the literary examination to be recognized. It is hard to separate the grains of truth from the mass of legend about Li Bai's brief period with Xuanzong.

Li Bai makes a hundred poems with one gallon of ale, in the marketplace of Chang'an he sleeps in the tavern. The Son of Heaven called for him, he wouldn't board the boat, declaring: "Your humble servant is an immortal in his ale."（天子

呼来不上船,自称臣是酒中仙。) A few years later, he left court, apparently no longer in favor, and continued his wanderings and his poetry. In striking contrast to Meng Haoran, Li Bai carefully conserved his work and twice asked friends to edit his literary collection (which would be complete only on his death).

Although his *yuefu*, "songs" (歌行体), and impromptu pieces are his best-known works, his poetry collection contains a large number of less-often read occasional pieces to "friends," many of whom were also probably patrons. We might see Li Bai as one of the first "professional" poets in China. Meng Haoran was probably supported by a local estate in Xiangyang; Li Bai, however, had no visible means to support himself, and his continuous travels throughout the greater part of his career were probably due less to wanderlust than to a continuing need to find new patrons, to get room and board and a tangible token of appreciation. His flamboyant poetic persona was part of his profession, as in the famous *yuefu* "Bring On the Ale" (《将进酒》):

> For satisfaction in this life taste pleasure to the limit
> and never let your golden cup be empty in the moonlight.
> Heaven bred in me talents, they must be put to use,
> I toss away a thousand in gold, it comes right back to me.
> So boil a lamb, butcher an ox, make merry for a while,
> in one sitting you must down three hundred cups.①

At the end of the *yuefu*, however, it is clear who should pay for the feast:

> So you, my host, why do you say you're short on cash?
> Go out right now, buy ale — and I'll do the pouring.
> Take the dapple horse,
> take the furs worth a fortune,
> just call for the boy to take them to pawn for fine ale,
> and here together we'll melt away the sorrows of eternity!②

---

① 《将进酒》李白:人生得意须尽欢,莫使金樽空对月。天生我材必有用,千金散尽还复来。烹羊宰牛且为乐,会须一饮三百杯。
② 《将进酒》李白:主人何为言少钱,径须沽取对君酌。五花马,千金裘,呼儿将出换美酒,与尔同销万古愁。

第五章 唐诗英译鉴赏实践（下）

Du Fu

[**Biography**]

Du Fu was forty-four when the civil war (An Shi Rebellion) that devastated China broke out in 755, and the dire social situation is a constant presence in his major poems, nearly all of which were written during these war years. Although there was a long tradition of certain established political themes in *yuefu* poems, Du Fu was the first poet to write extensively about real, immediate social concerns, and as a result he is often referred to as the "poet-historian." After rebel armies overran the capital, Du Fu was caught in the city, where he hid in monasteries. After somehow escaping, he tried to do his share in the government's campaign to rescue the country, but after much frustration and little success, he resigned in the hope of establishing a more reclusive life devoted to his art. Du Fu succeeded spectacularly as an artist, but his was not to be a settled life of tranquil dwelling far from human affairs. He never stopped agonizing over his country's struggles, which are a constant presence in his poems. And though the fighting had appeared to be nearly over when he resigned, it was not. Du Fu did manage to settle his family several times, but they were always driven on—either by the incessant fighting that kept flaring up all around the country or by his longing to return to his home in the capital and assist the government in its struggle to salvage the situation.

Du Fu spent these years wandering the outer fringes of the Chinese cultural sphere: the far west and Chengdu in the southwest; then Kuàijī（会稽）, perched above the Yangtze's spectacular Triple Gorge, in territory populated by non-Chinese aboriginal people; and beyond into the south, where he finally died in a boat on Dongting Lake（洞庭湖）. It was this exile wandering that provided him with his unique perspective. Though he responded poetically at the level of immediate experience, Du Fu achieved in his late poems a panoramic view of the human drama: He saw it as part of China's vast landscape of natural process. Poised between black despair and exquisite beauty, his was a geologic perspective, a vision of the human cast against the elemental sweep of the universe.

[Du Fu's Poetry]

Scholars usually divide Du Fu's poetry into four periods: his "early" work, the poems during the rebellion before he left for Sichuan, the poems he wrote in Chengdu, Sichuan, and the poems of his long, slow journey down the Yangtze in his final years.

Du Fu was not known for his interest in Daoism, and in this, one of his earliest poems, the sacredness of the temple is inseparable from his reverence for the dynasty, whose former rulers were painted on the walls by one of the most famous Tang painters, Wu Daozi (吴道子).

Daoism's arcane terminology and rich pantheon had a particular aura for Tang readers (though it was not popular in later ages). Li Bai often used his knowledge of Daoism in his poetry, but he remained, above all, a secular poet. Others, like his friend Wu Yun (吴筠), wrote an essentially religious poetry of mystical vision. Xuanzong welcomed Daoist adepts; Wu Yun arrived at court at about the same time as Li Bai and, like Li Bai, was given a position in the Hanlin Academy (翰林院). While Li Bai was making a legend of himself by drinking and writing poetry, Wu Yun was writing discourses to instruct the emperor in Daoist mysteries. In 754, he presented Xuanzong with the *Arcane Net* (《玄纲论》) in three volumes. We cannot date Wu Yun's sets of Daoist as always in Du Fu, there is a level of personal detail that is unmatched by other writers. When those details intersected with large political events, Du Fu earned the name later given him, "poet-historian" (诗史). Having taken his family to safety and returned to the capital, Du Fu found himself in the city under occupation by An Lushan's troops. Xuanzong's hasty and secret flight from the capital had left behind most of the large imperial family, who were hunted down by An Lushan's soldiers. In "Lament for a Prince" (《哀王孙》), Du Fu chances on such a prince in Chang'an attempting to hide.

In "Lament by the Riverside" (《哀江头》), Du Fu is in the Winding River Park (曲江池) of Chang'an and recalls the visits of Xuanzong and Lady Yang, whose "wandering soul is stained with blood and cannot return" (血污游魂归不得). News of the major imperial defeats at the battles of Greenslope (青坂之战) and Chentao (陈陶之战) get back to the city:

第五章　唐诗英译鉴赏实践（下）

　　The moors vast, the sky clear, no sounds of battle—
forty thousand loyalist troops died on the very same day. ①

　　Eventually Du Fu escaped from the city and made his way to Suzong's（肃宗）temporary capital, where he was given the court post of Reminder（左拾遗）, whose task was to point out errors in documents and imperial decisions. After a while Du Fu's unfortunate political associations and inexperience earned him imperial permission to go and visit his family, which in turn gave us one of Du Fu's longest and most famous poems, "Journey North"（《北征》）, bearing witness to a land in which "Heaven and Earth bear scars"（天地则创痍）. "Journey North" characteristically weaves together immediate experience with larger political issues. Emperor Suzong had been compelled to ask for help from his Uighur（回鹘）allies, a decision that was as politically unpopular as it was necessary in military terms.

　　Du Fu comments with wonderful ambiguity: "of this sort few are valuable"（此辈少为贵）. We can read this as praise of their prowess（"even a few are valuable"）or as "the fewer the better".

　　In 757 the capitals were retaken, though the rebellion was far from over, and never again would the Tang have full control over all the rich provinces of the northeast. Du Fu joined the restored court in Chang'an, but his support for a minister out of favor led to his transfer to a low-ranking post away from the capital. During that period, on an extended trip to Luoyang, he wrote his famous "Three Subalterns"（三吏:《新安吏》《潼关吏》《石壕吏》）and "Three Partings"（三别:《新婚别》《垂老别》《无家别》）, giving vivid accounts of the devastation and social dislocation of the rebellion.

　　Dissatisfied with his post and perhaps hoping for help from a relative, in 759 Du Fu set off for the town of Qinzhou（秦州,今甘肃天水）, northwest of Chang'an. His Qinzhou poems（《发秦州》）represented a major transformation of his style into an austere regulated verse, sometimes on unusual topics such as "Taking down a Trellis"（《除架》）, in which dismantling a gourd trellis becomes a figure for discarding something or someone that has served its purpose.

　　Sticks lashed together are falling apart,

---

① 《悲陈陶》杜甫：野旷天清无战声，四万义军同日死。

> the gourd leaves grow ever more withered and sparse.
> Right when the white flowers have done forming fruit,
> how can it object that its green vins be removed?
> The voices of fall insects have not left it,
> What is on the minds of the twilight wrens?
> The cold now makes thing leafless and bleak —
> human life too has its beginning. ①
>
> (Tr. by Stephen Owen)

By the end of 759 he again set out with his family for Chengdu; employment by the local commander and figures like Gao Shi (高适) in service there contributed to make this the happiest phase of his later poetry. He built his famous "thatched cottage" (an imagined reconstruction of which is still a local site, 草堂) near the city. Again he had colleagues with whom to write poetry, but, from the rebellion on, Du Fu was essentially an isolated poet, developing his own idiosyncratic style outside the context of social exchange that had largely defined Tang poetry. There is often an understated lightness about his Chengdu poems, balancing perfect formal control with wry monologue. A local flood, excitedly reported by his son, rises swiftly before the contemplative and unhurried witness: Du Fu is sometimes the visionary, but throughout his later work we sometimes find a gentle self-mockery that gives his poetry a rare human depth. Driven temporarily from Chengdu by a rebellion of the garrison, he returned to find his little boat sunk in the mud and waterlogged. He laments the loss, saying how he planned to sail down the Yangtze river (扬子江) to warm and idyllic Jiangnan.

The conclusion is characteristic:

> ...
> Perhaps I could dig up the old one,
> and a new one is easy to find.
> What grieves me is often running away to hide,

---

① 《除架》杜甫:束薪已零落,瓠叶转萧疏。幸结白花了,宁辞青蔓除。秋虫声不去,暮雀意何如。寒事今牢落,人生亦有初。

第五章 唐诗英译鉴赏实践（下）

  that in this plain cottage I can't stay long. ①

(Tr. by Stephen Owen)

  He has learned that he less wants to set sail down the Yangtze river than to be able to stay in one place, sitting in his boat and inventing poems about sailing down the Yangtze. Eventually in 765 he did set out from Chengdu, stopping in Kuizhou（夔州）at the head of the Three Gorges. His few years in Kuizhou were his most productive. It was here that he wrote his sequence of eight "Autumn Meditations"（《秋兴八首》）, using the parallel structure of regulated verse and its mirror image in eight regulated poems to contrast the present world and the past of Xuanzong's reign, the "here" of Kuizhou in autumn and the "there" of old Chang'an in spring, the mortal world and the world of Heaven. This is Chinese poetry at its thickest, dense with patterns that recur in changing forms.

  Although there are some lighter pieces from Kuizhou, their tone is much darker than that of the Chengdu years. The relative solitude of composition liberated him; he became visionary, using parallelism and the inherent indeterminacy of poetic Chinese to produce couplets unlike anything done before:

  Myself and the age: a pair of tangled tresses,

  Earth and Heaven: a single thatched pavilion. ②

(Tr. by Stephen Owen)

[Comments]

  Du Fu is generally described as the greatest Chinese poet. Although he is much admired for the erudition and formal virtuosity of his poetry, neither of which are translated to their full artistic beauty. Du Fu's most important achievements lie elsewhere, and fortunately they were satisfactorily translated by some reputed translators home and abroad. Aside from the immediate impact of his work, Du Fu's renowned works derive most fundamentally from a realism that opened poetry to all aspects of human experience, from the intimate and concrete to the political and abstract, as well as new depths of subjective experience. Indeed, these different dimensions are often combined in a single

---

① 《破船》杜甫：故者或可掘，新者亦易求。所悲数奔窜，白屋难久留。
② 《暮春题瀼西新赁草屋五首》杜甫：身世双蓬鬓，乾坤一草亭。

poem, a poetic artistry which itself was a substantial innovation. And although the innovative nature of his poetry denied his recognition during his own lifetime, Du Fu soon became an awing poet, his works inspiring such dissimilar poetics as Bai Juyi's(白居易) plainspoken social realism and Meng Jiao's(孟郊) black, quasi-surreal introspection.

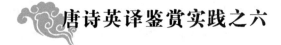 唐诗英译鉴赏实践之六

望庐山①瀑布

李　白

日照香炉②生紫烟③，
遥看④瀑布挂前川⑤。
飞流⑥直⑦下三千尺⑧，
疑⑨是银河⑩落九天⑪。

【注释】

①〔庐山〕又名匡山，中国名山之一，位于今江西省九江市北部的鄱阳湖盆地，耸立于鄱阳湖、长江之滨。
②〔香炉〕指庐山香炉峰。香炉峰有四，此指南香炉峰。因烟云聚散，如香炉之状，故名。关于香炉峰的位置，各注本有多种说法。
③〔紫烟〕指日光透过云雾，远望如紫色的烟云。
④〔遥看〕从远处看，遥望。
⑤〔挂〕悬挂。〔前川〕一作"长川"。川，河流，这里指瀑布。
⑥〔飞流〕快速降落的瀑布。
⑦〔直〕笔直，垂直向下。
⑧〔三千尺〕夸张手法，形容山高，为虚指。
⑨〔疑〕怀疑。
⑩〔银河〕古人指银河系构成的带状星群。

第五章　唐诗英译鉴赏实践（下）

⑪〔九天〕极言天高。古人认为天有九重，九天是天的最高层，九重天，即天空最高处。

白话释义

　　阳光照耀，香炉峰上紫烟袅袅，
　　遥望瀑布，好似绵绵白绢垂落山前。
　　瀑布湍急，如千尺白练，飞泻山涧，
　　就好像是银河从天上落到人间。

主题鉴赏

　　唐代大诗人李白曾创作两首《望庐山瀑布》，其一为五言古诗，其二为七言绝句，即这首最为人称道的《望庐山瀑布》。这两首诗一般认为是唐玄宗开元十三年前后李白出游金陵途中初游庐山时所作。

　　无论作于何时并不重要，重要的是《望庐山瀑布》成为李白山水诗歌中的经典佳作。整首诗采用夸张的艺术手法，把庐山瀑布气势磅礴的壮阔画面惟妙惟肖地展现在读者眼前，即使读者从未目睹过庐山瀑布的盛景，也一定在脑海里留下了深刻的印象。诗人首先描绘高耸的香炉峰，在阳光的照耀下，香炉峰放射出紫色的烟雾，远远望去，瀑布好像一条白练从悬崖的最顶端飞泻而下。瀑布的流速是那么湍急，从雄伟峻拔的山峰上流下来，似乎有几千尺高，让人恍惚觉得是银河从天上泻落到人间。李白素有诗仙之称，其丰富的想象力，和比喻、夸张手法的娴熟运用，再现了庐山瀑布绮丽雄伟的景象，展现出李白开阔的胸襟和非凡的"仙家"形象，也唤起读者对祖国大好河山的热爱之情。

　　这首诗，紧扣题目中的"望"字，以庐山的香炉峰入笔描写庐山瀑布之景。一个"挂"字，突出表现了瀑布如珠帘垂空的瑰丽景观。虚实结合的艺术表现力，将飞流直泻的瀑布描写得雄伟奇丽，气象万千，宛如一幅生动的山水画，因此千余年来，成为人们广为传诵的唐诗上品。

　　诗歌前两句描绘了庐山瀑布的奇伟景象，既有朦胧美，又有雄壮美；既有色，又有形；既有静，又有动。寥寥数笔，便将香炉峰和山巅飞泻的瀑布这一幅山水画勾勒而出。一座高耸入云的香炉，冉冉地升起了团团白烟，缥缈于青山蓝天之间，在红日的照射下化成一片紫色的云霞。这不仅把香炉峰渲染得更美，而且富有浪漫主义色彩，为不寻常的瀑布创造了不寻常的背景。接着诗人又把读者的视线带向悬崖顶端的瀑布:"遥看瀑布挂前川"。前四字是点题,"挂前川",这是"望"的第一眼形象,瀑布像是一条巨大的白练高挂于山川之间。"挂"字很妙,它化动为静,惟妙惟肖地表现出倾泻的瀑布在"遥看"中的形象。

　　后两句用夸张的比喻和浪漫的想象,进一步描绘瀑布的形象和气势,可谓字字珠玑。第三句极写瀑布的动态:"飞流直下三千尺"。一笔挥洒,字字铿锵有力:一个"飞"字,精妙绝伦,瀑布喷涌而出的景象被描绘得淋漓尽致,动态感直逼人眼;"直下",既写出山之高峻陡峭,又可以见出水流之急,那高空直落。势不可挡之状直击人面。然而,诗人犹嫌未足,接着又写上一句"疑是银河落九天",真是想落天外,惊人魂魄。"疑是"值得细味,诗人明明说得恍恍惚惚,而读者也明知不是,但是又都觉得只有这样写,才更为生动、逼真,其奥妙就在于诗人前面的描写中已经孕育了这一形象。巍巍香炉峰藏在云烟雾霭之中,遥望瀑布就如从云端飞流直下,临空而落,这就自然地联想到像是一条银河从天而降。可见,"疑是银河落九天"这一比喻,虽是奇特,但在诗中并不是凭空而来,而是在形象的刻画中自然地生发出来的。它夸张而又自然,新奇而又真切,从而提摄全篇,使得整个形象变得更为丰富多彩,雄奇瑰丽,既给人留下了深刻的印象,又给人以想象的余地,显示出李白那种"万里一泻,末势犹壮"的艺术风格。

　　宋人魏庆之说:"七言诗第五字要响。……所谓响者,致力处也"(《诗人玉屑》)。这个看法在这首诗里似乎特别有说服力。比如一个"生"字,不仅把香炉峰写"活"了,也隐隐地把山间的烟云冉冉上升、袅袅浮游的景象表现出来了。"挂"字前面已经提到了,那个"落"字也很精彩,它刻画出高空突兀、巨流倾泻的磅礴气势。很难设想若换掉这三个字,这首诗将会变成什么样子。

　　中唐诗人徐凝也写了一首《庐山瀑布》。诗云:"虚空落泉千仞直,雷奔入江不暂息。千古长如白练飞,一条界破青山色。"场景虽也不小,但还是给人局促之感,原因大概是它转来转去都是瀑布……,显得很实,很古板,虽是小诗,却颇有点大赋的气味。比起李白那种入乎其内、出乎其外,有形有神,奔放空灵,相去实在甚远。无怪苏轼说:"帝遣银河一派垂,古来唯有谪仙词。飞流溅沫知多少,不与徐凝洗恶诗"(《戏徐凝瀑布诗》)。话虽不无过激之处,然其基本倾向还是正确的,这也说明苏轼不仅是一位著名的诗人,也是一位颇有见地的鉴赏家。

　　一首篇幅短小的七言绝句,艺术容量却并不显逼仄狭窄,夸张和比喻手法的巧妙交织把自然景物幻化到更高的想象空间,达到写瀑布的极致,极为夸张,但又清新自然,浅显生动,同时具有动荡开阔的气势。这种飞动流走的章法,跳跃腾挪,纵横捭阖,显示出歌行的大气和高格。

　　李白一生遍访祖国的名山大川,所见之景不在少数,而能入其诗者,定为非同

第五章 唐诗英译鉴赏实践（下）

常景。庐山以雄、奇、险、秀闻名于世，从古至今享有"匡庐奇秀甲天下"之美誉。巍峨挺拔的青峰秀峦、喷雪鸣雷的银泉飞瀑、瞬息万变的云海奇观、俊奇巧秀的园林建筑，均使庐山名扬天下。而庐山瀑布乃庐山奇景中最负盛名者，历朝历代的文人墨客到此访游者络绎不绝，为其赋诗者也不在少数，但以李白的《望庐山瀑布》为最佳，故而传颂千载而不绝。

总体而言，这首七言绝句，可谓想象丰富，奇思纵横，气势恢宏，感情奔放，似江河奔腾，又自然清新，似云卷风清，其诗歌的审美特征是自然美、率真美和无拘无束的自由美。历代诗词品评家对此诗赞不绝口，宋代葛立方："徐凝《瀑布》诗云：'千古犹疑白练飞，一条界破青山色。'或谓乐天有赛不得之语，独未见李白诗耳。李白《望庐山瀑布》诗云：'飞流直下三千尺，疑是银河落九天'。故东坡云：'帝遣银河一派垂，古来唯有谪仙词。'"（《韵语阳秋》卷十二）。清代宋宗元："非身历其境者不能道"（《网师园唐诗笺》）。

英译实践版本选读

译文 1　王守义　约翰·诺弗尔

Watching the Lu Mountain Falls

Purple smoke rises from the mountain top,
The peak looks like an incense burner in the sunlight.
Far away I see the valley stretching before me,
The whole waterfall hangs there.
The torrent dropping three thousand feet,
Straight down to the valley floor.
I think it must be the Milky Way,
Spilling to the earth from the heavens.

译文 2　许渊冲

Cataract on Mount Lu

The sunlit Censer Peak exhales a wreath of cloud;
Like an upended stream the cataract sounds loud.
Its torrent dashes down three thousand feet from high;
As if the Silver River fell from azure sky.

译文 3　刘军平

Observing the Lushan Waterfall

The incense smoke curls up from the furnace in the sun,
The cataracts of a river in front of the mountain hang.
The torrential waters rush down of bottomless depth,
I wonder if the Milky way descends from the zenith.

第五章 唐诗英译鉴赏实践(下)

唐诗英译鉴赏实践之七

将进酒①(节选)
李 白

君不见②黄河之水天上来③,
奔流到海不复回。
君不见高堂④明镜悲白发,
朝如青丝⑤暮成雪⑥。
人生得意⑦须尽欢,
莫使金樽⑧空对月。
天生我材必有用⑨,
千金⑩散尽还复来。

【注释】

①〔将进酒〕劝酒歌,属于古乐府诗题,原是汉乐府短箫铙歌的一种曲调。《乐府诗集》卷十六引《古今乐录》曰:"汉鼓吹铙歌十八曲,九曰《将进酒》。"《敦煌诗集残卷》三个手抄本此诗均题作"惜樽空"。《文苑英华》卷三三六题作"惜空樽酒"。
②〔君不见〕乐府诗常用作提醒人语。
③〔天上来〕黄河发源于青海,因地势极高,故有此称。
④〔高堂〕房屋的正室厅堂。一说指父母,不合诗意。一作"床头"。
⑤〔青丝〕形容柔软的黑发。一作"青云"。
⑥〔成雪〕一作"如雪"。此指头发变白。
⑦〔得意〕适意高兴的时候。
⑧〔樽(zūn)〕中国古代的盛酒器具。
⑨〔天生我材必有用〕一作"天生我材必有开",一作"天生我身必有财",一作"天生吾徒有俊才"。
⑩〔千金〕一作"黄金"。

白话释义

　　　　　　难道你没有看见：
　　　那黄河之水犹如从天上倾泻而来，
　　　波涛澎湃奔流入海不再往回流。
　　　　　　难道你没有看见：
　　面对着高堂上的明镜，叹息那满头华发生！
　　　早晨还是满头黑发，到了傍晚却霜白如雪。
　　　　人生快意之时就要尽情地享乐欢愉，
　　　不要让金杯无酒空对皎洁的明月。
　　　上天造就了我的才干就必然是有用处的，
　　　千两黄金花完了也能够再次获得。

主题鉴赏

　　《将进酒》是唐代大诗人李白沿用古乐府诗题创作的一首七言歌行体诗，因篇幅原因，此处节选前四行作为鉴赏实践的主要内容。

　　关于这首诗的写作时间，说法不一。郁贤皓《李白集》认为此诗约作于开元二十四年前后，黄锡珪《李太白编年诗集目录》认为此诗系天宝十一载所作。一般认为这是李白天宝年间离京后，漫游梁、宋，与友人岑勋、元丹丘相会时所作。

　　唐玄宗天宝初年，李白由道士吴筠推荐，进京做翰林供奉。不久，因权贵的谗毁，于天宝三载，李白被排挤出京，唐玄宗赐金放还。此后，李白在江淮一带盘桓，思想极度烦闷，又重新踏上了云游祖国山河的漫漫旅途。李白作此诗时距他被唐玄宗"赐金放还"已有数年。这一时期，李白多次与友人岑勋（岑夫子）应邀到嵩山另一位好友元丹丘的颍阳山居为客，三人登高饮宴，借酒放歌。诗人在政治上被排挤，受打击，理想不能实现，常常借饮酒来发泄胸中的郁积。人生快事莫若置酒会友，作者又正值"抱用世之才而不遇合"之际，于是满腔不合时宜借酒兴诗情，以抒发满腔不平之气。

　　李白深知生命有限、价值无限的道理，把人生从头到尾看了个通透。黄河之水、镜中白发，都引起他对生命、人生的深刻思考。而其思考，并非停留在一般意义上的对时光匆匆流逝及人生短暂的哀叹惋惜，而是从更高层面去拷问自我存在的价值。"对酒当歌，人生几何。譬如朝露，去日苦多"，如果说曹操把其感叹和忧思

第五章 唐诗英译鉴赏实践（下）

浓缩在一滴朝露上，那么李白则是将之寄托于江海与生命本身。"人生如逆旅，我亦是行人"，任何人都不过是历史长河中一粒微不足道的尘土，区别只在于你在这条道路上留下的足迹的深浅。人既然存在，他就不得不存在；人既然活着，他就不得不活着。既然存在，既然活着，就应当做点什么吧。在李白看来，这正是其自我存在的价值所在。因此，可以说李白是一个具有历史情怀的人。他的思考和忧虑，不仅仅是针对个人，还针对个体。他所高唱的"人生得意须尽欢，莫使金樽空对月"，并非如某些人所指责的消极的享乐主义的人生态度，相反，李白是在鼓励人应当积极把握现实人生，努力创造自我价值。如果仅仅从诗句字面上作出负面的解读，则难得诗旨，违背了"诗仙"本意。

李白生性孤傲，强烈的自信以及狂傲不羁的处世态度凸显了他的个性，也使他成为中国古代文人不合流俗不愿委身世俗权贵的一张身份名片。"天生我材必有用"，我才天生也，天授我才，必定对国家对社会有价值。敢自许"天生我才"，放眼古今，恐怕唯李白一人而已。这种狂傲不羁源自强烈的自信，而这种自信乃是大唐帝国的文化心理，是华夏子孙的民族性格。李白对自己充满信心，丝毫也不怀疑，甚至认为获得表现自己施展才华的机会是理所当然的事，是天命所归。因此他敢在天子面前撒狂，敢叫高力士提鞋，更不在乎钟鼓馔玉，千金散尽。他始终把自己看成是一个具有独立人格的独立个体，才华固然天授，也是其安身立命之本，是其狂放不羁的凭靠。当然，这也是李白悲剧性格的因素之一。当自我实现的强烈需求没有得到及时满足或是根本就无法得到满足时，矛盾和痛苦也就产生。需求越强烈，矛盾越深，痛苦越盛。

事实上，李白一直希望在政治上有所作为，但尽管才高八斗却难以如愿。上层官僚的排挤和打压使得他不得不远离政治。面对这种施不开手脚的窘境，李白也许感到很意外，"唯才是用"的政策之外，原来还有另一股力量左右着。这让他颇觉郁闷，心理上承受着来自现实厚重的压抑感，也迫使他作出了强烈的反弹，即承袭魏晋之风，以一种独特方式来表达对现实的愤怒和不满，以及对岁月蹉跎、时光流逝的叹惋："朝如青丝暮成雪。"所以，他自我安慰道："人生得意须尽欢，莫使金樽空对月。"官场失意的李白，似乎只能以喝酒来排遣内心的压抑和苦闷，暂时忘却政治人生的失败，在醉眼蒙胧中纵声放歌，恢复本真性情，获得精神上的愉悦和超脱。

李白的一生与酒有不解之缘，自然与当时的酒文化有关，但他嗜酒如命甚至不要命，则是因为其个人遭遇。所谓"抽刀断水水更流，举杯浇愁愁更愁"，喝酒本为排忧，却反如火上加油。李白一头栽进了酒坛子，在他看来，也许真的是"何以解忧，唯有杜康"了。李白的任性放纵，李白的自我麻醉，实际上仍是由于他对现实的绝望。尽管如此，绝望的李白并不是消沉堕落的李白。当酒成为他人格的一个部分,李白寻找到了生活的另一面,寻找到源源不断的诗歌创作灵感。他借酒浇愁,饮酒赋诗,恃才傲物,笑傲江湖,深得魏晋风度;他纵酒任性,挥洒笔墨,慷慨豪迈,视金钱如粪土,则是对现实政治的强有力的嘲弄与讽刺。

诗歌后半部分说"岑夫子,丹丘生,将进酒,杯莫停",一杯复一杯,到"与君歌一曲,请君为我倾耳听",李白醉矣!后面皆为"酒话",却是李白心声。俗语说:酒后吐真言。李白趁醉将满腹真言全盘吐出。"钟鼓馔玉不足贵,但愿长醉不复醒",李白追求高级层面的精神生活,藐视庸俗的物欲和感观刺激。宁愿长醉而不愿清醒,因为所见皆俗物,不堪入目:权奸当道,能才委屈,宫廷声色犬马,歌舞升平,只顾追求享乐。李白鄙视这样的生活,自然不能与此类人同道。他有种曲高和寡的孤独感,一方面蔑视官僚们的庸俗,一方面为自己没有机会施展抱负而无可奈何。所谓"古来圣贤皆寂寞,唯有饮者留其名",那是李白自我安慰之言罢了。他自比圣贤,与俗人不能共舞,从古圣贤那里倒可觅得知音。李白是寂寞的,但他又难忍寂寞,所以便学陈王曹植斗酒十千,不作圣贤作酒仙。即便如此,他仍至始至终在出世入世间痛苦徘徊。入世不得也不甘放弃,心中仍有期待;出世也难,求仙访道终成空,名山大川走遍也不能彻底脱离俗世。

这首诗意在表达"人生几何,及时行乐;圣者寂寞,饮者留名"的虚无消沉思想,愿在长醉中了却一切。诗的开头六句,写人生寿命如黄河之水奔腾入海,一去不复重返,如此,应及时行乐,莫负光阴。"天生"十六句,写人生富贵不能长保,因而"千金散尽""且为乐"。尤其"天生我材必有用"句,是诗人自信为人的自我价值,也流露怀才不遇和渴望入世的积极思想感情。

总体而言,本诗深沉浑厚,气象不凡。情极悲愤狂放,语极豪纵沉着,大起大落,奔放跌宕。诗句长短不一,参差错综;节奏快慢多变,一泻千里。李白的人生,可谓是悲剧的人生。《将进酒》一诗,是其悲剧人生的写照。有人称《将进酒》是李白诗歌艺术的巅峰之作,也有人称那不过是他醉酒后的胡言乱语。其人,其诗,其酒,三位一体,方是真正的李白。

此诗思想内容非常深沉,艺术表现非常成熟,在同题作品中影响最大。诗人豪饮高歌,借酒消愁,抒发了忧愤深广的人生感慨。诗中交织着失望与自信、悲愤与抗争的情怀,体现出诗人强烈的豪纵狂放的个性。全诗情感饱满,无论喜怒哀乐,其奔涌迸发均如江河流泻,不可遏止,且起伏跌宕,变化剧烈;在手法上多用夸张,且常以巨额数词修饰,既表现出诗人豪迈洒脱的情怀,又使诗作本身显得笔墨酣畅,抒情有力;在结构上大开大阖,张弛有度,充分体现了李白七言歌行的豪放特色。

杜甫曾这样评价李白的诗:"笔落惊风雨,诗成泣鬼神",李白自己也十分自负

第五章　唐诗英译鉴赏实践（下）

地说"兴酣落笔摇五岳，诗成啸傲凌沧洲"。李白的诗极富浪漫主义色彩，想象丰富，极尽夸张之能事，一旦诗兴大发之时，豪情便喷薄而出，一泻千里，但又收放自如，达到了极高的艺术境界，《将进酒》即为明证。

叔本华说，"使我们生存充满烦恼与苦痛的东西，无一不是出自时间无休止的压迫。"具有历史情怀的李白就在时间无休止的压迫中唱出了生命的绝望之歌——《将进酒》。

学生英译实践园地

英译实践版本选读

译文 1 亚瑟·韦利

Drinking Song (Excerpt)

See the waters of the Yellow River leap down from Heaven,
Roll away to the deep sea and never turn again!
See at the mirror in the High Hall
Aged men bewailing white locks—
In the morning, threads of silk;
In the evening flakes of snow!
Snatch the joys of life as they come and use them to the fill;
Do not leave the silver cup idly glinting at the moon.
The things Heaven made
Man was meant to use;
A thousand guilders scattered to the wind may come back again.

译文 2 伯顿·华兹生

Bring the Wine (Excerpt)

Have you never seen
the Yellow River waters descending from the sky,
racing restless toward the ocean, never to return?
Have you never seen
bright mirrors in high halls, the white-haired ones lamenting,
their black silk of morning by evening turned to snow?
If life is to have meaning, seize every joy you can;
do not let the golden cask sit idle in the moonlight!
Heaven gave me talents and meant them to be used;
gold scattered by the thousand comes home to me again.

第五章 唐诗英译鉴赏实践(下)

译文 3　迈克尔·富勒

Bring in the Ale (Excerpt)

Don't you see:
Yellow River's waters that come from Heaven,
Rush to the sea and never return.
Don't you see:
Before the bright mirror in the tall hall, grieving at white hair:
In the morning like dark silk, by dusk, changed to snow.
In life, when it meets your inclination, you must exhaust the pleasure.
Don't let the gold beaker stand empty facing the moon.
Heaven gave birth to my talent:
it must have a use:
A thousand pieces of gold tossed away,
it shall return again.

译文 4　蔡宗齐

Bring in the Wine (Jiang jin jiu) (Excerpt)

Can't you see:
The waters of the Yellow River coming down from heaven,
swiftly rushing to the sea, never to return?
Can't you see:
In the bright mirrors of lofty halls, grief over graying hair:
blue-black silk in the morning, turned to snow by nightfall?
For satisfaction in this life, we must go to the limits of pleasure,
Never face the moon, your golden goblet empty!
The talents that Heaven instilled in me must be put to use—
Squander a thousand pieces of gold, they will yet be returned.

译文5　许渊冲

Invitation to Wine (Excerpt)

Do you not see the Yellow River come from the sky,
Rushing into the sea and ne'er come back?
Do you not see the mirrors bright in chambers high
Grieve o'er your snow-white hair though once it was silk-black?
When hopes are won,
O Drink your fill in high delight,
And never leave your wine-cup empty in moonlight!
Heaven has made us talents, we're not made in vain.
A thousand gold coins spent, more will turn up again.

唐诗英译鉴赏实践之八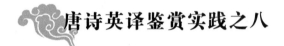

春夜喜雨

杜　甫

好雨知时节①，

当春乃发生②。

随风潜③入夜，

润物④细无声。

野径⑤云俱黑，

江船⑥火独明。

晓⑦看红湿处⑧，

花重⑨锦官城⑩。

第五章 唐诗英译鉴赏实践(下)

【注释】

① 〔知〕明白,知道。说雨知时节,是一种拟人化的写法。
② 〔乃〕就。〔发生〕萌发生长。春天是万物萌芽生长的季节,正需要雨,雨就下起来了。
③ 〔潜(qián)〕悄无声息地。这里指春雨在夜里无声无息地随风而下。
④ 〔润物〕使万物受到春雨的滋养。
⑤ 〔野径〕田野间的小路。
⑥ 〔江船〕江面上停泊的渔舟。
⑦ 〔晓〕天刚亮的时候。
⑧ 〔红湿处〕雨水湿润的花丛。
⑨ 〔花重〕重(zhòng),沉重。花沾上雨水而显得沉重。
⑩ 〔锦官城〕成都旧有大城、少城。少城古为掌织锦官员之官署,因称"锦官城",后用作成都的别称。晋常璩《华阳国志·蜀志》:"其道西城,故锦官也。"

白话释义

及时雨好像知道下雨的时节,
春天刚到,细雨伴着春风,
在宁静的夜晚悄然飘落,
无声无息地滋润着大地万物。
乌云覆盖着田野小路,一片漆黑,
只有江面上的渔舟里有点点微光。
拂晓时分,处处都是细雨浸润的湿润花瓣,
锦官城好一派姹紫嫣红。

主题鉴赏

《春夜喜雨》是唐代大诗人杜甫创作的一首诗,大致写于上元二年春。此前,杜甫在颠沛流离中辗转多地,终于来到成都安顿下来,创作此诗时,他已在草堂定居两年。初到一个地方,人们对当地的天气和物候现象是最有新奇感的。成都地处秦岭之南,四川盆地西部,阴湿多雨是其特点。阴湿多雨如果发生在春季,自然"春雨贵如油",对亲自耕作、种菜种花、与农民几乎融合的杜甫来说,那就更加受其欢迎了,遂写下了这首描写春夜降雨、润泽万物的美景佳作。此诗以极大的喜悦之情细致地描绘了春雨的特点和成都夜雨的景象,热情地讴歌了来得及时、滋润万物的春雨。诗人运用拟人手法描写春雨,体物精微,细腻生动,绘声绘形。全诗意境淡雅,意蕴清幽,诗境与画境浑然一体,是一首传神入化、别具风韵的咏雨诗。

  本诗最突出的是感物之微,体物之细。一开头就用一个"好"字来赞美"雨"。在生活里,"好"有"美好;及时;吉祥"等等语义,常常被用来赞美好人好事好物。而杜甫用"好"来修饰雨,而不是用"细""柔"等其他词语,即显得与众不同,独辟新语。自然会引起读者无限美好的联想。接下来,又把雨拟人化,说它"知时节",懂得满足客观需要。其中"知"字用得传神,简直把雨给写活了。春天是万物萌芽生长的季节,正需要下雨,雨就下起来了,的确很"好",很及时。

  颔联写雨的"发生",进一步表现雨的"好",其中"潜""润""细"等字生动地写出了雨"好"的特点。雨之所以"好",好就好在适时,好在"润物"。春天的雨,一般是伴随着和风滋润万物的。它不同于夏天的暴雨、秋天的连阴雨和冬天的冻雨,它温润绵软,珍贵如油,对农作物和植物的生长十分有益,而又悄无声息。这些特点全被诗人捕捉并巧妙呈现在读者眼前。然而也有例外:有时候,它会伴随着冷风,受到冷空气影响由雨变成雪;有时候,它会伴随着狂风,下得很凶暴。这时的雨尽管下在春天,但不是典型的春雨,只会损物而不会"润物",自然不会使人"喜",也不可能得到"好"评。所以,光有首联的"知时节",还不足以完全表现雨的"好"。等到颔联写出了典型的春雨——伴随着和风的细雨,那个"好"字才落实了。

  "润物"一句几乎是出神入化般的准确和细腻。这句仍然采用拟人手法,"潜入夜"和"细无声"相配合,不仅表明那雨是伴随和风而来的细雨,而且表明那雨有意"润物",无意讨"好"。如果有意讨"好",它就会在白天来,就会造一点声势,让人们看得见,听得清。唯其有意"润物",无意讨"好",才会选择在一个不妨碍人们工作、劳动的时间悄悄地来,在人们酣睡的夜晚无声地、细细地下。

  雨这样"好",就希望它下多下够,下个通宵。倘若只下一会儿,就云散天晴,那"润物"就不很彻底。诗人抓住这一点,写了颈联。在不太阴沉的夜间,小路比田野容易看得见,江面也比岸上容易辨得清,但此时放眼四望,"野径云俱黑,江船火独明。"这一句诗写实,四野"俱黑",只有渔船上点点灯火,除此之外,连江面也看不见,小路也辨不清,天空里全是黑沉沉的云,地上也像云一样黑。言下之意,这雨准会下到天亮。这两句写出了夜雨的美丽景象,"黑"与"明"相互映衬,不仅点明了云厚雨足,而且给人以强烈的美感。明暗对照法的采用,营造了"好雨"将至的夜晚静谧无声的自然景象。

  尾联是想象中的情景,紧扣题中的"喜"字写想象中的雨后锦官城(成都)之晨

第五章 唐诗英译鉴赏实践（下）

的迷人景象。如此"好雨"下了一夜，万物就都得到了润泽，发荣滋长起来了。万物之一的花，最能代表春色的花，也带雨开放，红艳欲滴。诗人说：等到明天清早去看看吧，整个锦官城杂花生树，一片"红湿"，一朵朵红艳艳、沉甸甸的花，汇成花的海洋。"红湿""花重"等字词的运用，令人耳目一新，言他人从未言，充分说明杜甫运用词语的能力非同一般。

清代浦起龙说："写雨切夜易，切春难。"（《读杜心解》）也是"好雨"这首"春夜喜雨"诗，不仅切夜、切春，而且写出了典型的春雨的高尚品格。诗人盼望这样的"好雨"，喜爱这样的"好雨"，所以题目中的那个"喜"字在诗里虽然没有露面，但"'喜'意都从罅缝里迸透（浦起龙《读杜心解》）"。中唐诗人李约有一首《观祈雨》："桑条无叶土生烟，箫管迎龙水庙前。朱门几处看歌舞，犹恐春阴咽管弦。"和那些朱门里看歌舞的人相比，杜甫对春雨"润物"的喜悦之情自然是一种很崇高的感情。

元代方回评价此诗说："'红湿'二字，或谓海棠可当。此诗绝唱"（《瀛奎律髓》）。明代胡应麟："咏物起自六朝，唐人沿袭，虽风华竞爽，而独造未闻。惟杜诸作自开堂奥，尽削前规。……《雨》：'野径云俱黑，江船火独明。'……精深奇邃，前无古人，后无来者"（《诗薮》）。明代王嗣奭："'野径云俱黑'，知雨不遽止，盖缘'江船火明'，径临江上，从火光中见云之黑，皆写眼中实景，故妙。……束语'重'字妙，他人不能下"（《杜臆》）。

学生英译实践园地

第五章　唐诗英译鉴赏实践（下）

英译实践版本选读

译文1　伯顿·华兹生

Spring Night, Delighting in Rain

(5-ch. regulated verse; in Chengdu, the "City of Brocade.")

The good rain knows when to fall,
stirring new growth the moment spring arrives.
Wind-borne, it steals softly into the night,
nourishing, enriching, delicate, and soundless.
Country paths black as the clouds above them;
on a river boat a lone torch flares.
Come dawn we'll see a landscape moist and pink,
blossoms heavy over the City of Brocade.

译文2　宇文所安

Delighting in Rain on a Spring Night

A good rain knows its appointed time,
right in spring it brings things to life.
It enters the night unseen with the wind
and moistens things finely, without a sound.
Over wilderness paths, the clouds are all black,
a boat on the river, its fire alone bright.
At daybreak look where it's wet and red—
the flowers will be heavy in Brocade City.

译文3　许渊冲

Happy Rain on a Spring Night

Good rain knows its time right;

It will fall when comes spring
With wind it steals in night;
Mute, it moistens each thing.
O'er wild lanes dark cloud spreads;
In boat a lantern looms.
Dawn sees saturated reds;
The town's heavy with blooms.

译文 4　大卫·杨

Rain on a Spring Night

Congratulations, rain,
You know when to fall coming at night,
Quiet walking in the wind
Making sure things get good and wet.
The clouds hang dark over country roads.
There's one light from a boat coming down river
In the morning everything's dripping red flowers everywhere.

唐诗英译鉴赏实践之九

春　望
杜　甫

国破①山河在②，
城春③草木深④。
感时花溅泪⑤，
恨别鸟惊心⑥。
烽火连三月⑦，

第五章 唐诗英译鉴赏实践(下)

家书抵万金⑧。

白头搔更短⑨,

浑欲不胜簪⑩。

【注释】

①〔国破〕国,此指大唐都城长安(今陕西西安)。破,陷落,被叛军占据。
②〔山河在〕旧日的山河仍然存在。
③〔城春〕此指春天的长安城。
④〔草木深〕指安史之乱导致长安城十室九空、人烟稀少的萧瑟。
⑤〔感时花溅泪〕为国家的时局动荡而感伤,连花儿都落泪了。〔溅泪〕流泪。
⑥〔恨别鸟惊心〕真痛恨战争,让人妻离子别,无家可归,连鸟儿都感到胆战心惊。
⑦〔烽火连三月〕古时边防报警的烟火,这里指安史之乱的战火。唐玄宗天宝十五载(756年)七月,安史叛军攻陷长安,太子李亨在灵武即位,是为肃宗,改元至德。杜甫闻知此消息,便把家小安顿在鄜州(今陕西富县)的羌村,前往灵武投奔肃宗,途中被叛军俘获押至长安,因其官卑职微,未被囚禁。《春望》即写于至德二年三月,因此,"连三月"是指757年3月,并非指三个月(正月、二月、三月)。
⑧〔家书抵万金〕家人的消息好比万贯金钱那么珍贵。抵,值,相当。
⑨〔白头搔更短〕心急如焚,抓耳挠腮,头发都越来越稀疏了。白头,白头发。搔,用手指轻轻抓挠头发。
⑩〔浑欲不胜簪〕头发稀疏,发簪都别不上。浑,简直。欲,想、要、就要。不胜,受不住,不能。簪,一种束发的首饰。

白话释义

长安城沦陷贼手,幸好山河依旧,
春天的京城却十室九空,荒草丛生。
见此情景,不觉内心伤感,花儿都为之流泪,
无家可归,亲人别离,连鸟儿都为此心悸。
三月时战火依然持续,如有家人的消息真是贵如万金。
心急如焚,抓耳搔头,头发稀疏,连发簪都别不上了。

主题鉴赏

  此诗作于唐肃宗至德二年三月。前一年,即唐玄宗天宝十五年六月,安史叛军越过潼关,直逼京师长安,七月,长安沦陷,太子李亨在甘肃灵武即位为肃宗,追封唐玄宗为太上皇,改元至德。叛军入城后,"大索三日,民间财资尽掠之",之后纵火焚城,昔日繁华壮丽的京都化为废墟。八月,杜甫将妻子安置于鄜州(今陕西富县)的羌村,准备北赴灵武投奔肃宗,但不幸途中被叛军俘获押送至沦陷后的长安,至此已逾半载。时值暮春,触景伤怀,思念家小,杜甫创作了这首被后世传诵千载催人泪下的诗篇,也是反映"安史之乱"历史大变动最为深刻的诗作之一。

  这首诗以诗人的儿女情长入手,但又完全跳出了传统以儿女情长为主题的窠臼,从更高层面反映了诗人热爱国家、眷念家人的美好情感,意脉贯通而不平直,情景兼具而不游离,感情强烈而不浅露,内容丰富而不芜杂,格律严谨而不板滞,以仄起仄落的五律正格,写得铿然作响,气度浑灏,因而千百年来一直脍炙人口,历久不衰。

  "国破山河在,城春草木深。"开篇即写春望之所见:国都沦陷,城池残破,虽然山河依旧,可是乱草遍地,林木苍苍。诗人记忆中昔日长安的春天是何等的繁华,鸟语花香,飞絮弥漫,烟柳明媚,游人迤逦,可是那种盛景今日已荡然无存。一个"破"字使人触目惊心,继而一个"深"字又令人满目凄然。诗人写今日景物,实为抒发人去物非的历史感,将感情寄寓于物,借助景物反托情感,为全诗创造了一片荒凉凄惨的气氛。"国破"和"城春"两个截然相反的意象,同时存在并形成强烈的反差。"城春"当指春天花草树木繁盛茂密、烟景明丽的季节,可是由于"国破"而失去了春天的光彩,留下的只是颓垣残壁,只是"草木深"。"草木深"三字意味深沉,表示长安城里已不是市容整洁,井然有序,而是荒芜破败,人烟稀少,草木杂生。这里,诗人睹物伤感,表现了强烈的"黍离"之悲。

  "感时花溅泪,恨别鸟惊心。"花无情而有泪,鸟无恨而惊心,花鸟是因人而具有了怨恨之情。春天的花儿原本娇艳明媚,香气迷人;春天的鸟儿应该欢呼雀跃,唱着委婉悦耳的歌,令人愉悦安详。"感时""恨别"都浓聚着杜甫因时伤怀、苦闷沉痛、家人分离的愁绪。这两句的含意可以这样理解:我感于战败的时局,看到花开而泪落潸然;我内心惆怅怨恨,听到鸟鸣而心惊胆战。人内心痛苦,遇到乐景,反而引发更多的痛苦,就如"昔我往矣,杨柳依依;今我来思,雨雪霏霏"(《诗经·采薇》)。杜甫继承了这种以乐景表现哀情的艺术手法,并赋予其更深厚的情感,获得更为浓郁的艺术效果。诗人痛感国破家亡的苦恨,越是美好的景象,越会增添内心的伤痛。这联通过景物描写,借景生情,移情于物,表现了诗人忧伤国事、思念家人的深沉感情。

第五章 唐诗英译鉴赏实践(下)

"烽火连三月,家书抵万金。"战火已经连续不断地持续到来年的春天,但仍然没有结束。就连一国之主的唐玄宗都被迫逃亡蜀地,唐肃宗刚刚继位,但是官军暂时还没有获得有利形势,至今还未能收复西京,看来这场战争还不知道要持续多久。诗人又想起自己流落被俘,好久没有妻子儿女的音信,他们生死未卜,也不知道近况如何。要能得到一封家信多好啊!"家书抵万金",含有多少辛酸、多少期盼,反映了诗人在消息隔绝、久盼音讯不至时的迫切心情。战争是一封家信胜过"万金"的真正原因,这也是所有受战争迫害的人民的共同心理,反映出广大人民反对战争、期望和平安定的美好愿望,很自然地使人产生共鸣。

"白头搔更短,浑欲不胜簪。"烽火连月,家信不至,国愁家忧齐上心头,内忧外患纠缠难解。诗人眼前一片惨戚景象,内心焦虑至极,不觉于极无聊赖之时刻,搔首徘徊,意志踌躇,青丝变成白发。自离家以来一直在战乱中颠沛流离,而又身困长安数月有余,人心焦虑,忧愤难离,头发变得更为稀疏,用手搔头,顿觉稀少短浅,简直连发簪也插不住了。诗人由国破家亡、战乱分离写到自己的衰老。"白发"是愁出来的,"搔"是欲解愁而愁更愁。头发白了,疏了,从头发的变化,表现了诗人内心的痛苦和愁怨,显示出诗人伤时忧国、思念家人的真切形象,这是一个感人至深、完整丰满的艺术形象。

这首诗全篇情景交融,感情深沉,而又含蓄凝练,言简意赅,充分体现了"沉郁顿挫"的艺术风格。诗歌结构紧凑,围绕"望"字展开,由登高远望到焦点式的透视,由远及近,感情由弱到强,就在这感情和景色的交叉转换中含蓄地传达出诗人的感叹忧愤。由开篇描绘国都萧索的景色,到眼观春花而泪流,耳闻鸟鸣而怨恨;再写战事持续很久,以致家里音信全无,最后写到自己的哀怨和衰老,环环相扣,层层递进,创造了一个能够引发人们共鸣、深思的境界。

明代徐用吾说:"子美此诗,幽情邃思,感时伤事,意在言外"(《唐诗分类绳尺》)。清代吴乔:"'烽火连三月,家书抵万金。'极平常语,以境苦情真,遂同于《六经》中语之不可动摇"(《围炉诗话》)。清代何焯评价说:"起联笔力千钧。……'感时'心长,'恨别'意短,落句故置家言国也。匡复无期,趋朝望断,不知此身得睹司隶章服否? 只以'不胜簪'终之,凄凉含蓄"(《义门读书记》)。清代纪昀也说:"语语沉着,无一毫做作,而自然深至"(《瀛奎律髓汇评》)。清代诗评家沈德潜道:"'溅泪''惊心'转因花、鸟,乐处皆可悲也"(《唐诗别裁》)。清代学者吴汝纶有言:"字字沉着,意境直似《离骚》"(《唐宋诗举要》)。

一代"诗史",名不虚传。仅仅四十字,却写尽了唐代"安史之乱"背景下人民流离失所的真实境况,表现了典型时代背景下的典型感受,反映了唐代民众热爱国家、期待和平的美好愿望,表达了无数普通民众的最强心音,也展示出诗人忧国忧民、感时伤怀的高尚情感和爱国情操。

学生英译实践园地

第五章 唐诗英译鉴赏实践(下)

英译实践版本选读

译文 1　伯顿·华兹生

Spring Prospect

(Written early in 757 when the poet was still a captive in chang'an. 5-ch, regulated verse.)

The nation shattered, mountains and rivers remains;
City in spring, grass and trees burgeoning.
Feeling the times, blossoms draw tears;
hating separation, birds alarm the heart.
Beacon fires three months in succession,
a letter from home worth ten thousand in gold.
White hairs, fewer for the scratching,
soon too few to hold a hairpin up.

译文 2　宇文所安

The View in Spring

A kingdom smashed, its hills and rivers still here,
spring in the city, plants and trees grow deep.
Moved by the moment, flowers splash with tears,
alarmed at parting, birds startle the heart.
War's beacon fires have gone on three months,
letters from home are worth thousands in gold.
Fingers run through white hair until it thins,
cap-pins will almost no longer hold.

译文 3　盖瑞·施耐德

Spring View

The nation is ruined, but mountains and rivers remain.
This spring the city is deep in weeds and brush.
Touched by the times even flowers weep tears.
Fearing leaving the birds tangled hearts.
Watch-tower fires have been burning for three months
To get a note from home would cost ten thousand gold.
Scratching my white hair thinner
Seething hopes all in a trembling hairpin.

译文 4　迈克尔·富勒

A Spring Vista

The capital is broken: mountains and rivers remain.
The city wall in spring: the grasses and trees grow thickly.
Moved by the times, flowers drenched with tears.
Resenting the parting, birds startle the heart.
Beacon fires burn for three months.
For a letter from my family, I'd pay ten thousand cash.
My white hair, as I scratch it, grows ever shorter,
So soon it won't sustain the clasp.

译文 5　许渊冲

Spring View

On war-torn land stream flow and mountains stand;
In towns unquiet grass and weeds run riot.
Grieved o'er the years, flowers are moved to tears;
Homes cut apart, birds cry with broken heart.
The beacon fire has gone higher and higher;
Words from household are worth their weight in gold.

第五章 唐诗英译鉴赏实践(下)

I cannot bear to scratch my grizzling hair;
It grows too thin to hold a light hair-pin.

唐诗英译鉴赏实践之十

月 夜

杜 甫

今夜鄜州①月,

闺中只独看②。

遥怜③小儿女④,

未解⑤忆长安。

香雾云鬟湿⑥,

清辉⑦玉臂寒⑧。

何时倚虚幌⑨,

双照⑩泪痕干⑪。

【注释】

①〔鄜(fū)州〕富县的古称,今陕西省北部。当时杜甫的家人在鄜州的羌村,杜甫在长安。
②〔闺中〕此指内室,卧房。〔看(kān)〕遥望。〔闺中只独看〕今夜,妻子只能在鄜州的房间内独自望月。
③〔怜〕想念,思念。
④〔小儿女〕年幼的子女。
⑤〔未解〕尚不懂得。
⑥此句写想象中妻子独自久立,望月怀人的形象。〔香雾〕发鬟中的香味散发到雾气中。雾本来没有香气,因为香气从涂有膏沐的云鬟中散发出来,所以说"香雾"。〔云鬟〕发鬟。古代妇女的环形发饰。

⑦〔清辉〕清澈明亮的光辉,多指日月之光。三国魏阮籍《咏怀》诗云:"微风吹罗袂,明月耀清晖。"
⑧〔玉臂〕古代多用以美称女子的臂腕。《群音类选·红蕖记·谐配》:"怕红绡误染,翻成玉臂珠痕。"张煮《题亚子分湖旧隐图》诗:"玉臂云鬟劳客梦,风流无奈让秦嘉。"此指妻子久久伫立于月夜中双臂寒凉。
⑨〔虚幌〕透明的窗帷。幌(huǎng),帷幔。
⑩〔双照〕与上面的"独看"对应,表示对未来团聚的期望。
⑪〔泪痕〕眼泪留下的痕迹。隋宫诗《杂曲歌辞·叹疆场》:"泪痕犹尚在。"

白话释义

今夜鄜州上空明月高悬,
你却在卧房中独自遥看。
远在他乡我想念着儿女,
她不懂你为何思念长安。
雾重香浓沾湿你的发髻,
清辉明月冰凉你的双臂。
何日能团聚双依在帷帐,
月华如练你我不再流泪。

主题鉴赏

天宝十五载春,安禄山叛军由洛阳攻破潼关,直逼京城长安。五月,杜甫从奉先移家至潼关以北的白水(今陕西白水县)的舅父处。六月,长安陷落,玄宗逃蜀,叛军入白水,杜甫携家眷逃往鄜州羌村。七月,肃宗在灵武(今宁夏灵武县)即位,杜甫获悉即从鄜州只身奔向灵武,不料途中被安史叛军所俘,押回长安。八月,杜甫被禁长安望月思家而作此诗。

这首诗借看月而抒离情,但抒发的不是一般情况下的夫妇离别之情。字里行间,表现出时代的特征,离乱之痛和内心之忧熔于一炉,对月惆怅,忧叹愁思,而希望则寄托于不知"何时"的未来。

在首颔两联中,"怜"字,"忆"字,都不宜轻易划过。而这又应该和"今夜""独看"联系起来加以品味。明月当空,月月都能看到。首句特指"今夜"的"独看",则心目中自然有往日的"同看"和未来的"同看"。未来的"同看",留待结句点明。往

第五章 唐诗英译鉴赏实践（下）

日的"同看"，则暗含于前两联之中。"今夜鄜州月，闺中只独看。遥怜小儿女，未解忆长安。"这透露出他和妻子有过"同看"鄜州月而共"忆长安"的往事。

安史之乱以前，诗人困处长安达十年之久，其中有一段时间，是与妻子在一起度过的。他和妻子一同忍饥受寒，也一同观赏长安的明月，自然就留下了深刻的记忆。当长安沦陷，一家人逃难到了羌村的时候，与妻子"同看"鄜州之月而共"忆长安"，已不胜其辛酸。如今自己身陷乱军之中，妻子"独看"鄜州之月而"忆长安"，那"忆"就不仅充满了辛酸，而且交织着忧虑与惊恐。这个"忆"字，是含意深广、耐人寻思的。往日与妻子同看鄜州之月而"忆长安"，虽然百感交集，但尚有自己为妻子分忧；如今，妻子"独看"鄜州之月而"忆长安"，"遥怜"年幼儿女们天真幼稚，只能增加她的负担，不能为她分忧。这个"怜"字，也是饱含深情、感人肺腑的。孩子还小，并不懂得想念，但杜甫不能不念。从小孩的"不念"更能体现出大人的"念"之深切。

颈联通过妻子独自看月的形象描写，进一步表现"忆长安"。月华如洗，秋气浓重，雾湿云鬟，月寒玉臂。望月愈久而忆念愈深，这完全是作者想象中的情景。当想到妻子忧心忡忡、夜深不寐的时候，自己也不免伤心落泪。两地看月而各有泪痕，这激起了作者想要结束这种痛苦生活的祈望，于是尾联以表现希望的诗句作结："何时倚虚幌，双照泪痕干？""双照"而泪痕始干，则"独看"而泪痕不干，也就意在言外了。

该诗题为"月夜"，字字都从月色中照出，而以"独看""双照"为一诗之眼。"独看"是现实，却从对面着想，只写妻子"独看"鄜州之月而"忆长安"，而自己的"独看"长安之月而忆鄜州，已包含其中。"双照"兼包回忆与希望：感伤"今夜"的"独看"，回忆往日的同看，而把并倚"虚幌"和对月抒愁的希望寄托于不知"何时"的未来。采用这种从对方设想的方式，妙在从对方那里生发出自己的感情，这种方法尤被后人当作法度。全诗主旨婉切，章法紧密，明白如话，感情真挚，没有被律诗束缚的痕迹。

明代谭元春云："'遍插茱萸少一人''霜鬓明朝又一年'，皆客中人遥想家中相忆之词，已难堪矣。此又想其'未解忆'，又是客中一种愁苦，然觉得前二绝意明，方知'遥怜''未解'之趣"（《唐诗归》）。钟惺云："'泪痕干'，苦境也，但以'双照'为望，即'庶往共饥渴'意"（《唐诗归》）。明代王嗣奭《杜臆》："'云鬟''玉臂'，语丽而情更悲。"

清代何焯《义门读书记》："衬拓'独'字，逼起落句，精神百倍，转变更奇（'香雾'二句下）。"清代李调元《雨村诗话》："诗有借叶衬花之法。如杜诗'今夜鄜州月，闺中只独看'，自应说闺中之忆长安，却接'遥怜小儿女，未解忆长安'，此借叶衬花也。总之古人善用反笔，善用傍笔，故有伏笔，有起笔，有淡笔，有浓笔，今人曾梦见否？"

近代李庆甲《瀛奎律髓汇评》："冯舒：……如此诗是天生成，非人工碾就，如此方称'诗圣'。""诗圣"并非浪得虚名！

学生英译实践园地

第五章 唐诗英译鉴赏实践(下)

英译实践版本选读

译文 1　伯顿·华兹生

Moonlight Night

(5-ch. regulated verse; written in 756
when Du Fu was being held captive in Chang'an.
His wife and family were in Fuzhou to the north.)

From her room in Fuzhou tonight,
all alone she watches the moon.
Far away, I grieve that her children
can't understand why she thinks of Chang'an.
Fragrant mist in her cloud hair damp,
clear lucence on her jade arms cold—
when will we lean by chamber curtains
and let it light the two of us, our tear stains dried?

译文 2　宇文所安

Moonlit Night

The moon tonight in Fuzhou
she alone watches from her chamber.
I am moved by my children far off there
who don't yet know to remember Chang'an.
Fragrant fog, her coils of hair damp,
clear glow, her jade-white arms are cold.
When will we lean at the empty window,
both shone upon, the tracks of our tears dried?

Du Fu managed to get his family to the relative safety of Qiang Village in Fuzhou, which soon fell to rebel forces moving on from conquered Chang'an. Suzong took the throne on August

11, 756, but was initially trying to gather support, and didn't yet have a headquarters. We don't know exactly what happened except that by the time Du Fu wrote "Moonlit Night," he was in rebel-held Chang'an, and it was autumn. He may have been captured and sent back to Chang'an (or Duling, just outside the city, where he would have been registered), but he was clearly not interned and had freedom of movement in the city.

译文 3 大卫·亨顿

Moonlit Night

Tonight at Fu-chou, this moon she watches
Alone in our room. And my little, far-off
Children, too young to understand what keeps me
Away, or even remember Ch'ang-an. By now,
Her hair will be mist-scented, her jade-white
Arms chilled in its clear light. When
Will it find us together again, drapes drawn
Open, light traced where it dries our tears?

译文 4 迈克尔·富勒

Moonlit Night

Tonight, the moon in Fuzhou:
From the bedroom [you] watch it alone.
I think fondly of my children far away:
They don't yet understand [your] recollections of Chang'an.
The fragrant mist of [your] cloud-ringlets has become damp.
The pure gleam of [your] jade arms is cold.
When, leaning on the empty gauze screen,
Will it shine [our] pairs of tear-tracks dry?

第五章 唐诗英译鉴赏实践(下)

译文 5　许渊冲

A Moonlit Night

Alone in your bed-chamber you would gaze tonight,
At the full moon which over Fuzhou shines so bright.
Far off, I feel grieved to think of our children dear,
Too young to yearn for their father in Chang'an here.
Your fragrant cloud-like hair is wet with dew, it seems;
Your jade-white arms would feel the cold of clear moonbeams.
When can we lean by the window screen side by side,
Watching the moon with tears wiped away and eyes dried?

单元扩展实践练习

一、请比较李白《静夜思》的两种英译文本,用英语谈谈您的看法。

静夜思
李　白

床前明月光,疑是地上霜。
举头望明月,低头思故乡。

【注】《静夜思》创作于唐玄宗开元十四年(公元726年)九月十五日的扬州旅舍,李白时年26岁。在一个月明星稀的夜晚,诗人抬望天空一轮皓月,思乡(nostalgia/homesickness)之情油然而生,写下了这首传诵千古、中外皆知的名诗。

译文 1　许渊冲

A Tranquil Night

Abed, I see a silver light,
I wonder if it's frost aground.
Looking up, I find the moon bright;
Bowing, in homesickness I'm drowned.

译文 2 翟理斯

Night Thoughts

I wake, and moonbeams play around my bed,
Glittering like hoar-frost to my wandering eyes;
Up towards the glorious moon I raise my head,
Then lay me down, — and thoughts of home arise.

第六章

宋词(豪放派)英译鉴赏实践

导 读

After its establishment, the Song Empire was not so strong in terms of its relations with foreign states, but it remained stable in its domestic ruling characterized by a high level of centralization of authority. During the Song dynasty, in addition to the remarkable development in the production of agriculture and handicraft industry, the advancement of urban and commercial economy also far exceeded previous ages, which may be seen if only in two examples, the use of paper money (also the earliest in world history) and the description in the hand-scroll "*Going up the River on the Qingming Festival*" (《清明上河图》). At the same time, as the printing industry began to serve its crucial function, the dissemination of culture became more extensive in range. It was also an age when people became more fastidious and tasteful about life's enjoyment.

With the upper social class, scholar officials were well treated by the imperial court; banquets with singing performances became an indispensable part of their life, wherein they were treated by entertainers trained exclusively for such occasions. With the lower social strata, a variety of entertainments, especially singing and dancing, were equally popular with the townspeople communities. All these made enormous demand for the song lyrics.

At the same time with the strengthening of centralization, scholar officials, more dependent on state power, also developed a higher consciousness of preserving, on their own initiative, current social structure and common value system. This generated a corresponding demand on literature. *Shi* poetry and prose, the "proper and right" (正宗) or canonical literary forms to scholar officials, clearly evolved in the direction of the graceful and upright, with a predilection for rationalization, shortly after the establishment of the state of the Northern Song.

However, aside from dignity and sobriety, scholar officials also had their individual and secular feelings, which also needed an outlet for representation. The song lyric (*ci*), in terms of its general nature, was the word text to be sung by singing girls, and it was a "small way" (小道) that had never had much to do with moral education, the running of the state and the harmony of the world, so these people did not have to treat it seriously. Precisely because of that, though, when the *shi* poetry began to turn more reserved, the song lyric made up for its insufficiencies. That was the reason behind the prosperity of the song lyric in the Northern Song.

The differentiation of *shi* poetry and the song lyric which first emerged in the Northern Song caused the differences between the two genres. To most men of letters, *shi* poetry was a more important literary form to which they devoted more of their effort and wrote more in number, and indeed, *shi* poetry of the Song dynasty also had its considerable achievements. Notwithstanding all this, though, the song lyric was more indicative of the creative power of Northern Song literature. In terms of liberal expression of feeling, it accorded with the characteristics of "poetry" in the wider sense of the word. The conventional saying, "the *shi* poetry of the Tang and the song lyric of the Song," is not without its reason.

Ci, or the song lyric, had been a kind of "light" literature (small way, 小道) from the Late Tang and the Five Dynasties all the way to the middle years of the Northern Song, primarily sung by singing girls to go along with drinking. Originally, there was probably only a weak and vague sense of the *ci* genre being independent of a host of other song forms to which words could be set. Through

第六章 宋词（豪放派）英译鉴赏实践

time, however, and certainly by the Five Dynasties period, the song lyric came to be recognized as a separate poetic genre, consisting of its own set of dozens of tunes. The musicality of the genre is a defining characteristic and sets it apart from *shi* poetry. *Shi* might be set to music and sing, but usually it was not. *Ci* in its early stages was always set to music and sing. Moreover, this was not just any kind of song. It was predominantly the song used in urban entertainment quarters, performed by professional female singers and dancers.

Scholars have long argued that the appearance of *ci*, with its separate topics and formal characteristics, influenced the development of the *shi* tradition in the Song dynasties by providing writers with an alternative genre in which to compose. Poets composed *shi* when their topic and occasion were best written in the *shi* form, but they wrote *ci* when the aesthetic impulse or the occasion called for *ci*.

Wen Tingyun（温庭筠）was said to be one of the first major writers to leave an important legacy of poetry within the ci genre. Most of Wen's extant lyrics come from the Five Dynasties anthology *Among the Flowers*（《花间集》）, compiled in the Later Shu（后蜀）court of Meng Chang（孟昶）in Sichuan in 940. This collection of ci lyrics contained 500 lyrics by eighteen poets and represented a major turning point in the development of ci as an elite poetic form. Among those writers, five, including Wen Tingyun（温庭筠）, Huangfu Song（皇甫松）, Wei Zhuang（韦庄）, Xue Zhaoyun（薛昭蕴）, Niu Qiao（牛峤）were from the Tang, although at least three of the five primarily were active at the very end of the dynasty and later.

Conventionally many of the graceful lyrics are slightly elegant and delicate descriptions of women or love affairs. Their central themes are usually restricted to romantic love, joy of reunion and sorrow of parting, and sentimentality about the changing seasons. They appear to focus less on the rather stereotypical figure of the woman herself than on combining the prosodic demands of the *ci* genre with technical aspects of representation in which the objects in the woman's apartment and the scenes that she views convey the emotion and ambience of the lyric.

Traditionally Wen Tingyun was considered one of the beginners of *Wanyue*, the Graceful and Restrained School（婉约派）, followed by the later lyricists like

Wei Zhuang (韦庄), Li Yu (李煜), Zhang Xian (张先), Yan Shu (晏殊), Liu Yong (柳永), Zhou Bangyan (周邦彦), Qin Guan (秦观) and Li Qingzhao (李清照), etc., who will be briefly introduced in the next chapter (*Wanyue* school). Among these *Wanyue* lyricists, Zhang Xian and Yan Shu were taken as the earliest notable song lyricists of the Northern Song, whose compositions are often said to be stylistically similar to those in *Among the Flowers* (花间派). The peculiar social context and function of the genre shaped its intrinsic non-formal characteristics. As with urban entertainment songs in many cultures, romantic love in its many moods and guises came to be a favorite subject. Consequently, in thinking about the song lyric in comparison to shi poetry, it became customary to observe that "whereas poetry is stern and correct, the song lyric is dainty" (诗庄词媚).

However, "romantic love" is certainly not the only subject treated in the *ci* lyrics. As a comparative sub-genre of *ci* lyrics, the *haofang* School, or the Bold and Unrestrained School (豪放派) actually displayed another panoramic masculine vision and heroic air of *ci* writing. Many of the *haofang* lyrics include not only those on the seasons, on aging and the passage of time, on flowering plants, on festivals, on travels, on farewells, on objects, but more on social, historical and political events as well, manifesting a much more grandeur and majestic inclination.

Among the *Haofang* lyricists, Su Shi in the Northern Song dynasty and Xin Qiji in the Southern Song dynasty were two leading figures who have greatly turned the themes of the *ci* writing away from the feminism and "womanly" style to the themes with more regard to social, political and historical events.

Su Shi

Su Shi (苏轼), also known by his literary name Dongpo (Eastern Slope, 东坡), was born in the family of a relatively poor and humble man of letters at Meishan, Sichuan (四川眉山). His father Su Xun (苏洵) and his younger brother Su Zhe (苏辙) were both famous literary authors of Northern Song. Together they were known as the "Three Su's." Among them, Su Shi made the highest accomplishments in Northern Song literature, and his poetry and prose had a

第六章 宋词（豪放派）英译鉴赏实践

deep influence on the later generations. In the field of song lyric, Su Shi brought the most distinctive changes and opened the path for this completely new style, carving out a special niche for himself throughout the history of the Chinese genre.

In his youth Su Shi gained the favorable recognition of Ouyang Xiu（欧阳修）, and he won the title of Presented Scholar（进士） at the civil service examinations. When he entered his official career, crisis began to arise in Northern Song politics and society. Scholar officials, according to their different political views and partisanship, formed various political factions（党派）, and Su Shi was drawn into the vortex of power struggle. Proposing to reform maladministration in a gentle and gradual way, he joined Ouyang Xiu and other officials in opposing the radical New Policies led by Wang Anshi（王安石新政）. When Wang Anshi was at the helm of the state, Su Shi offered to get himself appointed at a regional position away from the capital, so he first served in Hangzhou, and later also served as the Prefect of several places. Notwithstanding that he was arrested and thrown into prison on the charge of attacking the New Policies in his poetry and prose in 1079, namely the "Case of Poetry at the Blackbird Pavilion（乌台诗案）". Subsequently he was demoted to serve at a junior post in Huangzhou（湖北黄冈）, which placed him under actual surveillance.

In the struggle between the so-called political factions, the "New Guards（新党）" and "Old Guards（旧党），" Su Shi always found it hard to please either party. But it reveals that he was an upright person who refused to mix up disagreement in political views and partisan struggle. On the other hand, though, Su Shi was also an open-minded man. While he claimed to be a Confucian himself, he had great interest in the thinking of Laozi and Zhuangzi, and in Buddhism. He was also fond of all kinds of "miscellaneous studies"（杂学）, engaging himself in them with a broad mind. Such a personality had a close relationship with the characteristics of his literary compositions. As a man with a liberal personality and the temperament of a genius, he was more acutely and deeply sensitive than others to life's vulnerability and fragility, the misery of people, and the pathetic condition of things that human has experienced in the world.

For instance, his "Riverside Town" is concerned with the "love" theme, which was composed in memory of his deceased wife to show his deep heartfelt grief. This lyric is reviewed as the most melancholy elegy on the history of Chinese classical literature:

> For ten years the living and the dead are set wide, wide apart,
> I've tried not to think about you,
> But I simply cannot forget.
> Your solitary grave is a thousand miles away:
> I have no place to go to talk about my misery.
> Even if we could meet, you'd fail to recognize me
> With dust all over my face
> And hair at my temples like frost. ①
> ...
> (Tr. by Ye Yang)

Su Shi's other best known song lyrics were composed under adverse political circumstances. Face to face with nature, musing on past and present life hardships and political setbacks, the poet comes to a philosophical understanding of life that blends pathos with broad-mindedness. For example, "Lovely Nian Nu: Recalling the Antiquity at Red Cliff":

> The great river runs east,
> Its waves have washed away
> Heroes of a thousand ages.
> West of the old fortress,
> I've been told,
> Lies the Red Cliff where Master Zhou of Three Kingdoms stood.
> Jagged rocks pierce the sky;
> Waves, slapping the banks as if agitated,
> Roll like thousands of snowdrifts.
> The river and the mountains: what a picture!
> At the time back then, so many great men were around.

---

① 《江城子·乙卯正月二十日夜记梦》苏轼:十年生死两茫茫,不思量,自难忘。千里孤坟,无处话凄凉。纵使相逢应不识,尘满面,鬓如霜。……

第六章 宋词（豪放派）英译鉴赏实践

...①

(Tr. by Ye Yang)

This song lyric was composed when he was demoted to serve as Vice Military Training Commissioner of Huangzhou（黄州团练副使）after he lived through the "Case of Poetry at the Blackbird Pavilion," during which he endured great humiliation and confronted threat of his life. In order to ward off all the blows from forces in real life, the author tried to seek transcendence in the magnitude of spatial and temporal consciousness.

Another good example is "Heading of Water Tune: Mid-Autumn Festival, 1076":

How long has the bright moon been up there?
Holding wine in hand, I ask the blue sky.
I know not, up in the celestial palaces,
What year is it tonight?
I'd like to ride the wind and go back,
Yet fear, in the marble towers and jade mansions,
It'd be too cold for me to stay.
I arise to dance with my shadow:
Nothing is like this human world of ours.

...②

(Tr. by Ye Yang)

This lyric was written when Su Shi went to serve as Prefect of Mizhou（密州）because of his opposition to the Reform during the Xining reign（熙宁年间）, during a time when he suffered a political setback in life.

"Lovely Nian Nu," from its very beginning, unfolds on the grand scale of centuries of years in time and thousands of miles in space. It not only expresses the speaker's admiration for gallant heroes, but also relieves the inner depression by seeing through life's illusion in the boundless spatial and temporal sphere. At

---

① 《念奴娇·赤壁怀古》苏轼：大江东去，浪淘尽，千古风流人物。故垒西边，人道是：三国周郎赤壁。乱石穿空，惊涛拍岸，卷起千堆雪。江山如画，一时多少豪杰。……

② 《水调歌头·明月几时有》苏轼：明月几时有？把酒问青天。不知天上宫阙，今夕是何年。我欲乘风归去，又恐琼楼玉宇，高处不胜寒。起舞弄清影，何似在人间。……

the beginning of "Heading of Water Tune," by asking the sky, the speaker places his personal life in the light of the eternal time. Set in contrast with the permanent existence of time, the moon takes its turns shining or hiding, getting full or waning, and human beings have their joy and sorrow, parting and reunion, all inevitably. Once one realizes that life is bound to have imperfections, then one had better give up futile ambitions and self remorse, and treasure some of the things worthy to be cherished that one can always find in life. Such a philosophy of life may lack the power of spirited resistance, but it still reflects Su Shi's proud and unyielding personality. The lyrics provide an extraordinarily wide world of imagination and show an astonishing range of emotions, making them something unprecedented in the entire history of the genre.

In conclusion, Su Shi's most important contribution to the song lyric lies in that he initiated a majestic, bold, unconstrained, broad-minded and candid artistic style that shares something in common with the *shi* poetry, while simultaneously he also composed lyrics in a variety of other styles. Su Shi creatively expanded the thematic range and emotional content of the song lyric, and he also accordingly enriched the language, world of imagination, and style of the genre. His song lyrics crossed the traditional boundary between the shi poetry and the ci lyric.

Xin Qiji

Xin Qiji (辛弃疾) was born in Licheng, Shandong (山东东路济南府历城县), which was then under the rule of the Jin (Jurchens, 女真). In the thirty-first year of the Shaoxing reign (绍兴年间), during a war between the Song and the Jin (金), Xin Qiji, twenty-two years old at the time, joined an army of volunteers against the Jin led by Geng Jing (耿京), and acted as Geng's representative to contact the Southern Song court. On his way back to the north, hearing that Geng Jing was killed by Zhang Anguo (张安国), a traitor, and that the army of volunteers was defeated and dispersed, he immediately led a small number of picked troops in a sudden attack of the enemy's camp, captured the traitor and took him back to Jiankang (建康). The heroic undertaking brought him a great fame.

第六章 宋词（豪放派）英译鉴赏实践

Xin Qiji was one of the most well-known statesmen with not only political ambition but literary talents. His life-long pursuit of resistance against the Jin and persistence of recovering the lost central land was more vigorous and more in accordance with his ambition, as a valiant person, to take advantage of the tide of events. Unfortunately Xin served the government only in low official positions in most of his lifetime, even in 1181, in the prime of his life, he was impeached and forced to retire. For about twenty years, he lived in a reclusive life in Shangrao, Jiangxi（江西上饶）far from the political center.

During his retirement, Xin Qiji devoted himself entirely to the composition of the *song* lyric describing the scenic beauty instead of *shi* poetry, because the former form was more suitable, vigorous and forceful to express his intense and ever-changing emotions and patriotism. In fact, the beauty of natural countryside scenery and seemingly peaceful retiring life in his *ci* lyrics fully displayed his expansive and heroic spirit and aspiration for a fruitful political and military career.

The following lines from a song lyric to the tune of "Congratulating the Groom" ("贺新郎") shows his thirst for the unification of the splitting country:

...
At midnight I sang wildly, as a stirring solemn wind rises —
I hear the clanking of the row of metal horses hung from the eaves.
　　The south and the north
　　Are still split at this moment. ①
　　　　(Tr. by Michael A. Fuller and Shuen-fu Lin)

Another "Congratulation to the Groom":

...
Man, it is said, holds a heart of steel until death.
　　Let's see how he tries his hand
　　At patching up the broken sky. ②
　　　　(Tr. by Ye Yang)

---

① 《贺新郎·用前韵送杜叔高》辛弃疾：夜半狂歌悲风起，听铮铮、阵马檐间铁。南共北，正分裂。
② 《贺新郎·同父见和再用韵答之》辛弃疾：道"男儿到死心如铁"。看试手，补天裂。

More examples include "Tune: Dance of the Cavalry" ("破阵子"):

Recovering the lost land for the sovereign,
'Tis everlasting fame that we would win.①

(Tr. by Xu Yuanchong)

And "Chanting of Dragon in Water: In Celebration of the Birthday of Minister Han of the Southern Creek in the Year of Jiachen" ("水龙吟"):

For me, to suppress foreign invaders over ten thousand miles
And gain fame and honor is by itself
Truly a Confucian task.
Don't you know, my Lord?②

(Tr. by Ye Yang)

Xin Qiji's song lyrics are always filled with fiery emotions, with their basic tone in heroism and the grief of a hero who fails to fulfill his ambition. In a word, in terms of the so-called *Haofang* School or the "bold and unconstrained" style of the song lyric, Xin Qiji has habitually been mentioned side by side with Su Shi as "Su and Xin" and he himself was reputed as the "Tiger of *Ci* Lyrics" (词中之龙). So it is no denying that the "bold and unconstrained" (*haofang*) style of the Song dynasty was majorly represented by Su Shi and Xin Qiji, and the dramatic changes to the the heroic style and the lofty themes were fairly embarked with Su Shi and Xin Qiji.

宋词(豪放派)英译鉴赏实践之一

水调歌头·明月几时有

苏 轼

丙辰①中秋，欢饮达旦②，大醉，作此篇，兼怀子由③。

---

① 《破阵子·为陈同甫赋壮词以寄之》辛弃疾：了却君王天下事，赢得生前身后名。
② 《水龙吟·甲辰岁寿韩南涧尚书》辛弃疾：算平戎万里，功名本是，真儒事，君知否。

第六章　宋词（豪放派）英译鉴赏实践

明月几时有？

把酒④问青天。

不知天上宫阙⑤，今夕是何年。

我欲乘风归去⑥，又恐琼楼玉宇⑦，高处不胜寒⑧。

起舞弄清影⑨，何似⑩在人间。

转朱阁，低绮户，照无眠⑪。

不应有恨⑫，何事长向别时圆⑬？

人有悲欢离合，月有阴晴圆缺，此事⑭古难全。

但愿⑮人长久，千里共婵娟⑯。

【注释】

①〔丙辰〕指宋神宗熙宁九年。这一年苏轼在密州（今山东省诸城市）任太守。

②〔达旦〕直到天亮。

③〔子由〕苏轼的弟弟苏辙，字"子由"。

④〔把酒〕端起酒杯。把，执、持。

⑤〔天上宫阙〕此指月中宫殿。阙，古代城墙后的石台。

⑥〔归去〕回去，这里指回到月宫里去。

⑦〔琼楼玉宇〕美玉砌成的楼宇，指想象中的仙宫。

⑧〔不胜〕经受不住。胜，承担、承受。

⑨〔弄清影〕月光下的身影也跟着做出各种舞姿。弄，赏玩。

⑩〔何似〕何如，哪里比得上。

⑪〔朱阁〕朱红的华丽楼阁。〔绮户〕雕饰华丽的门窗。

⑫〔不应有恨〕不要有什么怨恨。

⑬〔何事〕为什么。

⑭〔此事〕指人的"欢""合"和月的"晴""圆"。

⑮〔但愿〕只希望。

⑯〔共〕一起欣赏。〔婵娟〕月亮的别称。〔千里共婵娟〕纵然相隔千里，也能一起欣赏这美好的月光。

白话释义

丙辰年(公元1076年)的中秋节,通宵痛饮直至天明,大醉,趁兴写下这篇文章,同时抒发对弟弟子由的怀念之情。

中秋佳节月儿圆,何时家人能团圆?
举起酒杯试问苍天。
天上仙宫,今日是否为佳节?
我想乘着风飞上月宫,
又怕美玉砌成的楼宇高耸,
寒冷寂寞难以承受。
伴着月华,与自己的身影一起舞动,
月宫再好,哪能胜过人间欢畅。

月移影动,转过了朱红色的楼阁,
雕花的窗户上,月影朦胧,今夜无眠。
明月该不会对人们心存怨恨,
偏偏在人们离别时又圆又亮呢?
悲欢离合人间事,月圆月缺乃无常,
(想要人团圆时月亮正好也圆满)
这样的好事自古就难以两全。
只愿世间的亲人都能平安健康,
纵使千里之遥也能把明月共赏。

主题鉴赏

这首词是宋神宗熙宁九年中秋苏轼在密州(今山东诸城)时所作,是一首被历代称颂并广为流传的中秋望月思乡怀人的上乘之作。词前的小序交代了写作此词的背景:"丙辰中秋,欢饮达旦,大醉。作此篇,兼怀子由。"丙辰,是北宋神宗熙宁九年。苏轼此前因为与当权的变法者王安石等人政见不同,自求外放,辗转在各地为官。熙宁四年,他以开封府推官通判杭州,是为了避开汴京政争的漩涡。他曾经多

第六章 宋词（豪放派）英译鉴赏实践

次要求调任到离苏辙较近的地方为官，以求兄弟多多聚会。熙宁七年朝廷同意他的请求，调任其为密州太守，虽说出于自愿，实质上苏轼仍是处于被外放冷遇的处境。尽管他当时"面貌加丰"，颇有一些旷达表现，也难以掩盖深藏内心的郁愤。赴任后，他与兄弟相聚的愿望仍无法实现。中秋月圆，万家团聚之夜，他却孤身一人，明月对酒，家人遥隔。此时此刻，此情此景，他举头望月，不仅心潮起伏，思绪万千，词人万分思念已阔别七年有余的胞弟苏辙，借着酒兴正浓，挥笔写就了这首旷达千年的《水调歌头》，词人运用形象描绘手法，勾勒出一种皓月当空、亲人千里、孤高旷远的境界氛围，不仅表达其对胞弟苏辙的无限思念之情，也道出了无数个无法与亲人在中秋佳节团聚赏月的人们的共情心理。

苏轼一生推崇儒学，讲究实务。但他也"龆龀好道"，中年以后，又曾表示过"归依佛僧"，经常处在儒释道的纠葛当中。每当挫折失意之际，则老庄思想上升，借以帮助自己消解穷通进退的困惑。这首中秋词，正是此种宦途险恶体验的升华和总结。"大醉"遣怀是主，"兼怀子由"是辅。对于一贯秉持"尊主泽民"节操的作者来说，手足分离和私情，比起廷忧边患的国势来说，毕竟属于次要的伦理负荷。此点在题序中有深奥微妙的提示。

在大自然的景物中，月亮是很有浪漫色彩的，很容易启发人们的艺术联想。一钩新月，可联想到初生的萌芽事物；一轮满月，可联想到美好的团圆生活；月亮的皎洁，让人联想到光明磊落的人格。在月亮这一意象上集中了古人无限美好的憧憬和理想，从古至今，以"月亮"为主题的诗词数不胜数，此篇可谓借月咏怀的神来之作。

苏轼是一位性格豪放、气质浪漫的文学家，当他抬头遥望中秋明月时，其思想情感犹如长上了翅膀，天上人间自由翱翔，反映到词里，遂形成了一种豪放洒脱与众不同的风格。

此词上阕望月，既怀超宜兴致，高接混茫，而又脚踏实地，自具雅量。一开始就提出一个问题：明月是从什么时候开始有的？"明月几时有？把酒问青天。"把酒问天这一细节与屈原的《天问》和李白的《把酒问月》有相似之处。其问之痴迷、想之逸尘，确实有一种类似的精、气、神贯注在里面。苏轼把青天当作自己的朋友，把酒相问，显示了他豪放的性格和不凡的气魄。李白的《把酒问月》诗说："青天有月来几时？我今停杯一问之。"不过李白这里的语气比较舒缓，苏轼因为是想飞往月宫，所以语气更强烈、更迫切。"明月几时有？"这个问题问得很有意思，好像是在追溯明月的起源，宇宙的起源；又好像是在惊叹造化的巧妙。读者从中可以感到诗人对明月的赞美与向往。

接下来两句"不知天上宫阙，今夕是何年"把对于明月的赞美与向往之情更推进了一层。从明月诞生之日起到现在已经过去很多年了,不知道在月宫里今晚是一个什么日子?诗人想象那一定是一个好日子,所以月才这样圆、这样亮。他很想去看一看,所以接着说:"我欲乘风归去,又恐琼楼玉宇,高处不胜寒。"唐人称李白为"谪仙",黄庭坚则称苏轼与李白为"两谪仙",苏轼自己也设想前生是月中人,因而起"乘风归去"之想。他想乘风飞向月宫,又怕那里的琼楼玉宇太高了,受不住那儿的寒冷。这几句明写月宫的高寒,暗示月光的皎洁,把那种既向往天上又留恋人间的矛盾心理十分含蓄地写了出来。这里还有两个字值得注意,就是"我欲乘风归去"的"归去"。飞天入月,为什么说是归去呢?也许是因为苏轼对明月十分向往,早已把那里当成自己的归宿了。从苏轼的思想看来,他受道家的影响较深,抱着超然物外的生活态度,又喜欢道教的养生之术,所以常有出世登仙的想法。他的《前赤壁赋》描写月下泛舟时那种飘飘欲仙的感觉说:"浩浩乎如冯虚御风,而不知其所止;飘飘乎如遗世独立,羽化而登仙。"也是由望月而想到登仙,可以和这首词互相印证。

　　词人之所以有这种脱离人世、超越自然的奇想,一方面来自他对宇宙奥秘的好奇,另一方面则是来自对现实人间的不满。人世间有如此多的不称心、不满意之事,迫使词人幻想摆脱这烦恼人世,到琼楼玉宇中去过逍遥自在的神仙生活。苏轼后来贬官到黄州,时时有类似的奇想,所谓"小舟从此逝,江海寄余生"(《临江仙·夜饮东坡复醉醒》)。然而,在词中这仅仅是一种打算,并未展开,便被另一种相反的思想打断:"又恐琼楼玉宇,高处不胜寒"。这两句急转直下,天上的"琼楼玉宇"虽然富丽堂皇,美好非凡,但那里高寒难耐,不可久居。词人故意找出天上的美中不足,来坚定自己留在人间的决心。一正一反,更表露出词人对人间生活的热爱。同时,这里依然在写中秋月景,读者可以体会到月亮的美好,以及月光的寒气逼人。这一转折,写出词人既留恋人间又向往天上的矛盾心理。这种矛盾能够更深刻地说明词人留恋人世、热爱生活的思想感情,显示了词人开阔的心胸与超远的志向,因此为词的创作带来一种旷达的文风。

　　"起舞弄清影,何似在人间!"苏轼毕竟更热爱人间的生活,与其飞往高寒的月宫,还不如留在人间趁着月光起舞呢!"清影",是指月光之下自己清朗的身影。"起舞弄清影",是与自己的清影为伴,一起舞蹈嬉戏的意思。李白《月下独酌》说:"我歌月徘徊,我舞影零乱。"苏轼的"起舞弄清影"就是从这里脱胎出来的。"高处不胜寒"并非作者不愿归去的根本原因,"起舞弄清影,何似在人间"才是根本之所在。与其飞往高寒的月宫,还不如留在人间,在月光下起舞,最起码还可以与自己清影为伴。这首词从幻想上天写起,写到这里又回到热爱人间的感情上来。从"我欲"到"又恐"至"何似"的心理转折开阖中,展示了苏轼情感的波澜起伏。他终于从

第六章 宋词（豪放派）英译鉴赏实践

幻想回到现实，在出世与入世的矛盾纠葛中，入世思想最终占了上风。"何似在人间"是毫无疑问的肯定，雄健的笔力显示了情感的强烈。

下阕怀人，即兼怀子由，由中秋的圆月联想到人间的离别，同时感念人生的离合无常。"转朱阁，低绮户，照无眠"中，"转"和"低"都是指月亮的移动，暗示夜已深沉。月光转过朱红的楼阁，低低地穿过雕花的门窗，照到了房中迟迟未能入睡之人。这里既指自己怀念弟弟的深情，又可以泛指那些中秋佳节因不能与亲人团圆以至难以入眠的所有人。月圆而人不能圆，这是多么遗憾的事啊！于是词人便无理地埋怨明月说："不应有恨，何事长向别时圆？"明月您总不该有什么怨恨吧，为什么总是在人们离别的时候才圆呢？相形之下，更加重了离人的愁苦了。这是埋怨明月故意与人为难，给人增添忧愁，无理的语气进一步衬托出词人思念胞弟的手足深情，却又含蓄地表达了对于不幸的离人们的同情。

接着，词人把笔锋一转，说出了一番宽慰的话来为明月开脱："人有悲欢离合，月有阴晴圆缺，此事古难全。"人有悲欢离合，月也有阴晴圆缺。她有被乌云遮住的时候，有亏损残缺的时候，她也有她的遗憾，自古以来世上就难有十全十美的事。既然如此，又何必为暂时的离别而感到忧伤呢？词人毕竟是旷达的，他随即想到月亮也是无辜的。既然如此，又何必为暂时的离别而忧伤呢？这三句从人到月、从古到今做了高度的概括。从语气上，好像是代明月回答前面的提问；从结构上，又是推开一层，从人、月对立过渡到人、月融合。为月亮开脱，实质上还是为了强调对人事的达观，同时寄托对未来的希望。因为，月有圆时，人也有相聚之时。这几句很有哲理意味。

词的最后说："但愿人长久，千里共婵娟。""婵娟"是美好的样子，这里指嫦娥，也就是代指明月。"共婵娟"就是共明月的意思，典故出自南朝谢庄的《月赋》："隔千里兮共明月。"既然人间的离别是难免的，那么只要亲人长久健在，即使远隔千里也还可以通过普照世界的明月把两地联系起来，把彼此的心沟通在一起。"但愿人长久"，是要突破时间的局限；"千里共婵娟"，是要打通空间的阻隔。让对于明月的共同的爱把彼此分离的人结合在一起。古人有"神交"的说法，好友天各一方，不能见面，却能以精神相通。"千里共婵娟"也可以说是一种神交了！这两句并非一般的自慰和共勉，而是表现了作者处理时间、空间，以及人生等一些重大问题时所持的态度，充分显示出词人精神境界的丰富博大。

初唐四杰的王勃《送杜少府之任蜀州》有："海内存知己，天涯若比邻。"意味深长，传为佳句，但"千里共婵娟"则比王勃句更富于想象力。另外，张九龄的《望月怀远》说："海上生明月，天涯共此时。"杜牧的《秋霁寄远》说："唯应待明月，千里与君同。"均有异曲同工之妙。但愿人们年年平安，相隔千里也能够共享这美好的月光，表达了诗人的祝福和对亲人的思念,反映出诗人旷达出世的态度和乐观豁达的精神。苏轼就是把前人的诗意化解到自己的作品中,熔铸成一种普遍性的情感。正如词前小序所说,这首词表达了对弟弟苏辙(字子由)的怀念之情,但并不限于此。可以说这首词是苏轼在中秋之夜,对一切经受着离别之苦的人表示的美好祝愿。

对于这首《水调歌头》历来都是推崇备至。胡仔《苕溪渔隐丛话》认为此词是写中秋的词里最好的一首。这首词仿佛是与明月的对话,在对话中探讨着人生的意义,既有理趣,又有情趣,很耐人寻味,因此历来传诵不衰。吴潜《霜天晓角》:"且唱东坡《水调》,清露下,满襟雪。"《水浒传》第三十回写八月十五"可唱个中秋对月对景的曲儿",唱的就是这"一支东坡学士中秋《水调歌》。"可见宋元时传唱之盛。全词意境豪放而阔大,情怀乐观而旷达,对明月的向往之情,对人间的眷恋之意,以及那浪漫的色彩,潇洒的风格和行云流水一般的语言,至今还能给人们以健康的美学享受。

第六章 宋词（豪放派）英译鉴赏实践

英译实践版本选读

译文 1　约翰·特纳

Remembrance in Mid-Autumn —
To the Tune of "Barcarole Prelude"

"When did this glorious moon begin to be?"
　　Cup in hand, I asked of the azure sky:
　　And wondered in the palaces of the air
　　What calendar this night do they go by.
Yes, I would wish to mount the winds and wander there
　　At home; but dread those onyx towers and halls of jade
　　Set so immeasurably cold and high.
To tread a measure, to support with fleshless shade,
　　How alien to our frail mortality!

Her light round scarlet pavilion, 'neath broidered screen, down streams
　　On me that sleepless lie.
　　Ah, vain indeed is my complaining:
But why must she beam at the full on those that sundered sigh?
As men have their weal and woe, their parting and meeting, it seems
The moon has her dark and light, her phases of fullness and waning.
　　Never is seen perfection in things that die.
　　Yet would I crave one solitary boon:
　　Long be we linked with light of the fair moon
　　Over large leagues of distance, thou and I.

译文 2　伯顿·华兹生

Tune: "Prelude to Water Music"

On mid-autumn night of the year bing-chen (1076), I drank merrily until dawn, got very drunk and wrote this poem, all the while thinking longingly of Ziyou.

Bright moon, when did you appear?
Lifting my wine, I question the blue sky.
Tonight in the palaces and halls of heaven
what year is it, I wonder?
I would like to ride the wind, make my home there,
only I fear in porphyry towers, under jade eaves,
in those high places the cold would be more than I could bear.
So I rise and dance and play with your pure beams,
though this human world — how can it compare with yours?
Circling my red chamber,
low in the curtained door,
you light my sleeplessness.
Surely you bear us no ill will —
why must you be so round at times when we humans are parted?
People have their griefs and joys, their joining and separations,
the moon its dark and clear times, its roundings and wanings.
As ever in such matters, things are hardly the way we wish.
I only hope we may have long long lives,
may share the moon's beauty, though a thousand miles apart.

译文 3　罗伯特·科特维尔　诺曼·史密斯

To "Water Song"

At the Mid-Autumn Festival in the year Bing-chen (1076) I enjoyed myself by drinking until dawn and became very drunk. I wrote this poem, thinking of Ziyou.

Bright moon, when wast thou made?
Holding my cup, I ask of the blue sky.
I know not in heaven's palaces
What year it is this night.
I long to ride the wind and return;
Yet fear that marble towers and jade houses,
So high, are over-cold.

第六章 宋词（豪放派）英译鉴赏实践

    I rise and dance and sport with limpid shades;
    Better far to be among mankind.
    Around the vermilion chamber,
    Down in the silken windows,
    She shines on the sleepless,
    Surely with no ill-will.
Why then is the time of parting always at full moon?
 Man has grief and joy, parting and reunion;
The moon has foul weather and fair, waxing and waning.
  In this since ever there has been no perfection.
   All I can wish is that we may have long life,
That a thousand miles apart we may share her beauty.

译文 4　艾朗诺

To the Tune, "Water Melody"

On the midautumn festival of Bingchen [1076]
I drank and amused myself all night until dawn.
Completely drunk, I composed this piece,
intending it also to express my longing for Ziyou.

How long has the bright moon existed?
  I lift my cup to ask azure Heaven.
In those Heavenly palaces, I wonder,
   What year it is tonight?
I long to mount the wind and return there
But fear those jeweled balconies and jade roofs
  So high aloft will be too cold.
I stand up to dance with my clear shadow,
 How could this be the world of men!

  It comes round the crimson hall,
   Dips to my painted doorway,

And shines on the sleepless one.
I should not resent it,
But why is it always full when we're apart?
Men have sorrow and joy, partings and reunions,
The moon is obscured or clear, waxing or waning.
Such things have never been perfect.
We can only hope through long lives
To share her charms across a thousand miles.

译文 5 许渊冲

Prelude to Water Melody

Sent to Ziyou on Mid-autumn Festival(1076)

When did the bright moon appear?
Wine-cup in hand, I ask the blue sky.
I do not know what time of year
It would be tonight in the palace on high.
Riding the wind, there I would fly,
But I'm afraid the crystalline palace would be
Too high and cold for me.
I rise and dance, with my shadow I play.
On high as on earth, would it be as gay?

The moon goes round the mansions red
With gauze windows to shed
Her light upon the sleepless bed.
Against man she should not have any spite.
Why then when people part is she oft full and bright?
Men have sorrow and joy, they part and meet again;
The moon may be bright or dim, she may wax or wane.
There has been nothing perfect since the olden days.
So let us wish that man live as long as he can!
Though miles apart, we'll share the beauty she displays.

第六章 宋词（豪放派）英译鉴赏实践

译文 6　朱纯深

Mid-Autumn Festival—
To the Tune of Shuidiaogetou

Mid-Autumn Festival. I drank in jubilation from evening till dawn. Intoxicated by wine, I wrote this piece, and thought of Ziyou, my brother, as well.

How often can we have
such a glorious moon?
Raising my goblet, I put
the question to Heaven.
Which year is it tonight,
in your celestial palaces?
I wish to ride the wind, and
return there, if not deterred
By the unbearable cold that must
prevail at that precarious height.
Aloof there, one could dance
but with a lonely shadow;
So why not
stay on this Earth?
Hovering round my chamber,
Sidling through my window,
a witness to my sleepless night.
You must bear no grudge,
but why should you turn so full
Every time when somebody's away?
This is, anyway, an eternal flaw —
an uncertain world
under an inconstant moon.
Nonetheless, may all of us remain
long in this world, and share

The immortal moon even though
thousands of miles apart!

宋词(豪放派)英译鉴赏实践之二

念奴娇·赤壁怀古①
苏 轼

大江东去②,

浪淘尽③,千古风流人物④。

故垒⑤西边,人道是:三国周郎赤壁⑥。

乱石穿空,惊涛拍岸,卷起千堆雪⑦。

江山如画,一时多少豪杰。

遥想公瑾当年,小乔⑧初嫁了,雄姿英发⑨。

羽扇纶巾⑩,谈笑间,樯橹⑪灰飞烟灭。

故国神游⑫,多情应笑我⑬,早生华发⑭。

人生如梦,一樽还酹江月⑮。

【注释】

①〔念奴娇〕词牌名,又名"百字令""酹江月"等。〔赤壁〕黄州赤壁,一名"赤鼻矶",在今湖北省黄冈市西。三国古战场的赤壁,一般认为在今湖北赤壁市蒲圻县西北。

②〔大江〕长江。

③〔浪淘尽〕江中大浪彻底冲刷。此处喻指历史的淘汰和筛选。

④〔风流人物〕杰出的历史名人。

⑤〔故垒〕过去遗留下来的营垒,推测此处是指古战场的遗迹。

第六章 宋词（豪放派）英译鉴赏实践

⑥〔周郎〕三国时吴国名将周瑜，字公瑾，少年得志，二十四为中郎将，掌管东吴重兵，吴中皆呼为"周郎"。下文中的"公瑾"，即指周瑜。

⑦〔雪〕比喻浪花。

⑧〔小乔〕周玄的小女儿，周瑜之妻，不仅有闭月羞花之容，且琴棋书画样样精通。"乔"原作"桥"。

⑨〔雄姿英发〕指周瑜仪表卓绝，谈吐不凡。英发(fā)，姿态焕然，精神饱满。

⑩〔羽扇纶巾〕古代儒将的便装打扮，手持羽毛扇，头戴青丝制成的头巾。纶(guān)，青丝。

⑪〔樯橹(qiánglǔ)〕此处指曹操水军。"樯橹"一作"强虏"，又作"樯虏"，又作"狂虏"。樯，挂帆的桅杆；橹，一种摇船的桨。

⑫〔故国神游〕"神游故国"的倒文，即想象中(我)游历古战场。

⑬〔多情应笑我〕"应笑我多情"的倒文。多情，多愁善感。

⑭〔华发(fà)〕白发。

⑮〔一樽还酹江月〕樽，酒杯。还(huán)，一说同"环"，往返，回环；或退身，返回。酹(lèi)，古人以酒浇于地上以示祭奠之意。这里指来回地洒酒，祭酒酬月，以寄托诗人怀才不遇怅然若失的感情。

白话释义

　　滚滚东流的长江水，淘尽了千古风流的人物。在那古战场的西边，据说是三国周瑜破曹军的赤壁。散乱而陡峭的山崖插入云霄，惊涛骇浪猛烈地拍打着江岸，卷起的浪花仿佛冬日的积雪。江山壮美如画，一时间涌出了多少英雄豪杰。

　　遥想当年的周公瑾，小乔刚刚嫁他为妻，英姿卓绝风度翩翩。手中执着羽扇，头上戴着纶巾，从容潇洒说笑闲谈之间，曹操水军顷刻间化为灰烬。如今我身临古战场神游往昔，可笑我有如此多愁善感，竟未老先衰鬓生白发。人生如梦，还是举起酒杯奠祭这万古的明月吧。

主题鉴赏

　　宋神宗元丰五年，时年四十七岁的苏轼因"乌台诗案"被贬黄州，并谪居于此两年有余。苏轼由于诗文讽喻新法，为新派官僚罗织论罪而被贬，心中郁郁不得志却无从诉说，于是四处游山玩水以舒缓压抑的情绪。一日，他正巧来到黄州城外的赤鼻矶，此处壮丽的风景使他感慨万千，在追忆三国将领周瑜潇洒从容地指挥战役并大获全胜的同时,慨叹时光易逝,表达了现实中壮志未酬的思绪。

《念奴娇·赤壁怀古》分上下两阕。上阕着墨于自然风景,意境开阔博大,笔锋洒脱不羁。开篇从滚滚长江磅礴气势着笔,接着"浪淘尽"将浩荡奔涌的江流和名垂千古的历史名人巧妙联系在一起,既使人看到壮阔奔腾的自然景观,又使人联想到曾经风华绝代的英雄人物。同时,苏轼亦感慨千古风流人物在历史长河中也会浮浮沉沉,个人一时的荣辱得失与之相比实在是微不足道。接着,"故垒"两句切入怀古主题,点出此地是传说中三国战场。"人道是"三字表明他其实对于此地是否是赤壁战场心存疑虑。苏轼写词之时,距离赤壁之战已经相距八百七十多年。此地是否是当年的古战场存在很大争议。湖北省境内共有四处地名同称赤壁,苏轼所到之处是黄冈赤壁,他并不能确定这就是当时的赤壁战场,所以"人道是"用得极有分寸(唐圭璋,1987),也和"怀古"的主题相呼应。"三国周郎赤壁"将年代、人物、地点交织在一起,向读者展现出一幅跨越时空的历史画卷。

"乱石"三句转而描写景物。"乱""穿""惊""拍""卷"等词语的运用,生动形象地勾画出赤壁雄奇壮观的景色,从陡峭的乱崖到汹涌的江水,再到拍打着江岸的雪浪,从不同的角度将视觉和声觉相糅合,将读者带入一个令人惊心动魄,精神为之振奋的恢宏场景之中。写景的这三句可谓激越昂扬,荡气回肠。上阕最后一句"江山如画,一时多少豪杰"是对上面壮阔山河景色的总括,同时又承接了从写景到写人物的转变,将"江山"与"豪杰"交织在一起,让读者在感怀壮美江山的同时,又对历史长河中无数英雄人物肃然起敬。

下阕着墨于"怀古",重点写历史人物,灵动逼真地刻画出周瑜潇洒从容的人物形象。"遥想"一词引领读者穿越了时空,将思绪带回到三国时期,仿佛见到了当年风华正茂、风度翩翩的周瑜周公瑾。在深入刻画周瑜的人物形象之前,插入"小乔出嫁了"这个生活细节,以小乔之娇美衬托周瑜之意气风发,年轻有为。"羽扇纶巾"描写出周瑜儒雅的仪容装束,衬托出他作为重大战役的指挥官临战时的那种从容潇洒、胸有成竹、胜券在握的风姿。"谈笑间,樯橹灰飞烟灭"的战争场面描写,突出了火攻水战的特点,寥寥数语,让读者看到了激烈宏大的战争场面。在滚滚奔流的大江上,周瑜沉稳不凡,谈笑自若,指挥东吴水军将不可一世的曹军一举击溃,万艘舳舻顷刻化为灰烬,如此气势是何等壮阔恢宏。"故国神游,多情应笑我,早生华发"这一句又将读者从三国时期带回了词人所在的现实。对历史人物和事件的回顾,引发了词人的无限感慨。"多情"是一种自嘲的表达,嘲笑自己的自作多情,因而难免长出了这许多花白的头发。

这种情绪和苏轼当时的经历不无关系。苏轼时年四十七岁,因"乌台诗案"被贬,谪居黄州已两年。在感怀周瑜年轻有为的同时,词人联想到自己空有报国之志

第六章 宋词（豪放派）英译鉴赏实践

却仕途坎坷,满腔热忱却无用武之地,于被贬之地不免怀古伤己,自叹自怨,与周瑜年少有为的典事形成鲜明的对照。"人生如梦,一樽还酹江月"是全词的收尾,是理想与现实的冲突在词人心理上的反映,既有感情上的起伏,也道出了词人面对现实的豁达。人生如梦,不必让消极的思绪萦绕于心。这滔滔江水犹如时间洪流,千古英雄人物都在时间长河中成为历史,更何况是自己呢？不如斟上美酒,祭奠这江上照耀古今的明月！

学生英译实践园地

英译实践版本选读

译文 1 肯尼斯·雷克斯洛斯

The Red Cliff

The River flows to the East.
Its waves have washed away all
the heroes of history.
To the West of the ancient
Wall you enter the Red Gorge
Of Chu Ko Liang of the
Days of the Three Kingdoms. The
Jagged peaks pierce the heavens.
The furious rapids beat
At the boat, and dash up in
A thousand clouds of spray like
Snow. Mountain and river have
Often been painted, in the
Memory of the heroes
Of those days. I remember
Long ago, Kung Ch'in newly
Married to the beautiful
Chiao-siao, shining in splendor,
A young warrior, and the other
Chu Ko Liang, in his blue cap,
Waving his horsetail duster,
Smiling and chatting as he
Burned the navy of Ts'ao Ts'ao.
Their ashes were scattered to
The four winds. They vanished away
In smoke. I like to dream of
Those dead kingdoms. Let people

第六章 宋词（豪放派）英译鉴赏实践

Laugh at my prematurely
Grey hair. My answer is
A wine cup, full of the
Moon drowned in the River.

译文 2　许渊冲

Tune: "Charm of a Maiden Singer"
Memories of the Past at Red Cliff

The Great River eastward flows,
With its waves are gone all those
Gallant heroes of bygone years.
West of the ancient fortress appears
Red Cliff Where General Zhou won his early fame
When the Three Kingdoms were all in flame.
Jagged rocks tower in the air,
Swashing waves beat on the shore,
Rolling up a thousand heaps of snow.
To match the hills and the river so fair,
How many heroes brave of yore
Made a great show!

I fancy General Zhou at the height
Of his success, with a plume fan in hand,
In a silk hood, so brave and bright,
Laughing and jesting with his bride so fair,
While enemy ships were destroyed as planned
Like shadowy castles in the air.
Should their souls revisit this land,
Sentimental, his wife would laugh to say,
Younger than they, I have my hair all turned gray.
Life is but like a passing dream,
I'd drink to the moon which once saw them on the stream.

译文 3　杨宪益　戴乃迭

Nian Nu Jiao
Memories of the Past at Red Cliff

East flows the mighty river,
Sweeping away the heroes of times past;
This ancient rampart on its western shore
Is Zhou Yu's Red Cliff of Three Kingdoms's fame;
Here jagged boulders pound the clouds,
Huge waves tear banks apart,
And foam piles up a thousand drifts of snow;
A scene fair as a painting,
Countless the brave men here in time gone by!

I dream of Marshal Zhou Yu in his day
With his new bride, the Lord Qiao's younger daughter,
Dashing and debonair,
Silk-capped, with feather fan,
He laughed and jested
While the dread enemy fleet was burned to ashes!
In fancy through those scenes of old I range,
My heart overflowing, surely a figure of fun.
A man grey before his time.
Ah, this life is a dream,
Let me drink to the moon on the river!

译文 4　张畅繁

Reflecting on the Red Cliff

Great river flows eastward.
Its waves have washed away all elegant
Men and heroes of past generations.

第六章　宋词（豪放派）英译鉴赏实践

West of the old fortress is said to be Zhou Yu's
Red Cliff at the Epoch of the Three Kingdoms.
Raveled rocks break through the clouds;
Billows smite the shore.
A thousand heaps of snow breaks off.
So picturesque are the rivers and mountains.
So many great men and heroes emerged.

I fancy at the time when Zhou was married to
Xiao Qiao, his young bride.
With a feather fan in his hand, and
a silken scarf on his head, he watched,
in between laughter and chats,
all enemy ships were destroyed in smoke and fire.

If they could revisit this land in spirit,
his passionate companion would have teased
me for being young and gray.
Life is like a dream.
Let me pour a bottle of wine
and salute the river moon bright.

宋词（豪放派）英译鉴赏实践之三

江城子① · 密州②出猎

苏　轼

老夫③聊发④少年狂⑤，
左牵黄，
右擎苍⑥，

锦帽貂裘⑦，
千骑卷平冈⑧。
为报倾城随太守⑨，
亲射虎⑩，
看孙郎⑪。

酒酣胸胆尚开张⑫。
鬓微霜⑬，
又何妨⑭！
持节云中⑮，
何日遣冯唐⑯？
会挽雕弓如满月⑰，
西北望⑱，射天狼⑲。

【注释】

① 〔江城子〕词牌名。又名"村意远""江神子""水晶帘"。兴起于晚唐，来源于唐著词（即酒令）曲调，由文人韦庄最早依调创作，此后所作均为单调，直至苏轼时始变单调为双调。有单调四体，字数有三十五、三十六、三十七三种；双调一体，七十字，上下阕各七句，格律多为平韵格，双调体偶有填仄韵者。代表作除这首《江城子·密州出猎》外，还有苏轼的《江城子·乙卯正月二十日夜记梦》（十年生死两茫茫）、《江城子·别徐州》（天涯流落思无穷）等。
② 〔密州〕今山东诸城，苏轼于宋神宗熙宁八年在此地任知州（太守）。
③ 〔老夫〕作者自称，时年大概四十。
④ 〔聊发〕聊，姑且，暂且。发（fā），抒发，表达。
⑤ 〔少年狂〕少年的壮志豪情。
⑥ 〔左牵黄，右擎苍〕黄，黄犬。苍，苍鹰。此句即左手牵着黄犬，右臂擎着苍鹰，形容围猎时用以追捕猎物的架势。
⑦ 〔锦帽貂裘〕名词作动词使用，头戴着华美鲜艳的帽子。貂裘，身穿貂鼠皮衣。此处描写的是汉羽林军穿的服装。

第六章 宋词（豪放派）英译鉴赏实践

⑧〔千骑卷平冈〕千骑，形容随从乘骑之多。平冈指山脊平坦处。此处形容狩猎的人马众多，所经之处尘土飞扬，掠过山脊的平缓处。

⑨〔为报〕为了报答，表示感谢。〔倾城〕全城的人都出来了，形容随观者之众。〔太守〕指作者自己。

⑩〔亲射虎〕我一定要（像孙权一样）亲自射杀老虎给大家看看。

⑪〔看孙郎〕孙郎，三国时期东吴的孙权。《三国志·吴志·孙权传》载："权将如吴，亲乘马射虎于凌亭，马为虎伤。权投以双戟，虎却废。"这里词人借孙权以自喻。

⑫〔酒酣〕极兴畅饮。〔胸胆〕胸怀和胆气。〔尚〕更。〔开张〕开阔，意即胸怀开阔，胆气豪涨。

⑬〔鬓微霜〕双鬓已开始长出白发。

⑭〔又何妨〕又能如何，有何关系。

⑮〔节〕兵符，传达命令的符节。持节，带着符节去承奉朝廷委派的重大使命。〔云中〕汉时郡名，今内蒙古自治区托克托县一带，包括山西省西北一部分地区。

⑯〔何日遣冯唐〕朝廷何日派遣冯唐去云中郡赦免魏尚的罪呢？典出《史记·冯唐列传》。汉文帝时，魏尚为云中太守。他爱惜士卒，优待军吏，匈奴远避。匈奴曾一度来犯，魏尚亲率车骑出击，所杀甚众。后因报功文书上所载杀敌的数字与实际不合，被削职。经冯唐代为辩白后，文帝认为判得过重，就派冯唐带着符节去赦免魏尚的罪，让魏尚仍然担任云中郡太守。苏轼此时任密州太守，故以魏尚自许，希望能得到朝廷的信任。

⑰〔挽〕拉。〔雕弓〕弓背上有雕花的弓。〔满月〕圆月。

⑰〔西北望〕即望西北，朝着侵犯者的方向。

⑲〔天狼〕星名，又称犬星。《楚辞·九歌·东君》："长矢兮射天狼。"《晋书·天文志》云："狼一星在东井南，为野将，主侵掠。"词中以之隐喻侵犯北宋边境的辽国与西夏。

白话释义

我也来抒发抒发少年志狂放，
左手牵着黄犬，右臂托起苍鹰，
华美的帽子戴头上，貂鼠皮衣披身上，
狩猎的人马欢腾，奔向平缓的山冈。
为了感谢全城老少随我出猎忙，
我要像孙权一样，亲自射杀猛虎。

美酒酣畅，心胸旷达，胆气豪壮，
虽然两鬓花白，又有何妨？
何时朝廷发赦命，
就像汉文帝派遣冯唐去云中赦免魏尚一样？
那时我将奋力拉弓，就像满月一样，
朝向西北方，歼灭"西北狼"。

主题鉴赏

这首词作于宋神宗熙宁八年苏轼任密州（今山东诸城）知州时，是一首抒发诗人爱国情怀的豪放诗篇，在题材和意境方面都具有开拓意义。词的上阕叙事，下阕抒情，气势雄豪，淋漓酣畅，读之令人耳目一新。首三句直出会猎题意，次写围猎时的装束和盛况，然后转写自己的感想：决心亲自射杀猛虎，答谢全城军民的深情厚谊。下阕叙述猎后开怀畅饮，并以魏尚自比，希望能够承担起卫国守边的重任。结尾直抒胸臆，抒发杀敌报国的豪情：总有一天，要把弓弦拉得像满月一样，射掉那贪残成性的"天狼星"，将西北边境上的敌人一扫而光。这首词在偎红倚翠、浅斟低唱之风盛行的北宋词坛可谓别具一格，自成一体，对南宋爱国词有直接而深刻的影响。

苏轼因此词有别于"柳七郎（柳永）风味"而颇为得意。他曾在《与鲜于子骏书》中自夸道："近却颇作小词，虽无柳七郎风味，亦自是一家。……数日前猎于郊外，所获颇多，作得一阕，令东州壮士抵掌顿足而歌之，吹笛击鼓以为节，颇壮观也。"

上阕主要描写"出猎"这一特殊场合下表现出来的词人举止神态之"狂"（豪放），词一开篇，"老夫聊发少年狂"，出手不凡，一个"狂"字统领全篇格局，借以抒写胸中雄健豪放的一腔磊落之气。接下去的四句写出猎的雄壮场面，表现了出猎者威武豪迈的气概：词人左手牵着黄犬，右臂擎举苍鹰，头上戴着锦缎织成的帽子，身上穿着貂皮做成的大衣，英气威武。出猎队伍，奔驰平冈，后面是倾城而出的观战百姓，这是怎样的一幅声势浩大的行猎图啊，作者倍受鼓舞，气冲斗牛，为了报答百姓随行出猎的厚意，决心亲自射杀老虎，让大家看看孙权当年搏虎的雄姿。作者以少年英主孙权自比，更是显出自身的"狂"劲和豪情。

下阕由实而虚："酒酣胸胆尚开张，鬓微霜，又何妨。"前三句是说，我痛饮美酒，心胸开阔，胆气更为豪壮，虽然两鬓微微发白，但这又何妨？东坡为人本来就豪放不羁，再加上酒酣，就更加豪情洋溢了。

第六章　宋词（豪放派）英译鉴赏实践

"持节云中，何日遣冯唐？"这两句是说，什么时候皇帝会派人下来，就像汉文帝派遣冯唐去云中赦免魏尚的罪名（一样信任我）呢？此时东坡才四十岁，因反对王安石新法，自请外任。此时西北边事紧张，熙宁三年，西夏大举进军环、庆二州，四年占抚宁诸城。东坡因这次打猎，小试身手，进而便想带兵征讨西夏了。汉文帝时云中太守魏尚抗击匈奴有功，但因报功不实，获罪削职。后来文帝听了冯唐的话，派冯唐持节去赦免魏尚，仍叫他当云中太守。这是东坡借以表示希望北宋朝廷委以边任，到边疆抗敌。一个文人要求带兵打仗，并不奇怪，唐代诗人多有此志。

"会挽雕弓如满月，西北望，射天狼。"末三句是说，我将使尽力气拉满雕弓如满月一样，朝着西北瞄望，射向西夏军队。词人最后为自己勾勒了一个挽弓劲射的英雄形象，英武豪迈，气概非凡。

此作是千古传诵的东坡豪放词代表作之一。词中写出猎之行，抒兴国安邦之志，拓展了词境，提高了词品，扩大了词的题材范围，为词的创作开创了崭新的道路。后又作出利箭射向敌人这种出人意料的结局，利用巧妙的艺术构思，把记叙出猎的笔锋一转，自然地表现出了作者志在杀敌卫国的政治热情和英雄气概。作品融叙事、言志、用典为一体，调动各种艺术手段形成豪放风格，多角度、多层次地从行动和心理上表现了作者宝刀未老、志在千里的英风与豪气。

学生英译实践园地

第六章 宋词（豪放派）英译鉴赏实践

英译实践版本选读

译文 1　宇文所安

Jiangchengzi

Lyric on Hunting

For a while this old fellow broke into the wildness of youth.
On my left I lead a yellow dog.
On my right, a gray hawk on the arm.
Brocade cap and sable furs,
a thousand riders roll over the level hill.
To repay the whole city
for following their governor,
they can watch a Sun Quan shoot a tiger himself?
Tipsy from drink, my sense of daring still expanded.
The hair at my temples was a little frosty.
But what did that matter?
When will they dis-patch this Feng Tang to take the
seal of authority to YunZhong?
I will surely bend the carved buw to the shape of the full moon,
and gazing northwest,
Shoot the Heaven Wolf.

译文 2　许渊冲

Tune: "A Riverside Town"

Hunting at Mizhou

(1075)

Rejuvenated, I my fiery zeal display,
On left hand leash, a yellow hound,
On right hand wrist, a falcon gray.
A thousand silk-capped and sable-coated horsemen sweep

Across the rising ground
And hillocks steep.
Townspeople pour out of the city gate
To watch the tiger-hunting magistrate.

Heart gladdened with strong wine, who cares
About a few frosted hairs?
When will the court imperial send
Me as envoy with flags and banners? Then I'll bend
My bow like a full moon, and aiming northwest, I
Will shoot down the fierce Wolf from the sky.

译文3 佚名

This old man is wild with adolescent bravado,
A leashed brown dog in the left hand,
And an eagle perched on the right.
Fitted out with brocade headgears and fur,
A legion of a thousand horses sweeping over rolling plains.
Get the whole city out in the wake of Gov'nor
To watch him shoot tigers,
A young Sun Lang.

Flushed with wine and chest bared in an expansive mood,
What does it matter
If only a little sideburn frost!
The imperial fiat at Yunzhong,
When would it be dispatched by my Feng Tang?
And I would draw the sculpted bow to a full moon,
With a northwest gaze,
To shoot the Celestial Wolf.
So, I want to follow our country.

第六章 宋词（豪放派）英译鉴赏实践

宋词（豪放派）英译鉴赏实践之四

定风波①·三月七日
苏 轼

三月七日，沙湖②道中遇雨。雨具先去，同行皆狼狈③，余独不觉。已而遂晴④，故作此。

莫听穿林打叶声⑤，
何妨吟啸且徐行⑥。
竹杖芒鞋轻胜马⑦，谁怕？
一蓑烟雨任平生⑧。

料峭⑨春风吹酒醒，微冷，
山头斜照⑩却相迎。
回首向来萧瑟处⑪，归去，
也无风雨也无晴⑫。

【注释】

①〔定风波〕词牌名。又名"卷春空""定风波令"等。双调六十二字，前段五句三平韵两仄韵，后段六句四仄韵两平韵。
②〔沙湖〕在今湖北黄冈东南三十里，又名螺丝店。
③〔狼狈〕因未带雨具而进退两难的困顿窘迫状。
④〔已而遂晴〕已（yǐ）而，不一会儿。过了一会儿天气就放晴。
⑤〔莫听〕不必在意。
⑥〔吟啸〕放声吟咏。〔徐行〕慢步而行。
⑦〔竹杖〕竹子做的手杖。〔芒鞋〕草鞋。

⑧〔一蓑(suō)〕蓑衣，用棕制成的雨披。〔一蓑烟雨任平生〕披着蓑衣在风雨里过一辈子也能泰然处之。
⑨〔料峭(liào qiào)〕微寒的样子。
⑩〔斜照〕偏西的阳光。
⑪〔向来〕方才。〔萧瑟〕风雨吹打树叶声。
⑫〔也无风雨也无晴〕意谓既不怕雨，也不喜晴。

白话释义

三月七日，在沙湖道上赶上了下雨，
拿着雨具的随从先已离开，
同行者进退两难，而我觉得挺好。
不一会儿天晴了，于是我写下这首词。

不必在意风吹雨打树叶响，
不妨放声吟唱从容慢行。
拄竹杖穿草鞋远比骑马更轻松，
也没什么好担心？
身披蓑衣随意自然度平生。

春风微寒，酒意全无，
身上感到微微冷，
仰头望山上有斜阳，
回想来时风雨路，
俱往矣，无论刮风或下雨。

主题鉴赏

《定风波·莫听穿林打叶声》是苏轼创作的一首风格比较婉约但思想豪放的记事抒怀之作，创作于宋神宗元丰五年春。当时苏轼因"乌台诗案"被贬黄州的第三个春天。苏轼与朋友相邀春日出游，恰逢风雨忽至，朋友深感狼狈，进退两难，唯有苏轼毫不在乎，泰然处之，吟咏自若，缓步而行，可谓宋词中写景寓情、抒怀状物的

第六章 宋词(豪放派)英译鉴赏实践

一篇绝好作品。

此词通过野外途中偶遇风雨这一生活中的小事,于简朴中见深意,于寻常处生奇景,表现出旷达超脱的胸襟,寄寓着超凡脱俗的人生理想。上阕着眼于雨中,下阕着眼于雨后,全词体现出一个正直文人在坎坷人生中力求解脱之道,篇幅虽短,但意境深邃,内蕴丰富,诠释着词人的人生信念,展现着词人的精神追求。

上阕首句"莫听穿林打叶声",一方面渲染出雨骤风狂,另一方面又以"莫听"二字点明外物不足萦怀之意。"何妨吟啸且徐行",是前一句的延伸。在雨中照常舒徐行步,呼应小序"同行皆狼狈,余独不觉",又引出下文"谁怕"即不怕来。"徐行"而又"吟啸",是加倍写;"何妨"二字透出一点俏皮,更增加挑战色彩。首两句是全篇枢纽,以下词情都是由此生发。

"竹杖芒鞋轻胜马",写词人手拄竹杖脚穿草鞋,迎着风雨,从容前行,以"轻胜马"的自我感受,传达出一种搏击风雨、笑傲人生的轻松喜悦和豪迈之情。"一蓑烟雨任平生",此句更进一步,由眼前风雨推及整个人生,有力地强化了词人面对人生的风风雨雨而我行我素、不畏坎坷的超然情怀。

以上数句,表现出旷达超逸的胸襟,充满清旷豪放之气,寄寓着独到的人生感悟,读来使人耳目为之一新,心胸为之舒阔。

下阕"料峭春风吹酒醒,微冷",饮酒忘忧、借酒消愁已成为苏轼在黄州时期的一种精神寄托,也是他逃避政治旋涡不得已而为之的嗜好。酒不醉人人自醉,酒醒奈何皆风雨,这位得不到赏识和重用的才子,无法找到政治上的人生定位和精神满足,似乎只能从平淡的生活里寻找些许慰藉。"山头斜照却相迎"三句,表面是写雨过天晴的自然景象,但实际也是诗人抒发情不得已、志气难酬的内心活动:既然得不到重用,那何不迎着傍晚的斜阳感受一下雨后的温暖。这几句既与上阕所写风雨对应,又为下文抒发人生感慨做好铺垫。

尾句"回首向来萧瑟处,归去,也无风雨也无晴"成为千古名句。这饱含人生哲理意味的点睛之笔,道出了词人在大自然微妙的一瞬所获得的顿悟和启示:自然界的雨晴既属寻常,毫无差别,朝堂上的政治风云、荣辱得失又何足挂齿?句中"萧瑟"二字,意谓风雨之声,与上阕"穿林打叶声"相和。"风雨"二字,一语双关,既指野外途中所遇风雨,又暗指几乎置他于死地的政治"风雨"和人生险途。

晚清词评家郑文焯说:"此足征是翁坦荡之怀,任天而动。琢句亦瘦逸,能道眼前景,以曲笔写胸臆,倚声能事尽之矣"(《手批东坡乐府》)。

学生英译实践园地

第六章 宋词(豪放派)英译鉴赏实践

英译实践版本选读

译文1　许渊冲

Calming the Waves
Caught in Rain on My Way to the Sandy Lake

On the 7th day of the 3rd month we were caught in rain
on our way to the Sandy Lake.
The umbrellas had gone ahead, my companions were quite downhearted,
but I took no notice. It soon cleared, and I wrote this.

Listen not to the rain beating against the trees.
I had better walk slowly while chanting at ease.
Better than a saddle I like sandals and cane.
I'd fain,
In a straw cloak, spend my life in mist and rain.

Drunken, I am sobered by the vernal wind shrill
And rather chill.
In front, I see the slanting sun atop the hill;
Turning my head, I see the dreary beaten track.
Let me go back!
Impervious to rain or shine, I'll have my own will.

译文2　杨宪益　戴乃迭

Ding Feng Bo

On the seventh day of the third month we were
caught in the rain on our way to shahu.
The umbrellas had gone already,
my companions were downhearted, but I took no notice.

It soon cleared, and I wrote this.

Forget that patter of rain on the forest leaves,
Why not chant a poem as we plod slowly on?
Pleasanter than a saddle this bamboo staff and straw sandals.
Here's nothing to fear.
I could spend my whole life in the mist and rain.

The keen spring wind has sobered me,
Left me chilly,
But slanting sunlight beckons from high on the hill;
One last look at scene behind
And on I go,
Impervious to wind, rain or sunny weather.

译文 3　卓振英

Taming the Waves and Winds

On 7th of the third moon, I was caught in rain on my way to Sandy Lake. As the rain-gear had been sent to the place in advance, all the company felt awkward except me. I composed this ci-poem when the rain stopped.

What matters if on the woods and leaves splatters th' rain?
I may well recite poems while pacing on the cane
And in sandals, which than horse back make me more eas'd.
Howe'er could one with dread be seiz'd,
Who's known in th' eventful life rain and wind and pain?

I feel the chill when th' breezes sober me from wine,
But then a soothing sun atop the hill does shine.
I glance back at the place that I am to return:
There's th' seclusion for which I yearn:
'Tis secure and quiet, be th' weather rough or fine!

第六章 宋词（豪放派）英译鉴赏实践

译文 4　赵彦春

Be Still

Don't listen if a rain does the leaves sway;
You'd better walk lightly singing a lay.
Sandals outdo saddles, cane as your aid,
Who's afraid?
A cape against mist and rain, come what may.

A spring wind blows me sober, blows away.
A chill day.
The sun uphill slants to me with a ray,
I turn around and feel a gentle sough,
Go back now.
No wind, no rain, nor shining light to stay.

宋词（豪放派）英译鉴赏实践之五

南乡子①·登京口北固亭有怀②

辛弃疾

何处望神州③？
满眼风光北固楼。
千古兴亡多少事④？悠悠⑤。
不尽长江滚滚流⑥。

年少万兜鍪⑦，
坐断东南战未休⑧。
天下英雄谁敌手⑨？曹刘⑩。
生子当如孙仲谋⑪。

【注释】

①〔南乡子〕词牌名,又名"好离乡""蕉叶怨",原为唐教坊曲名。原为单调,始自五代十国后蜀词人欧阳炯,直至南唐冯延巳(903—960)始增为双调。以欧阳炯《南乡子·画舸停桡》为正体:"画舸停桡,槿花篱外竹横桥。水上游人沙上女。回顾,笑指芭蕉林里住。"单调,二十七字,五句两平韵、三仄韵。单调有二十八字、三十字等变体,平仄换韵。双调有五十四、五十六、五十八字等变体。南乡子定格为双调五十六字,上下片各四平韵,一韵到底。代表作有冯延巳《南乡子·细雨湿流光》、辛弃疾《南乡子·登京口北固亭有怀》等。

②〔京口〕京口为江苏镇江古称。缘起于汉代京口里,东吴孙权称霸江东,设为京口镇。晋时置晋陵郡,南朝宋置南徐州,隋置润州,宋升润州为镇江府,并一直沿用至今。北固亭位于镇江东北方固山上,下临长江,三面环水,自古为江防战略要地。

③〔神州〕神州是中国汉地九州的代称,在概念和含义上,趋近于"华夏""中华""九州"等地理概念。此代指中原地区。

④〔千古兴亡多少事〕指国家兴衰,朝代更迭。

⑤〔悠悠〕连绵不尽的样子,一语双关,既指时间的久远,也指词人思绪万千。

⑥〔不尽长江滚滚流〕似化用杜甫《登高》一诗的尾联"不尽长江滚滚来",抒发了词人对古往今来国家兴衰变化无常的无限感慨。

⑦〔年少万兜鍪〕此指千军万马。〔年少〕年轻。此指孙权十九岁继父兄之业统治江东。〔兜鍪(dōu móu)〕古代士兵作战用的头盔,秦汉以前称胄,后称为兜鍪。种类多以形象设定,有虎头兜鍪、凤翅兜鍪、狻猊(suān ní,中国古代神话中的神兽,也是"龙生九子"中的第五子,形似狮子)兜鍪等。

⑧〔坐断〕坐镇,占据,割据。〔东南〕三国时吴国地处中国东南方。〔休〕停止。

⑨〔天下英雄谁敌手〕天下英雄谁是与孙权旗鼓相当的敌手呢?

⑩〔曹刘〕指曹操、刘备。

⑪〔生子当如孙仲谋〕孙权,字仲谋,吴郡富春(今浙江杭州富阳区)人,三国时期东吴的建立者。《三国志·吴主(孙权)传》记载:曹操尝试与孙权对垒,"见舟船、器杖、队伍整肃,叹曰:'生子当如孙仲谋,刘景升(即刘表,字景升)儿子若豚犬(猪狗)耳。'"东汉末年宗室刘表据地千里,称雄于荆州,为荆州牧。刘表卒,其次子刘琮承继刘表官爵。曹操进军襄阳时,刘琮不战请降,被曹操封为青州刺史。词

第六章 宋词（豪放派）英译鉴赏实践

人以此典故来暗讽当今的（宋）朝廷比不上能与曹操刘备抗衡的东吴，今天的皇帝也不如孙权。

白话释义

中原大地，风光旖旎，而今又在何处？登临北固楼，千里江山风光无限。从古到今，有多少王朝兴衰更迭，此起彼伏？谁能说清道明。唯有长江流水，滚滚向东。

遥想当年，孙权年少有为，指挥千军万马，占据东南，抗敌无休。天下英雄，谁能与孙权争雄？唯有曹操和刘备。即使曹操都说："生儿子就要像孙仲谋。"

主题鉴赏

提起宋词中堪称"大气"或"格局非凡"者，莫过于山东的"济南二安"：有"婉约词宗"之称的李清照（号"易安居士"）和被称为"词中之龙"的辛弃疾（字"幼安"），可谓南宋词人中最具忧国伤怀情结的代表性人物。

传统以为"婉约者"，多儿女情长呢喃燕语之作，但实际上，李清照虽为女流却同样心怀家国，情笃故土：

窗前谁种芭蕉树，阴满中庭。阴满中庭。叶叶心心，舒卷有余情。

伤心枕上三更雨，点滴霖霪。点滴霖霪。愁损北人，不惯起来听。

（《添字丑奴儿·窗前谁种芭蕉树》）

"愁损北人，不惯起来听"之句，字表借北人听不惯南国雨打芭蕉之声的含蓄，巧妙却深刻地勾起北人离乡背井之苦，的确是神来之笔。虽是女词人惯用的凄婉悱恻之笔调，却道尽了壮士般慷慨难平之绪，格调非同一般。

相比之下，"表故国深情，思旧土之念，抒亡国之痛，盼家国统一"的主题在"提笔能文，拔剑能武"的辛弃疾笔下，却是另一种气质。《南乡子·登京口北固亭有怀》即是辛氏爱国词作中最上乘之作，也是其暮年离世前不久的作品之一。

南宋宋孝宗淳熙八年，时年 42 岁的辛弃疾被弹劾免职，开始了长达 20 余年的赋闲生涯，其间虽曾两度赴外就职，但大部分时间都退隐于江西上饶铅山的乡村牧野，宝剑尘封，烈士伏枥，壮心难酬。南宋宋宁宗嘉泰三年六月，64 岁的辛弃疾终于等到了南宋朝廷的新任诏书，被任命为绍兴知府兼浙东安抚使。上任后，他立即招兵买马，收集情报，认真仔细地为作战做准备。在备战的过程中，辛弃疾发现南宋朝廷并不是真正的信任倚重他，而是利用辛弃疾在金国的名气高位，为北伐装点门面而已。第二年三月，朝廷又改派他为江苏镇江知府。镇江在历史上曾是英雄用武和建功立业之地,此时成了与金人对垒的第二道防线。每当他登临京口(即镇江)的北固亭时,遥望处于金人控制之下的中原大地,不禁感慨万千,英雄迟暮,壮志未酬,胸中块垒无处倾诉!这首词就是在这一背景下写成的。这首词委婉地表达了词人对于朝廷的不满,同时也倾吐了自己满腔爱国豪情却无处发挥的怅惘和无奈。

"何处望神州?满眼风光北固楼。"极目远眺,中原故土遥不可及,哪里能够看到?映入眼帘的只有北固楼周遭一片美好的风光了!此时南宋与金以淮河为界,辛弃疾站在长江之滨的北固楼上,翘首遥望江北金兵占领之处,固然中原山川景色秀丽如此,却落入金人之手。开首一问:"何处望神州?"不啻为棒喝之声,不仅质问自己,更是质问当朝皇帝、满朝官员,还有天下之人。

再看这眼前的北固楼,风物依旧迷人。那些消失在历史长河深处的英雄们,是否还记得曾在这里叱咤风云,立下帝国霸业,都已化作烟尘:"千古江山,英雄无觅,孙仲谋处。舞榭歌台,风流总被,雨打风吹去"(辛弃疾《永遇乐·京口北固亭怀古》)。词人接下来再问:"千古兴亡多少事?"世人们可知道,千百年来在这块土地上经历了多少朝代的兴亡更替?这句疑问展现出辛弃疾高远的历史观:兴亡成败,起伏更迭,无有定数,一切都会成为过往。"悠悠。不尽长江滚滚流。""悠悠"者,兼指时间之漫长久远和词人的心绪万千。"不尽长江滚滚流",似借用杜甫《登高》诗句:"无边落木萧萧下,不尽长江滚滚来。"千古多少兴亡事,逝者如斯乎?而词人胸中意绪难抑的不尽愁思和感慨,又何尝不似这长流不息的大江之水呢!"大江东去,浪淘尽、千古风流人物(苏轼《念奴娇·赤壁怀古》)",想当年,在这江防战略要地,多少英雄"金戈铁马,气吞万里如虎(辛弃疾《永遇乐·京口北固亭怀古》)"。三国时代的孙权就是其中最杰出的一位。"年少万兜鍪,坐断东南战未休。"他年纪轻轻就统率千军万马,雄踞东南一隅,奋发自强,战斗不息,何等英雄气概!据历史记载:孙权十九岁继父兄之业统治江东,西征黄祖,北拒曹操,独据一方。赤壁之战大破曹兵,年方二十七岁。因此可以说,上面这两句是实写史事,因为它是千真万确的历史,因而更具有说服力和感染力。作者在这里一是突出了孙权的年少有为,"年少"而敢于与雄才大略、兵多将广的强敌曹操较量,这就需要非凡的胆识和气魄;二是突出了孙权的盖世武功,他不断征战,势力不断壮大,而他之"坐断东南",形势与南宋政权相似。显然,稼轩热情歌颂孙权的不畏强敌,坚决抵抗,并战而胜之,正是反衬当朝文武之辈的庸碌无能、怯懦苟安。

接下来,辛弃疾进一步渲染其英雄之气,不惜以夸张之笔极力渲染孙权不可一世的英姿。他异乎寻常地第三次发问,以提请人们注意:"天下英雄谁敌手?"若问天下英雄谁能与孙权一决高下?作者自问又自答曰:"曹刘",唯曹操与刘备耳!据

第六章 宋词（豪放派）英译鉴赏实践

《三国志·蜀书·先主传》记载，曹操曾对刘备说："今天下英雄，唯使君（刘备）与操耳。"辛弃疾便借用这段故事，把曹操和刘备请来给孙权当配角，说天下英雄只有曹操、刘备才堪与孙权争胜。

《三国志·吴主（孙权）传》中有记载，曹操有一次与孙权对垒，见吴军乘着战船，军容整肃，孙权仪表堂堂，威风凛凛，乃喟然叹曰："生子当如孙仲谋，刘景升（刘表）儿子若豚犬耳！"一世之雄如曹操，对敢于与自己抗衡的强者，投以敬佩的目光，而对于那种不战而请降的懦夫，若刘景升儿子刘琮则十分轻视，斥为任人宰割的猪狗。把大好江山拱手奉献敌人，还要为敌人耻笑辱骂，这不就是历史上所有屈膝乞和、缺乏骨气的人的可悲命运吗！

曹操所一褒一贬的两种人，形成了极其鲜明、强烈的对照，在南宋摇摇欲坠的政局中，不也有着主战与主和两种人吗？这当然不便明言，只好由读者自己去联想了。聪明的词人只做正面文章，对刘景升儿子这个反面角色，便不指名道姓以示众了。然而妙就妙在纵然作者不予道破，而又能使人感到不言而喻。因为上述曹操这段话众所周知，虽然辛弃疾只说了前一句赞语，人们马上就会联想起后面那句骂人的话，从而使人意识到辛弃疾的潜台词：可笑当朝主张议和的众多王公大臣，不都是刘景升儿子之类的猪狗吗！词人此种别开生面的表现手法，颇类似歇后语的作用，是十分巧妙的。而且，在写法上这一句与上两句意脉不断，衔接得很自然。上两句说，天下英雄中只有曹操、刘备配称孙权的对手。连曹操都这样说，生儿子要像孙权这个样呢！真是曲尽其妙，而又意在言外，令人拍案叫绝！再从"生子当如孙仲谋"这句话的蕴含和思想深度来说，南宋时代的人如此看重孙权，实是那个时代特有的社会心理的反映。因为南宋朝廷实在太萎靡庸碌了，在历史上，孙权能称雄江东于一时，而南宋历宋高宗赵构、宋孝宗赵昚、宋光宗赵敦、宋宁宗赵扩四朝皇帝，均为苟且怯懦之徒！所以，"生子当如孙仲谋"这句话，辛弃疾借曹操之语，表达了他希望朝廷能于危难时机任用贤能力挽狂澜的政治诉求，也代表南宋子民盼望君民同心、驱除鞑虏、拯救社稷的坚定意志和决心。

公元1205年，宋宁宗召集大臣开始秘密商讨北伐之事，辛弃疾盼望着能够作为前线将军亲自收复失地，但命运之神再次与他擦肩而过，朝廷并未重用他。这位满怀期待的老英雄满含遗憾与悲愤离开了。当时的绝望和寂寞可能只有辛弃疾自己知道。同年，辛弃疾再赋北固亭词——《永遇乐·京口北固亭怀古》，格调更为高远，情绪更为激昂，意绪更为不平。不过气宇轩昂的背后，却是英雄难为，无奈退场的绝望和呼喊：

千古江山，英雄无觅孙仲谋处。舞榭歌台，风流总被，雨打风吹去。斜阳草树，寻常巷陌，人道寄奴曾住。想当年，金戈铁马，气吞万里如虎。

元嘉草草,封狼居胥,赢得仓皇北顾。四十三年,望中犹记,烽火扬州路。可堪回首,佛狸祠下,一片神鸦社鼓。凭谁问,廉颇老矣,尚能饭否?

两年后,1207年的秋天,当南宋朝廷再次想起辛弃疾时,他已病入膏肓,不久后便与世长辞,享年68岁。最终,他带着无尽的遗憾走了,想了一生,也盼了一生。这位一生都在梦想着收复失地统一中华的英雄还是没有站在战场上,所以"廉颇老矣,尚能饭否?"既是对庸庸无为苟且偷生的当权者的诘问,也是词人虽已年老却仍心怀天下壮志未酬的扼腕之叹,读来不觉令人潸然泪下。拟古诗一首,以追缅稼轩先生的在天之灵:"故国北望路漫漫,英雄寂寞泪阑干。人生若是堪回首,铁马金戈捍江山。"

两首"北固亭",一样报国心,伤怀悼今,笔法不同,却格调相似,立意相同,均不失刚健有力之风骨,不落无病呻吟之窠臼。明代杨慎评价辛词说:"辛词当以京口北固亭怀古《永遇乐》为第一(《词品》)",若如此,《南乡子》该排在第几?

学生英译实践园地

第六章 宋词（豪放派）英译鉴赏实践

英译实践版本选读

译文 1　蔡宗齐

To the Tune of "South Village":
Meditation on the Past on the Beigu Pavilion

Where to look for the Divine State?
A boundless scene meets the eye
here in the Beigu Tower.
Of all the rise and fall since antiquity,
how many stories can be told?
Boundless and endless,
The unending Yangtze surges forward,
waves upon waves.

At a young age he commanded
an army of ten thousand helmets;
Occupying the Southeast
he never stopped fighting his enemies.
Of the great heroes in the world,
who were his adversaries?
Cao and Liu.
If one is to have a son,
he should be like Sun Zhongmou!

译文 2　许渊冲　许明

Song of the Southern Country
Thoughts of Mounting on the Northern Tower

Where is the Central Plain?
I gaze beyond the Northern Tower in vain.
It has seen dynasties fall and rise.

As time flies,
Or as the endless river rolls before my eyes.

While young, Sun had ten thousand men at his command;
Steeled in battles, he defended the southeastern land.
Among his equals in the world, who were heroes true,
But Cao and Liu?
And even Cao would have a son like Sun Zhongmou.

译文 3　赵彦春

Climbing North Firm Tower at Townmouth —
To the Tune of Southerner

No home, where can I cast my eyes?
On North Firm Tower one sees everything glow.
Since of yore, how many a fall and rise?
So broad, vast!
Without end, the Long River pours to flow.
The youth could a million command;
Southeast he sits while wars go on and on.
Of all heroes, who can wave a hard hand?
Cao and Liu.
One should have borne a Quan Sun, such a son.

译文 4　秦大川

Reflections at the Beigulou Tower, Jingkou
(to the tune of Nan Xiang Zi)

Where to look out to the Divine Land's views,
At Beigulou Tower, eye-feasting sights one beholds.
How many dynasties were there that rose and fell?
Long long ago.
The Great River is surging with unending flow.

第六章 宋词（豪放派）英译鉴赏实践

When young, with ten thousand strong to hold,
He commanded in the Southeast, fought battles times untold.
Who could be his rivals that were deemed great heroes?
　　Cao and Liu.
"O, one should have his sons like Sun Zhongmou!"

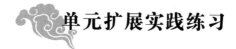

单元扩展实践练习

一、请翻译陆游的《诉衷情》，并在课堂上分享你的翻译过程和感想。

诉衷情

陆游

当年万里觅封侯①，
匹马戍梁州②。
关河③梦断④何处？
尘暗旧貂裘⑤。
胡⑥未灭，
鬓先秋⑦，
泪空流。
此生谁料，
心在天山⑧，
身老沧州⑨。

【注释】

①〔万里觅封侯〕奔赴万里外的疆场寻找机会建功立业。
②〔梁州〕古九州之一，指华阳一带。具体指汉中南郑（今陕西汉中市南郑区），因境内有梁山，故名梁州。陆游于1172年在南郑担任四川宣抚使王炎的幕僚。
③〔关河〕关塞，河流。此处指汉中前线险要之地。

④〔梦断〕梦醒。
⑤〔尘暗旧貂裘〕貂皮裘上落满灰尘,颜色暗淡。
⑥〔胡〕泛称西北各族,此处指金入侵者。
⑦〔秋〕秋霜,比喻年老鬓白。
⑧〔天山〕南宋与金国相持的西北前线。
⑨〔沧州〕靠近水的地方,指作者位于镜湖畔的家乡(越州山阴,今浙江绍兴)。

第七章

宋词(婉约派)英译鉴赏实践

导 读

  The Southern Song and the Jin were two states that existed almost at the same time but ruled the south and the north of China respectively. The Jin dynasty of the *Nüzhen* (Jurchen) nationality was founded in the year 1115 and within a matter of more than ten years attacked and wiped out, one after the other, Liao and Northern Song. In 1127, the Jin troops marched south and seized Bianjing (汴京), the capital of Northern Song. They captured Emperors Huizong (宋徽宗) and Qinzong (宋钦宗), and declared that Northern Song had come to an end. After Zhao Gou (赵构), Prince of Kang, assumed the throne, he passed through many places in an exodus to the south before he settled down in Lin'an (临安). He continued the rule of the Song court, known in history as the southern Song. Southern Song and Jin took turns fighting against or making peace with each other, but roughly speaking they maintained the situation of confrontation along the Huai River. Eventually, both Jin and southern Song were eliminated by the Yuan court.

  Although Southern Song and Jin were respectively under the control of different nationalities, both claimed to be the caretaker of Chinese cultural tradition. Literati and popular literature of both the north and the south developed on the same inherent basis of Northern Song, and each made some of its own achievements. In popular literature, the new and different elements of the Jin literature were more remarkable. *Medley of the Western Chamber* (西厢记), which emerged in the later years of the Jin dynasty, was significant in Chinese literary history. In addition, some of the masters of the variety play (杂剧) of Early Yuan dynasty, such as Guan Hanqing (关汉卿) and others, all entered the Yuan from the Jin, which also proved that important changes were brewing in the literature of Late Jin. Incidentally, due to insufficient materials, it is difficult to differentiate in details the evolution of drama and fiction from Northern Song to Southern Song and Jin.

Ci, also known as "Lyric with a melody," "Yuefu Poetry," or "Long and Short Verses," was originated in the Tang and the Five Dynasties, and developed to maturity as a new literary form and genre in the Northern Song and Southern Song dynasties. Its main feature is that it is set to music and singing. Each piece of *Ci* has a name for its tune, which is categorized with strict requirements for the number of lines and the characters as well as the fixed tone pattern and rhyming in terms of different tunes. In terms of the length, *Ci* is divided into short lyrics, medium lyrics, and long lyrics. In terms of musical system, a piece of *Ci* is usually divided into two stanzas of *que* (阕), as ancient Chinese called them. In terms of style, *Ci* falls into the Bold and Unconstrained School (豪放派) and the Graceful and Restrained School (婉约派). The former is bold and free, often expressing one's vision about some major social issues or changes like the fate of the nation and the warfare, while the latter is delicate and sentimental, often describing family life, romantic love or parting sorrow, featuring nuanced expressions of one's feelings, graceful and melodious metric patterning, and mellow and subtle use of diction. Therefore, their *Ci* poems were stereotypically regarded as lacking of vigor or too much with femininity. Whereas it should be mentioned that *Ci* poets of the Graceful and Restrained School were also deeply concerned about the fate of the nation and some social transformations, but they tended to express their concerns in a personal and more sentimental way, often through depicting scenery or individual destiny.

Many literati and scholars of the Northern Song and Southern Song dynasties

第七章 宋词（婉约派）英译鉴赏实践

composed *Ci* lyrics, which played a significant part in promoting the development of this literary genre with specific features and stylistics of the age. Some renowned lyricist or *Ci* poets include:

Wen Tingyun（温庭筠）and Li Yu（李煜）of the Five Dynasties period; Liu Yong（柳永）, Yan Shu（晏殊）, Ouyang Xiu（欧阳修）, Yan Jidao（晏几道）, Qin Guan（秦观）, He Zhu（贺铸）, Zhou Bangyan（周邦彦）, and Li Qingzhao（李清照）of the Northern Song dynasty, as well as Jiang Kui（姜夔）, Wu Wenying（吴文英）, and Zhang Yan（张炎）of the Southern Song dynasty.

Li Yu

Li Yu（李煜）, also known as Li Houzhu ("Li, the Last Monarch", 李后主）, was the last ruler of the Southern Tang dynasty, the sixth son of Li Jing（李璟）, Emperor Yuanzong of the Southern Tang dynasty. He assumed the throne at the age of twenty-five. When he was thirty-nine years old the Southern Tang was eliminated by the Song, and Li Yu was taken as a prisoner to Bianjing. More than two years later, he was poisoned to death by the order of Emperor Taizong of the Song（宋太宗）. He was an artist with multiple attainments and talent in calligraphy, painting, intonation and poetry, especially in *Ci*, though an incompetent ruler. The military power of the Southern Tang was no match against that of the Song, so its downfall was simply unavoidable. However, the traumatic experience of his degeneration from a sovereign to a prisoner provided Li Yu with a deep understanding of "the agony and regret of life" and precisely due to that, his status as a first-rate major poet in the history of the song lyric was established. It's said that Li Yu's most representative song lyrics are actually those he wrote after he was taken as a prisoner to Bianjing. The most reputed was admittedly the following one:

The Beautiful Lady Yu

When will there be no more autumn moon and spring flowers
For me who had so many memorable hours?
The east wind blew again in my garden last night.
How can I bear the cruel memory of bowers

And palaces steeped in moonlight!

Carved balustrades and marble steps must still be there
But rosy faces cannot be as fair.
If you ask me how much my sorrow has increased,
Just see the overbrimming river flowing east! ①

Yan Shu

  Yan Shu's（晏殊）song lyrics mainly accord with the refined taste of senior scholar officials. In his early youth Yan Shu was recommended to the court as a "prodigy" and he served at a series of distinguished positions until he became the Prime Minister. Yan Shu's life experience may be counted as quite successful among scholars of the imperial ages, so his song lyrics are often permeated with a sense of satisfaction and a dignified, graceful and leisurely disposition. Yan Shu's works served as a linkage between the song lyrics of the Five Dynasties, especially the Southern Tang, and those of the Northern Song.

Silk-Washing Stream

One song with new words, one cup of wine;
Climate just like last year; pavilion and terrace, as before.
The sun sets in the west.
When shall it return?
Helpless: flowers fade and drop;
Returning swallows look like old acquaintances.
Along a fragrant path in the small garden,
I walk to and fro, alone. ②

---

① 《虞美人·春花秋月何时了》李煜：春花秋月何时了？往事知多少。小楼昨夜又东风，故国不堪回首月明中。雕栏玉砌应犹在，只是朱颜改。问君能有几多愁？恰似一江春水向东流。
② 《浣溪沙·一曲新词酒一杯》晏殊：一曲新词酒一杯，去年天气旧亭台。夕阳西下几时回？无可奈何花落去，似曾相识燕归来。小园香径独徘徊。

第七章 宋词（婉约派）英译鉴赏实践

Liu Yong

The years of Liu Yong's (柳永) birth and death remain unknown, though he was perhaps a contemporary of Yan Shu and Zhang Xian, and was active primarily during the reigns of Emperors Zhenzong and Renzong. In his early years, he sat for the civil service examinations several times with no success, and became a Presented Scholar only in his late years, after which he only served at a number of lowly positions. In his youth Liu Yong lived in the marketplace for a long time where he got to know many singing girls, for whom he composed song lyrics and sometimes used them as his objects. It is common to write about women and romantic love in the song lyrics of the literati, but Liu Yong's works have a flavor of their own. On the one hand, he is quite explicit and bold. On the other hand, he treated the singing girls with a commoner's sense of equality rather than with the condescending attitude as a scholar official, so his description of their emotions is often realistic and passionate. So his song lyrics were characterized by their vivacious, explicit, and thorough expression of feelings. The following lyric was one of his most remarkable works describing the scenes of the flourishing metropolis Lin'an (临安):

Watching the Sea Tide

Superb scenic place in southeast,
Capital city of the three Wu provinces,
This city by the Qiantang River has flourished since ancient times.
Look at the misty willows, painted bridges,
Wind shades, emerald green canopies,
And rows upon rows of a hundred thousand homes.
Cloud-capped trees stand around the sandy embankments;
Roaring waves rise like swirling frost and snow;
The natural moat runs on without end.
Pearls and jewels are on display in markets,
Silk clothes fill up the stores,
All competing in luxury and pomp.

Twin lakes and ranges of hills look so refreshing,
With all the cassia blossoms in the autumn months,
And lotus flowers that spread for ten miles.
On sunny days, one hears the playing of flutes,
On evenings, the singing of lotus-picking songs.
Both old fishermen and young boat girls rejoice.
A thousand horsemen surround the tall banner of the commander
Who listens to pipes and drums in intoxication
And chants while watching the mists and clouds.
Some day, he'd have the great view drawn in a painting
And bring it to the imperial court to boast of the experience. [①]

Jiang Kui

Born in the family of a junior bureaucrat, Jiang Kui (姜夔) was known for his talent when he was young, but he tried his hand at quite a number of civil service examinations with no success. He was skilled in calligraphy and painting, very good at music, capable of writing poetry, song lyric and prose. Some of Jiang Kui's song lyrics expressed his concern and worry of the nation, but even the style of works under this category remains essentially that of his own. Take, for instance, the "Yangzhou Man" which he composed when he passed by Yangzhou in the third year of the Chunxi reign (淳熙三年):

Yangzhou Man

At the famous city east of Huaihe River
And west of a stretch of bamboo
(Where the first stage of my journey ends),
I dismount to rest.

---

① 《望海潮·东南形胜》柳永:东南形胜,三吴都会,钱塘自古繁华。烟柳画桥,风帘翠幕,参差十万人家。云树绕堤沙,怒涛卷霜雪,天堑无涯。市列珠玑,户盈罗绮,竞豪奢。重湖叠巘清嘉。有三秋桂子,十里荷花。羌管弄晴,菱歌泛夜,嬉嬉钓叟莲娃。千骑拥高牙。乘醉听箫鼓,吟赏烟霞。异日图将好景,归去凤池夸。

第七章 宋词（婉约派）英译鉴赏实践

As I walk along the road
Once bathed in a reach of vernal breezes
I see green field cress on all sides.
Since Tartar cavalry pressed upon the Yangtze,
The city with abandoned moat and towering trees
Still hates all mention of the war.
As evening sets in, in the empty city
Chilly horns are echoing.

If Du Mu the connoisseur of bygone beauty
Returned to life, he'd lament the lost glory.
His magic pen that described a cardamom-like girl
And dream-like time in blue mansions
Can no more tell a romantic story.
The twenty-bridges,
Upon which fairies once played their flutes,
Are still there;
And below, in ripples the silent moon glows.
But, oh, for whom the red peonies by the bridges
Bloom every spring? Who knows? Who knows?[①]

This song lyric describes the desolate scene after the Jin troops invaded the south at Yangzhou, a famous city, and tells people's fear of and weariness about war. In that year, Jiang Kui was in his twenties, but the song lyric does not show any excitement of a young man. All it reveals is a sense of helplessness and sighs of grief. The world it represents is a desolate one, and somewhat illusionary. It is a kind of psychological trauma left by the war, and also a reflection of the author's personal character.

---

① 《扬州慢·淮左名都》姜夔：淮左名都，竹西佳处，解鞍少驻初程。过春风十里。尽荠麦青青。自胡马窥江去后，废池乔木，犹厌言兵。渐黄昏，清角吹寒，都在空城。杜郎俊赏，算而今，重到须惊。纵豆蔻词工，青楼梦好，难赋深情。二十四桥仍在，波心荡、冷月无声。念桥边红药，年年知为谁生？

Li Qingzhao

Li Qingzhao（李清照）was born in a family of government officials with a heavy cultural atmosphere, and was gifted and talented since childhood. After she grew up, she married Zhao Mingcheng（赵明诚）, also from an official family, who was fond of the study of inscriptions on ancient bronzes and stone tablets. After their marriage, the couple often stayed together, composing poetry and song lyric in exchange, purchasing books, and enjoying the study of bronze and stone inscriptions. In short, her work was the typical life experience of a talented daughter from the family of a senior scholar-official.

At the downfall of the Northern Song, Li Qingzhao fled south with her husband who served as the Prefect of Jiankang, but Zhao died shortly afterwards. During the several years when the Jin troops marched deep down the south, and before the Southern Song regime was firmly established, she constantly led a life of wandering from place to place and endless frustrations. Later, she settled down in Lin'an, but still under straitened circumstances all the time. It was said that she experienced an unsuccessful second marriage. In contrast to her early years, the life of her later period was particularly lonely and dreary.

Li Qingzhao was known by her song lyrics, but there are also masterpieces among the few texts of her extant poetry and prose. The famous "Epilogue to *Notes on Bronze and Stone Inscriptions*" (《<金石录>后序》) using as a common thread of ideas the process of how the couple built up and then lost their collection of bronze vessels, stone tablets, paintings and calligraphy pieces, reflects the loss of cultural relics and the grief of personal fortunes caused by the upheaval of times. It shows true emotions and is quite moving in some of its details. The virile fervor of "Quatrain on a Summer Day" is rarely found even from male poets of the Song dynasty:

While alive, one should be a hero among men.

To die, still a gallant one among spirits.

Even today I have in mind the great Xiang Yu

第七章 宋词（婉约派）英译鉴赏实践

Who refused to move to the east of the Yangtze. ①

On the art of the song lyric, Li Qingzhao put forward, in her "Discussion of the Song Lyric" (《词论》), a somewhat integrated set of ideas. In the essay, she emphatically argues that the song lyric "is a different kind by itself (别是一家)." She criticizes Liu Yong's song lyric for being "inferior and vulgar in language (词语尘下)," which indicates that she opposes the tendency of excessive use of the vernacular and catering to the taste of the townsfolk. She chides the song lyric of Su Shi and others for being "all poetry in lines of uneven length, and frequently failing to observe the prosody," which shows that she is against the mixture in style of poetry and song lyric and looseness in the observation of prosody. She reproves Yan Jidao's song lyric for "suffering from the absence of elaboration," and Qin Guan's for "focusing on emotions only but lacking in solid content," which demonstrates how she believes that the song lyric should not only have elaboration and emotions, but also carry deep cultural implications. These quibbles reveal that this female song lyric author held a high opinion of herself, and also define her own pursuit in the genre. Her works are generally consistent with her theories.

Due to the agitating changes in life, there is a striking difference between Li Qingzhao's earlier and later song lyrics in the expression of feeling. In her early song lyrics there is a flavor of life of the gentry. For instance, her "Dreamlike Tune" adopts the conventional theme of springtime lament; with an ingenious dialogue, it uses a careless and indifferent servant maid to serve as a foil to the idle, delicate, spoiled young lady who is sensitive to the fleeting time:

  Last night, amid patchy rain and gusty wind,
  I had a heavy sleep, but still suffer from a hangover.
  I try to ask the one who is rolling up the hanging screen
  Who just says: "The crabapples remain the same."
  "Don't you know? Don't you?
  The green must have grown thicker, but thinner, the red." ②

---

① 《夏日绝句》李清照：生当作人杰，死亦为鬼雄。至今思项羽，不肯过江东。
② 《如梦令·昨夜雨疏风骤》李清照：昨夜雨疏风骤，浓睡不消残酒。试问卷帘人，却道海棠依旧。知否，知否？应是绿肥红瘦。

The phrasing of "thicker green and thinner red" is both original and sensual. For another example of the author's talent in using poetic language, there are the lines from her "Drunk in the Shade of Flowers": "Say not that no one is overwhelmed with sorrow: / The hanging screen rolls up in west wind; / Someone is thinner than the yellow flowers."① An unspeakable melancholy, which is a representation of the author's complex and intense emotions and her acute sensitivity, may be felt between the lines in these song lyrics.

As a female writer, Li Qingzhao managed to be ranked, without any scruples, among the great song lyric masters of the Song dynasty, with some of her own idiosyncrasies. Like that of Li Yu, her song lyric has a simple, pure lyricism of its own, and at its very center is always her innermost emotionality. However, after many years of artistic exploration, compared to earlier song lyric authors like Li Yu, she devoted more assiduous attention to the techniques of the genre. In accordance with her idea that the song lyric "is a different kind by itself," Li Qingzhao was particularly sensitive to the different ways in expressing feeling between the song lyric and *shi* poetry, and as a woman, she succeeded in making it even more subtle, mild, and tactful. She is good at grasping the state of her mind through vivid, original details, and at revealing the nuances of her emotional changes through multi-layered dramatic structure with one climax after another.

Li Qingzhao also devotes much of her attention to the singularities of language in the song lyric. Her song lyric is well wrought in language, but unlike that of Zhou Bangyan, shows no trace of meticulous artistry, but tries, as much as possible, to sound easy and natural. She is fond of using literary language in a spontaneous way and spoken language in a graceful manner; when the two are integrated into unity, they create a special style of her own. The adoption of some ingenious and lively vernacular expressions in her song lyrics accounts for their tremendous vigor.

In short, in Li Qingzhao's song lyrics, one may see the combination of some of the original features of the genre at its early formation and full-fledged artistic techniques.

---

① 《醉花阴·薄雾浓云愁永昼》李清照：莫道不消魂，帘卷西风，人比黄花瘦。

第七章 宋词（婉约派）英译鉴赏实践

宋词（婉约派）英译鉴赏实践之一

如梦令① · 昨夜雨疏风骤
李清照

昨夜雨疏风骤②，

浓睡不消残酒③。

试问卷帘人④，

却道海棠⑤依旧⑥。

知否，知否⑦？

应是绿肥红瘦⑧。

【注释】

①〔如梦令〕又名"忆仙姿""宴桃源"。五代时后唐庄宗李存勖(xù)创作的《忆仙姿·曾宴桃源深洞》为正体，单调三十三字。后嫌其名不雅，故改为《如梦令》。代表作除李清照这首词外，另有《如梦令·常记溪亭日暮》一首，及吴文英《如梦令·秋千争闹粉墙》。

②〔雨疏风骤〕雨点稀疏，晚风急猛。疏，指稀疏。

③〔浓睡不消残酒〕虽然睡了一夜，仍有余醉未消。

④〔卷帘人〕有学者认为此指侍女。

⑤〔海棠〕产于中国落叶灌木至小乔木，春季开花，花未开时深红色，开后粉红色。果实球形，黄色，味酸甜，可食，也可供观赏。海棠花是一种雅俗共赏的名花，素有"花中神仙""花贵妃""花尊贵"之称，海棠有"国艳"之誉。历来为文人墨客所喜爱。

⑥〔依旧〕还是如此；像过去一样。

⑦〔知否〕文言文的委婉问法，意为"你知不知道？"

⑧〔绿肥红瘦〕绿叶茂盛，花渐凋谢。或指暮春时节，形容春残的景象。

白话释义

昨夜雨点稀疏风却不停,
酣睡一夜酒意难消。
我问正在卷帘的侍女,
外面的景色如何,
她却说海棠花依然如故。
你知不知道,知不知道?
这个时节应是绿叶繁盛,红花凋零!

主题鉴赏

《如梦令·昨夜雨疏风骤》是李清照的早期作品之一。据陈祖美教授《李清照简明年表》考证,此词大致作于宋哲宗元符三年(1100)前后。李清照虽然不是一位高产的作家,其词流传至今的只不过四五十首,但却"无一首不工""为词家一大宗矣"。这首《如梦令》,便是"天下称之"的不朽名篇。这首小令,有人物,有场景,还有对白,充分显示了宋词的语言表现力和词人的才华。

此词借宿酒醒后询问花事的描写,委婉地表达了作者怜花惜花的心情,充分体现出作者对大自然和春天的热爱,也流露出其内心的苦闷和幽怨。全词篇幅虽短,但语言清新,词意隽永,以景衬情,委曲精工,轻灵新巧,对人物心理情绪的刻画栩栩如生,以对话推动词意发展,跌宕起伏,极尽传神之妙,显示出作者深厚的艺术功力。后人对此词评价甚高,尤其是"绿肥红瘦"一句,更为历代文人所激赏。

起首两句,词面上虽然只写了昨夜饮酒过量,翌日晨起宿酒尚未尽消,但背后还潜藏着另一层意思,那就是昨夜酒醉是因为惜花。这位女词人不忍看到明朝海棠花谢,所以昨夜在海棠花下才饮了过量的酒,直到今朝尚有余醉。

三四两句所写,是词人惜花伤春心理的折射。尽管饮酒致醉一夜浓睡,但清晓酒醒后所关心的第一件事仍是窗外的海棠。词人情知海棠不堪一夜骤风疏雨的揉损,窗外定是残红狼藉,落花满眼,却又不忍亲见,于是试着向正在卷帘的侍女问个究竟。一个"试"字,将词人关心花事却又害怕听到花落的消息、不忍亲见落花却又想知道究竟的矛盾心理,表达得贴切入微,曲折有致。"试问"的结果——"却道海棠依旧。"原本词人的意思是海棠花经夜里突然而至的雨水打湿之后会花落满地,一派萧瑟,海棠花明显比在阳光下绽放所呈现出的娇嫩、娇艳的状态清瘦很多,侍

第七章 宋词（婉约派）英译鉴赏实践

女的回答却让词人感到非常意外。本来以为经过一夜风雨，海棠花一定凋谢得不成样子了，可是侍女卷起窗帘，看了看外面之后，却漫不经心地答道：海棠花还是那样。一个"却"字，既表明侍女对女主人委屈的心事毫无觉察，对窗外发生的变化无动于衷，也表明词人听到答话后感到疑惑不解。她想："雨疏风骤"之后，"海棠"怎会"依旧"呢？这就非常自然地带出了结尾两句。

海棠花开的季节因品种不同而时间不同，但大多数为暮春孟夏开放，因此古人往往用它来表达"伤春""惜春"等更深的文化含义。古代歌咏海棠的作品并不鲜见，但称得上佳作的为数不多。北宋词人苏轼曾作《海棠》一诗："东风袅袅泛崇光，香雾空蒙月转廊。只恐夜深花睡去，故烧高烛照红妆。"苏轼因乌台诗案被贬黄州，他经过人生起伏，但并未沉沦。他在黄州夜不能寐，燃起高高的红蜡烛，不愿放弃这良辰美景，为了留住这人世间的刹那芳华，秉烛赏花，被高高举起的蜡烛，照亮了海棠娇羞的脸庞。"只恐夜深花睡去，故烧高烛照红妆"，这一句脍炙人口，写出了苏轼对海棠花的爱恋，写出了诗人的一片痴情，通过这首诗我们也能到苏轼的达观、潇洒的胸襟。除此之外，南宋诗人王淇有《春暮游小园》诗："一从梅粉褪残妆，涂抹新红上海棠。开到荼䕷花事了，丝丝天棘出莓墙。"另外，"凡有井水处，皆能歌柳词"的"行吟词人"柳永也写过海棠——《木兰花·海棠》："东风催露千娇面。欲绽红深开处浅。日高梳洗甚时欢，点滴胭脂匀未遍。霏微雨罢残阳院。洗出都城新锦段。美人纤手摘芳枝，插在钗头和凤颤。"海棠花在风流潇洒的柳永笔下，瞬间变成千娇百媚，惊艳红尘的"美人"，她随手摘下一朵海棠花，插在头上，就连风都有了万般风韵。

相比苏东坡，李清照眼里的海棠花俨然化身为不胜酒力、风姿绰约的魅力女词人。相比王淇，李清照没有"荼䕷花事了"那么悲戚。相比柳永，李清照也没有他的黏腻和暧昧。同样写海棠，男性与女性的视角和笔触为读者带来的阅读体验不尽相同。不过，这几首词也许是描绘海棠最耐读的作品吧。

尾句实为经典之中的经典："知否？知否？应是绿肥红瘦。"这既是对侍女的反诘，也像是自言自语：这个粗心的丫头，你知道不知道，园中的海棠应该是绿叶繁茂、红花稀少才是。这句对白写出了诗画所不能道，写出了伤春惜春的闺中人复杂的神情口吻，可谓"传神之笔"。"应是"，表明词人对窗外景象的推测与判断，口吻极当。因为她毕竟尚未目睹，所以说话时要留有余地。同时，这一词语中也暗含着"必然是"和"不得不是"之意。海棠虽好，风雨无情，它是不可能长开不谢的。一语之中，含有不尽的无可奈何的惜花情结，可谓语浅意深。而这一层惜花的殷殷情意，自然是"卷帘人"所不能体察也无须更多理会的，她毕竟不能像她的女主人那样感情细腻，那样对自然和人生有着更深的感悟。这也许是她之所以作出上面的回答的原因。末了的"绿肥红瘦"一语,更是全词的惊艳之笔,历来为世人所称道。"绿"代替叶,"红"代替花,是两种颜色的对比;"肥"形容雨后的叶子因水分充足而茂盛肥大,"瘦"形容雨后的花朵因不堪雨打而凋谢稀少,是两种状态的对比。本来平平常常的四个字,经词人的搭配组合,竟显得如此色彩鲜明,形象生动,这实在是语言运用上的一个创造。由这四个字生发联想,那"红瘦"正是表明春天渐渐消逝,而"绿肥"正是象征着绿叶成荫的盛夏即将来临。这种极富概括性的语言,实在令人叹为观止!

这首小词,只有短短六句三十三言,却写得曲折委婉,极有层次。词人因惜花而痛饮,因情知花谢却又抱一丝侥幸心理而"试问",因不相信"卷帘人"的回答而再次反问,如此层层转折,步步深入,将惜花之情表达得摇曳多姿。历朝历代诗词评论家对这首小令赞不绝口。宋代胡仔说:"近时妇人能文词,如李易安,颇多佳句,小词云:'昨夜雨疏风骤……','绿肥红瘦',此语甚新"(《苕溪渔隐丛话》前集卷六十)。宋代陈郁:"李易安工造语,故《如梦令》'绿肥红瘦'之句,天下称之"(《藏一话腴》内编卷下)。明代沈际飞:"'知否'二字,叠得可味。'绿肥红瘦'创获自妇人,大奇"(《草堂诗馀正集》卷一)。当代词学研究专家、李清照学会副会长吴熊和先生说:"这首词表现了对花事和春光的爱惜以及女性特有的关切和敏感。全词仅三十三字,巧妙地写了同卷帘人的问答,问者情多,答者意淡,因而逼出'知否,知否'二句,写得灵活而多情致。词中造语工巧,'雨疏''风骤','浓睡''残酒'都是当句对;'绿肥红瘦'这句中,以绿代叶,以红代花,虽为过去诗词中常见(如唐僧齐己诗"红残绿满海棠枝"),但把'红'同'瘦'联在一起,以'瘦'字状海棠的由繁丽而憔悴零落,显得凄婉,炼字亦甚精,在修辞上有所新创。"当代红学专家周汝昌先生评价说:"一篇小令,才共六句,好似一幅图画,并且还有对话,还交代了事情的来龙去脉。这可能是现代的电影艺术的条件才能胜任的一种'镜头'表现法,然而它却实实在在是九百年前的一位女词人自'编'自'演'的作品,不谓之奇迹,又将谓之何哉?"

第七章 宋词（婉约派）英译鉴赏实践

学生英译实践园地

英译实践版本选读

译文 1　肯尼斯·雷克斯洛斯

Spring Ends
To the Tune "A Dream Song"

Last night fine rain, gusts of wind,
Deep sleep could not dissolve the leftover wine.
I asked my maid as she rolled up the curtains,
"Are the begonias still the same?"
"Don't you know it is time
For the green to grow fat and the red to grow thin?"

译文 2　许渊冲

Tune: Like A Dream

Last night the wind blew hard and rain was fine;
Sound sleep did not dispel the aftertaste of wine.
I ask the maid rolling up the screen;
"The same crab-apple tree," she says, "is seen."
"But don't you know,
O, don't you know,
The red should languish and the green must grow?"

译文 3　杨宪益　戴乃迭

To the Tune of Ru Meng Ling

Last night the rain was light, the wind fierce,
And deep sleep did not dispel the effects of wine.
When I ask the maid rolling up the curtains,
She answers, "The crab-apple blossoms look the same."
I cry, "Can't you see? Can't you see?
The green leaves are fresh but the red flowers are fading!"

第七章 宋词（婉约派）英译鉴赏实践

译文 4　叶　扬

Dreamlike Tune

Last night, amid patchy rain and gusty wind,
I had a heavy sleep, but still suffer from a hangover.
I try to ask the one who is rolling up the hanging screen
Who just says: "The crab-apples remain the same."
　　"Don't you know? Don't you?
The green must have grown thicker, but thinner, the red."

译文 5　徐忠杰

Rumengling

Last night was windy with intermittent rain.
I've slept sound; but the effects of drink remain.
I ask how the flowers are of the curtain-drawer,
　　She says, "Begonias are e'er as before."
　　"Don't you recognize it for a fact at all：
Now leaves should be large and flowers should be small?"

宋词(婉约派)英译鉴赏实践之二

一剪梅①·红藕香残玉簟秋

李清照

红藕香残玉簟②秋，
　轻解罗裳③，独上兰舟④。
云中谁寄锦书⑤来？
　雁字⑥回时，
　　月满西楼。

花自飘零⑦水自流，

一种相思，两处闲愁⑧。

此情无计⑨可消除，

才下眉头⑩，却上心头。

【注释】

①〔一剪梅〕词牌名。双调小令，六十字，有前后阕句句用叶韵者，而此词上下阕各三平韵，应为其变体。每句并用平收，声情低抑。此调因此词而又名"玉簟秋"。

②〔玉簟(diàn)〕竹席的美称。

③〔轻解〕轻轻地提起。〔罗裳(cháng)〕犹罗裙。

④〔兰舟〕船的美称。《述异记》卷下谓："木兰洲在浔阳江中，多木兰树。昔吴王阖闾植木兰于此，用构宫殿也。七里洲中，有鲁班刻木兰为舟，舟至今在洲中。诗家云'木兰舟'出于此。"一说"兰舟"特指睡眠的床榻。

⑤〔锦书〕书信的美称。《晋书·窦滔妻苏氏传》云："前秦秦州刺史窦滔被徙流沙，其妻苏氏思之，织锦为回文璇玑图诗以寄滔，可宛转循环读之，词甚凄婉，共八百四十字。"这种用锦织成的字称锦字，又称锦书。

⑥〔雁字〕雁群飞行时，常排列成"人"字或"一"字形，因称"雁字"。相传古人以雁传书信。

⑦〔飘零〕凋谢，凋零。

⑧〔闲愁〕无端无谓的忧愁。

⑨〔无计〕没有办法。

⑩〔眉头〕两眉及附近的地方。

白话释义

荷花凋谢香气消，竹席冰冷如凉秋，
轻提罗裙，独自登上小舟。
遥望远天，白云舒卷，有谁给我寄锦书？
雁群南飞，队列齐整，
月色如华，洒满孤独的亭楼。

第七章 宋词（婉约派）英译鉴赏实践

花已飘零水在流。
离别之苦搅起无边的愁绪。
相思与离愁，无法去除，
刚离开眉宇，又填满了心头。

主题鉴赏

《一剪梅·红藕香残玉簟秋》是李清照前期的作品，当作于婚后不久词人与丈夫赵明诚离别之后。题名为元人伊世珍作的《琅嬛记》引《外传》云："易安结缡未久，明诚即负笈远游。易安殊不忍别，觅锦帕书《一剪梅》词以送之。"而现代词学家王仲闻编著的《李清照集校注》卷一提出了不同意见："清照适赵明诚时，两家俱在东京，明诚正为太学生，无负笈远游事。此则所云，显非事实。而李清照之父称为李翁，一似不知其名者，尤见芜陋。《琅嬛记》乃伪书，不足据。"

根据李清照带有自传性的《金石录后序》所言，宋徽宗建中靖国元年李清照嫁与赵明诚，婚后伉俪之情甚笃，有共同的兴趣爱好。而后其父李格非在党争中蒙冤，李清照亦受到株连，被迫还乡，与丈夫时有别离。这不免勾起她的许多思念之情，写下了多首词篇。这首《一剪梅》是李清照离别词中的名作，此词通过女词人独特的感受和体验另辟蹊径地揭示出中华民族的女子多愁善感的心理共性，既有精微的审美体验，又有精妙的审美传达，堪称一首工致精巧的别情佳作。

此词，先写清秋时节与爱人别后，独上兰舟以排遣愁怀，西楼望月恨雁来无书，再以两地相思之情如同花飘零、水流东那样出之自然来说明此情无由消除，寄寓着词人不忍离别的一腔深情，反映出初婚少妇沉溺于情海之中的纯洁心灵。全词不事雕琢，明白如话，以女性特有的真挚情感，丝毫不落俗套的表现方式，展示出一种婉约之美，格调清新，意境幽美。

起句"红藕香残玉簟秋"，领起全篇。它的上半句"红藕香残"写户外之景，下半句"玉簟秋"写室内之物，对清秋季节起了点染作用，说明这是"已凉天气未寒时"（韩偓《已凉》）。全句设色清丽，意象蕴藉，不仅刻画出四周景色，而且烘托出词人情怀。花开花落，既是自然界现象，也是悲欢离合的人事象征；枕席生凉，既是肌肤间触觉，也是凄凉独处的内心感受。这一兼写户内外景物而景物中又暗寓情意的起句，一开头就显示了这首词的环境气氛和它的感情色彩，具有多重妙处。这句中的"秋"字，是女词人情怀触发的景点，是缘景生情的契机。女词人把季节用具有感性色彩和具体特征的"红藕香残"表达出来，因而，"秋"就不是抽象的，而是具象的了。此为妙处之一。妙处之二是，"香"是女词人得来的嗅觉感受，她不是对节候作判断性的说明,而是独特地用感觉器官去感受,从"香残"的"残"中感知到凉秋降临了。这种感知方式与众不同,颇有特色。而女词人所感知到的对象的属性,又起到了暗暗提示的作用,暗示着"秋"已来临。妙处之三是,凉秋的"香残"景象和清飒氛围最容易激惹人们的愁情幽绪,这在古典诗词中例证甚多。这种手法说明了审美上的对象特征和心理意绪的对应同构关系。女词人并没有让自然景象淹没主体的心理意绪,使读者产生审美上的偏向,如张若虚的《春江花月夜》;而是把客体的自然物象作为引发情绪的媒介,既非意大境小,亦非境大意小,而是微衰的秋境和幽幽的秋思的两相契合。

　　女词人淡淡地起笔,先勾勒季节特征,然后微微推出抒情主人公的形象。"轻解罗裳,独上兰舟"二句,写的是白昼在水面泛舟之事。"轻",言其悄悄;"独",标示仅己身一人。这里可引人悬思主人公这些行动的原因和目的所在。词中可谓不着一字,而意脉潜隐。到"云中谁寄锦书来",原先潜隐着的意脉开始显豁,上升到表层意象。女词人眺望秋际云天,原来是期待着丈夫的"锦书来",所以,紧接着才有"雁字回时"一句。"雁字"可以是眼前实景,雁阵回归,嘹唳长空;亦可以是寄兴之景,因为鸿雁传书,已成为具有民族色彩的传统意象,含有象征意义。当翘首企足,引领秋空,是为着等待丈夫的书信的意识一旦成为显性意识时,前两句"轻解罗裳,独上兰舟"所包蕴的深意也就得到解释。"轻",悄然而行,"独",独自一人,是为着在一个幽静的环境里,在孑然只身中,去慢慢等待那雁传的尺素,去细细咀嚼那离别的伤情,去悄悄排遣那铭心的思念。这种情绪只属于她,因而无须有人结伴同来,更不必张扬开去。一切只有在"轻"中、"独"中,才会回味、咀嚼,才会体验、领略得到。唯其如此,方显出思妇之情的独特,益见其情之深挚。

　　上阕的煞尾处,突然跳成一个景象描述句:"月满西楼。"这一收煞,不但呼应了起笔"红藕香残"的景象,而且组合成了一个空间系列环境:红藕、兰舟、雁字、西楼。占据这空间一角的则是满怀幽思的女词人。如果化为丹青,就是一幅绘画,产生出绘画美。"月满西楼",以空间感透现出时态感。"满"字显示出时间的推移。女词人独上兰舟,引领眺望,已有相当长的时间了。她深情、缱绻、执着,直等到"月满西楼"。这里汩汩流转的是女词人的情和意,于是前述的绘画美便上升到一个更高的美学层次——意境美。

　　如果说,上阕更多的是从境中隐隐约约地透出相思之意,那么,下阕则侧重于直宣情愫。换头"花自飘零水自流"一句,承上启下,词意不断。它借眼前之景来抒发,暗合流水落花的伤感和无奈,既是即景,又兼比兴。其所展示的花落水流之景,是遥遥与上阕"红藕香残""独上兰舟"两句相拍合的;而其所象喻的人生、年华、爱情、离别,则给人以"无可奈何花落去"(晏殊《浣溪沙·一曲新词酒一杯》)之感,以

第七章 宋词（婉约派）英译鉴赏实践

及"水流无限似侬愁"（刘禹锡《竹枝词九首》其二）之恨。"相思"的全词意脉径露纸面。上阕的一切描述汇聚到这里，为它下了注脚。词的下阕就从这一句自然过渡到后面的五句，转为纯抒情怀、直吐胸臆的独白。

"一种相思，两处闲愁"二句，在写自己的相思之苦、闲愁之深的同时，由己身推想到对方，深知这种相思与闲愁不是单向的，而是双向的，女词人和丈夫在两处作同一的感受、感应，表明女词人和丈夫的心灵感应是同一个节拍，可见两心之相印。这两句也是上阕"云中"句的补充和引申，说明尽管天长水远，锦书未来，而两地相思之情初无二致，足证双方情爱之笃与彼此信任之深。前人作品中也时有写两地相思的句子，如罗邺的《雁二首》其二"江南江北多离别，忍报年年两地愁"，韩偓的《青春》诗"樱桃花谢梨花发，肠断青春两处愁"。这两句词可能即自这些诗句化出，而一经熔铸、裁剪为两个句式整齐、词意鲜明的四字句，就取得脱胎换骨、点铁成金的效果。这两句既是分列的，又是合一的。合起来看，从"一种相思"到"两处闲愁"，是两情的分合与深化。其分合，表明此情是一而二、二而一的；其深化，则诉说此情已由"思"而化为"愁"。下句"此情无计可消除"，紧接这两句。正因人已分在两处，心已笼罩深愁，此情就当然难以排遣，而是"才下眉头，却上心头"了。

这首词的结拍三句，是历来为人所称道的名句。王士禛在《花草蒙拾》中指出，这三句从范仲淹《御街行·秋日怀旧》"都来此事，眉间心上，无计相回避"脱胎而来。这说明，诗词创作虽忌模拟，但可以点化前人语句，使之呈现新貌，融入自己的作品之中。成功的点化总是青出于蓝而胜于蓝，不仅变化原句，而且高过原句。李清照的这一点化，就是一个成功的例子。王士禛也认为，相对于范句，李句"特工"。两相对比，范句比较平实板直，不能收醒人眼目的艺术效果；李句则别出巧思，以"才下眉头，却上心头"这样两句来代替"眉间心上，无计相回避"的平铺直叙，给人以耳目一新之感。这两句词是女词人对相思情的独特体验和捕捉。相思之情，特别是心心相印的思念情，是人类最普遍的情感之一。它"剪不断，理还乱"，一旦萌发，难以消遣，它铭心刻骨，像游丝一般地黏附着。它可以从外在情态的"眉头"消除，却又会不自禁地钻入"心头"。女词人对这种情感作了独特、深细的体察和把握。这里，"眉头"与"心头"相对应，"才下"与"却上"成起伏，语句结构既十分工整，表现手法也十分巧妙，因而就在艺术上有更大的吸引力。当然，句离不开篇，这两个四字句只是整首词的一个有机组成部分，并非一枝独秀。它有赖于全篇的烘托，特别因与前面另两个同样工巧的四字句"一种相思，两处闲愁"前后衬映，而相得益彰。同时，篇也离不开句，全篇正因这些醒人眼目的句子而振起。

女词人以独特的方式感知到人类最普遍存在的一种情感，又以独特的技巧表达出这一情感，凝为审美的晶体，于是这首词就产生了永久的艺术魅力，也获得了不少名家的点评。明代杨慎批点杨金本《草堂诗馀》卷三："离情欲泪。读此始知高则诚、关汉卿诸人，又是效颦。"明代王世贞《弇州山人词评》曰："李易安'此情无计可消除，方下眉头，又上心头。'可谓憔悴支离矣。"清代万树《词律》卷九："'月满楼'，或作'月满西楼'。不知此调与他词异。如'裳''思''来''除'等字，皆不用韵，原与四段排比者不同。'雁字'句七字，自是古调。何必强其入俗，而添一'西'字以凑八字乎？人若欲填排偶之句，自有别体在也。"清代陈廷焯《云韶集》卷十："起七字秀绝，真不食人间烟火者。梁绍壬谓：只起七字已是他人不能到。结更凄绝。"《白雨斋词话》卷二："易安佳句，如《一剪梅》起七字云：'红藕香残玉簟秋'，精秀特绝，真不食人间烟火者。"清代况周颐《〈漱玉词〉笺》："玉梅词隐云，易安精研宫律，所以何至出韵。周美成倚声传家，为南北宋关键，其《一剪梅》第四句均不用韵，讵皆出韵耶？窃谓《一剪梅》调当以第四句不用韵一体为最早，晚近作者，好为靡靡之音，徒事和畅，乃添入此叶耳。"

第七章 宋词（婉约派）英译鉴赏实践

学生英译实践园地

英译实践版本选读

译文 1　肯尼斯·雷克斯洛斯

To the Tune, "Plum Blossoms Fall and Scatter"

The perfume of the red water lilies dies away.
The Autumn air penetrates the pearl jade curtain.
Torches gleam on the orchid boats.
Who has sent me a message of love from the cloud?
It is the time when wild swans return.
The moonlight floods the women's quarters.

Flowers, after their nature, whirl away in the wind.
Split water, after its nature, flows together at the lowest point.
Those who are of one being can never stop thinking each other.
But, ah, my dear, we are apart, and I have been become used to sorrow.
This love — nothing can ever make it fade or disappear.
For a moment it was on my eyebrows,
now it is heavy in my heart.

译文 2　许渊冲

A Twig of Mume Blossoms

Pink fragrant lotus fade; autumn chills mat of jade.
My silk robe doffed, I float alone in orchid boat.
Who in the cloud would bring me letters in brocade?
When swans come back in flight, my bower's steeped in moonlight.

As fallen flowers drift and water runs its way,
One longing overflows two places with same woes.
Such sorrow can by no means be driven away;
From eyebrows kept apart, again it gnaws my heart.

第七章 宋词（婉约派）英译鉴赏实践

译文 2　叶　扬

A Sheaf of Plum Flowers

A sweet smell still lingers from the pinkish lotus root,
Autumn is felt in the jade mat.
Gently loosening my silk robe
I get on a boat alone.
In the clouds, who is sending a letter?
The swan geese are on their way home.
Moonshine is all over the western tower.

Flowers keep falling, waters keep flowing.
It's the same lovesickness
Shared by two, each in their melancholy and idleness
There is no way one can dispel such a feeling:
As soon as one gets rid of it from one's brows,
It goes right into one's heart.

译文 4　王季文

Key: I Chien Mei

Lotus flowers fade as fall is felt on the bamboo mat.
Gently taking off the silk coat;
Lonesomely embarking the orchid boat.
Who's to send me love letters from the cloud or mist?
When it's time that one person returnest,
Full moon shall fill my chamber with joy amidst.

Let the flowers wither and water by itself drift,
For love, there is only one sort,
But sorrow has made two places its resort.
'Tis all in vain trying to dispel this sentiment:
No sooner was it loosened from the brows,
Than up to my heart a new one grows.

译文 5　朱曼华

To the Melody: A Blooming Plum

The fragrant red lotuses have withered away,
My jade-like mat turns cool on autumn day.
Lightly putting off my skirt or silky coat,
Alone I boarded on the pretty boat.
Looking back, the wild geese fly,
Who's to send me a letter through clouds' sky?
My west chamber window's full of moonlight.

Flowers drift alone out of the smell,
The creek running alone is natural.
There's one kind of lovesickness,
Coming from two places with sadness.
No way could cure such a sickness,
Just falling down from my eyebrows,
into my heart with sorrows.

译文 6　何赵婉贞

To the Tune of
A Spray of Flowering Plum

Falling fragrance of pink lotus,
jade-green reeds of autumn.
Gently I unfasten my robe of sheer silk,
And step aboard the orchid boat all by myself.

Who will bring me embroidered letters from the clouds?[①]
When the wild geese return,
The west balcony is flooded with moonlight.

第七章 宋词（婉约派）英译鉴赏实践

  Flower petals drifting, water flowing,
    One and the same longing
  Makes two hearts sad with yearning.
  There is no way to dissipate this grief：
    As the brow ceases frowning,
      The heart begins aching.

---

① During the 2nd century B.C., Su Wu, when he was a captive of the Huns, conveyed his loyalty to the Han Emperor by tying a letter to the foot of a wild goose. In time, the expression "the wild goose brings letter from the clouds" has become a customary usage in referring to the delivery of any letter or message.

宋词（婉约派）英译鉴赏实践之三

鹊桥仙①·纤云弄巧

秦　观

纤云弄巧②，
飞星传恨③，
银汉迢迢暗度④。
金风玉露⑤一相逢，
便胜却人间无数。

柔情似水，
佳期⑥如梦，
忍顾鹊桥归路⑦。
两情若是久长时，
又岂在朝朝暮暮⑧。

【注释】

① 〔鹊桥仙〕词牌名，又名"鹊桥仙令""忆人人""金风玉露相逢曲""广寒秋"等。以欧阳修《鹊桥仙·月波清霁》为正品。双调五十六字，上下阕各两仄韵，一韵到底。上下阕首两句要求对仗。代表作另有宋代苏轼的《鹊桥仙·七夕》。

② 〔纤云〕轻盈纤小的云彩。〔弄巧〕指云彩在空中幻化成各种巧妙的花样。

③ 〔飞星〕流星。一说指牵牛、织女二星。

④ 〔银汉〕银河。〔迢迢〕遥远的样子。〔暗度〕悄悄渡过。

⑤ 〔金风玉露〕指秋风白露。李商隐《辛未七夕》："恐是仙家好别离，故教迢递作佳期。由来碧落银河畔，可要金风玉露时。"

⑥ 〔佳期〕美好的时光；婚期；男女约会的日期。屈原《楚辞·九歌·湘夫人》："登白蘋兮骋望，与佳期兮夕张。"

⑦ 〔忍顾〕怎忍回头看。〔鹊桥〕中国神话传说中每年的农历七月七日，即七夕节，会有来自不同地方的喜鹊在银河身体紧贴架起一座桥梁，让牛郎和织女得以相见，称作鹊桥，后来此一名词便引申为能够联结男女之间良缘的各种事物。

⑧ 〔朝朝暮暮〕原指每天的早晨和黄昏，后指从早到晚，也指情侣相聚的时间极其短促。语出战国宋玉的《高唐赋》："妾在巫山之阳，高丘之阻，旦为朝云，暮为行雨。朝朝暮暮，阳台之下。"

白话释义

纤薄的云彩在天空中变幻多端，
天上的流星传递着相思的愁怨，
遥远无垠的银河今夜我悄悄渡过。
在秋风白露的七夕相会，
就胜过尘世间那些长相厮守却貌合神离的夫妻。

缱绻的柔情像流水般绵绵不断，
重逢的约会如梦影般缥缈虚幻，
分别之时不忍去看那鹊桥路。

第七章 宋词（婉约派）英译鉴赏实践

只要两情至死不渝，
又何必贪求卿卿我我的朝欢暮乐呢。

主题鉴赏

《鹊桥仙·纤云弄巧》是宋代词人秦观的名作。这首词歌咏七夕佳节，借牛郎织女悲欢离合的神话故事，讴歌了真挚、细腻、纯洁、坚贞的爱情。上阕写牛郎织女聚会，下阕写他们的离别。全词哀乐交织，熔抒情与议论于一炉，融天上人间为一体，优美的形象与深沉的感情结合起来，起伏跌宕地讴歌了美好的爱情。此词用情深挚，立意高远，语言优美，议论自由流畅，通俗易懂，却又显得婉约蕴藉，余味无穷，尤其是末二句"两情若是久长时，又岂在朝朝暮暮"，使词的思想境界升华到一个崭新的高度，成为千古佳句。

借牛郎织女的故事，以超越人间的方式表现人间的悲欢离合，古已有之，如《古诗十九首·迢迢牵牛星》，曹丕的《燕歌行》，李商隐的《辛未七夕》等。宋代的欧阳修、张先、柳永、苏轼等人也曾吟咏这一题材，虽然遣词造句各异，却都因袭了"欢娱苦短"的传统主题，格调哀婉、凄楚。相形之下，秦观此词堪称独出机杼，立意高远。

词一开始即写"纤云弄巧"，轻柔多姿的云彩，变化出许多优美巧妙的图案，显示出织女的手艺何其精巧绝伦。可是，这样美好的人儿，却不能与自己心爱的人共同过美好的生活。"飞星传恨"，那些闪亮的星星仿佛都传递着他们的离愁别恨，正飞驰长空。接着写织女渡银河。《古诗十九首》云："河汉清且浅，相去复几许？盈盈一水间，脉脉不得语。""盈盈一水间"，"咫尺"之间，似乎连对方的神情语态都宛然在目。这里，秦观却写道："银汉迢迢暗度"，以"迢迢"二字形容银河的辽阔，牛女相距之遥远。这样一改，感情深沉了，突出了相思之苦。迢迢银河水，把两个相爱的人隔开，相见多么不容易！"暗度"二字既点"七夕"题意，同时紧扣一个"恨"字，他们踽踽宵行，千里迢迢来相会。

接下来词人荡开笔墨，以富有感情色彩的议论赞叹道："金风玉露一相逢，便胜却人间无数！"一对久别的情侣金风玉露之夜，碧落银河之畔相会了，这美好的一刻，就抵得上人间千遍万遍的相会。词人热情歌颂了一种理想的圣洁而永恒的爱情。"金风玉露"化用李商隐《辛未七夕》诗句，用以描写七夕相会的时节风光，同时还另有深意，词人把这次珍贵的相会，映衬于金风玉露、冰清玉洁的背景之下，显示出这种爱情的高尚纯洁和超凡脱俗。

"柔情似水"，那两情相会的情意啊，就像悠悠无声的流水，是那样的温柔缠绵。

"似水"照应"银汉迢迢",即景设喻,十分自然。一夕佳期竟然像梦幻一般倏然而逝,才相见又分离,怎不令人心碎!"佳期如梦",除言相会时间之短,还写出爱侣相会时的复杂心情。"忍顾鹊桥归路",转写分离,刚刚借以相会的鹊桥,转瞬间又成了和爱人分别的归路。不说不忍离去,却说怎忍看鹊桥归路,婉转语意中,含有无限惜别之情,含有无限辛酸眼泪。

回顾佳期幽会,疑真疑假,似梦似幻,及至鹊桥言别,恋恋之情,已至于极。词笔至此忽又空际转身,爆发出高亢的音响:"两情若是久长时,又岂在朝朝暮暮!"秦观这两句词揭示了爱情的真谛:爱情要经得起长久分离的考验,只要能彼此真诚相爱,即使终年天各一方,也比朝夕相伴的庸俗情趣可贵得多。这两句感情色彩很浓的议论,成为爱情颂歌当中的千古绝唱。它们与上阕的议论遥相呼应,这样上、下阕同样结构,叙事和议论相间,从而形成全篇连绵起伏的情致。这种正确的恋爱观,这种高尚的精神境界,远远超过了古代同类作品,是十分难能可贵的。

总观全词,每片前三句皆为写景抒情,后两句均作议论。这些议论,自由流畅,通俗易懂,却又显得婉约蕴藉,余味无穷。一是因为有前三句做精彩的铺垫,令后两句的议论自然流出,尤觉深沉真挚。二是立意高妙,既能收得住前句,又能荡开,融汇情理,醒明本旨。作者将画龙点睛的议论和散文句法,与优美的形象、深沉的情感结合起来,起伏跌宕地讴歌了人间美好的爱情,取得了极好的艺术效果。

明代李攀龙《草堂诗余隽》卷三眉批:"相逢胜人间,会心之语。两情不在朝暮,破格之谈。七夕歌以双星会少别多为恨,独少游此词谓'两情若是久长'二句,最能醒人心目。"明代卓人月《古今词统》卷八:"(末句)数见不鲜,说得极是。"明代沈际飞《草堂诗余四集·正集》:"(世人咏)七夕,往往以双星会少离多为恨,而此词独谓情长不在朝暮,化臭腐为神奇!"近代俞陛云《唐五代两宋词选释》:"夏闰庵云:'七夕之词最难作,宋人赋此者,佳作极少,惟少游一词可观,晏小山《蝶恋花》赋七夕尤佳。'"近代吴梅《词学通论》第七章:"《鹊桥仙》云:'两情若是久长时,又岂在朝朝暮暮。'……此等句皆思路沉着,非如苏词之振笔直书也。北宋词家以缜密之思,得道炼之致者,惟方回与少游耳。"

第七章 宋词（婉约派）英译鉴赏实践

学生英译实践园地

英译实践版本选读

译文 1　宇文所安

To 'Gods on the Magpie Bridge'

Fine wisps of cloud sport their craft,
shooting stars bear word of the lovers' pain,
and now far off in the River of Stars
they are making the crossing unseen.
To meet just once in fall's metal wind
and in the jade white dew
turns out to be better by far
than the countless meetings of mortals.

Their tender feelings seem like water,
this sweet moment is as in dream—
how can they bear to turn their heads
to the path leading back over Magpie Bridge?
But so long as both of them love
and so long as their love lasts on,
it does not need to be done
every night and every morning at dawn.

译文 2　许渊冲

The Double Seventh
Tune: "Immortal at the Magpie Bridge"

Clouds float like works of art;
Stars shoot with grief at heart.
Across the Milky Way the Cowherd meets the Maid.
When Autumn's Golden Wind embraces Dew of Jade,
All the love scenes on earth, however many, fade.

第七章 宋词（婉约派）英译鉴赏实践

Their tender love flows like a stream;
This happy date seems but a dream.
How can they bear a separate homeward way?
If love between both sides can last for aye,
Why need they stay together night and day?

译文 3 王宏印

The Magpie Bridge Rendezvous

Slender Clouds gather into nature's fine needle works;
Love Stars message their sorrows for long separation.
Once the Cowherd and the Girl Weaver crossed the Milky Way,
They embrace in gentle breeze, wet with dew of tears!
How can the date in the human world be compared?

A tender heart grows a tender love, but lasting all.
A good date is but a good dream, once a year. Alas!
Never look back at the Magpie Bridge where you meet!
People acclaim: "It's a better couple to miss and meet
Than to simply stay together from morn to night."

译文 4 曾冲明

Meeting at Magpie Bridge

A few clouds play still in the sky bright;
Stars twinkle to send love likely with griefs.
The cowboy and the sewer-girl meet tonight
In the Milky Way and during the golden autumn.
Their meeting once a year is far better
Than living together always on earth.

Their love is as tender as water;

Their meeting as short as a dream.
They fear to think of their new separation.
But if their love lasts long and forever,
Why should they live always together?

译文 5　许景城

The Magpie-Bridge Lore

Clouds fine like art,
stars flying with rue,
the Cowherd is inching across the Milky Way.
When the Golden Breeze meets with the Jade Dew,
it wanes all romances on earth in play.

Love like streams soft,
Date like dreams due,
Magpie Bridge sees them homeward reluctant to part away.
Were mutual love to last for good and true,
why should they conjoin always night and day?

宋词（婉约派）英译鉴赏实践之四

蝶恋花① · 伫倚危楼风细细

柳　永

伫倚危楼②风细细，
望极③春愁，
黯黯生天际④。
草色烟光⑤残照里，
无言谁会凭阑意⑥。

第七章 宋词（婉约派）英译鉴赏实践

拟把疏狂图一醉⑦。

对酒当歌，

强乐⑧还无味。

衣带渐宽终不悔⑨，

为伊消得⑩人憔悴。

【注释】

①〔蝶恋花〕原唐教坊曲名，后用为词牌名。又名"鹊踏枝""凤栖梧"。《乐章集》《张子野词》并入"小石调"，《清真集》入"商调"。双调六十字，上下阕各四仄韵。

②〔伫(zhù)倚危楼〕长时间倚靠在高楼的栏杆上。伫，长时间站立。危楼，高楼。

③〔望极〕极目远望。

④〔黯(àn)黯〕神情沮丧，情绪低落。〔生天际〕从遥远无边的天际升起。

⑤〔烟光〕飘忽缭绕的云霭雾气。

⑥〔会〕理解。〔阑〕同"栏"。

⑦〔拟把〕打算。〔疏狂〕狂放不羁。〔图一醉〕一醉方休。

⑧〔强(qiǎng)乐〕勉强欢笑。强，勉强。

⑨〔衣带渐宽〕指人逐渐消瘦。语本《古诗十九首》："相去日已远，衣带日已缓"。〔终不悔〕也无怨无悔。

⑩〔消得〕值得。

白话释义

伫立高楼上，柔柔春风迎面来，

极目远望，道不尽春愁无限，

弥漫了整个天际。

斜阳夕照，草色空蒙，

谁懂我独倚栏杆倚心意愁？

真想一醉方休大醉一场。

举杯低吟浅唱，
勉为其乐强颜欢笑又为何。
行消人殒无怨无悔，
只为你甘愿满身憔悴。

主题鉴赏

《蝶恋花·伫倚危楼风细细》是宋代词人柳永的代表作之一。此词采用"曲径通幽"的表现方式，写出了抒情主人公的落魄感受和缠绵情思，抒情写景，感情真挚，令人感伤不已。此词上阕写词人登高望远所引起的无尽离愁，以迷离的景物描写渲染出凄楚悲凉的气氛；下阕写主人公为消释离愁决意痛饮狂歌，但强颜为欢终觉索然无味，最后以健笔写柔情，自誓甘愿为思念的伊人日渐消瘦憔悴而无怨无悔。全词巧妙地把漂泊异乡的落魄感受，同怀恋意中人的缠绵情思融为一体，表现了主人公坚毅的性格与执着的态度，成功地刻画了一个钟情男子的柔美形象。

上阕首先说登楼引起了"春愁"："伫倚危楼风细细。"全词只此一句叙事，便把主人公的外形像一幅剪纸那样突现出来了。"风细细"为这幅剪影添加了一点背景，使画面立刻活跃起来。

"望极春愁，黯黯生天际。"极目天涯，一种黯然魂销的"春愁"油然而生。"春愁"，又点明了时令。对这"愁"的具体内容，词人只说"生天际"，可见是天际的什么景物触动了他的愁怀。从下一句"草色烟光"来看，是春草。芳草萋萋，刬尽还生，很容易使人联想到愁恨的连绵无尽。柳永借用春草，表示自己已经倦游思归，也表示自己怀念亲爱的人。至于那天际的春草，所牵动的词人的"春愁"究竟是哪一种，词人却到此为止，不再多说。

"草色烟光残照里，无言谁会凭阑意"写主人公的孤单凄凉之感。前一句用景物描写点明时间，可以知道，他久久地站立楼头眺望，时已黄昏还不忍离去。"草色烟光"写春天景色极为生动逼真。春草，铺地如茵，登高下望，夕阳的余晖下，闪烁着一层迷蒙的如烟似雾的光色。一种极为凄美的景色，再加上"残照"二字，便又多了一层感伤的色彩，为下一句抒情定下基调。"无言谁会凭阑意"，因为没有人理解他登高远望的心情，所以他默默无言，有"春愁"又无可诉说。这虽然不是"春愁"本身的内容，却加重了"春愁"的愁苦滋味。作者并没有说出他的"春愁"是什么，却又掉转笔墨，埋怨起别人不理解他的心情来了。词人在这里闪烁其词，让读者捉摸不定。

下阕词人写他如何苦中求乐。"愁"，自然是痛苦的，那还是把它忘却，自寻开

第七章 宋词(婉约派)英译鉴赏实践

心吧。"拟把疏狂图一醉",是写他的打算。他已经深深体会到了"春愁"的深沉,单靠自身的力量是难以排遣的,所以他要借酒浇愁。词人说得很清楚,目的是"图一醉"。为了追求这"一醉",他"疏狂",不拘形迹,只要醉了就行。不仅要痛饮,还要"对酒当歌",借放声高歌来抒发他的愁怀。但结果却是"强乐还无味",他并没有抑制住"春愁"。故作欢乐而"无味",更说明"春愁"的缠绵执着。

至此,词人才透露这种"春愁"是一种坚贞不渝的感情。他的满怀愁绪之所以挥之不去,正是因为他不仅不想摆脱这"春愁"的纠缠,甚至心甘情愿为"春愁"所折磨,即使渐渐形容憔悴、瘦骨伶仃,也决不后悔。"为伊消得人憔悴"才一语破的:词人的所谓"春愁",不外是"相思"二字。

这首词紧拓"春愁"即"相思",却又迟迟不肯说破,只是从字里行间向读者透露出一些消息,眼看要写到了,却又煞住,调转笔墨,如此影影绰绰,扑朔迷离,千回百折,直到最后一句,才使真相大白。在词的最后两句相思感情达到高潮的时候,戛然而止,激情回荡,具有很强的感染力。清末学者俞陛云评价说:"长守尾生抱柱之信,拼减沈郎腰带之围,真情至语。此词或作六一词,汲古阁本则列入《乐章集》"(《唐五代两宋词选释》)。当代词学大家唐圭璋批:"此首,上片写境,下片抒情。'伫倚'三句,写远望愁生。'草色'两句,实写所见冷落景象与伤高念远之意。换头深婉。'拟把'句,与'对酒'两句呼应。强乐无味,语极沉痛。'衣带'两句,更柔厚。与'不辞镜里朱颜瘦'语,同合风人之旨"(《唐宋词简释》)。王国维一语点破:"专作情语而绝妙者。……求之古今人词中,曾不多见"(《人间词话删稿》)。

学生英译实践园地

第七章 宋词（婉约派）英译鉴赏实践

英译实践版本选读

译文1 克拉拉·凯德琳

The Butterfly Loves the Flowers

In solitude I lean
Against the ruined tower
Soft breezes blow.
But hope has reached its end
In parting grief.
The border of the sky
Begets dark night.
The slow of hills：
The Hue of grass.

Have intermingled in the dusk.
My thoughts to none are known
As here I rest
Against the balustrade.
Shall I then madly drink,
And sing before the wine?
The boundary of bliss
Is joyless still.
My girdle grows
Too spacious as my form Diminishes.
Until the end
My love will never change.
For you
I pine.

译文 2 许渊冲

Butterflies in Love with Flowers

I lean alone on balcony in light, light breeze;
As far as the eye sees,
On the horizon dark, parting grief grows unseen.
In fading sunlight rises smoke over grass green.
Who understands why mutely on the rails I lean?

I'd drown in wine my parting grief:
Chanting before the cup, strained mirth brings no relief.
I find my gown too large, but I will not regret;
It's worthwhile growing languid for my coquette.

译文 3 赵彦春

A Butterfly's Love for Flowers

I lean on the wall to hear wind sigh
And peer at Spring,
Whose gloom permeates the sky.
Toward the dusk the grassy smoke curls high.
No words to say
who'll on the rail rely?

To forget the love, I'd get drunk and lie;
I sing loud before wine,
but it's tastelessly dry!
My gown's getting loose, no regret, o why!
Loving her, I'm growing gaunt by and by.

第七章 宋词（婉约派）英译鉴赏实践

译文 4　佚　名

Standing in a Tower, Breeze Gently Wafting

Standing in a tower, breeze gently wafting,
My gaze reaches the horizon,
Where a sense of spring-sorrow is creeping.
The grass and the haze are now in fading light;
Who knows why I linger mute by the railings?

I want to drown my ruffled feeling in wines,
So to turn my sorrow merry,
But labored cheerfulness is so cheerless.
I never regret my clothes are getting loose,
For I am eager to pine for you, in truth.

宋词（婉约派）英译鉴赏实践之五

鹤冲天① · 黄金榜上
柳　永

黄金榜②上，
偶失龙头③望。
明代暂遗贤④，
如何向⑤？
未遂风云⑥便，
争不恣游狂荡⑦？
何须论得丧⑧。
才子词人，
自是白衣卿相⑨。

烟花巷陌⑩，

依约丹青屏障⑪。

幸有意中人，

堪⑫寻访。

且恁偎红倚翠⑬，

风流事⑭，

平生畅⑮。

青春都一饷⑯。

忍把浮名⑰，

换了浅斟低唱⑱！

【注释】

① 〔鹤冲天〕词牌名，始于柳永，以他的《鹤冲天·闲窗漏永》为正品，双调八十四字，前段九句五仄韵，后段八句五仄韵。另有词牌《喜迁莺》《风光好》的别名也叫"鹤冲天"。

② 〔黄金榜〕录取进士的金字题名榜。

③ 〔龙头〕旧时称状元为龙头。

④ 〔明代〕圣明的时代。一作"千古"。〔遗贤〕抛弃了贤能之士，指自己为仕途所弃。

⑤ 〔如何向〕向何处。

⑥ 〔风云〕际会风云，指得到好的际遇。此指科举成功。《周易·乾·文言》："云从龙，风从虎，圣人作而万物睹。"

⑦ 〔争不恣游狂荡〕一作"争不恣狂荡"。〔争不〕怎不。〔恣（zì）〕放纵，随心所欲。

⑧ 〔得丧〕得失。

⑨ 〔白衣卿相〕指自己才华出众，虽不入仕途，也有卿相一般尊贵。〔白衣〕古代未仕之士着白衣。

⑩ 〔烟花〕代指歌伎。〔巷陌〕街头巷尾。

⑪ 〔丹青屏障〕彩绘的屏风。〔丹青〕绘画的颜料，这里借指画。

⑫ 〔堪〕能，可以。

⑬ 〔恁（nèn）〕如此。〔偎红倚翠〕指出入烟花巷。宋陶谷《清异录·释族》载，南唐后

第七章 宋词（婉约派）英译鉴赏实践

主李煜微行烟花巷,自题为"浅斟低唱,偎红倚翠大师,鸳鸯寺主"。
⑭〔风流事〕风流浪荡,不拘一格。
⑮〔平生〕一生。
⑯〔饷(xiǎng)〕片刻,极言青年时期的短暂。
⑰〔忍〕忍心,狠心。〔浮名〕功名。
⑰〔浅斟低唱〕对着浅浅的酒杯吟唱。

白话释义

我只不过偶然错失金榜题名的良机。
即使在贤君的时代,贤能之才也可能无人问津,
那该何去何从?
既然天不眷顾,为何不随心畅游?
得失随它去。
才子当风流,
不入仕途,也不输那诸侯将相。

烟花巷里,绣屏幔帐,
把那佳人寻访。
互诉女儿情长,
人生才算欢畅。
青春年华,稍纵即逝,
不如把功名利禄,
换成薄酒一杯,伴着低吟浅唱。

主题鉴赏

《鹤冲天·黄金榜上》是柳永早年参加科举考试落榜而写就的作品。词的上阕叙写词人科考落第的失意不满和恃才傲物,下阕叙写了词人放浪形骸、出入风月场中的颓废生活。全词表现了词人恃才傲物、狂放不羁的个性与怀才不第的牢骚和感慨。此词的特点是率直,无必达之隐,无难显之情,语言质朴。名落孙山之后,心中有所不甘,因为科举的仕途之路仍然是他实现自我价值的最佳选择,但是失落、激愤和难堪之情,必须要有所排解,词人于是写下这首词。

"黄金榜上,偶失龙头望",考科举求功名,开口辄言"龙头",词人并不满足于登进士第,而是把夺取殿试头名状元作为目标。落榜只认作"偶然","见遗"只说是"暂",其自负可知。词人把自己称作"明代遗贤",这是颇有讽刺意味的。宋仁宗朝号称清明盛世,却不能做到"野无遗贤",这个自相矛盾的现象就是他所要嘲讽的。"风云际会",施展抱负,是封建时代士子的奋斗目标,既然"未遂风云便",理想落空了,词人就转向了另一个极端,"争不恣游狂荡",表示要无拘无束地继续过自己那种为一般封建士人所不齿的流连坊曲的狂荡生活。"偎红倚翠""浅斟低唱",就是对"狂荡"的具体说明。词人这样写,是恃才负气的表现,也是表示抗争的一种方式。科举落第,使他产生了一种逆反心理,只有以极端对极端才能求得平衡。他毫不顾忌地把一般封建士人感到刺目的字眼写进词里,恐怕就是故意要造成惊世骇俗的效果以保持自己心理上的优势。还应看到,"烟花巷陌"在封建社会是普遍存在的,这是当时的客观事实,而涉足其间的人们却有着各自不同的情况。柳永与一般"狎客"的不同,主要有两点:一是他保持着清醒的自我意识,只是寄情于声伎,并非沉湎于酒色,这一点,他后来登第为官的事实可以证明;二是他尊重"意中人"的人格,同情她们的命运,不是把她们当作玩弄对象而是与她们结成风尘知己。可见,词人的"狂荡"之中仍然有着严肃的一面,狂荡以傲世,严肃以自律,方能不失为"才子词人"。

"何须论得丧。才子词人,自是白衣卿相",真切细致地表述了词人落第以后的思想活动和心理状态。言得失何干,虽是白衣未得功名,而实具卿相之质,这是牢骚感慨的顶点,也是自我宽慰的极限。这些话里已经出现了自相矛盾的情况,倘再跨越一步,就会走向反面。"何须论得丧",正是对登第与落第的得与丧进行掂量计较;自称"白衣卿相",也正是不忘朱紫显达的思想流露。词人把他内心深处的矛盾想法抒写出来,说明落第这件事情给他带来了多么深重的苦恼和多么繁杂的困扰,也说明他为了摆脱这种苦恼和困扰曾经进行了多么痛苦的挣扎。写到最后,词人好像得出了结论:"青春都一饷,忍把浮名,换了浅斟低唱。"谓青春短暂,不忍虚掷,为"浮名"而牺牲赏心乐事。其实,这仍然是他一时的负气之言。

这首词可以说是柳永进士科考落第之后的一纸"抗议书",在宋元时代有着重大的意义和反响。它正面鼓吹文人士子与统治者分离,轻视功名利禄,主张人性自由,有一定的思想进步性。这首词的构思、层次、结构和语言均与柳永其他作品有所不同。全篇直说,绝少用典,不仅与民间曲子词极为接近,而且还保留了当时的某些口语方言,如"如何向""争不""且恁"等。全词写得自然流畅,平白如话,读来琅琅上口。

清代叶申芗评论:"此亦一时遗怀之作"(《本事词》)。清代陈廷焯批评道:"耆卿'忍把浮名,换了浅斟低唱',荒漫语耳,何足为韵事?"(《白雨斋词话》卷六)。

第七章 宋词（婉约派）英译鉴赏实践

学生英译实践园地

英译实践版本选读

译文1　赵彦春

The Crane Darting to the Sky

On the Roll of Grand Test,
I've won no place, not so depressed.
E'en a good reign may lose the best.
What should I do next?
Since I can't sail before the wind,
Why don't I have fun, throwing a chest?
Why should I care loss or gain?
As a man of letters,
Compared with courtiers I am more blessed.

The misty rosy lanes
See rooms full of screens and scrolls well dressed.
Sure, I could find a pretty one,
I'll go there to quest.
Clinging to the buds and roses there
What bliss I enjoy,
Caressing and caressed!
How long can we stay on life's crest?
Go away, you vain world,
Why not drink and sing, all to our zest?

译文2　杨宪益　戴乃迭

He Chong Tian

On the golden list of candidates,
I lost the chance to come first.
And am briefly a deserted sage during this enlightened time,

第七章　宋词（婉约派）英译鉴赏实践

What should I turn to?
Failing to achieve my ambition,
Why not indulge in passions and run wild?
No need to worry about gains and losses.
As a gifted scholar and writer of lyrics,
I am like an untitled minister.

In the singsong houses and brothels,
I keep a rendezvous behind painted screens;
My old acquaintances are to my liking.
They are worthy of my visits.
Better to take comfort in the arms of the girls in red and green,
And enjoy the distractions and hours of dalliance,
Thus compensating for my disappointment.
The prime of one's life is too short.
Better to barter empty fame,
For the pleasures of good wine and sweet song.

单元扩展实践练习

一、王国维在《人间词话·二十四》中有如下文字，请结合你的专业或科研经历，用英文谈谈你对这三句宋词的理解。

"古今之成大事业、大学问者，必经过三种之境界。'昨夜西风凋碧树，独上高楼，望尽天涯路'①，此第一境也；'衣带渐宽终不悔，为伊消得人憔悴'②，此第二境也；'众里寻他千百度，回头蓦见，那人正在灯火阑珊处'③，此第三境也。"

---

① 选自晏殊《蝶恋花·槛菊愁烟兰泣露》
② 选自柳永《蝶恋花·伫倚危楼风细细》
③ 选自辛弃疾《青玉案·元夕》

附 录

阅读文献

曹道衡,2000.乐府诗选[M].北京:人民文学出版社.
陈伯海,1995.唐诗汇评[M].杭州:浙江教育出版社.
陈国林,2012.高中生必背古诗文[M].北京:龙门书局出版社.
陈新璋,1986.唐宋咏物诗赏鉴[M].广州:广东人民出版社.
陈贻焮,2011.杜甫评传[M].北京:北京大学出版社.
陈子展,杜月村,2008.诗经导读[M].北京:中国国际广播出版社.
陈祖美,1992.李清照作品赏析集[M].成都:巴蜀书社.
迟文浚,许志刚,宋绪连,1992.历代赋词典[M].沈阳:辽宁人民出版社.
崔钟雷,2009.唐诗三百首[M].长春:吉林美术出版社.
戴燕,2006.历代诗词曲选注[M].杭州:浙江文艺出版社.
范国平,2010.初中生必背古诗词[M].北京:新世界出版社.
方玉润,1986.诗经原始[M].李先耕,点校.北京:中华书局.
葛晓音,2003.杜甫诗选评[M].上海:上海古籍出版社.
谷玉婷,2016.宋词三百首详注[M].北京:中国华侨出版社.
管士光,2014.李白诗集新注[M].上海:上海三联书店.
郭茂倩,2014.乐府诗集[M].崇贤书院,释译.北京:新世界出版社.
郭预衡,2020.汉魏南北朝诗选注[M].上海:东方出版中心.
韩成武,1997.杜甫诗全译[M].石家庄:河北人民出版社.
韩盼山,1986.品花诗译[M].郑州:河南人民出版社.
蘅塘退士,2009.唐诗三百首・宋词三百首・元曲三百首[M].北京:华文出版社.

黄岳洲,2013.中国古代文学名篇鉴赏辞典[M].北京:华语教学出版社.
霍松林,2018.历代好诗诠评[M].西安:陕西师范大学出版社.
蒋风,1990.新编文史地词典[M].杭州:浙江人民出版社.
蒋锡金,1990.文史哲学习词典[M].长春:吉林文史出版社.
康志梅,2017.从目的论看诗经·蒹葭的三种英译文[J].山西煤炭职业技术学院学报,(S8):30.
柯汉琳,王荣生,2019.高中语文选择性必修:上册[M].北京:人民教育出版社.
李炳海,冯克正,傅庆升,1996.诸子百家大辞典[M].沈阳:辽宁人民出版社.
李晨阳,黄辛,2022.不拘一格的他,这样回应"要教授"的年轻人[N].中国科学报,07-28(004).
李承林,2011.中华句典中华文典[M].北京:高等教育出版社.
李春祥,1990.乐府诗鉴赏词典[M].郑州:中国古籍出版社.
李存仁,2011.新编初中古诗文一看通[M].广州:暨南大学出版社.
李静,2009.唐诗宋词鉴赏大全集[M].北京:华文出版社.
李山,2017.诗经节选[M].北京:国家图书馆出版社.
李一鸣,2009.大学语文[M].济南:山东人民出版社.
李泽厚,汝信,林丽珠,1990.美学百科全书[M].北京:社会科学文献出版社.
刘向,2017.战国策[M].鲍彪,注,吴师道,校注.上海:上海古籍出版社.
刘勇刚,2018.秦少游的鹊桥仙为谁而歌?[N].中国艺术报,08-17(08).
陆林,1992.宋词白话解说[M].北京:北京师范大学出版社.
罗立刚,2014.倚天万里须长剑·豪放词[M].济南:山东文艺出版社.
马景霞,李月,2018.从"音象美、视象美"解读望庐山瀑布两个英译本[J].青年文学家,(09):84-85+87.
马玮,2014.柳永[M].北京:商务印书馆国际有限公司.
聂巧平,2012.崇文国学经典文库·唐诗三百首[M].武汉:崇文书局.
裴斐,1988.李白诗歌赏析集[M].成都:巴蜀书社.
彭定求,1986.全唐诗:上[M].上海:上海古籍出版社.
彭玉平,2014.唐宋词举要[M].北京:商务印书馆.
钱穆,2011.庄子纂笺[M].北京:九州出版社.
乔继堂,2012.国人必读唐诗手册[M].上海:上海科学技术文献出版社.
段玉裁,2013.说文解字注[M].北京:中华书局.
马瑞辰,1989.毛诗传笺通释[M].陈金生,点校.北京:中华书局.
任国绪,1989.卢照邻集编年笺注[M].哈尔滨:黑龙江人民出版社.

沈德潜,2016.古诗源[M].北京:中华书局.
史杰鹏,2014.宋词三百首正宗[M].北京:华夏出版社.
唐圭璋,1988.唐宋词鉴赏辞典:唐·五代·北宋[M].上海:上海辞书出版社.
唐圭璋,1988.唐宋词鉴赏辞典:南宋·辽·金[M].上海:上海辞书出版社.
唐圭璋,潘君昭,曹济平,2019.唐宋词选注[M].北京:北京十月出版社.
唐圭璋,1965.全宋词[M].北京:中华书局.
滕征辉,2014.做东[M].南京:江苏文艺出版社.
田荣昌,冯广宜,2021.诗国圣坛:汉诗英译鉴赏与评析[M].西安:西安交通大学出版社.
王强,左汉林,2008.唐诗选注汇评[M].成都:巴蜀书社.
王先谦,1987.诗三家义集疏[M].吴格,点校.北京:中华书局.
王云五,1970.礼记今译今注[M].王梦鸥,注译.台北:台湾商务印书馆.
吴世常,陈伟,1987.新编美学词典[M].郑州:河南人民出版社.
吴小如,1992.汉魏六朝诗鉴赏辞典[M].上海:上海辞书出版社.
吴熊和,2004.唐宋词汇评·两宋[M].杭州:浙江教育出版社.
西北师范学院中文系文艺理论教研室,1985.简明文学知识词典[M].兰州:甘肃人民出版社.
奚少庚,赵丽云,1992.历代诗词千首解析词典[M].长春:吉林文史出版社.
夏承焘,2013.宋词鉴赏辞典:上[M].上海:上海辞典书出版社.
夏征农,2000.辞海缩印本[M].上海:上海辞书出版社.
姜亮夫,1998.先秦诗鉴赏辞典[M].上海:上海辞书出版社.
萧涤非,1983.唐诗鉴赏辞典[M].上海:上海辞书出版社.
徐公持,1986.中国大百科全书·中国文学[M].北京:中国大百科全书出版社.
徐培均,2003.秦观词新释辑评[M].北京:中国书店.
徐中玉,1999.中国古代文学作品选[M].上海:华东师范大学出版社.
许渊冲,1992.中诗英韵探胜[M].北京:北京大学出版社.
许渊冲,2009.诗经:汉英对照[M].北京:中国对外翻译出版公司.
许子东,2011.许子东讲稿:张爱玲·郁达夫·香港文学(第2卷)[M].北京:人民文学出版社.
姚际恒,1958.诗经通论[M].顾颉刚标点.北京:中华书局.
叶嘉莹,陈祖美,2003.李清照词新释辑评[M].北京:中国书店.
衣兴国,1988.实用中国名人辞典[M].长春:吉林文史出版社.
于海娣,2010.唐诗鉴赏大全集[M].中国华侨出版社.

附录 阅读文献

余冠英,1979.三曹诗选[M].北京:人民文学出版社.

余冠英,1979.诗经选[M].北京:人民文学出版社.

余恕诚,2006.中国古代诗歌散文欣赏[M].北京:人民教育出版社.

詹福瑞,1997.李白诗全译[M].石家庄:河北人民出版社.

张国举,2010.唐诗精华注译评[M].长春:长春出版社.

张屏,2014.认知翻译观下蒹葭四种英译文的比较[J].西华大学学报(哲学社会科学版),(33):4.

张忠纲,2005.杜甫诗选[M].北京:中华书局.

赵海菱,2012.李白将进酒新考[J].社会科学辑刊,(2):182-185.

赵则诚,张连弟,毕万忱,1985.中国古代文学理论词典[M].长春:吉林文史出版社.

中国历史大词典编纂委员会,2000.中国历史大辞典[M].上海:上海辞书出版社.

钟基,李先银,王身刚,2009.古文观止[M].北京:中华书局.

周汝昌,1988.唐宋词鉴赏辞典:唐·五代·北宋[M].上海:上海辞书出版社.

周啸天,1990.诗经楚辞鉴赏辞典[M].成都:四川辞书出版社.

朱熹,1987.诗经集传[M].上海:上海古籍出版社.

祝总斌,1992.中国大百科全书·中国历史[M].北京:中国大百科全书出版社.

Arthur W, 1996. The Book of Songs: The Ancient Chinese Classic of Poetry [M]. New York: Grove Press Inc.

Cleanth B, 2004. Understanding Poetry[M]. Beijing: Foreign Language Teaching and Research Press & Thomson Learning.

James L, 1871. The Chinese Classics, Vol. 4, The She King, or the Book of Poetry[M]. London: Frowde.

John F N, 1983. Western Wind, an Introduction to Poetry, second edition[M]. New York: Random House, Inc.

Kang-I S C, Stephen O, 2011. The Cambridge History of Chinese Literature Volume I[M]. New York: Cambridge University Press.

Paul W K, 2015. Reading Medieval Chinese Poetry: Text, Context, and Culture [M]. Leidon & Boston: Koninklijke Brill NV, Leiden.

Ronald C E, 1994. Word, Image, and Deed in the Life of Su Shi[M]. Cambridge (Massachusetts) and London: Harvard University Press.

William J, 1891. The Shi King, the Old "Poetry Classic" of the Chinese [M]. A Project Of Liberty Fund, Inc.

Xu Y C, 1992. On Chinese verse in English rhyme: From the Book of Poetry to the Romance of the Western Bower[M]. Beijing: Peking University Press.
http://www.moe.gov.cn/srcsite/A13/s7061/201403/t20140328_166543.html
http://www.chinaknowledge.de/Literature/Classics/shijing.html
http://www.moe.gov.cn/srcsite/A13/s7061/201403/t20140328_166543.html
https://upimg.baike.so.com/doc/1440243-1522442.html